THE

GREEN

VIRGIN

CORPORAL

REX D. ENSIS

For my daughter Debbie, my wife Pearl,
Frank, Jake and all
my family and friends

Acknowledgement and Thanks.
Without the inspiration and help from my daughter and technical assistance from my friend Dennis Hughes this story would never have been told or published. I thank both of them for their invaluable help and advice.

FOREWARD

In January 2016 my 50 year old plus daughter came up from Bristol for the weekend to visit me in Nottingham. After dinner and over drinks she told me that she knew nothing at all about my early childhood. She added that although relatives had told her certain things about my National Service days and my service in Malaya during the Malayan Emergency, and how I had married a Malaysian princess that I had never ever mentioned anything about these subjects to her and she asked me to tell her about them.

Over the next two hours and over a few whiskies I proceed to tell my daughter about my early childhood. My daughter listened patiently over her gins and tonics. The following morning, my daughter, before leaving back to Bristol told me that on her following visits that she expected me to tell her everything I could remember about my service in Malaya.

I remembered only too well the things that I had done, the names of the people that I had met and the places I had visited in Malaya during my tour there during the Malayan Emergency, but to be on the safe side I read through all my old diaries in order to get all the dates correct. I was then fully prepared to give an accurate account of my service in Malaya to my daughter when she next visited me.

During the next few months my daughter visited me frequently and listened patiently whilst I told her about my adventures in Malaya. It was in December 2016 when I had finished telling my daughter everything about my service in Malaya that my daughter made me promise to put everything down in writing so that she and her son could read it all. I promised her that I would and over the next few months I wrote over forty chapters or more and gave them to her in late 2017

On reading the written chapters my daughter showed the chapters to a few of her friends to read. My daughter then told me that she and her friends thought that these chapters were excellent book material and that they should be published as a book for all to read. Perhaps my daughter and her friends were too kind and too biased in recommending that my story be published as a book, but in the end I agreed to their request.

The story has been written exactly as I told it to my daughter over her many visits and it is how I would have told it to any audience. The incidents I experienced are all fact. The places I visited are all fact. Although I told my daughter the real names of all the people I met and got involved with, I have changed all the names of the people in the book in order to save them or their relatives any embarrassment.

I thank my daughter for all the help and encouragement which she has given me in writing this book and without her this book would never have been written.

As the motto of the RADC is "Ex Dentibus Ensis" I have chosen to write this book under the pseudonym of Rex D. Ensis.

The following chapters are exactly what I told my daughter.

1

EARLY CHILDHOOD

I was born in Hackney, a little hamlet in Derbyshire in 1937. My father died at the age of 32 years leaving my mother with five children; two sons and three daughters to feed. I was the oldest of the five children, aged just eight years when he died. In order to cope and to feed her family my mother went out to work as a waitress in a hotel and as she often did not get back home from work until around 9pm. I had to learn to cook and feed my brother and three sisters before putting them to bed. Our house did not have any electricity or even a flushing toilet inside the house and we had to make do with a "Thunder Box" type of toilet, which was outside and to gain access to this we had to climb the steps and the side of the house and down the steps at the other side of the house - no mean achievement especially on those dark and windy nights when we attempted this with a lighted candle in one hand and a piece of newspaper in the other hand. The "Thunder Box" was emptied once a week by the Council. Cooking for my brother and sisters was relatively easy as my mother provided me with a good range of cookery books but the difficulty was that we did not have a gas stove as such but just an old black leaded cooking range which seem to eat loads and loads of coal. Many times we could not afford coal so my brother and I used to steal wood logs .

from various places, but logs were never as good as the coal. On the subject of stealing, as were very poor and often hungry my brother and I often stole milk and other things from neighbour's doorsteps and eggs from the farmer's fields. Eggs were easily available as there were no such things as battery eggs in those days. Our egg stealing came to an end when my brother stole about 30 eggs and tried to sell them in the hamlet. Of course everybody knew where the eggs had come from and he was reported and the next thing we knew was a policeman appearing at our house. We also stole turnips out of the farmer's fields and ate those.

At first we didn't know the difference between mangels and turnips, but soon learned that mangels with their bitter taste were farmed as a cattle food to feed the cows with. Summer was good as there was a plentiful supply of apples, pears and plums to scrump. Scrumping came to a drastic end though when my brother and I raided the school headmaster's garden one day and the local magistrate's orchard the following day and we got cornered by his ferocious Alsatian dog. Those two incidents entailed the local policeman visiting our house yet again. Growing up in those days, at our age, without a father, meant that my brother I were very venerable to aggressive neighbors who took every opportunity to dish out quite a few beatings to us, on a regular basis.

On the subject of the local policeman or "the Bobby" as he was called. I recall that he called at our house so many times that neighbours thought he was having an affair with my mother and strangers to the hamlet thought he lived at our house. My brother but mainly I, got blamed for everything bad thing that occurred in the area. When a snooker cue was stolen from a nearby snooker hall; when neighbour's windows were broken as a result of catapult actions; when somebody let the handbrake off of Fred Bond's car (he had the only car in the hamlet) and it ran down the steep hill and crashed; when the church collection box was robbed; when somebody telephoned the school headmaster from the local telephone call box and speaking through a handkerchief or a similar thing and called him some awful names; when somebody set fire to the local magistrate's garden shed, the local Bobby always came to our house first. The only thing I was actually responsible for – which I should have admitted to was letting the handbrake off of Fred's car, which was his prize and joy!

At school the girls aged 12 to 16 had no busts and were very flat chested. Even the girls aged 17 to 18 had no busts, unlike the girls of that age today, who would put Marilyn Monroe or Jayne Mansfield to shame. If you tried to "chat" them up you could expect a strapping or a caning with a bamboo stick from their fathers. I lost count of the number of these I got from Fred Bond, our next door neighbour, because I spoke to his daughter Mavis. (I was to get even with Fred Bond much later in life when I came home from the army on leave and gave him a pasting). In the end after suffering quite a few beatings I stopped talking to girls and became very frightened and very shy when I was in their company. This was not to change until after I reached the age of 21. My brother was much different though as he always seemed to have a secret girlfriend.

Come to think of it he had quite a few - perhaps this was because he had a better personality than me; was better looking than me ; was not as shy; was more confident than I was or was just a better talker than I was! Women of all ages didn't seem, to deter my brother as I found out when a forty year old plus farmer appeared at our door with a double barreled shotgun asking for my brother! The farmer told me that he had found out that he had been seeing his wife and had some sort of involvement with her.

Life from the age of 8 years old until I was 15 seem to drag. At weekends and during the school holidays we either stole or entertained ourselves with catapults, bows and arrows and pea shooters; sometimes we just lay around in our dens. During the evening I used to sit in what my mother called the sitting room waiting for her to come home. The two most frightening nights were on Tuesday when the wireless broadcast 'Appointment with Fear' and on a Thursday night when they broadcast 'Arm Chair Detective'. 'Arm Chair Detective' was very scary and came on at 9.30pm and always opened with something like "turn your gas lamps down low...". Once when listening to this programme the gas ran out and the gas light went off and I couldn't find any coins to put in the gas meter. It was a very frightened young boy who listened to the rest of the programme in complete darkness. Following that frightening night I asked my mother to ensure that there was a supply of coins to put into the gas meter. You also had to ensure that your wireless accumulator was topped up with acid and that you had a supply of gas light mantles.

On reaching the age of 15 I started work at local butchers. That soon ended when I accidently chopped one of the butcher's fingers off as he was holding a side of pork when he asked me to use the cleaver to chop the head off. Of course I was immediately sacked and had to find another job. The Co-Op took me on in their warehouse. Whilst working there at the age of 16 the foreman insisted that I took driving lessons. My driving instructor was a nice young man named John Fearn. Alas the driving lessons came to an abrupt end and my employment ended following two incidents; the first was when I pulled the gear stick out of its socket when driving through a town and we had to be towed back to base and the second incident was when I accelerated down the hill in the van which then overturned and caught fire.

Soon I was in my third job at the age of nearly 17 where I was employed by the leading and a famous High Class Grocer in the county. I was happy that I ended my employment with them without any incidents, when my National Service call up papers arrived at the house.

During my age of 15 to 18 the only thing I used to look forward to was my weekly game of football when I played for a good nearby village team. The team was captained by a lovely chap named Charles, who was not only a great footballer, but also became a professional footballer later on in life. Besides playing for quite a few professional teams, Charles also captained the Combined Services later on, which was a marvelous feat considering there were so many top professional footballers in those National Service days. I was to meet Charles again in Malaya, much later on in life.

Looking back on my life aged 8 years old to 18 years I cannot say that I really enjoyed it. It was a very hard and lonely life. I was always in trouble of some kind or other, if not for stealing off neighbour's doorsteps, it was for raiding the neighbour's orchids and allotments, or for stealing the turnips, eggs and the odd chicken from the farmer's fields. Come to think of it I got blamed for everything that was stolen in the hamlet! The only good thing about my early childhood is that you could go out and play all day safely — which unfortunately cannot be said about the present day.

Just after reaching the age of 18 I received my National Service Call Up papers telling me to report to the Royal Army Dental Corps (RADC) Depot, at Connaught Barracks in Aldershot. My tearful mother packed a suitcase for me, took me to the local railway station and put me on the train, which was my first railway journey. I arrived at Aldershot railway station and caught a bus to the RADC Depot, to start a new life. "Welcome to the real world" I was told by the corporal I encountered at the guardroom. My life was to change dramatically from that day!

2

INTO THE ARMY

The following morning I, along with another 30 squaddies were made to form up in three ranks, given an army number and then marched to the Quartermasters store to be kitted out with our army kit. We were told by a sergeant that we would not need our civilian clothes for the next 12 weeks. Our training at the RADC Training Centre was no different from any other Regiment or Corps and it consisted of marching, shooting, trade training and many, many hours of fatigues. Fatigues usually meant painting coal white; spending hours in the cookhouse, washing and cleaning dirty greasy dishes or anything else those awful NCOs could find for us. We worked for seven days every week and it was a relief to be able to sit in the classroom on various days to do our trade training. The NCOs on the Depot believed they were the Sons of God. The exception was Sgt Frank Bramley, who came from Whatstandwell, a small hamlet in Derbyshire. Apart from Frank we found all the NCOs to be inhuman. We soon christened our Depot "Stalag 15" and we gave all the NCOs, apart from Frank Bramley, pet names – such as Adolf, Hitler, Goering, Himmler, Heinrich, Reinhardt, Eichmann, Muller and Goebbels. These pet names came in very handy for if we were talking about a certain NCO nobody not in the know knew which NCO we were talking about. Wednesday afternoon was always a recreational afternoon and if you were lucky enough to play sport you were alright, but if you did not play any sport then it was another afternoon doing fatigues. I was lucky enough to be a decent footballer and Frank Bramley and Major Cox always made sure that I played for the depot team every Wednesday. Major George Cox, the Depot Adjutant, had come through the ranks and had represented the Medical Services at both football and cricket in his prime days. George had been unkindly nick-named "Guts and Gaiters" by many soldiers on the depot, but not by me I hasten to add. I was to meet Major Cox a few years later when I was posted to Chester and sent to the depot to do some courses. Major Cox was the very first AUC cricket umpire in the entire HM Services and he later took me under his wing and I became the second ACU cricket umpire in HM Services. George and I were qualified to umpire any first class cricket match and indeed we umpired at many of those first class matches together.

Our squad finally finished all our training on 18 December 1955 and we were assembled that morning and informed of our first posting. All of us were hoping for exotic postings like Germany, Hong Kong, Singapore, Tripoli, Malta, Kenya, just to name a few of the overseas posting which were available. An overseas posting meant that you received a tax free Local Overseas Allowance (LOA), which was an amount not only much more than your weekly basic pay of 28 shillings (£1.40 today's rate), but cheaper cigarettes, alcohol and other items. The postings were read out and I was disappointed not to get an overseas posting, but a posting to Northern Ireland instead. Later on in the morning I was called into the pay office and given rail warrants from Aldershot to Matlock and another from Matlock to Belfast, via the ferry from Liverpool and a posting order which stated that I had to report to the dental centre in Thiepval Barracks, Lisburn by 27 December 1955. I was then sent home on seven days embarkation leave before departing for Belfast on Boxing Day, 26 December 1955. I found it wonderful once again to be able to wear civilian clothes during my 7 days embarkation leave.

On Boxing Day I put on my battle dress (BD) uniform and started the long journey from Matlock to Belfast. On boarding the Ferry at Liverpool I had never heard of the Irish Sea let alone seen it. I soon found out that it was an awful and very rough sea and I was so violently sick that I slept on the toilet floor for the whole journey.

On arriving at Thiepval Barracks I was escorted to the dental centre which was a three chair dental centre and staffed by three dentists, 4 dental clerks and a dental technician. I was met by Sgt John Markham, the NCO in charge of the dental centre. During the time I spent at this dental centre I was to find that I learnt more from John Markham, than I had done in my previous 18 years. After my time at "Stalag 15" I found army life at Thiepval Barracks to be very good; no parades (apart from Sunday Church Parade), no regimental duties, never hungry with lots of good food available; plenty of time off and being able to wear civilian clothes when I was not working at the dental centre. John Markham was a real decent and friendly Sgt, unlike those Sgts and other NCOs (apart from Frank Bramley) I had served under at "Stalag 15". John and I became good friends and in some of the spare time I had in the evenings I used to babysit for John and his German born wife, Hannah.

One of the first pieces of advice John gave me was to warn me about the local Irish girls whom he told me were always looking for invites to the weekly dances which we had in the camp and also quite a few of them wanted to marry British soldiers, get a fully furnished married quarter and then accompany their husbands on an exotic overseas posting. I never went out of the barracks during my first two months until I decided to go to the local cinema. Coming out of the cinema, on the other side of the road were a crowd of at least 20 young girls who saw me and screamed "Cliff Richard" and started chasing me up the road. I legged it as fast as I could back to Thiepval Barracks, breaking every possible Olympic running record at the time. I was still a very shy guy and frightened of girls, after my experiences before I joined the army. Not being big-headed, but this was not to be the first time that I was to mistaken for Cliff Richard, as a similar thing was to happen to me at the Military Hospital, Chester some years later and I was also told by a few of my friends that I did indeed look a lot like Cliff!

The thing I always looked forward to were Wednesdays when I played football for the garrison team. The coach of the garrison team was Paddy Ryan. Paddy was a civilian who worked in the QM stores in the barracks and who in addition to running and coaching the garrison football team also coached and ran a local team which played every Sunday morning in a local league. Paddy asked me to play to play for his local team. I told him that I would love to, but unfortunately was not in a position to do so as every Sunday I had to dress in my best uniform, march down with other soldiers to the garrison church and attend the 75 minute service. Paddy often came around to the dental centre for a cup of coffee on some mornings and it was on one of these mornings he mentioned to me, in front of John Markham, that it was a great pity that I could not play for his local team as he was missing a good centre forward. I thought no more of our conversation at the time. Later that afternoon John invited me up to his married quarter for dinner and beers. Later that evening John asked me if I really wanted to play for Paddy's local football team. I said I would love to but was unable to do so because of those weekly church parades. John knew that my religion was stated on my personal documents as being Church of England (CE) and asked me if I was religious. I told him that I was not but when I was at the "Stalag 15" the docs clerk who filled in our documents form listing all our personal details had asked me what religion I had was. I told him that I was an agnostic and that I had never been to church in my life (except for the occasional visit to see if the collection boxes had been emptied). He told me that he could not put agnostic down and I had to pick a religion from RC, Methodist or Church of England. I had already been warned about attending church parades on Sundays, and indeed I had to attend one every Sunday when I was at "Stalag 15". I asked the docs clerk which was the shorter service - RC, Methodist or Church of England? He told me thought it was Church of England, so I told him to put me down as such. Having heard all this John Markham told me not to worry as he had a solution. He asked me what I wanted to be a Buddhist or a Muslim and he explained that if I was listed as one of them I would not have to attend any church service on Sundays and that I would be free to play local football on Sundays. The Muslims were well respected at the time so I chose Muslim and John told me to leave everything to him. The following morning John published a part 2 order stating that I had changed my religion from CE to Muslim.

John got the Part 2 Order signed by the National Service dental Officer and sent it off to WRAC and Medical Services records at Winchester. Of course I was very worried that there would be serious repercussions when the Records Office received the Part 2 Order. What if they asked where I had converted from CE to Muslim; what if they asked what my Muslim name was; what if they asked if I had been circumcised!. John told me not to worry as the Officer in Charge (OIC) at records was a retired Lieut Colonel, who was seldom there as he was always out playing golf or drinking and that all his staff, apart from a Warrant Officer, were all civilians anyway who did all the work. John was an absolute genius because the records office accepted the Part 2 Order without any comment and the religion on my personal documents was changed and the Garrison Sgt Major was informed. The good news was that from that day I never had to attend any church parade and could therefore play football for Paddy's local team on most Sundays. The bad news was that every time I passed the Garrison Sgt Major in the camp he used to address me as "Mohammad". Apart from leaving the garrison on most Sundays in order to play football I did not venture from the garrison at all, so not only did I avoid the mass of screaming young Irish girls looking for marriage, but I was able to save a little money out of the 28 shillings (£ 1.40) I earned each week.

John Markham usually took me in his car to local football match on Sundays and I believe it was after the last match of the season in late April 1956, when I was having a drink with John and Paddy in the local pub, that I mentioned life in the garrison was going to a bit quiet and a bit boring for the next few months until the new football season started in September. John advised me not to worry as something would be sorted out. The following day John called me into his office and asked me if I would like an overseas posting. He told me some of the advantages of an overseas posting, like a very attractive local overseas allowance which was free from income tax; of cheap cigarettes and booze; of lovely sunshine if I got posted to the Far East or Middle East;

lots of time off with reduced working hours if I got a posting in a tropical country; of the exotic food available in these exotic countries; the advantages went on and on! What John failed to mention was that if he did manage to get me an 'exotic' overseas posting, it could turn out to be in Kenya where the British were fighting the Mau Mau, or in Cyprus where the British were fighting EOKA, or in Malaya where the British were fighting the Communist terrorists. Perhaps the posting could be to one of those isolated places in Germany where the winters were often extremely hostile and freezing with lots and lots of snow. I told John that I had heard that no National Service guy from our Corps in Northern Ireland had ever managed to get an overseas posting from there. John told me not to worry. In order to get an overseas posting a soldier had to write to his CO/OIC and then his CO/OIC would forward the soldier's letter onto his Records Office. John asked me if I wanted to volunteer for an overseas posting. I replied that I did. He then drafted a letter for me which I signed which John handed to our National Service OIC. The letter was forward to our records office at Winchester. Two days later I was having coffee in John's office when the telephone rang and on the line at the other end was a woman from the Record Office at Winchester.

After about 10 minutes discussion John informed me in order to get an overseas posting I had to sign on as a regular soldier and she would then organize a posting for me to the Far East within two to three months. John informed me that was a promise and not just idle chatter. I signed the form ten minutes later that afternoon and John sent it immediately off to records at Winchester. From that day my weekly pay immediately doubled from 28 shillings (£1.40) a week to 56 shillings (£ 2.80) per week.

True to her promise, a few days later, we received from the woman in question, my posting order to the Far East, which stated that I was to take a week's embarkation leave in July and then report to a certain officer at an assembly point on Southampton docks and would eventually sail on the 'Empire Fowey', which was a troopship at anchor in Southampton Docks. Goodbye Ireland and Singapore or Hong Kong here I come or so I thought!

3

THE TROOPSHIP "EMPIRE FOWEY"

I arrived back at my little hamlet on a week's embarkation leave. I was very excited and looking forward to the next three years in the tropical sunshine of Singapore or Hong Kong. I had never travelled overseas before so that meant I had to arrange to get a passport which the Army did for me in very quick time. When I told my mother of my posting to the Far East she was quite disappointed as it meant that I would not be seeing her or my brother and sisters for the next three years. Obviously Fred Bond and his aggressive neighbours were over the moon because it also meant that they would not be seeing me for at least another three years. I explained to my mother that I would be travelling to the Far East in a large troopship.

As it happened there was a wealthy Australian couple staying at the hotel where my mother worked and she told them that I was going to the Far East on a liner. They told her that they had done a few long sea cruises and informed her that I was an extremely lucky lad, as not only was it a most wonderful experience, but also those cruises were very expensive and that I was going to be able to do one completely free of charge. When my mother relayed this news to me I became very excited and could not stop dreaming about the time I would be sunning myself on the top deck of the liner which was to take me to the Far East and the wonderful exotic places I would see on route. Nobody in our hamlet had ever been on a sea cruise, let alone being able to afford one. Come to think of it, to my knowledge nobody from our hamlet had ever travelled further than Blackpool. Lucky, Lucky me! Whilst on my week's embarkation leave and dreaming of the wonderful cruise I was going to have; the exotic places I was going to see; and spending the next 3 three years in Singapore or Hong Kong, I avoided those flat chested girls and spent most of my time at the Church, which in fact was a pub which was called 'The Church Inn' in a nearby village which I hasten to add was the only 'church' I enjoyed being in.

The day finally arrived when I had finished my embarkation leave. I packed my kitbag and bade farewell to my brother and sisters.

My mother accompanied me to Matlock railway station where I exchanged my rail warrant for a rail ticket to Southampton. After a very tearful goodbye with my mother the express train pulled out of the station and I was on my way to paradise, or so thought!

Arriving at Southampton railway station I eventually found my way to Southampton docks in the early afternoon and, as instructed by my army movement order, I eventually reported to a major at the reporting station. He informed me that I would be embarking on the 'Empire Fowey', at approximately 5pm, meanwhile I was required to report to the Sgt who was in charge at assembly point D1 who would give me all the necessary instructions for embarkation etc. I made my way through the many assembly points until I found assembly point D1 and was met by an elderly Royal Artillery (RA) Sgt, who informed me that I could wander around, get myself a cup of tea (char) but had to report back to him by 3pm where I would be given instructions for embarkation. Whilst wandering around I kept on looking for a large ocean-going liner, named 'Empire Fowey', but the only ship I could see docked about 300 yards or more away, was a ship with smoke coming out of its one funnel and which looked like a large tramp steamer. I reported back to assembly point D1 at a few minutes before 3pm and was pleased to see that there were another five RADC soldiers also waiting there with the Sgt.

The Sgt then explained the embarkation procedure and informed us that we were to be accommodated in H.2.B deck. The Sgt knew that all the six of us were from the Royal Army Dental Corps (RADC) but with his warped sense of humour he asked if RADC stood for Richard Attenborough's Dancing Class. He asked us what kind of duties we did in the RADC and we explained working in dental surgeries, helping the dentist by mixing filling materials, sterilizing the instruments and keeping the surgeries cleaned etc. So you are all very keen on hygiene he asked us. In harmony we replied that we were. The Sgt continued in his warped sense of humour by then telling us that as we were so good at hygiene we would employed in the kitchen of the 'Empire Fowey' throughout the whole voyage where we would wash all the all greasy crockery, cutlery, and pots and pans and dry them - and this is what we eventually did, wearing our fatigue clothing every day. This was my first encounter ever with anybody from the RA and I found this RA Sgt to be an obnoxious nasty little man with a warped sense of humour. I therefore told myself the RA did not stand for Royal Artillery but Right Arseholes and I must admit that for the rest of my 27 years which I served in the army, that I never met a decent soldier from the RA. To me they were all Right Arseholes!

We were taken to the quayside where the ship was anchored and to my horror I saw the ship that we were to embark on - It was the 'Empire Fowey'. This was the ship which I had seen hours before in the distance and which I thought was a large tramp steamer. Going up the gangway and onto the ship all my illusions of going on a luxury sea cruise on some kind of liner vanished within seconds. On board I thought that the ship was quite dirty and smelt quite a lot. After finding our way to Deck H.2.B our party of six RADC soldiers found to our horror that this despicable RA Sgt was the sergeant in charge of Deck H.2.B and he continued to make life as miserable as possible for us six RADC soldiers. That was until two weeks later when he was reduced to the rank of corporal. After a few days at sea a Warrant Officer who was one of the permanent staff on the ship told us that the ship had built in Germany and was originally named Potsdam and had been launched in 1935. He added that the ship's tonnage was 17, 728 and that its passenger capacity was just 286. That figure of 286 did not make any sense at all because I was sure that there between over 1000 to 1500 officers and soldiers on our ship.

The ship sailed to Port Said where it berthed and great number of soldiers were allowed ashore for a time. The RADC personal were not. We sailed through the Suez Canal and berthed again at Aden. Once again many soldiers were allowed a few hours ashore, but once again the RA Sgt did not include us RADC lads in that number. I was told much later on that our trip on the 'Empire Fowey' was the last trip that that ship made through the Suez Canal due to the Suez war that was to take place a few weeks after our sailing. After our sailing the 'Empire Fowey' sailed via South Africa where she docked at Capetown for three days and all the soldiers were allowed ashore for those three days. These soldiers had the time of their lives as they were wined and dined by the expats in Capetown for the whole three days, as these expats had not seen British soldiers for many, many years. Very unlucky for us to be on the 'Empire Fowey's' last sailing through the Suez Canal, and not on that her first voyage around South Africa. I guess we were just two months two early!

Although we did not manage to get off the ship at Port Said or Aden we did manage to see the sea, daily and to see Port Said and Aden from the open top deck, because that was the only place we were allowed to smoke, so we all became regular smokers in order to gain access to the top deck. Nobody however was allowed on the top deck when we sailed through the Suez Canal as snipers had shot at people who were on the top deck on other ships which had gone through the canal months earlier. Following the awful dirty and smelly conditions of the ship my RADC mates and myself soon rechristened the ship "Empire Phoo-ey" and although we did not know it at the time, our rechristening of the ship was going to hold us in good stead in the near future. Meanwhile the Right Arseholes Sgt continued to give us RADC lads a very torrid time but unknown to him he was soon going to wish he had never met us.

As I have mentioned smoking was taboo on the lower decks but the RA Sgt - who was a forty a day smoker - was far too lazy to go up to the top deck for his smoke, and used to sneak into the toilet on our deck and smoke on a regular basis there. The ship had left Aden and was in the Arabian Sea heading towards Colombo which was to be out next port of call, when a major in the Royal Engineers came into our deck very early one morning and asked where the RA Sgt was. A volley of voices from the RADC lads informed the major that the Sgt was in the toilet smoking. More voices added that he was always in the toilet smoking. The major rushed into the toilet and within a minute the red faced Sgt, followed by the major came out of the toilet. The major marched the Sgt from our deck and we never saw him again.

During that part of the voyage between Aden and Colombo we had been given two postcards each with a photo of the 'Empire Fowey' on the front. These postcards were intended for us to complete and send to our families and were to be posted to them when the ship docked at Colombo. I completed my two postcard by crossing out 'Fowey' on the front and writing the word 'Phooey'. Overleaf, in the limited space, I wrote to my mother about the voyage and mentioned that I had not been allowed off the ship so far, so that I had seen nothing of Port Said and Aden, etc . I then put the postcards in the post box at the end of our deck and thought nothing more about it. The following morning a very friendly postal Sgt from the Royal Engineers came into our deck looking for a guy who came from Hackney in Derbyshire who was accommodated on deck H.2.B. I immediately informed him that it was me.

He proceeded to tell me that the Royal Engineers were responsible for the postal services in the army and that he was the permanent postal Sgt on the ship and that when collecting the postcards from the deck post box he noticed that my postcards were addressed to an address in Derbyshire, and had become interested (as he had been born in Buxton, Derbyshire which was about 20 miles from Hackney where I lived) and had read my postcards and had found them disturbing when I had 'lied' about my RADC mates and myself not being allowed off the ship throughout the voyage so far, as every soldier was either allowed to go ashore off the ship at either Port Said or Aden. My RADC mates had soon gathered around the RE Sgt and myself and they confirmed that we had not been allowed off the ship so far. We all went onto explain about the horrible RA Sgt and that he had ensured that we spent all our time below deck and were not allowed off the ship. On hearing our story the RE Sgt told all six of us RADC lads to report to him at the ship's RE Postal Office immediately the ship docked at Colombo, which we did at 6am on the morning our ship docked at Colombo. The RE Sgt told us that were going to spend the day ashore with him in Colombo and that we would be the first soldiers off of the ship. We explained to him that we were required in the ship's kitchen as we had to wash and clean all the pots and pans etc. The Sgt told us not to worry as everything had been taken care of and other arrangements made. We, along with the RE Sgt were in fact the first soldiers off the ship. The Sgt took us all on a guided tour of Colombo, where we were pestered every step of the way by locals asking if we wanted to go with their sisters, or buy some dirty cigarette/postcards which featured pictures of naked women. John Emerson, who was one of our party of six actually did buy a pack of these pictures. After a morning's tour the Sgt took us to a lovely restaurant/bar, where obviously he was well known from previous visits, and sat us down and told us that all drinks and food were to be on him. I remember ordering my first chicken curry ever and it was hot and delicious. The beers tasted like nectar as well. After finishing our food and during our drinking session John Emerson opened his pack of cards which he had purchased from one of the locals and distributed them amongst us. I was flabbergasted when I was handed one and saw the picture of a completely naked girl on it. I had never seen either an actual naked girl or even a photo of a naked girl before. It was during these drinks that the Sgt told is that we were "heroes" and when we asked why he told us that we were responsible for getting the RA Sgt reduced from Sgt to Cpl as a result of being found smoking in the toilets. He went on to tell us that the Sgt had been charged and brought before the OC of the ship who had reduced him in rank.

The Sgt explained further that the RA Sgt was the most hated senior rank in the Sgt's Mess on the ship and that he was continuously causing trouble and causing hardship to many of the soldiers on the ship. After the most wonderful and most delightful day in my life, at least until then, I finally boarded the ship with my colleagues and the ship left Colombo at 5pm for Singapore. The evening before we were due to dock in Singapore, we were told over the tannoy system that personal who were being posted to Singapore or Malaya (Whoops first time I had heard Malaya mentioned) would disembark first. A list of the units and names of some individuals were then read out. The names of four RADC personnel were then read out, which included my name. That meant at least two RADC would be going on to Hong Kong. Jolly for those two lucky lads I thought. We all embarked early in the morning and eventually on the quayside we were found by WO2 Harry Roper (later to be commissioned and to reach the rank of major before he sadly died as a result of a brain tumor). Harry, who we found to be a very decent guy, was very witty with a wicked sense of humour and he took us to the NAAFI canteen which was one the quayside. Over our cups of char Harry told us that two of us were going to spend the next couple of years holidaying in Singapore whilst the other two were being posted to Malaya (God that word again) and would be fighting for Queen and Country. Harry looked at John Emerson and myself and declared that we had drawn the short straws and would be leaving shortly for Nee Soon Transit Camp. Several 3 ton vehicles arrived shortly afterwards and all the personnel who were being posted to Malaya piled into these vehicles for the short journey to Nee Soon Camp. I never saw the other four RADC lads who had luckily managed to get postings to Singapore and Hong Kong again. I was to meet Major Roper six years later when he was the depot Quartermaster and I was posted into the depot as the QM's Sgt. It was a great pleasure to serve under Major Roper, who I subsequently discovered during my 27 years service in the army, that he was one of the finest British Army Officers I had the pleasure of ever meeting. Major Roper died in 1963 and I was one of his pall bearers at his military funeral.

As regards that friendly RE Sgt who helped us so much, I later found that in all my 27 years in the army that the every single RE officer or soldier I had the pleasure to meet were not only intelligent, but were 'top notch'. From that very day since I met that RE postal Sgt I have thought of the REs as Royal Excellence or Right

Excellent. I also had the pleasure to serve with 28 RE Regt in Tidworth, much later in my career.

During my service I made up many nicknames for the various Corps in the army I served with. Many QARANCs served as Dental Hygienists with the RADC at dental centers and in military hospitals so in addition to the REs and RA which I had nicknames for, I christened the QARANC (Queens Alexandra's Royal Army Nursing Corps), as 'Quick And Ready And Never Caught'. Alas, this was not to be true as I was to find out to my cost later on!

4

NEE SOON TO SEREMBAN

The 3 tonners soon arrived at Nee Soon camp and John Emerson and I were told, along with a few other guys who were on individual postings to report to a major, who was the Weapons Training Officer, at the armoury which was at the far end of the camp. We duly did that. A Sgt who was the major's assistant gave us a .303 rifle each, with oil, cleaning rods and cloths and demonstrated to us how to clean a rifle and he told us to clean our rifles. That done the Sgt inspected our rifles and then told us to remember the number which was marked in white paint on our rifle as that would be the rifle we would be issued with later on. He added that the rifle would be of more use than any woman we had been with! The Sgt made a list of our names with our rifle number marked against our names. All the rifles were put back in the armoury. We were told that later on we would be taken back to the armoury and issued with that rifle and a magazine containing 10 rounds of ammunition. The major then informed us that the magazine was not to be loaded into the rifle unless instructed by an officer or NCO. I asked the major why he had issued rifles to John Emerson and I, as being part of the Medical Services we were classed as non combatant soldiers. The major immediately informed us that the "war" against the communist terrorists (MNLA -

Malayan National Liberation Army) was not actually a war but had been termed to be a guerilla type conflict and that the British Government had termed it The Malayan Emergency. This being the case he added, the Geneva Convention did not apply and therefore every soldier was considered to be a combatant. I later found out the British Government had termed this Emergency as a guerilla conflict as the rubber plantations and tin-mining industries had pushed for the use of "Emergency" since their losses would not have been covered by Lloyd's insurers if it had been termed as a war.

Perhaps this was another excuse for the British Army, when they became the very first army to use Agent Orange Herbicides and defoliants to destroy bushes and food crops. These chemicals were dropped from helicopters or fixed wing aircraft. Many British soldiers who handled Agent Orange during the conflict suffered seriously in decades to come. The major went to explain that if we "managed" to lose a single bullet, or could not account for all our 10 rounds, that it would an automatic Court Martial with an automatic sentence of 28 days detention (jankers) in the military prison. I remembered then what the major had told us a few minutes before in that we could only load our rifles if instructed by an officer or NCO and I thought what do we do if no officer or NCO was around and if we are attacked by the Communist terrorists (CT's) . I never did get an answer to this. We were then told to leave the armoury but ensure that we reported back there at 6pm in order to collect our rifles and ammunition. Meanwhile the major told us that we were free to wander around the camp and that lunch and dinner would be served at certain times.

We reported back to the major at the armoury just before 6pm and we were issued with our rifles and ammunition. We then boarded the 3 ton lorries again for our journey to Singapore railway station. On arriving at Singapore rail station we were shown to the platform where the train which was to take us up country into Malaya was standing. The train certainly did not look like any of the express trains I had travelled on in the UK. In front of this train there was a armoured vehicle which looked like a mini tank. It had a search light on it and also machine guns mounted on its turret. We were informed by one of the Sgts who was waiting to board the train with us, that it was a Wickham Trolley which ran on rails and ran in front of the train to see if any of the rail line had been tampered with or damaged by the CTs, who would then lay in wait to ambush the train and its passengers.

On the end of the main train was an armoured type of carriage which also had machine guns mounted on its roof. After seeing all this I thought that at least we were going to be well protected on our train journey through Malaya, but on the other hand I thought there must have been quite a good number of trains already ambushed by the CTs, in order to have so much protection on our train. I was later to find out that a good number of trains had been ambushed by the CTs and a good number of British soldiers and other passengers killed as a result of those ambushes.

On getting settled in one of the train's carriages I noticed that we had a Gurkha soldier at both ends of the carriage and both these Gurkhas were armed with Sterling sub-machine guns. The infantry Sgt who was in charge of our carriage told us to try and keep away from the windows as much as possible and also in the event of an ambush to lie on the floor and wait for necessary orders from him. He told us that we could continue to carry on smoking and he wished us a "pleasant" trip. I must admit that I was chain smoking before the train left the station at well past 9pm. Welcome to Paradise I thought once again. Our first stop was Johor Bahru, just a few miles over the causeway which separates Singapore and Malaya, and this was where John Emerson got off. So it was a sad farewell I bade to John and I was never to see him again. The journey through the night passed without incident and we arrived at Seremban station in the early hours on the morning. I got off the train, with a couple of other guys and wondered how I was going to find my way to Rasah Camp. My fear was unfounded however, for Cpl Graham Purcell RADC , with Terry Diamond, RASC, the land rover driver were there to meet me. Graham shook my hand and told me "welcome to heaven, because it is heaven here" . We both got into the land rover and Terry Diamond drove us to Rasha Camp.

5

RASHA CAMP, SEREMBAN

I was very impressed when we arrived in Rasah Camp for the camp looked spotless and in addition to having a few stone buildings there were also many more wooden buildings which resembled luxury wooden holiday homes. The Dental Centre, the Medical Reception Station (MRS) and the RAMC Hygiene Unit were based at the very end of the camp, right next to the perimeter wire, which I was to find out later was the very best place in the camp to based and as far apart as possible from the guardroom, GSM (Garrison Sgt Major) and the Officers Mess. After handing my .303 rifle and my loaded magazine in at the guardroom Graham Purcell took me to one of the two accommodation buildings, known as billets and told me that each billet had very comfortable accommodation for 8 soldiers. The RADC soldiers and the soldiers from the MRS and RAMC Hygiene Units were based in these two billets. I was shown to the building that I was to be accommodated in which was only about 20 feet from the dental centre. Like every other wooden building in the camp our accommodation had a very nice wide verandah with tables and chairs on it. After unpacking my kitbag and finding my bed which I was to use for the next few years, Graham took me to the dental centre to meet the CO, who was Lt Colonel WC Hull. After a very brief introduction he then took me to the kitchen and dining room which was attached to the end of the dental centre.

Over breakfast Graham explained that Lt Col Hull was not only the CO of the dental centre but was also in charge of all dental centres and dental personnel in Malaya and only answerable to Colonel Green, who was based at GHQ FARELF (Far Eastern Land Forces) in Singapore. Colonel Green was not only a full colonel, but he was also the Deputy Director of Dental Services (DDDS) for all dental centres and dental personnel in the Far East - which covered Malaya, Singapore, Brunei and Hong Kong.

He added that in addition to the RADC having its own CO, that also the MRS had its own CO as did the Hygiene Unit and that these three units did not come under the Camp CO for discipline of any kind. Good news I thought. Therefore all three units were completely independent, and these three units shared a separate kitchen and dining room at the end of the dental centre and was not part of the main kitchen and dining room on the camp. More good news I thought. After breakfast Graham gave me a walking tour around the camp finishing up with seeing the GSM who insisted on seeing every soldier who was to be accommodated in Rasha Camp. The GSM was WO 1 Andrews of the Royal Artillery and he was commonly known by the lads as the 'poisoned dwarf' due to being only about five foot three. Graham told me the GSM was married to a large

German woman who gave him a very hard time at home, and he, in turn took it out of the lads in the camp whenever he had the chance to do so. Graham also explained that whilst the GSM was responsible for allocating duties and overseeing discipline in the camp, that soldiers of the independent units in the camp who had their own Commanding Officers, did not come under the GSM for any duties. If the soldiers of any independent units were to be charged by the GSM for any offence, then they would appear in front of their own Commanding Officers and not the Camp Commandant. Graham warned me to be very wary of the GSM who did not like the 'untouchable' soldiers of those independent units.

During the evening whilst drinking on the verandah of my wooden billet with some of the soldiers I was told by one of them that they always referred to Lt Col Hull as 'Shithouse' due to his initials being WC. Obviously this name was never used when Lt Col Hull was in hearing range. Lt Col Hull was about aged 45 plus I guess and I was told that he was a single man, a woman hater and his main hobbies were photography, sailing, fishing, golf and gardening. In fact he was always supervising the Officer's Mess gardeners, much to the annoyance of the local gardeners. He also grew his own prize orchids of which he was very proud. The lads told me that I was going to have a very cushy time at the dental centre in Rasha camp during my time there as I would only have to do my clerical duties and no regimental duties and I went to bed thinking that this could be paradise after all.

I was woken next morning in the billet by Kristen, one of our civilian cooks who gave me a cup of char. The lads in my billet told me that one of the cooks came round every morning and woke us with a cup of char.

God I thought this is better than Butlins Holiday Camp. After ablutions and getting dressed, Graham took me to the dental centre to meet the staff. The dental staff consisted of Lt Col Hull the CO, and two National Service dental officers, a Captain John Horne who ran the dental centre when the CO was away on many of his trips. Horne not only was in charge when the colonel was away but he thought he was a colonel and he played the part to a tee. Horne kept a pet monkey at the dental centre that he called 'Kong'. Perhaps he named this primate after King Kong, as this creature was as strong as a young gorilla, as I was to find out to my cost later on. This ape like monkey was smart as he got on well with the officers and civilians, but always showed his big fang like teeth to all soldiers and hissed at them. Another arse crawler I thought! He had already bit two of the RADC lads I was told. The second dental officer was Captain Churchyard and his pet was an Alsatian. This Alsatian was smart as well and was always in trouble as he always went down to the Services school to where the bottles of milk had been left outside and took the tops off the milk bottles with his tongue and then sipped the milk. At the time I thought that I had come to a mini zoo and not a dental centre. I was then to meet the three National Service RADC lads who worked at the dental centre. First I was taken to the dental laboratory to meet the dental technician corporal whose name was Ian Alistair Malcolm Andrew Pratt. What a mouthful! Pratt was the son of a well known Scottish laird. I was soon to find out that this guy was Pratt by name and nature! The next two guys I met were dental clerks Cpl Johnny Hart and Cpl Harry Hughes. None of the RADC lads did any surgery work or any clinical duties as the dental centre employed three Malay male civilians, Ramasammy, David and Harris to do those tasks. I was to find that both David and Harris were top guys but that Ramasammy was not only a trouble maker, but a snitch who told the 'Shithouse' everything when the colonel returned from his many trips; he was, naturally the CO's favorite. He ceased to be the colonel's favourite within a few weeks of my arrival at the unit! Ramasammy was also Horne's favourite as he always looked after the monkey. The dental centre had a very impressive set-up and basically consisted of 3 surgeries, an x-ray room, a darkroom, a large waiting room, the COs office, an office/restroom for the dental officers, a large general office, a dental laboratory and a large storeroom. All good news! More good news came when Cpl Purcell handed me two stripes and congratulated me on becoming acting paid full Corporal.

Graham explained that he was due to be posted to the dental centre at Kuala Lumpur a few days later and that I, being the only regular RADC soldier, would be the NCO I/C office and responsible for all the administrative work. Graham explained further that the establishment at the dental centre was for 3 full corporals and that the part 2 order had already gone off to records confirming my promotion. Lucky me I thought a full Cpl just a couple of months after my 19th birthday and a nice pay rise! Life was going to be far much better than I ever anticipated I thought.

Next it was off to meet the two military guys in the Hygiene Unit. S/Sgt Gil Meek RAMC was a married accompanied NCO and the NCO in charge of the unit and it was to turn out that he was to become not only a very good friend but my main mentor. Later on I often did baby-sitting duties for Gil. His assistant was Cpl Chico Burrell RAMC. Chico and I were to become the best of friends and indeed Chico was bunked next to me in our billet. The rest of the Hygiene staff were local Malay lads (basically "coolies") who carried the mosquito sprayers on their backs most of the time and did the necessary daily spraying, where and when, when directed by Gil or Chico. The CO of the Hygiene Unit was based in Kluang and was an officer I never did meet.

Onto the MRS where I was introduced to three doctors, including the CO, whose names I do not recall now as I had very little to do with them from that day on. The main RAMC soldiers whom I was introduced to were S/Sgt Sexton RAMC, who was the NCO I/C, and a really nice guy. Other RAMC guys were Cpls Derek Underwood, John Bates, and L/Cpls John Briggs and Terry Foad. I was introduced to the two MRS RASC drivers, L/Cpl 'Tich' Marshall and L/Cpl Terry Diamond (whom I had already met). Most of the clinical work and nursing duties were done by Malay male nurses. The startling two things about the set-up of these three units were that all its soldiers were NCOs and that all civilian staff was Malay males. There could not have been any similar set-up like that anywhere in the British army.

6

FIRST FEW DAYS IN RASAH CAMP

I started work and Graham Purcell showed me the ropes before he disappeared to Kuala Lumpur on his new posting. The work was very easy and I was mainly responsible for maintaining an orderly office, writing and typing letters, keeping up to the date the personal records of all the officers and soldiers, indenting for all dental equipment and maintaining stock records of such, publishing Part 2 Orders and submitting weekly and monthly returns to GHQ in Singapore. The hours were very cushy as well with 90 minutes off for lunch and like all the other soldiers I took the opportunity after lunch to have 30 minutes kip (sleep) on top of my bed, as often I felt quite tired due to the high humidity, which was always over 60%. Each of the four RADC soldiers were required to work one Saturday in every four weeks, so we had plenty of time off.

It was during my first week at the dental centre that I was taken down in Seremban town and showed all the bars that the lads drank at. There were quite a few and we sampled the beer at a few of them. The two drinking establishments which were to become my favourites were The Mee Lee Hotel and The Yam Yam Cabaret. More on these two establishments later.

L/Cpl John Briggs of the MRS was a bit of a queer guy and he was nicknamed "the Mad Professor", or "Professor". Every spare moment he had he would wander into the jungle looking for large insects, small reptiles and snakes which he collected. Once he had caught them he brought them back to camp and put the larger insects into jars with formalin. The snakes he caught, and he caught quite a few on a frequent basis, he sold to the Chinese guy in Seremban who sold snakes to his customers. The lads from the Dental Centre, Hygiene Unit and MRS were accommodated in two billets and it was unfortunate that Briggs was accommodated in my billet as he often came in at all hours with those pests from the jungle in his basket he always seem to be carrying. It was during my first week in the camp when I was having a kip on the top of my bed after lunch that I woke up to find a viper snake on my chest. Without thinking I jumped off my bed like lightening. On landing down from the ten feet I had jumped up I saw Briggs and another soldier in hysterics and screaming with laughter at the far end of the billet. I knew immediately what had happened. I rushed over to Briggs and grabbed him by the throat and asked him what he thought he was playing at. He croaked that it was only a joke and that he had anesthetised all the snake's head by spraying it with Ethyl Chloride. Whilst he was croaking all this to me I noticed that the snake was slithering away on the floor; obviously the snake had come out of the anesthetic much quicker than Briggs had thought. I then instructed Briggs to catch this poisonous snake and to put it back in his basket, which he did. For the uneducated Ethyl Chloride spray is a skin refrigerant. It works by freezing and numbing the skin. It is not a local anesthetic and the mad professor should have known this. I certainly knew what Ethyl Chloride was because we used quite a bit of the stuff in dentistry. I marked Briggs's card and knew that my opportunity would come for revenge in the future at sometime or other.

At the dental centre we had a Jectaflo anesthetic machine which had two blue nitrous oxide (laughing gas) cylinders and two black oxygen cylinders attached to it. By using this machine a dentist could administer mild inhalation sedation with nitrous oxide and oxygen, in order to keep his patient in a conscious state while depressing the feeling of pain. The dentist usually used this machine when he had to do a difficult extraction. The alternative was to send the patient to the dental specialist at a dental department in a British military hospital (BMH) where he would be given a general anesthetic. As the nearest BMH was about 50 miles away most of our patients who had to have difficult extraction done, chose to them done under the anesthetic machine. As these machines were never considered to be safe a second dentist was always required to be present and he administered the anesthetic whilst the 2nd dentist did the difficult extraction. (In later years these machines were banned in the army and most civilian dental establishments as they were deemed to be unsafe and liable to explode).

Unknown to the CO and his dentists these machines had another excellent use. When one of our lads had a very bad hangover from a heavy night boozing we used to give him a good whiff of oxygen from the machine the following morning. The soldier was soon back to normal and was "walking on air". A few days later after the "snake incident" Briggs celebrated his birthday at the bars in town. I was told that it was a right booze up by all those who attended.

It so happened that the mad professor made a very big mistake when he came to see me with a massive hangover the following morning and asked me if I could give him a good whiff of oxygen. Sure I told him. I sat him in the dental chair and put the machine's mask over his nose, but instead of switching the black oxygen (CO_2) cylinder on I switched the blue Nitrous Oxide (N_2O) cylinder on. Soon he was screaming his head off with laughter so loudly that I thought he would wake up the dead. I switched the cylinder off and Briggs got out of the chair and ran outside, laughing and swearing like a trooper for about five minutes. When assisting the dentist we often found that a patient would often swear and say awful things when going under the anesthetic. The worst case I ever encountered was when one of the dentists administered this type of anesthetic to a matron. The language was the worst I had ever heard in the life. For the uneducated Nitrous Oxide (N_2O) was commonly known as "laughing gas".

Of course Briggs, after he stopped laughing and swearing and had come back to normality had a go at me so I reminded him about the snake episode and that the "score" was 1-1. He saw the point and we shook hands and I never had any trouble from Briggs after that we became quite good friends.

7

FIRST MONTH IN RASAH CAMP

My first month in the dental centre in Rasha Camp was not to end before another incident involving me took place. This time it was a serious incident and was to be the very first time that I had been wounded 'in action'. As I previously mentioned, Captain Horne kept a pet monkey called Kong at the dental centre and this monkey was never allowed anywhere near the Officers Mess. During the day on dry days he would be a on long lead and tied to one of the palm or papaya trees on the large lawn which was in front of the dental centre, the MRS and the Hygiene Unit. On wet days he would be on a shorter lead and chained to one of the posts on the verandah. At night he would be put in his cage in the large dental centre store room.

The dental store was a large store and contained all metal enclosed shelving where the drugs, dental expendables and dental instruments were kept. The only things that "Shithouse" (The CO) allowed on the floor were a small cage which had straw on the floor which housed the money at nights and the wooden boxes which came to us from CMED (Command Medical Equipment Depot) in Singapore, which contained the medical supplies which we had indented for. Even these boxes had to be opened and the items checked against the invoices and put in the enclosed metal cabinets within 24 hours of their arrival. There were no exceptions and the CO always inspected the store room daily, around 11am when he was in the dental centre.

In addition to Captain Horne, the other person who looked after Captain Horne's monkey was Ramasammyy. Ramasammy who was the favourite of both the CO and the captain was also the surgery assistant who worked with Captain Horne in his surgery. I suspect that Captain Horne gave Ramasammy quite a bit of money, in addition to his free tin of 50 cigarettes for doing these non-official duties.

Ramasammy usually got to the dental centre just after 8am. He then got the surgery ready and switched the sterilizer on which took 30 minutes to sterilize the instruments and he then took the monkey outside and tied it up. He then ensured that the monkey's cage was clean. Captain Horne started work at 9am and he would generally arrive at about 8.45am in order to play and feed his pet monkey. During lunchtime Captain Horne never went to the Officer's Mess for food as he brought sandwiches and fruit in and he fed himself and his monkey on the lawn. When the dental centre was due to close Captain Horne would feed and play with his monkey again until Ramasammy took the monkey away and put him in his cage in the store room. On Sundays and Public holidays Ramasammy would always come in and do his monkey duties. We used to joke that Horne kept two pet monkeys in Kong and Ramasammy. I suspect that Ramasammy would have looked after the monkey without any payment as he was always trying to curry favour with the CO and Horne. If Ramasammy was absent for any reason then some other poor RADC would have to do the monkey business.

It was about the 3rd week of my time at the dental centre when I came into the office at 8am. Horne telephoned me at my office and told me that Ramasammy had telephoned him at the Officer's Mess and had informed him that he was unable to come to work that day as he had to take his wife to the local hospital after she had been violently sick during the night. Horne told me or rather ordered me to take over the monkey duties of Ramasammy, tie the monkey outside then to ensure that its cage was clean. Obviously I reluctantly agreed as I had only been in the unit for 3 weeks and I did not want to get off to a bad start and cause trouble.

I unlocked the storeroom and switched the light on. The monkey's cage door was open, (I suspected later that Ramasammy had left it open on purpose) and I could not see the monkey anywhere. Knowing that I had put two large 4 feet tall wooden boxes behind the door which had arrived from CMED at 5pm the night before and which I was going to unpack and check the following morning, I stooped down a little and peered around the door. I caught a quick glimpse of the creature and he was stood on one of the wooden boxes holding the 12in crowbar (which I used to use to open the wooden boxes) in his right hand. The monkey was faster than lightening and in one foul swoop he hit me on the head with the force of a gorilla and split the top of my skull open.

I saw stars and I let out an almighty scream as blood flowed down my face, into my eyes and onto the floor. Johnny Hart who was in the office heard my scream and came running in order to see what had happened. He came into the storeroom where I still was and the monkey tried to castrate him by giving him a massive swipe with the crowbar he was still holding at Johnny's wedding tackle. Johnny managed to put the creature back in its cage but not before getting bitten. I was drenched in blood, and there was also lots of blood all over my spotless storeroom floor. Johnny saw that I was bleeding like a pig and he took me to the medical surgery in the MRS which was only 10 yards away. One of the doctors examined me and then proceeded to put 10 stitches into the top of my head. The doctor thought that I may have suffered concussion so to be on the safe side he told me he had to keep me overnight in the MRS for observation. He therefore admitted me to one of the hospital beds in the ward of 12 beds. The MRS had a ward of 12 beds for minor cases. All major cases were referred to BMH Kinrara in Kuala Lumpur which was some 50 miles away. Some 60 years later I still have that very nasty, awful scar on the top of my head covered with the bit of grey hair I have left and I am dreading going bald as I would look like Frankenstein!

"Shithouse" was away in Penang at the time inspecting the dental centre up there so Captain Horne was in charge of the dental centre. Horne was told what had happened immediately he entered the dental centre, but he obviously knew something was amiss before he entered the dental centre as there was no monkey tied up outside. Horne did not come to see me in the ward right away but left it until he had seen the patients on sick parade. I reckon he visited me around 11am but I could not be sure as I was still feeling a little hazy. I do remember the 'sweet' words he spoke to me however! He said that he was sorry that such an unfortunate accident had taken place. He spoke of 'esprit de corps' and all that rubbish and what such a happy unit the dental centre was etc. He asked if I was going to make a fuss or report the matter to the CO on his return from Penang. Knowing that Horne could be very vindictive and nasty when it suited him I agreed with him that it was indeed an accident and that I may frightened the monkey too much etc. I confirmed to him that I would indeed not be reporting the matter and that it was just one of those things. Horne left my bedside a happy man. Whether the CO ever got to hear about the matter I do not know as he certainly never heard anything from me.

Of course, irrespective of what I had told Horne, I had not intentions whatsoever of letting the matter rest there and I spent the rest of the day and the evening plotting revenge and the early departure from Seremban of both Horne and his pet gorilla. All that time

I kept of thinking about that famous idiom "softly, softly catchee monkey" or was it "Slowly, slowly catchee monkey"? Either way I knew I would have an opportunity at some time or other, but I did not realise at the time that that opportunity it would come so quickly. Whist thinking I thought that perhaps Ramasammy had planned the whole thing all along. He had certainly left the cage door open (most likely deliberately) when had put the money into its cage. More than likely his wife had not been violently sick overnight and that he did not take her to hospital the following morning before telephoning Horne up and informing him that he would not be able to come to work that morning. Ramasaamy knew that Horne would arrange for one of the RADC lads to perform the monkey duties in his absence that day. The more I thought about it the more I was convinced that my suspicions were well founded, especially when he kept well away from me when I returned to duty and when I also noticed his sly smirk and grin he gave me when he thought I was not looking, so to be on the safe side I added Ramasammy to my hit list!

8

INTRODUCTION TO THE YAM YAM CABARET

The remainder of 1956 passed without any incidents, but little did I suspect at the time that 1957 was going to be a lot more interesting. During the months leading up to the new Year I did a good job in the dental centre according to the CO. I spent a lot of my spare time reading, listening to music and babysitting for Gil Meek and Sgt Bill Chester RAOC. I went into the town twice a week to sample the exotic food, or for drinks at the bars or even a visit to the cinema. Life was certainly good. My tax free Local Overseas Allowance (LOA) was about three times my weekly pay and for the first time in my life I was able to save money. In addition to this the army gave us a free weekly ration of a tin of 50 cigarettes and you could pick from John Players, Capstan and a whole range of brands. As Chico Burrell did not smoke he gave his weekly tin of 50 to me and as it turned out I never had to buy a cigarette whilst I was in Malaya, which was a great saving. The army also gave you an extra tin of 50 cigarettes, termed "patients comforts" when you were in hospital. As the MRS always had a more than adequate supply I always had as many cigarettes as I ever wanted. How times change. The army encouraged us to smoke and smoke even more when we were hospitalized. Nowadays, it is virtually a crime to smoke a cigarette and I believe that smoking is banned from all barracks now. I have often thought about suing the army for encouraging me to smoke and for giving me all those cigarettes! Smoking was a habit I have never been able to stop.

Drinks were cheap in the bars in town and often when I was with Chico, which was most of the time, we got many free beers from the bar owners. Food was not only exotic but was also cheap and the Malay foods, especially the Malaya curry become my favourite food for the rest of my life. All these bars, restaurants and open air restaurants remained open until the early hours of the morning, which was a massive change from Hackney where everything closed down at 9.30pm every night. Rasha Camp and Seremban certainly seemed the nearest thing to paradise.

Gil Meek of the Hygiene Unit spent a lot of his time doing mosquito control and supervising the coolies who sprayed various areas inside and outside the camp daily. He left Chico to do a weekly inspection of all the local bars to see that they were sufficiently clean for British troops to drink and eat in. Chico had an army motor bike which he used for his visits and often when I was not busy he used to take me and I rode pillion on the bike. At every bar Chico used to enter he started sniffing very loudly before he inspected the kitchen, bar area and toilets, looking for rats, mice and cockroaches etc. If Chico was not satisfied that the bars were not up to standard he would place the bars out of bounds to the troops and a large notice would be placed on the front door or front window of the bar stating "Out of Bounds" to all Service personnel. As these bar owners relied on most of their business from service personnel they did everything possible to remain on the right side of Chico. This meant lots of free beers on Chico's visits, whether it was on his weekly inspection or his night time drinking. Delicious curries were also free for Chico. Of course being Chico's best mate meant that whenever I was with him I was included in those freebees. What could I spend my money on I asked?

When Chico was not visiting the bars he was generally out during the day visiting a variety of different soldiers' wives! Chico told me that whilst he preferred white women to Asian women and that he had a regular supply from the two white women; he was not averse to going with a really good looking Asian girl if the opportunity arose. One embarrassing thing happened one morning when Chico took me on his motor bike and inspected one of the bars. Afterwards he said that as we had plenty of time left he thought he would visit his latest mistress who was married to the REME L/Cpl. I asked him what I was going to do whilst he was with her and he replied that he was taking me to see the wife of the RAPC Sgt, another of his mistresses and that he would collect me from her house when he had finished. He knocked at the door and introduced me to the woman and I spent the next embarrassing hour drinking coffee with her and ignoring her innuendos and suggestions until Chico called to collect me. I was still scared of women and was still a virgin. The woman must have thought I was a right Charlie, or even queer not to accept her 'offers' I guess.

Chico had two favourite places where he used to like drinking at nights. The Mee Bar was his favourite and both Chico and I spent many happy hours there.

The Yam Yam Cabaret was a close second and we also spent many happy hours there drinking and dancing. The name Cabaret was a misleading name, for the Yam Yam was simply a dance hall, with a bar and 42 dancers, who were prostitutes. The dancers were seated on numbered seats 1 to 42 which were in a U shape on the dance floor. There were many tables behind the dancers for customers to sit and drink. The idea was that if you wanted to dance you had to go to the little ticket office next to the bar and buy 5 tickets for M $2. When you wanted to dance with a certain girl you would then approach her give her one of your tickets. The girl would then put the ticket down her bra and dance with you for one dance. If you wanted to take the girl out for either a meal or to bed you would then agree on a price and she could leave the Yam Yam at any time after midnight. Of course most of the guys who booked the girls out had only one thing on their mind and that was to sleep with them, for who wants to go out for a meal after midnight?

The youngest and prettiest girls were seated in the low numbered chairs 1 to 10. From chairs 11 to chair 30 the girls were older but still quite attractive. Once you got past chair 30 then you were into the much, much older women who had lost their looks a few years ago. No 42, the last chair was taken by a woman who was 50 if she was a day. Of course the ladies who occupied chairs 1 to 10 were always the popular, danced the most and were booked out the most, for obvious reasons.

All the girls had nice names of course but some of them changed them to names of famous female Hollywood stars who were popular at the time. All the girls were given nicknames of course by the soldiers and I guess that I will remember most of the girls names until my dying day. I can still remember what numbered chairs they used to sit in as well. In the first ten chairs sat, No 1 was Rose; No 2 Tina; No 3 Jane ; No 4 Sue; No 5 Doris; No 6 Gina; No 7 Betty; No 8 Lucy; No 9 Lisa; No 10 Nina;

No 1 "Randy" Rose. She was a beautiful Eurasian girl aged about 19. She was also one of the best looking girls I ever saw in Asia. Obviously she was the most popular girl in the dance hall and was always in great demand. She was called "randy" as she always chatted up the guys if they did chat her up and she promised them a lot of Eastern Promise if they went with her.

No 2 "Tiny Tina". She was aged 18 or so and was a very petite Malaya girl who only stood 5ft high, thus her name. The guys said that "tiny" not apply to the rest of her anatomy though!

No 3 "Calamity" Jane. Aged about 19 and Malay. According to my mates she was called Calamity because she always wanted to be in the saddle and to do all the riding!

No 4 "Sexy" Sue. A very young looking Chinese girl who always wore a cheongsam. She certainly looked very sexy that was for sure!

No 5 "Dirty" Doris. Another very attractive Chinese girl under 20 years. I am not sure if she was nicknamed "Dirty" because there was always a whiff of BO under her armpits when you danced with her, or whether it was because she knew a lot of dirty tricks in bed which the other girls didn't.

No 6. "Gee Spot" Gina. Aptly named for obvious reasons. Gina was also an extremely attractive Eurasian girl under the age of 20.

No 7. "Busty" Betty. This Indian lady was the tallest out of the 10 and she was nicknamed as a result of her large bust. It was very hard to dance with Betty and whisper in her ear as due to her very large bust you could never get close so we had to speak louder to her than we would have liked.

No 8. "Juicy" Lucy. Another very attractive Chinese lady who always wore a Cheongsam, which showed her beautiful slender legs off. There were many girls named

Lucy in the various dance halls and to my knowledge they were all called "Juicy".

No 9."Lester" Lisa. A very attractive Malay girl. She was nicknamed because she was another girl who liked to be in charge in the bed and on top and the guys reckoned that she could ride better than Lester Piggott who was one of the best flat jockeys the world has ever seen.

No 10. "The Nymph". Lisa was another attractive Malay who the lads told me was a nymphomaniac. Chico once told me that she could never get enough of it and would sometime offer the guys a freebee if she had not been propositioned or booked out.

I used to dance with all these ten girls on a regular basis. I had never danced with any girl, or even had held one in my arms until I started dancing in the Yam Yam but these girls taught me to dance and dance well and according to the lads I became one of the best dancers seen on the floor in the Yam Yam. I am not saying that I was as good as Fred Astaire but I knew I was a good dancer. I spent quite a bit of money buying the tickets in order to dance, but whenever I was with Chicko, the manager of the Yam Yam always gave us loads of free tickets.

The girls liked dancing with me I knew, but not because I was a good dancer. Chico knew all the girls so well and he told them all that I was a "Virgin Boy", not gay, but a soldier or had never had sex with any girl. This being the case the girls used to chat me up all the time and offered me free sex anytime and anywhere. The used to bet which girl would be the first girl who takes my virginity so that they could brag about it afterwards. They all lost their bets! From the day Chico told these girls my secret I was always called "The Virgin Boy" by them and never by my Christian name

Every three months at the camp we were given lectures and presentations on drugs and venereal diseases.

The lectures on drugs were given to NCOs and WO's (Warrant Officers) by the Military Police (MPs) and after the lecture we were shown slides and films of the drugs; what they were and frightening pictures of what those drugs could do to people. The WO's and NCO's had to attend these lectures every three months without fail and we were told of the many signs to look out for if we suspected any solider who was taking drugs we were told to report it immediately to the MP's. I would state that in all my 27 years that I never saw or knew of any soldier who had taken drugs or who was taking drugs.

Just as frightening as the drugs lectures, the lectures on venereal diseases (VD) which were given by the doctors every three months and were compulsory for all soldiers to attend.

At the very first of these lectures I attended the doctor went to great length to destroy two myths. The first one was that you could catch VD from toilet seats. The doctor added that you could only catch VD if you had been with a woman and not for any other reason. The second myth (used in the army a lot) he destroyed was that a blobby knob meant demob (discharged from the army).

The doctor informed us that this myth was completely untrue and it was not an offence if you reported you had VD as you would be treated by a doctor and you would continue your service in the army, but he warned us that it was an offence not to report if you had VD. We were also told (how true it was I never did find out) that in the American forces it was the complete opposite and it was an offence to report you had VD, but not an offence if you did not report it. Perhaps this is why so many American servicemen in the years to come spread so much VD around Asia when they were on R&R leave. I fully remember the doctor only ever talking about two types of VD and these were Syphilis and Gonorrhea. Gonorrhea was noticed after 10 days you had been with a woman and this disease could easily be treated by "magic bullets", (penicillin injections). Syphilis was far more dangerous and came in two stages. The first stage was seen after 28 days and had to be treated very quickly over a longer period. If the first stage was not treated then the second stage went into operation and could lead to death. We were shown slides and films of people with these two diseases and these pictures were frightening and enough to put you off sex for life, especially if you were a young virgin boy! I well remember that the doctor only spoke about these two diseases and did not mention about many of the other types of VDs, like Chlamydia, Herpes, HPV, HIV/AIDS, just to name a few. Perhaps those diseases had not been discovered at that time! The doctor concluded his lecture by reminding all of us that on every camp there was a Prophylactic Station where you could pick up a packet of 3 (durex) before you went out, or you could use these stations when you returned to camp having been with a woman. I thought at the time that it was useless going to these stations to clean up when you had been with a woman and done the "dirty deed" as it was far too late by then. I came out of these lectures much wiser and vowed that it would be years and years before I went with any woman! The funny part of these lectures was leaning the word gonorrhea for the first time, for in the camp was Gunner Hera who was in the RA and who had recently been posted out to Malaya. The lad got so depressed when we started taking the "Mickey" out of him that the Camp Commandant soon promoted him to Lance Bombardier (L/Bdr).

That night, following the lectures on "social diseases" a few of us went into town with "Tich" Marshall, the driver who was due to back to the UK (Blighty) a couple of days later after finishing his service in Malaya. We had a good sent off party for him and as usual we most of our drinking in the Mee Lee bar before hitting the Yam Yam Cabaret. "Tich" assured us that he was going to get laid that night by one of the girls and we left him dancing away with "Lester" Lisa. I just hope when "Tich" arrived back in the UK that he was free of any unwanted present from any of the Yam Yam girls. "Tich" was great guy and an excellent driver and he was going to be sadly missed, but unknown to us at the time, his replacement, a L/Cpl "Geordie" Shaw, a giant of a man was also going to be a top guy and a lot of fun.

9
MONKEY BUSINESS

Christmas 1956 and the New Year 1957 came and went and I guess that I had been enjoying my job and my life in Rasah Camp and in Seremban of just over four months by this time. The week started very badly for Ramasammy the snitch, but unknown to me at the time it was going to be an excellent week for me.

Monday was quite a busy day as the staff in the centre were getting everything ready and tipsy turvy for the six monthly visit of Col Green the DDDS from Singapore. The DDDS was due to arrive at the Officer's Mess in Rasah Camp at about 12.30pm and our CO was due to meet him there at that time. From what I gathered later on the DDDS did arrive on time but the CO did not. After lunch they had planned a game of golf and the DDDS was due to carry out his inspection of our centre the following day.

The CO arrived at the dental centre dead on 9am and he was annoyed to find out that the surgery was not ready for him, as Ramasammy had forgotten to switch on the sterilizer, let alone not putting the instruments out ready for the 9am patient. Ramasammy got a deserved rocket from the CO. Worse was to follow when the CO found out that Ramasammy had doubled booked two officer patients for a 10am appointment. The rollicking that Ramasammy got for that was heard loud and clear in my office. Even worse was to follow when the Garrison Adjutant arrived for his 11.30am appointment. The appointment had been made for the usual 30 minutes, but as the CO was to perform a root treatment on the patient, the appointment should have been made for 60 minutes and not just 30 minutes. The CO was already running late due to the double booking of the 10am appointment and he was in a foul mood when he eventually saw the Garrison Adjutant 30 minutes late. The CO told Ramasammy in no uncertain terms that he was an idiot to only book the Garrison Adjutant in for a 30 minutes appointment instead on 60 minutes.

Ramasammy was in a foul mood that morning, due to the two previous rollicking he had already received from the CO, and he started to argue with the CO in front of the Garrison Adjutant telling the CO that he had not mentioned the root canal treatment. One thing you should know and if you don't, you learn very quickly, is that you as a, subordinate never ever argue with a colonel, as colonels are never wrong and you will never win. Another thing is that you never argue with an officer when he is in presence of another officer. Suicide! The CO was swearing and ranting at Ramasammy; the air was blue and we could hear instruments being thrown in the surgery. Music to the ears of us in the general office. The CO eventually completed the treatment on the Garrison Adjutant at 1.00pm and by this time he was running 30 minutes. The CO made quick haste for the Officer's Mess order to meet the DDDS and I reckon he must have been 40 minutes by the time he reached the Officer's Mess. We did not see our CO and DDDS that afternoon as they had planned that game of golf in Seremban.

On Tuesday the DDDS spent most of the day inspecting our dental centre, checking records, documents and returns, checking the precious metals register and the secrets documents registers and doing a spot inventory check and talking to every member of the staff. We received a really excellent report from him.

So by Wednesday I was in a very good mood when I woke up as the inspection had gone well and that we would not see the two colonels until the following Monday as they were then going to Malacca early on Wednesday morning to do some sailing , returning to the Officer's Mess late afternoon. Then they had planned to depart on Thursday morning going up to Penang for three days to play golf and go fishing. This meant that we would not see the CO for five days until Monday morning. Unbeknown at the time, they were never to make that trip to Penang! I was also looking forward to playing football for the garrison team of which I was a regular player. Johnny Hart and our new driver, Geordie Shaw would also be in the team. I was especially looking forward to this particular match as we were we were due to play against Kuala Lumpur (KL) Garrison and I knew that Graham Purcell the dental clerk at the dental centre at KL was the goalkeeper for this team.

I did my normal dental duties and after a light lunch I went off to my billet to change into my football gear. The match went exceptionally well and we won 5-0 of which I scored two goals.

The other three goals were scored by Geordie who had been on Newcastle United books before he got called up for National Service. After the match we had a couple of beers with the opposing team and took the "mickey" out of Graham. Soon the opposing team were on their way back to KL and Johnny, Geordie and myself made our way back to our billets in order to get a shower, change into our civvies and go for dinner, which was always served between 5.30pm to 6.30pm. It had been a great day so far but unknown to me at the time it was going to get even better later on.

The MRS was always manned for 24 hours a day and there was always a NCO on duty overnight from 5pm until 8am the following morning. As it happened it was Gil Meek who was on duty on that particular day. Although Gil was married and lived out in Army married quarters and like all married NCOs who did night duties at the MRS who lived out, he ate his meals (dinner and breakfast) in the MRS/Dental dining room. It was at dinner that Gil came in for his dinner and sat next to Johnny Hart and myself and whispered to me that Lt Col Hull had telephoned him about 15 minutes earlier asking if the dental keys had been handed in. Gil informed the colonel that Ramasammy had handed the keys for the dental centre into the MRS at 5pm that evening. Gil added that Lt Col Hull had informed him he would be coming down to the dental centre with Col Green the DDDS after dinner in the Officer's Mess had finished in order to use the darkroom and develop some films that they had taken. They expected to arrive at the MRS shortly after 8pm. This being the case he asked Gil to ensure that somebody was in the MRS at that time so that he could collect the keys. Gil was giving me all this information as a friendly warning to stay away from the dental centre and not be in there drinking tea or messing around when the two colonels arrived. I was a bit disappointed to hear that the CO would be coming down as we had not expected to see him again until the Monday. I was determined to keep out of his way when he did come down that evening.

There were two sets of keys to the dental centre, Johnny Hart had one set and I had the other set. One set was always kept in our billet and the second set was always taken to the MRS in case of emergencies and when Johnny and I were not available. On this particular Wednesday I had left my keys in the dental centre and informed Cpl Hughes that I would not be back as I was playing football and I instructed that whoever was the last person to lock up was to take the keys to the MRS reception.

After we had finished our dinner Johnny and I went back to our billet at around 6.30pm. I looked at him and told him what a great opportunity had arisen with the CO coming down and Ramasammy having been the last to leave the dental centre, lock up and hand the keys into MRS reception. Johnny soon got my drift and remembering that both of us had been bitten by the bloody monkey we both went into immediate planning some monkey business. With our plans formulated we grabbed Johnny's keys and started to put our plan into operation.

Johnny and I crept into the dental centre but we did not put any lights on. I opened the CO's office door and left it open whilst Johnny went into the store room. The monkey was in his cage. Johnny shouted for me to stand by the front door and make sure the monkey did not get outside as he was about to let the creature out. Johnny unlocked the door of the cage and left the store room door open and bolted for the front door of the dental centre. We locked the dental centre up and looked through the darkened windows of the dental centre and caught a glimpse the monkey coming out of the store room and strolling down the corridor. Johnny and I beat a hasty retreat and went back to our billet. Nobody had seen Johnny and me enter the dental centre and the operation had taken under three minutes.

Johnny and I then went into the second stage of our planning. We knew that the CO would come down the path which was in between the MRS and the Dental Centre. The MRS and Dental Centre were six feet on opposite sides of the path. We decided to sit on our verandah of our billet knowing that the CO would see us before he reached the MRS reception. We grabbed a couple of beers and lemonade from the fridge inside our billet and drank shandies on the verandah whilst we waited.

The CO came strolling down the path with Colonel Green at around 8.15pm. He immediately saw us and he bade us Good Evening. (He was always polite when senior officers were around). Johnny and I returned the salutation. The CO then told us that he and the DDDS had come to develop three films they had taken in Malacca and he asked me if the developer in the darkroom was "fresh". I told him that it was old and that it was due to be changed the following morning. The CO asked me if I would mind opening up the dental centre and make some fresh developer for him.

Of course I said I would and that it would only take me 5 minutes to mix a lot of new developer up. Johnny went into the billet to get the keys and returned and handed me the keys.

I opened the front door of the dental centre and stood back to let the two colonels into the building. I presumed they would be going into the CO's office whilst I made up some new developer. I had just finished closing the front door when I heard an almighty scream from the CO who had just entered his office. I immediately went into the CO's Office to see what had happened, but of course I found what I had anticipated. On hearing the very loud scream of the CO, Johnny came running from the verandah. We both witnessed the sight in the CO's office. The pots holding the ten prize orchids which the CO had on the shelves by the windows had been thrown onto the parquet floor and had broken into pieces. The orchids had been chewed and pulled to bits. The diary, the blotting pad, the in and out trays along with his expensive sterling silver pens had been thrown from the CO's immaculate desk onto the floor. On the desk sat the monkey and in his hands he had the CO's expensive gold half-moon glasses. Johnny and I had to bite our tongues to stop laughing.

The CO then made a very stupid mistake when he reached towards the monkey in order to retrieve his expensive glasses. As quick as lightening the monkey dropped the glasses leapt forward to bite the CO's thumb taking a little piece off in the process. Having done that the monkey leapt onto the DDDS's shoulders and bit him on his ear. God this was so much better than the Benny Hill Show! Of course both the injured colonels were hysterical by this time and Johnny and I were biting our tongues very hard in order to stop laughing, which was extremely hard to do. We had to look "concerned". After a few minutes the colonels had simmered down. The monkey ran out of the office along the corridor. The CO asked us to grab the monkey and put him back in its cage. Johnny went down to the laboratory and got some thick cloth gloves, which the dental technician used in his work. Johnny put the gloves on and went into the storeroom where the monkey was jumping squealing and jumping around in the corner. Johnny managed to put the creature back in his cage without getting himself bit.

Meanwhile the two injured colonels were in need of urgent medical attention and I accompanied them to the MRS reception and went to find Gil Meek the duty NCO. I found Gil doing his rounds in the ward checking on the patients he had in the ten ward centre. I explained to Gil what had happened. Gil immediately went into the reception area and looked at the wounds of the colonels. He told both of them of course that he would have to call out one of his doctors as both the colonels needed stitches. Whilst waiting for the doctor to arrive Gil gave both the colonels tetanus injections. The doctor eventually arrived and he put eight stitches into the CO's hand and six into the DDDS's ear. Whilst the doctor was doing his business the CO asked me if Johnny and I would mind cleaning up his office etc. No problem Sir I informed the CO. I then went off to find Johnny and we started to clean the CO's office.

The two colonels returned to the dental centre approximately about a hour later. The CO informed me that he had spoken to S/Sgt Meek and asked if he could use to the duty driver to drive one of the land rovers in order to take the monkey out of the dental centre and miles away from Rasah Camp. The CO then asked me if I would accompany the driver and ensure that he drove at least 20 miles down the road away from the camp and to release the monkey into the jungle. The CO emphasized that he wanted to do this right away as he did not want the monkey in the dental centre when Captain Horne arrived the following day for work. I readily agreed and got myself more brownie points. Terry Diamond the duty driver and I put the cage with the monkey in it into the land rover and Terry drove the land rover a good 20 miles down the road. We stopped and took the cage out of the land rover and laid the cage at the side of the road with the door facing the jungle. I stood behind the cage and opened the door. The monkey scuttled off into the darkened jungle. Terry and I drove back to camp arriving back at just after midnight. Johnny was still awake with a couple of other lads and he told me that the CO and the DDDS were cancelling their trip to Penang as the CO could not hold a golf club let alone play golf and that the DDDS was cutting his official visit (holiday he meant) short and that he would be returning to Singapore the following day. The CO added that he would be coming down to the dental centre the following morning and that he would be holding an investigation into the matter. I had a good sleep that night, but could not help wondering whether or not Johnny and I had covered all our tracks

10

THE BOARD OF INQUIRY

I awoke on the Thursday morning and was given my cup of char by Kristen. I then went off to the ablutions, washed and got changed into my uniform. I sat on my bed thinking what a wonderful week it had been so far. It was even going to get better, although I did not know it at the time. Gil Meek came into our billet at 7.30am and told me that our CO had telephoned him at the MRS Reception and had asked him if he would relay a message to me stating that he would be arriving at the dental centre at 8am prompt and could I ensure that I opened the dental centre for him at 8am. Gil added that the CO had also asked him if he would kindly see him in the dental centre at 8am before going off duty. I thought that the CO was coming down very early in order to talk to the staff before they got together and agreed on their stories. I had a very quick breakfast and duly opened the centre up at 7.50am. The CO arrived dead on 8am and went into his office which had been cleaned and tidied up (less the rare orchids) by Johnny Hart and myself the night before. The CO asked Gil to step into his office shortly after 8am and he asked Gil to confirm that Ramasammy had handed the dental keys into the MRS reception at 5pm the evening before. Gil confirmed this. The CO then handed Gil two tins of cigarettes containing 100 cigarettes and asked him to give them to L/Cpl Terry Diamond, the driver who had taken the monkey and me 20 miles down the road and disposed of the creature the evening before.

Just shortly after 8am Cpl Harry Hughes, Cpl Hart and Cpl Pratt and the two civilian surgery assistants Harris and Ramasammy, arrived at the dental centre. Ramasammy immediately went to the store room in order to take the monkey outside, tie him up and feed him, but of course there was no monkey. Ramasaamy ran into our office and told us that the monkey had escaped. I told him nothing of course, but Johnny could not himself and told him that "he was in deep shit". The CO and Gil came out of the CO's office and he looked at Ramasammy and if looks could have killed, Ramasammy would have perished on the spot. The CO told Ramasammyto go into his surgery and not move from there until he called him. Ramasammy immediately went into the CO's surgery. The CO told us all to ensure that Ramasammy stayed in the surgery until he called him out.

Harry Hughes was the next to be called into the office and he informed the CO that he had left the centre at 4.30pm and instructed Ramasammy to lock the place up and take the keys to the MRS reception after he had fed the monkey and put the monkey back in his cage in the store room.

Next in were Johnny Hart and myself. The CO asked us to confirm our stories which we had told him the night before, which we did. The CO told us that he was very grateful for the help we had given him the night before in cleaning up his office and disposing of the money. The CO then handed us two tins of cigarettes each. Who says that Crime does not pay?

Johnny and I went back to our office. The CO stood by the door waiting for his officers to arrive. The first officer to arrive was Captain Horne who was in the garden searching for his monkey. The CO called to Captain Horne to go into his office immediately. Captain Horne was not given the chance to ask any of us where his monkey was. We heard a loud heated conversation going on in the CO's office very shortly afterwards. A very red faced, and an obviously disturbed Captain Horne came out of the CO's office about 15 minutes later and immediately went into his surgery. I would add that it was not only the staff who heard all the heated conversation, but about six dental patients who were waiting to be treated.

The CO then went into his surgery and virtually dragged Ramasammy into his office.

All of us in the office plus the patients could hear was our CO ranting and raving in his office. His voice was very, very loud and the air was very blue! The CO came out of his office and informed me that Captain Horne was being posted to BMH Kluang the following Monday and that Captain Paul Summers would be posted from Kluang to our dental centre with effect from Monday and he told me to prepare the necessary posting and movement orders for his signature. which I did with the greatest of pleasure. The CO added that Ramasammy would not be working for him in the future but would be working with Captain Churchyard and that Harris the surgery assistant of Captain Churchyard would then be working for him. A very subdued Ramasammy was as quiet as a church mouse for the remainder of the day and made himself as scarce as possible. Later on Captain Horne managed to get hold of Ramasammy and asked him what had happened. Naturally Ramasammy denied that he was to blame and stated that he thought that somebody else had let the money out of his cage. Captain Horne did not dare to say anything to us, as, although he suspected that it was not Ramasammy but one of us who had let the monkey out. The CO went off shortly afterwards to the officers mess in order to see the DDDS off.

Johnny and I went down to the Mee Lee Hotel that night and drank more than normal whilst celebrating what had happened and how the outcome had ended. I believe it was Johnny and not me who exclaimed that it had been an excellent couple of days in which we had managed to kill two monkeys off in one foul swoop.

We found out a few days later that the CO had initially suspected Ramasammy had done the dirty deed and got his revenge because of the three rollockings he had been given on the Monday. According to the CO, the facts, or stories told by all of us who were interviewed confirmed the CO's suspicion.

Friday was a very quiet day and passed without incident. I believe that after he had finished his surgery that Captain Horne took Ramasammy out for a drink somewhere.

Over the weekend, like ships crossing during the night Captain Horne made his way down to Kluang, whilst Captain Summers made his way from Kluang to Seremban.

Captain Paul Summers, a National Service dental officer arrived at our dental centre the following Monday ready to start work in his new centre. Little did I know it at the time, but Paul's posting to us was the best thing which had happened to me during my spell in Malaya. Life for me was going to get even much better!

11

CAPTAIN PAUL SUMMERS

Captain Paul Summers walked into the Dental Centre on the Monday morning and it was just like a breath of fresh air had come through the door. He greeted everyone in the office with a cheery smile and a Good Morning to everybody, before making his way to the CO's office.

We were to find out that Paul was a National Service officer, who was not only an excellent dentist, but that he did not have much time for the army or the Officer's Mess. Word soon got around that Paul was a superb dentist and that his chair side manner was second to none. Senior officers and their wives and kids were soon making dental appointments to see him instead of the CO. This suited the CO of course as the less dentistry he did meant he could spend more time fishing, sailing, golfing or talking to his prize orchids.

In the RADC, a dental officer was expected to see an average of 200 patients each month and to do an average of 200 fillings a month. Other treatments like gold inlays, crowns, bridges, root treatments and dentures were a bonus. I was responsible for submitting a monthly return to the DDDS at GHQ FARELF in Singapore at the end of each month. These returns from all the Dental Centres in the Far East were then forwarded to the Director of Dental Services at the Ministry of Defence (MOD) in London. The returns always showed that Paul had seen more than 200 patients each month and that he had done at least 200 fillings or more.

The CO was not expected to see 200 patients each month or to do 200 fillings as in addition to his dentistry he had to visit the various Dental Centres in Malaya on a regular basis. Often he combined these visits with a trip to the golf course or a visit to his boat which was berthed at Malacca.

The CO usually only saw senior officers, their wives and children, plus a few British civilian school teachers, and government officials, and their families. With Paul being so popular quite a good number of the CO's patients were switching to him which meant that the CO was seeing less and less patients. This did not worry the CO as the less patients he saw meant that more time could be spent swanning off. The problem for me of course was was when I had to complete the monthly returns at the end of the month showing what work each dentist had done. No problem doing the returns in respect of

Captain Summers or Captain Churchyard, but big problems when I came to do the return for the CO.

During the second month of Paul's time at the Dental Centre I completed the monthly returns as normal and I typed the return with very accurate figures showing the CO had seen 47 that particular month and had done 38 fillings. I took the monthly return to the CO to sign and he looked at it and he told me that he thought I had made some tying errors. I asked him why and he told me that he thought I had missed a 1 in front of the 47 and a 1 in front of the 38. In other words the returns should have read 147 patients seen and 138 fillings completed. I retyped the monthly return and he signed it and I posted it off. I certainly got the message from the CO and from that month and I always typed a 1 in front of actual figure in respect of patients seen and fillings completed. After all who was I to rock the boat and corporals always did what colonels tell them to, or else!

Paul was very happy doing his dentistry for Queen and Country and he was very popular with all the staff and patients alike. He was always smiling and never in any bad mood. He once told me that he was happy when he was doing dentistry but that he had no time for the army. He accepted that he was a National Service officer and that he had to do his two years in the army like all others, whether they were the "riff raff" or the cream of the country.

Paul spent as little time as possible in the Officer's Mess and as he loved the Malayan food he was often seen in the restaurants, the open air restaurants and the bars in the town by myself and my mates when we were in town. Paul was usually in the company of Lieut (Lt) Jones RMP or Lt Barker of the Intelligence Corps. Both these officers were also National Service officers and were due to depart back to the UK (Blighty) in the very near future. No matter who Paul was with when he saw us in the restaurants or bars he always sent over a few beers to my mates and myself.

The following month Lt Barker departed for Blighty which meant that Paul only had one dining or drinking partner in Lt Jones when he was available. Paul then started asking me if he could join my friends and myself in the restaurants and bars whenever we were in the town, which was always on a Thursday, Friday, Saturday and Sunday. Sure, I told him and it was to be a regular occurrence during the next 15 months or so.

It was on my 20th birthday on Monday 17 June 1957 that Paul took me down to the town to celebrate my birthday. Chicko and Johnny Hart had also been invited. After superb curry at one of the open air restaurants we all hit the Mee Lee bar. During drinks Paul mentioned that Lt Jones who would be leaving for Blighty two weeks later and would be selling his MGTD green sports car at a very fair price before he left. I thought nothing about it until Chicko mentioned that as I had saved a lot of money since I had been in Malaya for nearly a year I should think about buying it. The more I drank the more the idea appealed to me. A lad from a tiny hamlet owner of a MGTD sport car at the age of 20; an impossible dream I thought. I enquired from Paul as to what price Lt Jones was selling the car for and having been told the price and knowing that I had more than sufficient money to buy the car I informed Paul that I was interested.

It was on the Friday morning that Paul told me that he had spoken to Lt Jones and informed him that I was prepared to buy the car from him. It was later that afternoon that Paul informed me that he would collect the car from the Officer's Mess, after work on Saturday afternoon and that he would collect me and take me for a test drive.

After the test drive Lt Jones had informed Paul that I could use the car all day on the Sunday and if I was happy with it, then we would complete the deal on the Monday.

Paul drove the car down on Saturday afternoon to my billet and picked me up and took me for a spin in the car. We did about 40 or 50 miles in the car with Paul driving and me in passenger's seat. I was very impressed with the car and its power to say the least. We got back to my billet in the early evening and Paul parked the car in the MRS car park and gave me the keys. Paul told me that the car was mine all day on Sunday and could take it for a drive, but warned me to be careful as the car was not really mine until I paid for it. I forgot to mention to Paul that I had no driver's licence or insurance and that the only time I had spent behind a steering wheel in a vehicle had been less than one week and had resulted in two accidents!

After Paul had taken me back to my billet on the Saturday evening I had dinner and got changed and arranged to go down town with Chicko and Johnny Hart. As usual we hit the Mee Lee Bar before going on to Yam Yam Cabaret. As I was with Chicko we did not have to buy any tickets as the manager gave Chicko a few free books. In between drinks Chicko was dancing with either "Randy" Rose or "Tiny" Tina, the No 1 and No 2 girls in the place whilst I was dancing with "Calamity" Jane, "Dirty" Doris or "Gee Spot" Gina. It was after one of the dances that Chicko told me that he had told "Randy" Rose that I had bought a MGTD and that she was very interested in me taking her for a ride in the car. Rose came over to our table later on and asked if I would take her for a ride the following morning. Sure I told her and I arranged to pick her up from her "residence" , for want of a better word the following morning at 11am. I planned a drive through the Lake Gardens and lunch at a nearby hotel or restaurant afterwards.

Sunday morning arrived and I got in the car and tried to start it. After a few hiccups when the engine started, spluttered and did I manage to get the engine going ok by pressing down on the accelerator and possibly revving the engine less. The problem which I then I encountered was that I found it hard to reverse as the gear started grinding and that I could not put the car in reverse.

I suddenly remembered from my week's previous driving experience that I had to double the clutch in order to get reverse. That done I tried to put the car into 1st gear only to find that the gear started grinding badly again and that it was impossible to put the car into 1st gear. I then doubled the clutch, put the car in 1st gear and drove out of camp.

Rasah Camp was only about 2 to 3 miles from Rose's shack and I managed to drive quite slowly down to meet her. She got into the car and we started on our drive. She soon asked me why a sports car went so slowly so I started to put my foot down on the accelerator a little more. We entered the Lake Gardens and I drove round the corner and put my foot down further on the accelerator. Suddenly I realised that I was going too fast and instead of breaking I tried to change down, forgetting that I had to double clutch again. The result was that the car was still going quite fast when it took off down the slope right into the lake. We landed in about three feet of water. We managed to get out of the car and Rose who was none too pleased, used words to me which were unbecoming from a Lady of the Night! Rose stormed off leaving me to sort out the problem of the sunken car.

I was never a slow thinker and having walked to the Government Rest House in Lake Gardens I telephoned Paul at the Officer's Mess who told me to go back to the car, but to stay out of sight, and not to talk to any police who may arrive and to wait for him to arrive. Within 30 minutes Paul had arrived in a land rover, with Lt Jones and two RMP lads. The MG was hooked up by a tow rope and pulled out of the water and towed back to camp. During this procedure nothing was said by the three MP guys and I stood aside with Paul. After the car was towed away Paul took me to the hotel and asked me what had happened. I told him what I thought had happened, omitting that Rose had been in the car with me. I also added that I had no driver's licence, and of course no insurance. Paul told me not to worry as he would sort the matter out. Of course I never purchased the car or indeed was never allowed to purchase the car. I never saw Lt Jones or even spoke to him again before he left for Blighty a few days later. I never knew what happened to the car on the end!

Obviously Paul true his promise had sorted out the whole matter for me. I was not to get behind a steering wheel in a car for another ten years.

The incident with the car did not spoil my friendship with Paul and we continued to go out to the restaurants and bars together. It was a few weeks later when I was drinking with Paul in the Mee Lee bar on a Sunday that we met a rubber planter named John Holliday. John was on the next table and during drinks he looked in severe pain and was holding his mouth. Paul being a dentist asked John what was the matter and John informed him that he had severe tooth ache and could get nothing done as all the dentists were closed on a Sunday. Paul told John that he had a solution and that he would take John up to his surgery in the camp and have a look at his tooth. Paul knew that he would not be disturbed by the CO as he was away on his boat for the weekend in Malacca. The three of us got into John's Land Rover and his driver drove us up to camp. In the surgery Paul looked at John's teeth and found out that he had two really bad teeth. Paul did the two extractions and I acted as Paul's surgery assistant. Obviously John tried to pay Paul but Paul refused to take any payment whatsoever. Paul told John that he also needed a couple of fillings and a root treatment doing and that he would do them for him at an appropriate time. A very grateful John left with his driver telling Paul that he would be getting an invite to his "bungalow" at the rubber plantation shortly.

A couple of days later Paul received a telephone call at the dental centre from John inviting both Paul and I down to his bungalow for a curry lunch on the coming Sunday. John informed Paul that his driver would collect us from the dental centre at 10am. Little did I know at the time that Paul and I were to receive many invites out to John's rubber plantation and neither did we know at the time that we were destined to meet a prince, a princess and other VIPs on future visits to John's plantation. Following these visits to John's plantations my life was going to be even more exciting that I could ever have imagined.

12

THE RUBBER PLATATION

John Holiday's driver picked us up at exactly 10am on the Sunday morning. Accompanying the driver was a Malayan bodyguard/escort from the rubber plantation. Both were armed with submachine guns (Sterling submachine guns I believe). Getting into the back of the land rover we found another two submachine guns with 6 magazines. The escort told us that we were to use them if we were ambushed by the CTs. The driver drove off with the four of us in the vehicle.

The rubber plantation of which John Holliday was the Estate Manager was deep inside Negri Sembilan and between Seremban and Malacca and about 25 miles of so from Rasah camp. After leaving the main road after about 20 miles or so we drove down a sandy dirt, single lane track for the remaining 5 miles of our journey. On either sides of the track was either thick jungle or rubber trees. On reaching John's house we saw John seated on his verandah, who immediately got up and came to greet us.

John took us inside and gave us a drink and afterwards took us on a guided tour of his large house. I had always thought that European rubber plantation managers lived in bungalows but John's house was far from being a bungalow. It was a very large two storey house with several bedrooms, bathrooms, a large dining room and lounge, study, kitchen and servants quarters. All the rooms had very high ceilings with ceiling fans. In fact the house was a residence fit for a king.

Over drinks and a lunch of chicken and king prawn curries John told us a lot about rubber plantations and the dangers of being a rubber estate manager. He told us that it was following the murder of three European rubber plantation managers on 18 June1948 in Sungai Siput, Perak, that the British declared a State of Emergency in Malaya the following day. He went to add that Malaya was the world's biggest producer of rubber and that it accounted for 75% of Malaya's income and was also the biggest dollar earner in the British Commonwealth.

Some other startling facts that John told us were that rubber plantations were the main targets for the terrorists because Malaya depended on the rubber industry; that 400 attacks on rubber plantation had taken place in one month in 1950; that 60 European rubber plantation managers had been murdered since 1948; that 70% of the rubber plantations were owned European owned with Dunlop having the most plantations with Sime Darby being the second biggest owner. The most startling fact, as far as John was concerned was the fact that many of the European managers were seeking early retirement due to the murders and that the rubber companies were finding it hard to recruit new managers.

After lunch John and Lou his assistant manager gave us a guided tour of the rubber plantation complex. In addition to John's large residence there were several small houses for the coolies (Tamil rubber tappers), smoke houses, an office, a small type of medical centre, and an armoury. This armoury contained several weapons including pistols or revolvers, rifles, submachine guns, ammunition for the weapons and grenades. The tour ended with a view of thousands and thousands of rubber trees as far as the eye could stretch. John's rubber plantation was a very, very large plantation.

Paul and I went back to the house with John and his assistant for a couple of beers before departing back to Rasah Camp. John told us a lot more about rubber, the rubber plantations and the dangers of working on a rubber plantation. Not only did the terrorists murder the European managers, but they also murdered anybody who worked on the plantations. One of the terrorists favourite tricks John told us was to nail the coolies to rubber trees. All very frightening stuff. It was at this stage that Paul remarked on the range of weapons in the armoury and was surprised that rubber plantations had their own armoury. John informed us that his estate had suffered two ambushes by terrorists during the past five years and that he had had four employees murdered by terrorists. This was one of the reasons that he always carried a pistol on his belt with several bullets, just like the cowboys in the Wild West. It was at this point that John's assistant informed us that John was always known as Doc Holliday, to his good friends. Lou jokingly mentioned that the famous or infamous 'Doc Holliday' in the Wild West always carried a gun and six bullets on his belt   From that day on Paul and I, like John's friends always addressed John as Doc.

Before we finally departed John told us that not only was he armed all the time, but whenever he went into town or anywhere, that he always ensured that he, his escort and his driver and any passengers were also fully armed with submachine guns and lots of magazines housing the bullets.

It was dusk when we finally departed and I must admit that Paul and I were a lot more nervous on our trip back down that isolated sandy 5 mile dirt track until we hit the main road. On the way back Paul and I agreed what an eye opening experience the visit to Doc's had been and that but that he would not wish to be a European manager of a rubber plantation.

During the next two months Paul did quite a bit of dentistry on the Doc and Paul and I were invited down to his rubber plantation on two occasions during July and early August. As before, Doc's driver and escort came to collect us and Paul and I sat in the back of the land rover and bearing in mind what the Doc had previously told us, our hands were never too far from the submachine guns and magazines. Unlike our first visit to the plantation when only the Doc, his assistant Lou, Paul and I were present, at these two further visits the Doc had also invited around a further six European guests. Great to meet different European expats and we spent quite a bit of time listening about their life in Malaya and what they did for a living. A superb choice of delicious curries and cold beers made these two visits very memorable for us two army guys. These European expats certainly lived in a much different and exciting world to that of Paul and I enjoyed.

It was on this third visit to the Doc's that he mentioned to Paul and I that he would be organising a special party for about 20 people or so to celebrate Hari Merdeka (Independence Day from the British) on 31st August 1957 and that he would be honoured if we came along to this party and also stayed the night. Paul told him that we would both be delighted.

Saturday 31st August 1957 duly arrived and as usual Doc's driver and escort collected us from the Dental Centre at around 10am and took us out to the plantation. When we arrived there at just after 11.30am what a sight met us. On the verandah was a selection of virtually every drink imaginable which were being served by two of Doc's maids. Paul and I met the Doc who told us that we were free to roam around and mix with the many guests who had already come. We went into the dinning and adjacent room and the sight that met us was the finest and biggest range of delicious Malayan dishes that we had ever seen.

During lunch and during the afternoon Paul and I met most of the many guests. Most of the guests were VIPs but Paul and I did not feel out of place as were treated on an equal basis by all. I felt privileged and honoured to be amongst some people as I knew that I was the only soldier at that wonderful party.

Evening came, more drinks consumed, more stories told and more superb food eaten before Paul and I toddled off to our bedrooms. The following morning after a SSSS (shit, shave, shampoo and shower) I went down to a superb breakfast to dine with the Doc and another four of his other guests. Paul soon joined us shortly afterwards. Later on after more drinks and food Paul and I left in Doc's land rover with his driver and escort back to Rasah Camp. Such a memorable way to celebrate Hari Merdeka and indeed a day that I will remember to my dying day.

What I did not know at the time was that Paul and I were to receive further invites out to the plantation from the Doc and that we would meet a lot more very interesting people, including royalty, plus become involved in a nasty incident

13

SNAKES IN THE YAM YAM CABARET

It was in early September 1957, shortly after we had celebrated Hari Merdeka that we organised a sad farewell for Cpl Harrry Hughes, Cpl Derek Underwood and L/Cpl Terry Diamond. All three of these good guys were due to finish their National Service in Seremban a few days later and were due to leave Malaya a few days later and would be sailing back on one of the troopships, back to Blighty and demob. Chicko and I were responsible for organising everything and we were both determined that it would be a party to remember and that we would give them a good send off.

The party included most of the lads from the Dental Centre, MSR and Hygiene Unit, plus the three guys who were due to leave and their three replacements, Cpl George Wilkie RADC, Cpl Joe Walters RAMC and L/Cpl Andy Andrews RASC. If I remember correctly all the lads except for S/Sgt Sexton and Cpl Bates from the MRS, who were on duty, attended the party. As I was very friendly with Paul Summers and was knocking around with him a lot I asked Paul if he would like to join us. He told me that he would be delighted and that he would have been offended if I had not asked him out to the farewell party for the three lads.

Chicko and I had planned a curry dinner at one of the open air restaurants, followed by drinks at the Mee Lee bar and finishing off the night at the Yam Yam Cabaret. The dinner and the drinks sessions went well and without any hitches, but problems arose when we hit the Yam Yam Cabaret at just after 10pm, as the place was full and there was not a vacant table in the place.

On all my frequent visits to the Yam Yam I had never ever seen the place packed to capacity. Our party, numbering about 15 stood by the bar drinking and waiting for some tables to clear, but to no avail, and it looked like all the customers were there for the night. Chicko and I were quite embarrassed, not only for the lads who were leaving and whom we wanted to have a really good send off and a night to remember, but also for Paul who was making his very first visit to the Yam Yam.

It was whilst I was on my second beer when I was thinking how to get tables for our party that an idea came to me and I mentioned it to Chicko who thought it was a brilliant idea. I got hold of the mad professor and told him what my idea was and he also said he thought it was great idea. I explained my plan very carefully and off he went.

In virtually every village, town or city in Asia there is a Chinese shop were the owner sells live snakes to his customers, as the Chinese believe that the snake meat helps to cure arthritis, eliminates toxins, cleans your skin and keeps you young. In Seremban there were at least two such shops and one of these shops was owned by Vincent Wong. The professor used to sell all the live snakes he caught to Vincent Wong so they knew each other very well.

The professor returned to the Yam Yam about 30 minutes later. He was in a very jovial mood and he looked smart in his safari suit, although I noticed that the two lower pockets on his safari suit were bulging a bit. I asked him if he had got the snake and he told me that for good measure that he had got two of them from Vincent's and that he had each one in a small cloth brown bag in each of his two pockets. He assured me that both snakes were Malayan bronzebacks, which were non venomous and were each about three feet in length.

Now we had to put the second part of our plan into action. How to release the snakes without being seen! Chicko suggested that five or six of the lads stand about three feet in front of the wall by the bar and that the mad professor would get between the lads standing and the wall and release the snakes and that is what happened.

Very, very shortly afterwards when the two snakes, coloured yellow and brown were slithering all over the floor there was pandemonium in the place with customers screaming snake or ular (snake in Malaya). People started rushing for the exits and although being a betting man, I would not bet who were the first to the exits, whether it was the small band, the girls or the customers. It was a close call! Of course all our party had to make for the exits quite quickly as well for had we had stayed, then the manager would most likely have guessed who was responsible for bringing the snakes into the Yam Yam.

Outside the cabaret many of the customers were not hanging around but were making headway for other bars. The band, the girls and a few customers stayed outside the exits waiting to see what was happening. By this time the mad professor had got rid of the two small brown bags he had brought the snakes in. Chicko went into the cabaret and spoke to the manager, whom he knew quite well of course and he told him that he had an expert medical man in his party who could catch snakes if he provided him with a cardboard box. The mad professor was then called back into the cabaret and handed a cardboard box and he managed to catch the snakes within ten minutes or so.

The manager then went outside and informed everybody that the snakes had been caught and that it was safe to return. The band, the girls and what few customers were outside then made their back into the cabaret. Even when everybody had filed back into the cabaret the cabaret was less than a third full. There were many vacant tables and as Michael Miles used to say, it was "Take Your Pick"! Our party sat down at three tables and the Manager came over and spoke to the mad professor and Chicko and thanked them for getting rid of the snakes and he handed them a stack of books containing free tickets for dancing with the girls. Also quite a few free beers arrived at our tables for the rest of the evening.

The manager told us afterwards that as far as he knew the Yam Yam had only been cleared in its history once before the "snake episode" and that was when a CT had thrown a grenade into the Yam Yam in an incident when luckily nobody had been killed.

A fantastic send off for the three lads who were due to leave for the UK shortly afterwards and a night that they would remember for the rest of their lives. I suspect that everybody in Yam Yam that night would also remember the incident for rest of their lives as well.

Paul, to my knowledge was the only officer in the Yam Yam that night and he told me afterwards that he had it had been a long time since he had experienced as much fun. I had never seen the mad professor have so much fun or not seen him laugh so much. He was also due to finish his National Service a couple of months later and I told him that he would miss all that kind of fun, the free cigarettes, the cheap booze, the superb Malayan curries and dancing with all those gorgeous girls when he went back to the UK. Over the weekend He obviously thought about what I had told him for on the Monday morning he went and saw S/Sgt Sexton and signed on as a regular soldier. Perhaps I should have been a recruiter for the army instead of being in the RADC.

I never asked or found out what the mad professor did with those two snakes he captured in the Yam Yam!

14

BMH KINRARA, KUALA LUMPUR

It was on a Friday in early October 1957 at just after 4pm when the body of a dead SAS soldier, who had been killed in an ambush nearby was brought into the MRS. The MRS did not have a mortuary and any bodies that were brought in had to be cleaned up and placed in a coffin and transported to the Kinrara British Military Hospital at Kuala Lumpur. There were strict standing instructions regarding bodies that were brought into the MRS in that, due to the high temperature and high humidity bodies had to be transferred to BMH Kinrara within an hour. Ambulances could not be used to transport the bodies but a suitable truck would be made available from the RASC transport pool for transportation. That in addition to the driver of the vehicle and his armed escort, a soldier, with a minimum rank of Cpl from the Medical Services had also to accompany the bodies.

It was during mid afternoon when the body of the dead SAS soldier was brought into the MRS. S/Sgt Gil Meek, my good friend and mentor came across to the Dental Centre and asked me if I would accompany the body in the coffin to BMH Kinrara. Gil explained that his two RAMC Corporals were out with ambulances at BMH Kinrara and BMH Kluang and that he had nobody else to turn to. I was reluctant to say yes because the last time when I had to accompany the body of a Gurkha soldier a couple of weeks before had been quite a bit of a disaster. I had also planned a 48 hour pass from that Friday night over the weekend.

My last visit to BMH Kinrara two weeks before had resulted in a bit of a comedy show. S/Sgt Harry Sexton had detailed me in the late evening at about 7pm to accompany the body of a dead Gurkha to BMH. Harry and his assistants had got a one ton vehicle from the transport pool and put the coffin in the back of the vehicle. I then had to trot down to the guardroom and armoury in order to collect a submachine gun and 3 magazines. I went back to the MRS and saw that the vehicle was ready to depart. The driver was a private in the RASC and the armed escort who was sat next to him was the RP (Regimental Police) Sgt from the guard room, who from past experience I had found to be a bit of a bastard. in the back quickly the Sgt told me and I jumped into the back of the one tonner, with my submachine gun, my three magazines and my tin of 50 fags and sat on the floor next to the coffin. The vehicle moved off on its journey to BMH Kinrara. The distance between Seremban and Kuala Lumpur was about 50 miles and usually took 60 minutes to 90 minutes depending on what traffic was on the road and also how fast our driver went. This particular journey was to take us well over two hours.

Midway between Seremban and Kuala Lumpur I wanted a fag again but I had run out of matches. I knew the Sgt smoked as I had seen him nervously chain smoking when the coffin was being put in the truck. It was pitch black on the roads which did not have any street lighting like the UK. The one tonner has two windows between the cab and the back; one window is immediately behind the driver and the other window is immediately behind the passenger seat. I knew the Sgt had matches and as I wanted some matches or a light for my cigarettes I hammered on the window behind him time and time again. I hammered and hammered and eventually the driver stopped. As soon as he stopped the Sgt was out of the vehicle in a flash and he sprinted off down the road like lightening. In fact he could have beaten Jessie Owens over 200 yards.

The driver and I were at a loss to know what had happened for the Sgt to take off like that. The driver and I lit up cigarettes and waited for about ten minutes for the Sgt to return. The Sgt did not return. The driver and I were not only very worried, but quite frightened, as not only was it pitch black everywhere, but we were in a terrorist activity area. We shouted his name repeatedly but to no avail. After a frightening 30 minutes or so when the Sgt had not returned I told the driver that we could not wait any longer and I instructed him to drive slowly and continue the journey.

I was hoping that we would find the Sgt somewhere further down the road. If we did not find him, then I would be in a bit of a quandary not knowing if to continue looking for the idiotic Sgt or carry on with our journey without him.

I got into the passenger's seat and we drove off. About a good two miles down the road I spotted the Sgt smoking and sitting down on the edge of the road. The driver stopped the vehicle and I got out and asked the Sgt what had happened. He whispered to at me to get back into the back of the vehicle and he told me that he had forgotten that I was in the back of the vehicle and that he thought the body of the Gurkha had come back to life!. He told me that he would speak to me later on. I got back into the back of the vehicle, with matches which the driver had given me and the Sgt got back into the passenger seat and we continued our journey.

We eventually arrived at BMH Kinrara about 10pm. In accordance with standing instructions we could not take the coffin and the body straight to the mortuary, but first had to report to the duty officer who would instruct us as to where we would take the body and coffin to. The Sgt and driver stayed with the body and I went into the reception of the BMH and I told the duty RAMC Sgt that we were delivering a body and had to report to the duty officer and I asked him who the duty officer was and he informed me that it was a Captain Kneebone and he pronounced her name as Knee Bone. The Sgt gave me instructions as to where I could find Captain Kneebone.

I found the duty officer's room and I saw two pretty captain QARANC officers in the room drinking tea. I presumed that one of them was Captain Kneebone. I was asked what I wanted and I informed them that I was looking for a Captain Kneebone, the duty officer. One of the officers jumped up immediately and screamed at me calling me a moron and shouting that her name was pronounced as Nee Boney and not Knee Bone. I told her that the duty RAMC Sgt had quite clearly pronounced her name as Knee Bone and not Nee Boney and she said that she would reprimand that bastard later. Captain Kneebone gave me instructions to take the body to the mortuary and that she would meets us there. At the mortuary the driver and I took the body into the mortuary and laid the coffin to rest. Captain Kneebone looked into the coffin, saw that a body was inside and signed a receipt as such.

The Sgt, who had not been seen since we landed at reception, suddenly appeared and we were on our way back to Seremban. Little did I know at the time that I was to meet Captain Kneebone under much more pleasant circumstances a few months later.

We arrived back in Rasah Camp well after midnight. We stopped at the armoury and my weapon and 3 magazines were signed in. I bade farewell to the driver and the RP Sgt and the Sgt informed me that he would come to the dental centre the following morning for a chat.

The RP Sgt was at the dental centre the crack of dawn and he got hold of me outside. He explained about his behavior the night before, informing me he had forgotten about my being in the back of the truck with the coffin and that in an absence of mind he thought the dead body had woken up. He went on to explain that since he had found his dead mother, who had been dead for at least 3 days when he visited her house, that he was always frightened of dead bodies after that. He told me that he had ordered the driver not to say anything to anybody or else. I told him that I would also not mention the matter. It was only when he threatened to make my life a misery if I did tell anybody else that I decided to tell everybody I talked to about what had happened, and tell everybody I did! Soon most of the people on Rasah Camp knew about what had happened and the Sgt became the laughing stock of the camp.

After all I did not worry about this Sgt or what he thought he could do, as the dental centre had its own CO and we did not come under the camp GSM or the Garrison Commander for any discipline. I just hoped that the Sgt learnt a valuable lesson that day, in as much not to threaten anybody unless you are capable of backing it up!

So after that awful day when I had to accompany the body of the Gurkha soldier to BMH Kinrara I was reluctant to go again so soon with yet another body, but as Gil Meek was my mentor, and a very good friend and as I owed him a few favours I agreed to accompany the body of the SAS lad up to BMH Kinrara. I suddenly remembered that I had not filled my 48 hour leave pass out and had it signed by one of the three dental officers who were working in the surgery at that time. This leave pass was most important because it allowed me to be out of the camp from after duty on the Friday evening until 8am on the Monday morning.

I quickly filled out my leave pass and as there was no dental officer available to sign it at the time I gave my filled out leave pass to Cpl Ian Pratt, the dental technician and asked him to get an officer to sign it. Sure Ian said and he told me that as he was going out himself that night and most likely would not see me that he would leave the signed leave pass on my bedside locker. Great I thought at the time!

Gil and I put the coffin containing the body of the SAS lad into the back of the one tonner which had come to the MRS, with its driver and armed escort. I sat in the back of the one tonner with the coffin once again. We stopped at the guardroom and armoury on the way out and I picked and signed for a submachine gun and three magazines, then we went on our journey to BMH Kinara. The journey to and from Kuala Lumpur went without any incident, as did our handover of the body at BMH Kinrara.

We all arrived back at camp shortly before 10pm. After checking my weapon and magazines back into the armoury I went to my billet and got showered and changed. To my delight I saw my leave pass on my bedside locker where Ian Pratt had promised to put it. I put the leave pass into the top pocket of my safari suit and was soon on my way to the Mee Lee bar, where I was to meet Johnny Hart and Chicko.

It was just after midnight when the door of the Mee Lee bar opened and a big RAF Sgt and a big RAF Corporal stormed through the door. These two RAF guys both had MP written in big letters on a band on their sleeves. I immediately knew that they were RAF Military Police. I thought that the presence of these two guys in Seremban must be something serious as there were no RAF stationed in Seremban, and that the nearest RAF station was in Kuala Lumpur. The two RAF MPs looked in a foul mood and very soon they were asking all us soldiers in the bar to produce our leave passes, as it was after curfew. There must have been about 15 to 20 soldiers in the bar. The MPs began checking all the leave passes and after they had checked most of them when they came to our table, at which sat Chicko, Johnny and myself. Chicko's pass was checked and given back to him as was Johnny's. My leave pass was the last to be checked in the bar. The MP Sgt snatched it out my hand read it and roared to the Cpl to put the handcuffs on me and to take me out to the duty land rover outside.

He instructed that I was to be charged with AWOL (Absence without Leave), taken back to the guardroom in Rasah camp and put in a cell overnight, when several charges would be made against me the following morning

I was marched outside quickly followed by the RAF MP Sgt and his RAF MP Cpl to the RAF land rover outside. I thought what the hell was going on? I wondered if something had gone wrong with the delivery of the body up to Kuala Lumpur, and as these RAF MPs had come down from Kuala Lumpur I was positive that this was the case. In front of the land rover stood a Cpl also with MP written in big letters on a band on his sleeve. He was Charles, my old football captain and friend from my nearby village. Charles immediately saw me and asked how I was and what had I been doing. The RAF MP asked Charles if he knew me. Charles told him that we were good friends, and that we played football for the same village team for three years before being called up into the Services. Charles asked his Sgt why I was in handcuffs and being arrested. The Sgt replied that my leave pass had not been signed by an officer but had been signed by I A M A PRATT, Cpl. I suddenly realised what had happened and I explained everything to the Sgt about my having to accompany a body to BMH Kinrara, not having the chance or time to get my leave pass signed and had asked Cpl Pratt to get it signed by an officer for me. The Sgt soon appreciated what had possibly happened in that Cpl Pratt had forgotten to get the pass signed by an officer and had therefore signed it illegally himself. The Sgt then became human and he told his Cpl to take the bracelets off me and he took me back into the bar with his Cpl and

Charles and brought us all a beer. Over the beers the Sgt explained that they were chasing a RAF deserter who had been spotted in Seremban so they had come down from Kuala Lumpur, liaised with the Army Military Police in Rasah camp and suggested that they could have the night off and that they would patrol Seremban that night looking for the deserter. After the beers and before the Sgt left he suggested that I get hold of Pratt by name and nature at the first opportunity and give him a right rollicking for serious trouble he could have got me into. As Charles was leaving he told me that he was due to finish in Malaya within the next month and would be going back home to our village. I asked Charles if he would look up my sister when he arrived home and let her know that I was fine and enjoying Malaya. This he promised to do.

After a weekend on the town with Chicko and Johnny I finally got back to Rasah camp and reported for duty at the dental centre at 8am on the Monday morning. I waited for Cpl Pratt and when I got hold of him I got stuck into him straight away and told him what had happened. Pratt told me what the RAF Sgt had suspected in that he forgotten to get my pass signed by an officer and when he realised this it was too late as all the officers had gone back to the officer's mess. He then thought that he would sign my pass as the Rasah Camp MPs knew us all and seldom checked out passes. Pratt had a black eye for the next few days which was well hidden by the sun glasses he always wore!

Charles did leave Malaya during the following month and returned to our village. It was much later that I learned that he had indeed met my sister on the local bus within a month of his returning to our village and that he had told her that he had seen me and shared a beer, and he had passed my regards onto her and assured her that I was doing okay in Malaya. From that meeting on the bus Charles and my sister started going out together. Charles got engaged to my sister and they eventually married a couple of years later. When they got married I had finished my tour in Malaya, or rather been deported if the truth be known and I was there at my sister's wedding in order to Give Her Away.

I believe that fate often takes a hand in life, when you least expect it and I have often wondered if Ian Pratt had not signed my leave pass and in fact had got it signed by an officer, then I would never have been taken outside in handcuffs and met Charles in Malaya. Had my leave pass had been in order I would never have left the bar that night, or marched outside and seen Charles and perhaps Charles would never have met my sister!

15
SCALE AND POLISH

The ten weeks leading up to Christmas and the end of 1957 were quite eventful in quite a few ways and full of fun.

It was on a Sunday afternoon during the latter part of October when Johnny Hart and myself had arranged to give "Randy" Rose and "Juicy Lucy" a scale and polish at our dental centre. This was not a new thing as both of us had done a scale and polish on a few of the girls from the Yam Yam before. These girls always gave us lots of free dances and I thought that Johnny often got additional free perks in addition to his free dances. Obviously we always made sure that the old "Shithouse", our CO was away for the weekend down in Malacca on his boat with his friends before we arranged any scale and polish for the girls. The reason we had to be careful is that our dental centre contained a darkroom in which we developed x-rays. The darkroom was also used by our CO when he was in camp, and also by a couple of lads to develop and print their photos. The only other darkroom on the camp was in the MRS which also had x-ray facilities. As there was little colour photography around at the time virtually all photographs at the time were in black and white. Once you knew how to develop, fix and print your black and white photos it was piece of cake and it certainly was for me as I was a qualified dental radiographer.

Rose and Lucy arrived at the dental centre in the early afternoon. Johnny took Rose into surgery No 1 which was the CO's surgery. Johnny always preferred to do his scale and polishing on his "patients" with the dental pump chair in the horizontal position for other reasons than just doing a scale and polish. I always had the chair in its normal upright position as I only ever did a proper scale and polish for the girls and nothing else. I took Lucy into surgery No 2, which was the surgery of Captain Summers.

I had just about finished my 30 minute scale and polish on Lucy when the door of the surgery opened and in walked Paul Summers. I was at a loss of what to say, as although I was a good friend of Paul's and that we used to go out together I knew that it was an offence for a non qualified person to do dentistry on anybody, and also, far more serious was the fact is that it was going to be very hard to explain why I had brought bar girls up from the Yam Yam to our dental centre anyway. Before I could think of anything to say, a smiling Paul just said if you are going to practice dentistry on your friends make sure that you do a damn good job!

Lucy was quite embarrassed whilst Paul and I were smiling and laughing at each other, but then Paul heard loud groaning and moaning sounds coming from surgery No 1. "Who is in the CO's surgery" he enquired and I told him that Johnny Hart was also giving one the girls a scale and polish. Paul said that he thought Johnny must be giving other parts of the girl's anatomy a good scale and polish as well. Johnny and I finished the scaling and polish on the two girls and they departed. Paul, Johnny and I went into the dental laboratory and made some tea and had a chat. Paul told us that he had come down to the dental centre in order to use the darkroom to do some developing and that as he thought we would not be around with the keys to the centre on a Sunday afternoon that he had collected the spare of keys which were always held in the MRS. Just imagine if it had been the CO who had walked in and caught you he said. He would have had a coronary and whilst he was in hospital you two would have been waiting a Court Martial. Paul's advice was always to ensure that we had all two sets of keys, those held by Johnny & myself before we decided to practice any further dentistry on the girls.

Good advice from Paul as to knowing where all the two sets of keys were, as Ian Pratt our dental technician had told me once he had gone back to the dental centre one night to complete an urgent denture job for a patient who was being seen by the dental officer the following morning and that after getting the keys from Johnny he had gone into the dental centre and found the CO and the Padre just coming out of the darkroom wearing only their underwear. Ian told me that the CO just remarked how very hot it was inside the darkroom and then asked Ian what he in fact he was doing in the centre so late at night!

The dental centre had a back passage leading to a back door, and Ian mentioned that he had seen the padre using the back passage before, to exit the dental centre. We continued to give the Yam Yam girls scale and polishes, but we always made sure that the back passage door was locked just in case that padre was around with the colonel somewhere. Best to safe than sorry I told Johnny!

16

REST AND RECUPERATION LEAVE

It was during the first week in November 1957 that old "shithouse", our CO, called me into his office and told me that he was going to give me an early Christmas present, as a result of the excellent work I had done for him over the past 15 months. I immediately thought that it must be because of all those 100 plus conservations (fillings) he had never done, or the 100 plus patients which he never seen, but which I had added to his monthly return which I had to submit to GHQ FARELF. Although I thought that my work at the dental centre was good I again thought that it could not because of that, as the CO, being an old miserable sod, and a selfish confirmed bachelor at the age of 45 + never gave any of us much credit. It certainly could not be because of all the undetected "minor" crimes I had managed to get away with during my 15 months with him I thought! He then told me that he was sending me up to the Cameron Highlands for two weeks on Rest and Recuperation (R & R) leave. I thought that this was no Christmas present at all because every soldier in our Corps serving in Malaya was entitled to a two week R & R tour in the Cameron Highlands during their tour in Malaya, so it certainly was not any kind of 'Thank You' from the CO to me. It was only later that I found out that it was Colonel Green from GHQ FARELF who instructed the CO to send me on R & R following his discovery that I had not taken any of my 42 days entitled privilege leave during the past year. The CO informed me that a Major JP Black, a dental officer from Jahore Bahru, would be accompanying me to the Cameron Highlands and that Major Black would be seeing just a few patients whilst he was up there and that I would be working as his chair side assistant. The CO added that Major Black would be arriving in Seremban on the Saturday evening in two days' time and that he would be staying in the Officer's Mess overnight and that we would be travel up to Cameron Highlands the following morning by land rover. I had mixed feelings because I had heard a lot about the Cameron Highlands and how nice it was, but I did not fancy doing any work during my R & R leave.

The Cameron Highlands is the most intensive hill station in Malaya and is some 6000 feet + above sea level. Its average temperature ranged between 9C to 18C with no humidity, and that the temperature could fall to as low as -4C overnight as opposed to the rest of Malaya where the average temperature is 27C with a high humidity of an average of 80%.

Major Black arrived two days later on the Saturday and stayed overnight in the Officer's Mess in Rasah Camp. He arrived at the dental centre at about 7am the following morning with his driver and land rover and collected me. We went down to the guardroom where the driver collected his .303 rifle and his rounds, whilst I collected the usual submachine gun with 3 magazines. Major Black was given a pistol and 6 rounds of ammunition. The reason I was always chose a submachine gun was that all corporals and above were entitled to carry a submachine gun as opposed to the .303 rifle. Whilst doing my training at the Depot RADC I had been taught to use both and had fired both and I was proficient in both the rifle and submachine gun. Whilst the Sterling (or Sten as we called them) submachine gun was nowhere near as good or accurate over longer distances, as the .303 rifle, the gun was not as bulky as the rifle and was much easier to carry. After collecting our weapons and ammunition we sat off on the 180 mile journey to the Cameron Highlands. There were only three of us in the land rover, so obviously the Major sat in the front next to the driver whilst I dived into the back.

We had a deadline to reach Tapah, which was about 140 miles from Seremban, in order to join the armoured convoy which would take us from Tapah to the Cameron Highlands. Very little was said by Major Black on our journey to Tapah.

We reached Tapah an hour before our deadline and Major Black instructed the driver to find and drive us to a decent eating place, which he did. The driver was then told by the major that he could go and join the other drivers who were waiting to join the convoy and who were gathered across the road in another cafe. That left just Major Black and myself and we soon found a vacant table and ordered some food and beers.

It was over our food and beers that Major John Black told me quite a bit about himself. He mentioned that he was not only a qualified dentist but also a qualified solicitor and that he had also joined the RADC with a 7 year ante date and had joined as a major. I reckoned that he must have been in the region of 40 to 45 years old but he never did mention his age to me. He said that he had been looking forward to his two week holiday up in the highlands as he had heard excellent reports about the place and that it would be a good thing to get after serving in the heat and high humidity of Johore Bahru after the past year or so. The major was not too pleased when I informed him that it would not be all holiday as the CO had told me that arrangements had been made for us to see a few patients. Let us wait and see what they have planned for us when we get to the dental centre at BMH Cameron Highlands, he told me.

We had finished our meal when our driver came over and told us that it was time to make our way to the assembly point and join the armed convoy that would leave at 3pm sharp and which would escort us up to the Cameron Highlands. We arrived about ten minutes before 3pm and Major Black and myself got out of the land rover and had a wander around. We saw a large notice by the assembly point which stated that the road up to the Cameron Highlands was a "Red" road and that no vehicle should proceed beyond that point without an armed escort. A Sgt from the convoy who was standing by us, told us that vehicles included, civilian cars, trucks and buses in the armed convoy, but that often the drivers of these civilian vehicles ignored the warning and went off on their own without an armed escort with the result that quite a number of them and their passengers had either been robbed or killed by the terrorists.

3pm arrived and the convoy had been formed and was ready to start the 40 mile journey to the Cameron Highlands. There must have been about 40 vehicles or more in the convoy, which included armoured personnel carriers, scout cars and two armoured cars (one at the front of the convoy and one at the rear) with 2 pounders and heavy machine guns. Half the convoy was made up of civilian vehicles. All very exciting I thought.

The first 20 miles of our journey was quite normal and not exciting at all and it was the last 20 miles or so when it got quite exciting for the road was winding, "U" turning backwards and forwards all the way up to the

Cameron Highlands. Our convoy was then driving at about 10 miles to 15 miles per hour. Thick jungle was on either side of the road and the Malayan jungle has some of the thickest jungle in the world. Major Black shouted to me that he could well understand why he had been told that so many ambushes by the terrorists had taken place on that last 20 miles up to the Cameron Highlands.

At frequent intervals we saw little brown men walking at the side of the road and these men carried blowpipes and darts. Behind them came their women who were all topless. It was the first time that I had ever seen any topless women and I was surprised to see the different sizes and shapes of their breasts. I was told later that these people were aborigines and were from a tribe called Sakias and that the darts they carried were always poisonous darts. We completed our 40 mile journey without incident and it was a journey that had taken us well over 2 hours to complete. Our convoy arrived in the Cameron Highlands and we were taken to the BMH. Major Black and I dropped off our weapons and ammunition at the guard room and we were shown to our accommodation. Major Black told me he would meet me at the dental centre the following morning at around 8.30am.

Monday morning came around and I got to the dental at just after 8am. Cpl Ernie Evans the dental centre technician was already at the dental centre and he told me the good news and the bad news. The good news he said was that there was plenty to see and do in the Cameron Highlands when one was off duty. There were many vegetable farms, strawberry farms, tea plantations, and lakes to visit. If we wanted to play golf he told us that there was also a 9 hole golf course where the military could play. The restaurants served excellent cheap food as well, plus there was an excellent English pub called "The Smokehouse", where one could get an excellent steak, or enjoy a few beers in front of a roaring log fire.

Now for the bad news he told me! Ernie then told me that the captain in charge of the dental centre had gone to Penang on leave and that he was a right, selfish and lazy individual and that he had told his surgery assistant, one Cpl Meadows to ensure that Major Black was fully booked up with patients during his two week stint at the dental centre. I asked Ernie where this Cpl Meadows was and he informed me that he had gone on leave to Singapore for two weeks. As it got dark at 6pm every night Ernie said that it did not leave the major and myself any time to visit any of the tourist attractions, as we did not finish work until 5pm and that there was not enough time to get changed into civvies (civilian clothes) and draw a weapon and ammunition before going out. We could go out at nights of course, but we had to be in civvies, carrying a weapon and in a party of at least 4 people. The "Smokehouse" was very popular. Unfortunately, Ernie added that nobody in uniform was allowed entry into the place.

Major Black arrived at around 8.30am to find out that he had been fully booked up with patients from 10am until 12.30pm, then from 2.00pm until 4.30pm. Sick parade lasted from 9am until 10am. The furious major told me that he thought we were supposed to on a two weeks R & R leave and not expected to serve a penal sentence of two weeks. It was a very subdued and furious major who worked throughout the day on the Monday and the Tuesday. On Tuesday Ernie suggested that after work the major, he and myself visited the "Smokehouse" for a steak and beers. Major Black agreed that this was an excellent idea. After work we all got changed into civvies, drew our weapons and ammunition and Ernie got us a jeep with a driver and all the four of us went into a very impressive "Smokehouse".

It was later on during the evening when Ernie was at the bar with the driver and I was sat with the major, drinking beer in front of the roaring log fire that the major remarked what a great pity it was that we were fully booked up with patients for the two weeks and had been left with so little time for recreation. A great, great pity all the equipment was working so well he added.

Whether this remark by the major was a suggestion or a hint, I do not know, but as the evening went on and after more beers, nasty little thoughts started to come into my head. One always seem to get 'brilliant' ideas when they are drinking alcohol!

Wednesday morning came and the major saw the patients who were on sick parade and his appointments. As Wednesday afternoon was a recreational after the major finished his patients by 12.30pm, he went off to lunch in the Officer's Mess and after lunch played a round of golf with one of this fellow officers. After lunch I returned to the dental centre as I had no intention whatsoever of doing any sport or recreation of any kind. I had other plans! I worked in the surgery and left after a couple of hours.

Thursday morning arrived and I opened the dental centre at just after 8am. Just before 9am there were only three patients on the daily sick parade for Major Black to see. I went into the surgery with the first patient and sat him in the dental chair. The major tried to switch the dental unit's light on in order to see into the patient's mouth. No light came on. Major Black then attached a dental handpiece to the machine and tried to switch on. Nothing happened. He told me that the dental unit was not working and was out of action and he instructed me to call the electro med technician out to have a look at the machine. Major Black then saw his three patients and did extractions on all three. It was a good job that the sterilizer was working at least! The major then went off back to the Officer's Mess and instructed me to call him after the electro med technician had visited and to bring him up to date with the latest state of affairs, which I did in the afternoon.

I went into the dental laboratory and spoke Ernie about the problem. Ernie told me that the REME workshops had a couple of electro med technicians at a small REME workshops which was situated in the Cameron Highlands and that these technicians were responsible for repairs any of the medical or dental equipment which needed repair in the Military hospital. Ernie made the telephone call to the REME workshop. A Cpl electro med technician arrived during our lunch break and was greeted warmly by Ernie. Over a cup of tea Ernie explained that the electro med technician was Horace Bradshaw and that he was good drinking mate of his. Both had lived in Brighton before joining the service and that they often went out together. Horace asked me what the problem was and I told him about the dental unit. Over further cups of tea Ernie told Horace about the dirty trick the resident dental captain had played on the major and myself by fully booking us up with patients for the fortnight. Do not worry stated a grinning Horace.

After a few more cups of tea and a few fags later Horace went into the surgery with me and tried to switch on the dental unit. Nothing switched on. I went back to the dental laboratory and joined Ernie whilst Horace unscrewed the large side panel of the unit. Horace returned to the lab after a few minutes and told us that he taken one look inside the unit and remarked that it was big trouble and that he had not seen such a mess like it in any dental unit before. He told us that three parts were blackened and burnt out and it looked like they had somehow fused together and burnt out. He said, with a wink, and that as the three items were beyond local repair (BLR) it was not possible to repair the unit as his small REME workshops did not carry any of the parts that were necessary to repair the unit. He would have to contact the large REME workshop in Singapore and find out if they carried such spares he told me. If not then they will have to contact the UK and get them flown out as quickly as possible.

Horace and I went back into the dental laboratory for more cups of tea and a few fags. Horace told Ernie the problem. Ernie then suggested that I cancel all the major's patients for the next few days and just get the major to see the patients who attended the sick parade who would possibly need extractions, which the major would be able to do.

Horace remarked that it could a lot longer than a couple of days to get the spare parts and repair the machine and he then left and went on his way. Ernie looked at me and the blowtorch which was the bench and remarked how dangerous those things were the wrong hands. I said nothing and went into the office and started cancelling the appointments for the rest of Thursday, Friday and the Saturday morning.

After a 'wasted' first part of the week, Thursday, Friday and Saturday became very enjoyable as we all finished work at 10am. Ernie had no work to do as there were no patients to make dentures for. There was no work for the major and myself to do because there were no patients to see. This being the case Ernie offered to show us around the Cameron Highlands and its beautiful attractions. Over the next three afternoons Ernie managed to get us a jeep and the three of us, together with the driver, spent quite a good few hours visiting the various restaurants, bars, the "Smokehouse" and some lakes. A superb three afternoons I thought on the Sunday evening.

I reported for duty at the dental centre at just after 8am on the Monday morning and by 9am we only two patients on the sick parade to see. It must have been just after 9am when Horace Bradshaw telephoned Ernie informing him that the required three spare parts would not be available for at least another week. I carried this message to a very delighted Major Black who instructed me to cancel the patients for the rest of week. This I did during that morning.

During the remaining days of that week we all finished work at 10am and changed into our civvies and drew our weapons and ammunition. Once again Ernie through his contacts had got us a jeep with a driver for the week. We visited many places including, a strawberry farm, markets, more lakes, bars and restaurants and of course a few visits to the "Smokehouse". The highlight of the week was a guided tour around a large tea plantation, which took most of the day to do. A wonderful and most enjoyable week I thought on the Saturday night and was very grateful to Ernie for arranging everything and showing us around the Cameron Highlands and organising everything. Perhaps I should also have been grateful for the dental unit being out of action and for any help that Horace Bradshaw may have given us.

Sunday morning arrived and it was soon time to get into uniform, draw our weapons and ammunition, meet out driver and join the convoy which was due to depart from the Cameron Highlands for Tapah at exactly 10am. Ernie was there to see us off and the major thanked Ernie for everything he had arranged before we both said a sad farewell to him. I was never to see Ernie again but he did telephone me at Rasha Camp on the following Tuesday morning to tell me that Horace had received the spares from Singapore and had repaired the dental unit on the Monday morning and that the unit was working properly again. What beautiful timing I thought!

Our journey down to Tapah was uneventful again and the highlight was seeing quite a few Sakias and their topless women whom we waved at. We left the armed convoy at Tapah and started our journey back to Seremban. About 10 miles from Seremban Major Black asked the driver to stop so that he could enjoy a smoke (although he did not smoke) and that he wanted a five minute break as his legs were tired and felt a little cramp coming on. The major and I got out of the land rover and he took me to one side and asked me for a cigarette which I gave him. He then told me that he noticed that the 6 bullets he had drawn with his pistol and had placed on a metal space between his passenger's seat and the driver's seat had disappeared. He noticed a large hole between these two metal spaces and thought that the bullets had dropped through the hole. The major asked me what we should do. I told the major that if a soldier lost a single bullet then it was a Court Martial with a mandatory sentence of 28 days detention, but that I did not know what happened if an officer lost a round. The major told me not to mention the matter to the driver. Whilst finishing our cigarettes I did some quick thinking and by the time I had finished my cigarette an idea had come into my head. I explained my idea. I told him that Captain Paul Summers, frequently went, during several evenings and at the weekends, to in the indoor pistol range in the camp in order to keep his eye in with the pistol. I added that Paul could get as much ammunition usually as he wanted when he went to the range and that perhaps he would give us 6 rounds we wanted. I suggested Paul would help us out because not only was he and I good friends, but that he, and the major were fellow dental officers.

The major then told me that he thought that I was a good organiser following the breakdown of the dental unit and our ten days holiday in the Cameron Highlands and that the idea may work. I suggested to the major that we carry on with our journey to Seremban, which was only 15 minutes down the road, find and restaurant, have some food, as we had not eaten since an early breakfast, and that I would try and contact Paul in the Officer's Mess by telephone.

We arrived in Seremban and found a restaurant on the edge of the town. The driver parked the car and we all got out and found a vacant table and ordered our food and coffees. Whilst we were waiting for the food to come I asked the waitress if I could use the telephone urgently and she took me to the telephone. I telephoned the Officers Mess in the camp. The mess steward answered the phone and I told him that I wanted to speak to Captain Paul Summers. The steward informed me that captain had had breakfast in the mess that morning and had told him that he would not be dining for lunch or dinner as the captain had told him he was going down to Port Dickson for the day and would not be returning until late evening. I thought Christ, so much for my bright plan. I thanked the steward and put the phone down. Time to do some more quick thinking I thought.

The only six telephone numbers I could always remember by heart were those of the dental centre, the MRS , the Officers Mess, the Mee Lee Bar, the Yam Yam Cabaret and Doc" Holliday's at the rubber plantation. I thought shit or bust and I picked the telephone up again and rang the Doc. Luckily he was at home and he picked the telephone up straight away. I told him the details and he replied that it was no problem at all. The Doc asked me which restaurant we were at and I told him. He told me to stay in the restaurant until one of his contacts, a Malayan Police Sgt contacted me, which would be inside the hour. I went back to our table, winked at the major and sat down and started on my food. I took my time over my food, ordered more coffee and waited.

About 40 odd minutes had passed when a Malayan Police Sgt in uniform came into the restaurant and immediately looked over at our table, as we were the only guys in army uniform in the restaurant.

The police Sgt nodded to us at our table and he went off to the toilet. I immediately got up telling the major that I was going to the toilet and I followed the police Sgt into the toilet. Once inside the toilet the police Sgt asked me to confirm who I was and I told him. He then introduced himself as Sgt Ahmad and said that we had a mutual friend in Doc and that the Doc had asked him to come to the restaurant and give me a present. He then handed me 6 bullets for the pistol. I thanked him and he left and I went back to join the major and the driver. The major asked me if everything was okay and I replied in the affirmative and suggested to the major that it about time we left and went on to Rasah Camp. The driver went outside to get the vehicle and it was then I passed the major the 6 bullets who put them into his pocket.

We arrived in Rash Camp about ten minutes later and the driver drove us straight to the guardroom and armoury where all the three of us checked our weapons and ammunition in. Before the driver drove the major to the Officer's Mess, the major told me that he would visit me in the dental centre the following morning before departing on the train journey back to Johore Bahru.

The driver and the major drove off and I walked back to my billet. The following morning I reported for duty at the dental centre just before 8am. Shortly after 8am Captain Summers and Major Black walked into the dental centre together and immediately went into Paul's office. I heard much laughter coming from Paul's office and I wondered if the major was telling Paul about the fun we had had in the Cameron or whether it was regarding his lost bullets. I never did find out why they laughed so much.

Paul went into his surgery at 9am to see the first patient on the sick parade and Major Black came into my office and we spoke to each other until the CO's arrival. The CO arrived just before 10am and called the major into his office. I presumed that the CO was asking the major about the two weeks trip to the Cameron Highlands. Obviously what the major told the CO pleased the CO because the CO never mentioned anything about the Cameron Highlands trip to me at any time afterwards.

Major Black left shortly afterwards on his journey back to Johor Bahru but before doing so he thanked me for all the help he had received from me in the Cameron Highlands. His parting comments to me were that he would never forget me and that he sincerely hoped that we would meet again someday. Little did I know at the time that I was going to be posted under Major Black's command in the future and that he would be a very great help to me.

On the many days and evenings that Paul and I spent together over the next few months, never once did he mention the subject of the lost bullets. A smiling Paul did, however mention a couple of times that if ever he wanted his dental unit fixed that he would have no hesitation in asking for my assistance. I gathered from those remarks that Major Black had told Paul, possibly in the dental centre on that Monday morning about the dental unit in Cameron Highlands and how it become so unserviceable. That was why so much laughter had come from Paul's office I suspected.

17

DECEMBER 1957

Doc Holliday invited Paul and I down to his Rubber Plantation during the first week in December. His driver picked us up early and we arrived at the plantation just after 10.30am. Brunch, a combination of breakfast and lunch, was then served and the Doc told us that he had arranged a shooting competition for his guests in his indoor pistol range. His guests included Lou his assistant manager, his driver/bodyguard, a Malayan Dato (a VIP), Paul, myself. The six of us made our way to the armoury which was next the indoor range. The Doc picked up a revolver and stacks of ammunition and we went off to the indoor range, This indoor range was a brick building and was about 25 yards long by about 6 yards wide. The back of the range was completely covered with sandbags as were the sides at the bottom part of the range.

At the bottom of the range I noticed that there was a bank of sandbags about 6 or 9 feet in front of the end of the range and that there were 6 tins cans perched at 12 inch intervals on top of the sandbags. The Doc explained that his driver/bodyguard would load the pistol, (I forget whether it was a Webley or Smith and Wesson), hand it to us and that we would each shoot in turn. We were to shoot three times each in sequence, using a total of 18 bullets each. Each can that was shot off the sandbags would count as one hit. A coolie was stationed at the bottom of the range, at the side, but well away from the targets. His job was to replace the tin cans when they were hit, after the shooter had finished his firing. The Doc explained that we would be shooting at three different distances. Our first session would be at 20 feet, the second session at 15 feet and the last session at 10 feet. The Doc suggested that for interest that we all put $20 into a kitty with the winner taking the pot.

I thought this was a good idea and that I most likely would be $100 richer at the end of it all. Paul put $20 into the kitty for me along with his $20.

I thought all this was going to be a piece of cake when it was my turn, for I was told on the depot that I was a good shot having hit the bulls eye with a .303 rifle from 100 yards and with the submachine gun from 30 yards quite frequently. Unfortunately I had never fired a pistol before and I was soon due for a nasty shock later on.

Paul shot first and hit one tin can from his 20 feet. The Doc, his assistant, The Datu, and the driver/bodyguard shot next and they did no better than Paul, only hitting 2 cans between them. I was the last to shoot and I fully remember my first shot hitting the lightshade covering one of the lights and ricocheting to the side of the range, way off target and just missing the Coolie who disappeared like lightening. I failed to hit a single can.

The second shoot soon started with Paul shooting from 15 feet. Paul managed to knock two cans off the sandbags. The others who followed only managed 4 cans between them with the Doc getting two of those four. I fired last, with the Coolie nowhere to be seen, and did not hit a single can.

Coffee was brought into the range by one of the servants and whilst we drank our coffee the Doc told us the state of affairs. The Doc and Paul were leading with 3 hits each, followed by his assistant and driver/bodyguard with 1 hit each.

With coffee finished it was time for the third and final session, shooting at 10 feet Paul shot three cans off their perch to make it a grand total of 6 hits for his three sessions.

The Doc who followed him and also hit three cans. Doc's assistant, his driver/bodyguard and the Datu managed to hit one can each. Shooting last I needed to hit all six cans from 10 feet in order to draw with Paul and the Doc. I missed every can! The Doc declared Paul and himself the winners and they shared the pot. I was the only person to have not hit a single can from 18 bullets!

Over a late lunch the Doc and Paul explained to a very embarrassed me that firing a handgun was very much different to firing a rifle or sub machine gun and that the handgun was not very accurate at all. In fact any handgun was only accurate up to about twelve feet he said. They told me to forget all about the cowboys in the Westerns which I had watched, when these cowboys could hit a man from 100 feet or so. It never happened they told me. So much for my love of Western films. The Doc told me that he heard that I was quite good with the rifle and sub machine gun and advised me to always to stick to these two weapons when travelling around Malaya and to forget about trying out any of the John Wayne stuff. Paul explained that his many trips to the indoor range at Rasah camp had paid dividends. Enough said I thought!

It was over this late lunch when the Doc told us that he would be having some very interesting guests & visitors over the Christmas period and he asked Paul and I if we would like to spend a week or so at the plantation with him during this period. Paul and both readily accepted the invitation.

We usually left the plantation during the early evening on our visits to the plantation, but on this day we left just after 4pm I guess. Doc's driver dropped us at the one of the bars in Seremban and we went in for a beer. Paul suggested that when we submitted our leave passes to cover our leave at Doc's that I apply for two weeks leave and put the plantation address on my leave pass and that he would apply for 10 days leave and that he would either put Penang or Kuala Lumpur on his leave application. This way Paul said, with the different dates and addresses on our leave passes that the CO would not suspect that we would be going on leave together.

During the following week Paul and I both submitted our leave passes for the CO to authorise and sign. Before signing my leave pass the CO asked me why I was going out to a rubber plantation for my leave. I reminded the CO that I had not taken any privilege leave so far in the year I had been in Malaya and that I had met a European Assistant Estate Manager in Seremban in a bar, who came from Derbyshire, the county I used to live in and that he had invited me out to the plantation.

I explained to the CO that I knew rubber was the main industry in Malaya and that I always wanted to know more about the industry, how rubber grew and how it was gathered and processed etc. All bullshit of course. The CO complimented me about wanting to know more about the industries in Malaya and about Malay culture and added that he wished more corporals had the same idea as I did. Paul got his leave pass signed telling the CO that he was planning a touring holiday and most likely would be visiting Kuala Lumpur, Ipoh and Penang.

18

THE PRINCE AND PRINCESS

The Doc had told Paul a few days before 24 Dec that his driver would pick us up from the Government Rest House in Lake Gardens, which was managed by a friend of his at 9am on Tuesday 24 December and that should not bother to bring any weapons as there would sufficient in the vehicle which was collecting us. The 24 December came and Paul and I made our separate ways to the Government Rest House with our suitcases, with sufficient clothes to last us for a week or so. Over breakfast we waited for Doc's driver to arrive which he duly did at just before 9am and he was accompanied by an armed bodyguard. Paul and I jumped into the back of the land rover and noticed that there were three sterling sub machine guns and a couple of revolvers with ammunition on the floor. We moved all that to one side and made ourselves comfortable for the drive to the rubber plantation. Our journey passed with incident.

The Doc was on the verandah of his residence drinking coffee when we arrived and that was where we joined him. Over the next hour or so and over more coffees and a couple of punch drinks the Doc told us what the format over the next week was going to be like and what guests would be coming. Quite a number of his guests over the Christmas would include a prince, a princess Malayan VIPs, a couple of estate managers from other rubber plantations and some personal friends the Doc added. The Doc explained that addressing a Malay was quite diverse and complicated. Family names are relatively unimportant as long as the title was used correctly. Improper use may cause offence. The Doc emphasized that when addressing either the prince or princess that we should always address them as tunku, tengku, as both these words were appropriate for either a prince or princess. Addressing the prince as prince, and the princess as princess would not cause any offence though the Doc added. Regarding the other guests the Doc told us to just listen to how his other guests addressed the VIPs.

As obviously the two most important guests were going to be the prince and the princess the Doc then went to great lengths to give us a decent background on the both of them.

This background of the prince was: The prince was very westernised and nearly always wore Western clothes and seldom wore Malay dress. His preference was Western woman to that of Asian women. The prince's father was a Sultan of one of the nine states in Malaya and lived in that particular state with his three wives, that the prince had chosen not to live in that state and therefore had two residences, one in Seremban and his main one in Malacca. He was a bit of a playboy and often his behaviour could be termed as outrageous. He spoke excellent English and liked to be in the company of Westerners. He smoked English cigarettes like a trooper and drank like a fish as well. He could be "one of the boys" but it should always be remembered that he was a prince!

This background of the princess was quite the opposite of the prince in many ways. Although her father was another Sultan of another state where he lived with his four wives the princess had chosen to live in Seremban where she had a residence. She always wore Malay dress and never wore Western clothes. She was a strict Muslim and never smoked or drank. Her English was excellent. She was also quite shy and reserved. The best friend of the princess was a lovely Eurasian girl called Diana who lived very near to the princess and it was Diana who seemed to accompany the princess everywhere she went. Diana's father was an English doctor who was married to an Eurasian lady and they both resided in Singapore.

With the backgrounds over Paul and I were shown to our rooms by one of the maids. Paul and I were the only guests at this time. We had lunch followed by a quiet afternoon whilst the Doc went around his rubber estate. During the afternoon Paul gave me some history lessons regarding Malaya explaining that there were nine states in Malaya and that each state was ruled by a Sultan. Penang and Malacca were not states and therefore did not have sultans as such. Malacca was termed as a Settlement of some kind Paul added. Paul said he thought he could understand why the prince chose not to live in his father's state, as if he was westernised and behaved outrageous at times, that his Sultan father being a strict Muslim would not tolerate such behaviour.

Christmas Eve dinner was a simple affair and enjoyed only by the Doc, his assistant, Paul and myself. Possibly it was the quietest Christmas eve dinner I had ever sat down to. Paul and I departed to our rooms just after 10pm.

Following Christmas day breakfast four of Doc's guests arrived and these were two European managers of rubber estates and their two assistant managers. We all sat down to Christmas dinner which was turkey and all the usual trimmings of course. After much talk, a lovely Christmas evening buffet dinner, more drinks and more talking Paul and I finally went to bed at just before midnight. I got into my bed thinking that it was easily the quietest Christmas I could remember and hoped that things would liven up for the rest of the week.

I went down to breakfast on Thursday 26 December and joined the Doc, Paul and the four European estate guys who had stayed the night. One of the rubber estate guys told me the Christmas Eve and day sessions had been quite quiet as the Muslims did not celebrate Christmas and that he had been told by the Doc that the Malay guests would be arriving during the next day. Shortly after breakfast the four European rubber estate managers departed.

It must have been around 11am when the first two vehicles arrived with the Doc's Malayan guests. The prince was in the first vehicle with his driver and bodyguard who was Sgt Ahmed of the Malayan Police force, who was the guy who had given me the six bullets for Major Black a month before. In the second vehicle was the princess, her driver, her bodyguard and a stunning Eurasian girl who I soon found out was called Diana! All the necessary introductions were made and we all sat on the verandah where coffee was served by one of the maids. I noticed that the prince carried a handgun, not a revolver and a type which I had not seen before. I obviously stared at the weapon too much for the prince remarked that it was a browning 9mm Hi Power weapon and was automatic and its magazine carried 13 rounds.

A couple of hours later over a superb selection of really delicious curries it was the prince who outlined the plans for the afternoon. There was to be a shooting competition in the afternoon in the indoor range in which he, the Doc, Paul and the two drivers and two bodyguards would participate. The prince added that Browning 9mm Hi power handguns were to be used and that proper cardboard targets and not tin cans would be shot at. The prince would not use his own weapon but all participants would use the two Browning 9mm Hi Power weapons which the Doc had in his armoury. Each participant would fire three magazines each in the competition.

The prince added that he was putting up a prize of a Rolex watch for the winner. I was a bit disappointed and wondering why I had been omitted from the competition and thought that it was perhaps because the Doc had told the prince about my awful pistol shooting ability, when the prince addressed me stating that he had not asked me to participate in the shooting competition as he wanted me to look after the princess and Diana whilst the shooting match took place. Looking over at the delightful princess and Diana at the table I immediately cheered up and thought it was great idea of the prince's.

The prince and his party disappeared to the armoury or range. I was left at the table with the princess, Diana, and Lou the Doc's assistant. Lou soon got up afterwards stating that he had to go around the estate and check it. That left a nervous me with the princess and Diana. We all adjourned to the large lounge and sat under the large ceiling fans which were going round. The princess was in a lovely blue sarong with a matching blue kebaya (blouse) whilst Diana wore a yellow loose dress. Over the next couple of hours Diana did most of the talking and she asked the usual questions where I had come from, what I was doing and what Paul was doing in Malaya. By the time I had I answered all her questions I reckon she possibly thought that it was Paul and I who ran the army dental service in Malaya and not Lt Col Hull our CO! The princess asked a few questions to which I replied. I must admit that I was thunderstruck by the princess and luckily I seemed to get on with her very well.

The maid served us all coffee a couple of hours later and the princess asked the maid if she could rest somewhere as she was tired. The maid took the princess away to one of the bedrooms which left just Diana and I alone. This is when Diana got really talkative and she told me quite a lot about the princess. The princess was the daughter of the 3rd wife of one of the sultans who lived in his own state. The princess did not get on with the sultan's first wife and could not stand her, therefore she resided in Seremban, instead of in the state of her father. Diana added that the princess lived in a large house in Seremban and that she had a smaller house in the same street as the princess. Diana added that she was the princess's best friend and indeed did accompany her most of the time. I asked Diana if she lived alone and she replied that she did and that her father, a doctor, and her mother used to live in Seremban but had moved to Singapore.

I asked Diana if the prince and the princess were related and she replied that they were distant relatives. Diana added that both the prince and princess had their own vehicles and drivers but that they often shared Sgt Ahmed as a bodyguard and it was Ahmed who looked after both of them full time and was also responsible for arranging their security at all times. Diana went on to add that the prince lived on a different street to herself and the princess but that his residence was only about

100 yards away from theirs. Paul seemed to be the topic of conversation after Diana had told me all about the prince and princess for she asked me many questions about Paul. I immediately thought what I had been told about Eurasian women and that their target in life was always to marry a Western guy and leave Malaya! The fathers of these lovely Eurasian women were always trying their hardest to get their daughters married of to Europeans. This was common knowledge. Little did I suspect at the time that this was also Diana's plan to get married to a European as soon as possible.

I reckon it was just after 6pm when the guys from the firing range joined us in the lounge. The prince declared that Paul had won the shooting completion and he presented Paul with the watch at the bar, which was at the end of the lounge. The princess came down from her nap and Lou also joined us in the lounge. We all adjourned into the dining room where the two maids served us from a superb buffet of delicious Malayan dishes. After the buffet we all went back into the lounge. The prince, The Doc and Paul went to the bar. I noticed that the prince seemed to be knocking back the whiskies as though were going out of fashion. He was in deep conversation with both Paul and the Doc. About an hour later the prince announced that it was time that he, the princess and Diana departed back to Seremban, which they duly did, bidding us all Goodnight!

The Doc, Paul and I went back to the bar and over beers during the next hour the Doc told us more about the prince and he finished up by informing us that the prince had invited all the three of us down to Malacca on Tuesday 31 December and that we would be having lunch with him at one of the restaurants. For New Year's Eve the prince had booked several rooms at one of the hotels, where we would be accommodated and attend the New Year's Eve party which was being held there. Great I thought it gets better and better!

The next four days passed without any incidents. A number of Malayan civilian visitors came and went. Some of them were possibly VIPs or Datos, but Paul and I had little contact with them and we replied to them when we were spoken to. Eating throughout the day, drinking during the evening and exchanging stories, whilst during the day we toured the estate with either the Doc of with Lou. I did notice that during our tour round the estate that Paul was carrying a Browning 9mm Hi Power whilst I was given my usual Sterling SMG.

Tuesday 31st Dec arrived and we set off for Malacca to meet the prince in the designated restaurant for lunch. The driver dropped us outside the restaurant and Paul looked through the window of the restaurant whilst I was listening to the Doc giving instructions to his driver. Paul returned in a flash telling the Doc that we could not go into the restaurant. The Doc asked Paul why and Paul told him that he had seen our CO and the padre at a table in the corner eating their lunch. Paul explained all about the CO and where we were supposed to be on leave and what the CO was like. The Doc told us that it was not a problem and he said that his driver would take us all to the prince's residence and that everything would be explained to the prince. The driver took us all off to the prince's and Paul explained everything to him. The prince thought that it was hilarious but soon said that we would all go off to another restaurant which would be far away from where the CO and the padre were dining at. The driver disappeared taking our things to the hotel which the prince had booked us for the night.

The prince soon found us another lovely restaurant where we had a lovely meal and wine before being driven to the hotel where we were booked in at.

The New Year's Eve party was attended by the prince and Elizabeth, the prince's British partner for the evening, the princess, Diana, the Doc, Paul and myself. We had a special table for seven and I was lucky enough to be seated next to the princess who wore a light beige sarong and matching kebaya, whilst Paul was seated next to Diana who wore a red evening dress. Perhaps the seating had all been arranged by Diana I thought! We really had an excellent evening. The band were superb, as was the food. All four men danced with the three girls, but Paul had the most dances with Diana whilst I had the most dances with the princess. I was complimented on my dancing ability and I thought I should have been after all the practice I had had at the

Yam Yam with those taxi dancers! Alas the lovely evening came to an end in the early hours of the morning and the Doc, Paul and I trooped off to our rooms. Presumably the prince and his party left for the prince's residence. Before leaving the prince told Paul and myself that he hoped we would all be seeing each other quite frequently in the future. I certainly hoped that I would be seeing the princess again.

After breakfast the following morning the Doc took Paul and I back to Seremban and dropped us at the Government Rest house in the Lake Gardens. Paul disappeared back to Rasah Camp and started work on Friday 3 January 1958. I left the Rest house about an hour after Paul and went back to Rasha Camp. I was not due to start work until Monday 6 January 1958 so I just stayed in the camp and did a few personal chores until the Monday.

19

FEBRUARY 1958

Following a very dull and uneventful January, February was to be quite exciting. A few days before Friday 14 February 1958 the Doc telephoned Paul up and told him that he was having a birthday party on Friday 14 February (Valentine's Day) and asked Paul if he would like to bring three or four of the lads from the dental centre and MRS to spend the weekend at the rubber estate and celebrate his birthday. Paul thanked the Doc for his kind invitation and said that the lads would delighted to spend a weekend with him at his rubber estate.

Paul asked me to ask around the lads to see who would like to go and who could get a 48 hour pass. Cpl George Wilkie was on duty at the dental centre on the Saturday morning so that let him out, but Johnny Hart jumped at the chance to go. The other two guys who wanted to go were Chicko Burrell and the professor. I told Paul the lads who wanted to go and he told me to tell them all to be in the Mee Lee bar by 5pm on the Friday where we would all be picked up.

We all were in the Mee Lee bar well before 5pm on the Friday. Our CO had left, the dental centre as usual at midday on the Friday, in order to go down to Malacca with the Padre. S/Sgt Sexton and S/Sgt Meek had also made sure that Chicko and the professor finished work very early on the Friday afternoon. Just before 5pm we were joined by the prince and his driver and the Doc and his driver. We finished our beers and got into the two land rovers which were outside. As usual there were sufficient weapons in the back of the land rovers.

The prince got into the first land rover and Paul and I sat in the back. The Doc got in the second land rover and Chico, Johnny Hart and the professor sat in the back. The Prince told the Doc that he would lead the way. I thought at the time that it was something like the Wild West with the prince leading a posse of some sort. The Doc's land rover did not immediately leave behind us as the Doc was waiting for some crates of beers and some bottles of whisky to be loaded into his land rover.

The rubber estate was about 25 miles from Seremban with 20 miles of good road and the remaining five miles a private sandy single lane leading from the main road to the rubber estate. On looking out of the back of the land rover I noticed that there was very little traffic behind us and that the Doc's land rover had not caught us up yet.

We must have gone about 15 miles down the main road I guess, when we came round a sharp left hand corner and we heard loud explosions. The prince immediately told the driver to stop the car and told us it was an ambush. The driver of the land rover brought the vehicle to a rapid halt. The prince jumped out instructing us all of us to get out of the vehicle and take cover behind the land rover. Before you could say Jack Robinson the prince was kneeling and firing at what appeared to be a red flag on the other side of the road. Paul and I got out of the land rover very quickly with our weapons. The prince was shouting for us to fire. I looked at Paul and Paul looked at me and I said to Paul that the loud explosions we had heard were not bullets or grenades, but dynamite as I heard very similar explosions in Matlock when they used dynamite to blow up the quarries. Although the prince kept on telling Paul and myself to fire we did not fire a single shot.

Within a few minutes of the prince stopping our vehicle and getting us out of the vehicle, the Doc's land rover arrived and immediately pulled up behind us. The Doc was out of the land rover in a flash and he asked the prince what he was doing. By this time the prince had used up one magazine, which I believed contained about 11 or 12 rounds and was fixing a second magazine into his Browning HP.

Another loud explosion went off and the prince said that we were caught in an ambush. The Doc told the prince in no uncertain terms that it was not an ambush but that it was workers from a government concern who were clearing part of the jungle and a rock formation with dynamite and that they had been doing this most of the day and indeed had been doing it when he had passed the place on his way from the rubber estate to Seremban to collect us. The Doc told the prince that the red flag which was very visible at the side of the road was to warn motorists and any pedestrians that blasting with dynamite was taking place. We all got back into our respective land rovers and continued on our journey.

It was a very embarrassed prince who told us at dinner that night, that it was better to be safe than sorry! I told Paul later on that evening that the communist terrorists never told you via a red flag that they were ambushing you. The only red you saw was a red star on their caps and that was if you were unlucky enough to get close to them to see it, and then you had not long left in this world!

We all sat down to dinner over a selection of wonderful, delicious Malay curries, and wines, served by two of the maids. After dinner we celebrated Doc's birthday over more alcoholic drinks into the early hours of the morning. For his party piece the prince, ever the showman, was lifted up onto the ceiling fan where he swung round and round several times. All of us declined his invitation to follow him!

Over a late breakfast on the Saturday morning the Doc asked us all what we fancied doing during the day. The professor told him that he would like to wander around the estate and go into the jungle and bush. Obviously he wanted to look for more snakes or large insects. The Doc said that Sgt Ahmed and his driver would accompany the professor on his travels. Paul, Chicko and I, who had all brought our cameras said that we would like to go around the estate and take photos of the various buildings and rubber tappers at work. Both the Doc and the prince said that they would come with us. Johnny Hart said that he had a bit of a hangover from the night before and that he would rest until lunch time. Knowing Johnny and his love of all women I suspected that he had his eye on one of the attractive maids who had served us dinner the night before and whom he was chatting up when we came down for breakfast.

The professor went off with Sgt Ahmed and the driver. The prince and the Doc, who were both armed with pistols accompanied Paul, Chico and myself went off in a different direction. We spent a good hour taking photographs of all the surrounding buildings and some of the workers in them, before we went off into the rubber estate.

We had spent another good hour deep inside the estate taking some wonderful shots of the female and male rubber tappers tapping the rubber. From what I could see nearly all these rubbers tappers were Indians or Tamils. The estate was very large but we soon came to the edge on part of the estate which was met with jungle and bush. One of the bushes moved quite a bit and the prince took out his pistol, took aim and fired a shot into the bush. Within a second of the shot being fired, up jumped a male Tamil from behind the bush who was bleeding from the ear. The Doc immediately rushed over to the Tamil who was dancing all over the place, to see what had happened. The Tamil told the Doc that he had been "caught short" and had sat down behind the bush and had just finished doing a crap and was wiping his backside when he had heard a bang and something had stung his ear. The prince was soon in discussion with a very annoyed Doc. The Doc explained the situation to the prince and the prince said that he would take care of everything. We all took the wounded Tamil back to the little medical hut on the estate. The medical set up did not have any doctor, just a nurse with some sort of qualification. Paul took a look at the bleeding ear of the Tamil and told the Doc that the Tamil had been "very lucky" in that the bullet had only clipped his ear and that there was a lot more blood than any damage. The nurse was not around so Paul told the Doc and the prince that he would treat the Tamil. Paul looked around the surgery, which had an excellent supply of various drugs, and he used something, which I believe was tannic acid, which we used in dentistry to stop bleeding, before giving him a penicillin injection.

The Doc and the prince took the Tamil to one side and spoke to him. It was afterwards at the bar in the evening that the Doc told Paul and me that the prince had agreed to give the Tamil a few thousand dollars, which was more than he could earn in five years as a rubber tapper.

A few months later the Doc told us that the rubber tapper was still working for him, and that the prince had kept his promise and thus made the Tamil easily the richest rubber tapper on the estate.

We all had lunch, apart from the professor, Sgt Ahmed and the driver who had still not come back. We all did our own thing in the afternoon. I wandered around and took some more photos and I did not know what the others did.

Later on during the late afternoon we were all sat on the large verandah drinking our coffees or beers when the professor arrived back with his two escorts. The professor was carrying a cardboard beer case which he put down on the table which was occupied by the prince, Chicko, and the Doc. A beaming professor told us all that he had caught two snakes and that inside the box was a baby Malayan cobra and a pit viper. On hearing this Chicko, the Doc and the prince jumped up like lightening, but the prince was easily the fastest up. The prince asked the professor what he was going to do with the snakes and the professor told him that he was going to sell them to Vincent Wong, the snake seller in Seremban, when he got back Seremban. The Doc refused to have the snakes lying around in any box during the rest of the weekend and he told the professor to kill them immediately. The Doc sent the professor off, with his two escorts to ensure that this was done, quite a long way from the house.

Another superb meal was served by the two maids at around 7pm. It was at dinner that prince told us that he was organising a card school for the evening and asked who would like to play for small stakes. Chicko, Johnny Hart and the professor immediately all told him that they would love to play. These three had never met a prince until yesterday, let alone played cards with one, so they were very quick to volunteer. Lou, the Doc's assistant said he would also like to play. Paul and the Doc said that they never played cards, which left just me to answer. However, before I could answer the Doc told the prince jokingly to be very careful with me as he had seen me perform many tricks with the cards and had seen me deal myself a full house time and time again when playing poker for fun and not money, and 3 x aces when playing 3 card brag. On hearing this the prince said that he had five players and that perhaps was enough. This meant, of course that I did not have to play cards, but could enjoy the rest of the evening drinking with the Doc and Paul.

The five card players made their way to the table in the lounge, whilst the Doc, Paul and myself went to the bar at the other end of the large lounge. Over drinks the subject or the prince and his "ambush" and the shooting of the Tamil came up and the Doc told us that the prince was a "bit of a loose cannon" and very trigger happy and that whilst walking around the estate that he would shoot at anything that moved, monkeys and snakes being his favourites. The Doc went on to say that the prince had been born 100 years too late and that he should have been born in the 1820's in the Wild West in America. Had he have been born in the Wild West, then you could guarantee that the trigger happy prince would have been either an infamous outlaw or a famous sheriff the Doc added. The Doc went on to tell us that the prince apart from his "minor deficiencies", was a very good friend, a very generous man and a good organiser.

Paul told the Doc that the prince had certainly been good to all us "squaddies".

I was about the last one down for breakfast on the Sunday morning and I noticed that the maids had set the breakfast up on the tables on the verandah. I sat down with the others and as I was eating my breakfast I noticed two coolies marking out some lines with whitewash on the sand. Before I could ask what they were doing the prince explained that he was organising a touch rugby match between the British Army v Malaya. The prince went to explain that the army side would consist of Paul, Johnny, Chico, the professor and myself and that the Malay side would consist of the "Doc", Lou, Sgt Ahmad, the driver and the prince. The rules the prince explained were that when a player was touched he immediately had to pass or get rid of the ball. The ball could only be passed sidewards or backwards. When a player went over the opponent's line and dropped the ball it would be one point. The prince concluded that he would also be the referee in addition to playing and that the game would finish when one team scored 6 points, or after ten minutes, whichever came the sooner. I knew that Paul had played rugby at university but that the rest of us in our team had never played any type of rugby in our lives. I thought anyway that it was only a game and would be over in ten minutes maximum.

We finished our breakfast and were ready to play the so called rugby match. The prince appeared back on the verandah carrying a very large frozen cabbage. The prince then told us that the "ball" was to be the frozen cabbage and that is what we would be playing with. We all took our places on the makeup sandy pitch which was alongside the verandah and the game started. Not only was the frozen cabbage very hard but it was bloody cold and you did not keep it long but got rid of it quickly. After about three or so minutes with the scores at 2 - 2, I was passed the frozen cabbage by the professor and immediately got rid of it by passing it to Chicko. Unfortunately the prince tried to intercept the flying cabbage and the cabbage hit him full in the face. Blood was pouring from the face and out of the mouth of the prince. The game was stopped and Paul took a look at the prince's face. After a quick examination the prince was helped to the little medical hut where Paul examined and cleaned the prince up. Paul then told the prince that he had very bad cuts on his lips that would required 4 of 5 stitches and in addition he had two chipped teeth. Whilst Paul had often done stitching (sutures) to the inside of his patient's mouths following extractions he was not qualified or confident to do any suturing of the lips or outside the mouth and he suggested that the prince went to a hospital and had the suturing done by a doctor. The prince agreed with

Paul. Paul told the prince that he would look at his chipped teeth after the suturing had been done by the doctor.

The Doc got the prince's driver to bring the land rover around and the prince, Paul and I got into the land rover and took off for Seremban hospital. Arriving at the hospital the prince, with his connections was soon seen by a doctor who put four stitches into the prince's swollen lips. After the suturing Paul looked at the prince's swollen lips and told him that it was not possible to do anything then about his two chipped two teeth as it would be far too painful. Paul suggested that he should see the prince in two weeks time at our dental centre on a Sunday. We all piled into the land rover again which took us to the prince's residence. Over a couple of whiskies the prince joked that he held no malice against me and joked that he had never seen anybody get rid of the "ball" so quickly.

The prince added that he had enjoyed the eventful weekend at the Doc's and that it was a pity it had finished so quickly, as he had planned other activities for us after the rugby match and in the afternoon. He never mentioned what his planned activities were!

The driver drove Paul and me back to Rasah Camp, dropping Paul off at the Officer's Mess and then taking me to my billet. I had to wait until around 8pm until the lads returned from the Doc's. They told me that it was one of the best weekends that they had ever had. An excited professor told me that he had won most of the money when they had played cards, whilst Johnny Hart could only rant and rave about the two maids. I often wondered what Johnny had been doing with those maids when he disappeared all the time, but he never let on to me

20

BACK TO BMH KINRARA

After Christmas, an exciting New Year, a very dull January and a quite exciting February it was back to more personal and exciting things for me in March. The CO called Captain Paul Summers into his office during the middle of March and told him that he would like him to go up to the Dental Department at BMH Kinrara in order to give a lecture and demonstration to the Dental Service of 3rd Royal Australian Regiment (3 RAR) on the latest dental equipment, materials which the British Army Dental Service were using. The CO said that Captain Summers was to take one Cpl from our dental centre with him and that a second Cpl would be Cpl Graham Purcell from the Army Dental Centre in Kuala Lumpur and that these two corporals were to assist Captain Summers in his lecture and presentation to 3 RAR.

Captain Summers chose me as the corporal from our dental centre to accompany him. I was not only the senior corporal, but obviously I was quite close to Paul. Paul explained to me that our dental service worked very closely with the dental service of 3 RAR and that the 3 RAR had informed our CO that they wanted to know the latest dental materials we were using; also what the contents of our latest dental panniers contained; also what were the latest accounting procedures we were using.

Paul said that two dental officers and two corporals of the 3 RAR would be attending the presentation. Paul then explained to me that the 3 RAR were based in Perek which was considered to be one of the main areas of communist activity. They were often on patrol near the Thai-Malay border and that they also did many distant patrols and they used dental panniers on their patrols.

Cpl Purcell was to collect our latest dental panniers from 16 Field Ambulance at Wardiburn camp in KL which they shared with 22 SAS. Paul asked me if I knew Cpl Purcell and I explained it was Graham who had picked me up from Seremban railway station when I had first arrived in Malaya and that we were not only good friends but also that we spoke on a regular basis on the telephone. Paul told them that this being the case that he proposed to split the presentation into three parts. Whilst he would demonstrate the latest dental materials we used in our service to the two 3 RAR dentists he would also show them the working procedure on the new anesthesia machine (which I believe was the McKesson) which was to replace the Jetaflo machine. Whilst he was doing this Cpl Purcell was to show all the items in our dental panniers, plus the latest foot treadle apparatus to the two Australian corporals and once that had finished I was to explain all the latest accounting procedures we used in the army dental service.

The demonstration was arranged to take place in the Dental Department at BMH Kinrara on the Saturday from 9am until 5pm with a break for lunch. On the Thursday afternoon, as directed by Paul I packed all the dental materials and the accounting books and forms, and put them into two boxes. These I loaded into the land rover with the new anesthesia machine and bottles of nitrous oxide and oxygen.

On Friday morning Paul and I set off for the Dental Department at BMH Kinrara. After lunch Paul laid out all the dental materials and the anesthesia machine. Graham laid out the contents of the dental panniers whilst I laid out all the accounting books, forms, indenting forms and the new cardex system for accounting for consumable items. We had all finished by 4pm. Paul told Graham and I that whilst he was going off to see a bit of Kuala Lumpur, with his camera, that we were free to do what we wanted and that he would see us the following morning at 8.30am. Graham took the opportunity of taking me around Kuala Lumpur, mainly showing me his favourite bars.

Paul, Graham and I met on the Saturday morning at 8.30am as planned. Paul explained to Graham and myself the format of the presentation and the presentation started off at 9am.

Paul was demonstrating to the two Australian officers in the dental surgery, whilst Graham was showing the two

Australian corporals the contents of the dental pannier and the demonstrating the use of the new foot treadle apparatus. Notes were taken and by 11am Paul and Graham had finished their demonstrations.

At exactly 11am coffee and biscuits were brought into the dental department for the seven of us by a QARANC captain and a QARANC corporal. I was shocked to see that the captain was Captain Kneebone, that aggressive woman who had given me a right rollicking five months before when I had reported to her with the dead body of that SAS soldier. Coffee and biscuits were served to the seven of us and I knew that Captain Kneebone had recognised me because she winked at me.

During the coffee and biscuits I was talking to the four Australians about all the accounting stuff I had laid out and I noticed that Paul was in deep conversation with Captain Kneebone and Graham at the other end of the room. Coffee was soon finished and Paul went into the office with the two Australian dentists. Graham disappeared somewhere. I started my talk and demonstration to the two Australian corporals on the latest accounting system used in the army dental service. More notes were taken. By 1pm it was time for lunch. Paul and the two Australian dentists came out of the office and Graham appeared out of thin air. After an exchange of words between the four Australians and Paul, Paul informed us all that the Australians had seen enough and that they were really pleased with the presentation and demonstration and that this being the case there was no need to continue after lunch and that we were all free to do what we wanted for the rest of the day.

Paul added that he was exceptionally pleased how the presentation had gone and that he wanted to take us all out in the evening for a Chinese meal. One of the Australian officers thanked Paul but stated that they would have to take a rain check as they had been invited out by staff of the Australian Embassy or Consulate that evening. That being the case Paul told Graham and me that he would take the both of us that evening. The Australians said farewell to us all and departed. Before Paul, Graham and I departed for lunch at our various messes Paul told me that he would see me at the restaurant at 7pm that evening and that Graham had all the details.

Over lunch Graham told me that Paul had asked him (being based in Kuala Lumpur) to pick a good Chinese Szechuan restaurant that served hot spicy Chinese food. Graham told me that he had chosen a Szechuan restaurant called Fook Yu, which was his easily his favourite restaurant. Graham and I finished our lunch and went back to the dental department and started packing the things back into the pannier and boxes. We finished at just after 4pm and we went back to rooms had a shower and got changed into civvies (civilian clothes). Graham and I then went into Kuala Lumpur and visited a couple of bars for a few beers before meeting Paul at the Fook Yu at 7pm.

Graham and I arrived at the Fook Yu at around 6.45pm and sat at the bar waiting for the arrival of Paul. At just before 7pm Paul arrived with two females, one whom I immediately recognised as the aggressive Captain Kneebone. Paul introduced the two females to both Graham and I as Captain Judith Kneebone and Captain Anna Willing. I knew Captain Kneebone of course but obviously I did not know Captain Anna Willing QARANC. Graham, I found out later knew both these QARANC captains more than well, but of course he did not let on at the time.

The waiter found us a table for five and I was seated next between Anna and Graham whilst Judith was seated between Paul and Graham. I was thankful at the time not to have been seated next to Judith. Before the evening was out perhaps I had wished I had have been seated next to Judith instead of being seated next to Anna. Paul on Graham's recommendation ordered about 10 different dishes. I thought it was going to be a long dinner and indeed it did last just over two hours.

There was plenty of talk and joking. On reflection perhaps the best talker out of all of us was Judith Kneebone with her wicked sense of humour and dirty jokes. She was certainly the life and soul of the party.
The drinks were flowing very freely and after about an hour I found that Anna kept on rubbing her left leg against my right leg under the table. As the evening went on and more drinks were being consumed Anna's

left leg was pressing much more heavily against my left leg. I started getting very embarrassed to the extent that my face was the colour of a cooked lobster. Paul, who sat immediately opposite me obviously noticed the colour of my face and asked me if the food was too hot and spicy for me.

Before I could tell Paul the food was okay, Anna replied to Paul stating that perhaps I was not used to it. Perhaps she meant the leg crush and not the food I thought.

The dinner finished at just after 9.30pm. Paul paid the bill and we all thanked him for a super meal and an excellent evening. We all got up from the table and Paul told us that he would be taking the ladies back to the Officer's Mess and he told me that he wanted to leave BMH Kinrara for Seremban at about 2pm the following day and to make sure that everything was packed and that we were ready to leave around that time. Paul and the two ladies then left the restaurant but not before Anna gave me several winks and a nice smile.

Graham suggested that as the night was still young, that before returning to BMH Kinrara that we hit another couple of bars, which we did. Over a beer at the first bar we hit I told Graham about Anna's behaviour in the restaurant and how her leg kept on crushing against mine. The longer the evening went on and the more she drank I told Graham the more force she put into the crushes. Graham then told me that he had never been with Anna, but that he had been told from excellent sources that Anna was known as a very 'ready willing and able' lady. Graham went to tell me that Judith was even a lot worse than Anna, as Judith was a nymphomaniac and more than 'willing'. Graham added that he had been with Judith a few times and that she "went like a bunny rabbit". All this sounded strange to me and I told Graham I thought Judith Kneebone was a stuck up aggressive bitch and that I had experienced her wrath in the past. Graham then explained that both Judith and Anna were aged 26 years old and that both these ladies were very quite timid and friendly and very popular with the staff they worked with and patients they cared for. I bet they were I thought! I could understand how Graham managed to be so popular with the ladies, as he was a very handsome lad with blue eyes and blonde hair. As good looking as Clark Gable that Hollywood heart throb at the time I thought.

Just before 11pm Graham and I decided to call it a day and we went back to our rooms in the hospital. Graham's room was next to mine and I heard the door of his room open and close at around midnight. Presumably he had gone out again somewhere I thought.

Graham and I had a late breakfast the following morning and Graham suggested that we go back to the dental department and make sure that we were leaving everything nice, clean and tidy. All the boxes were packed into the corner with the anesthesia machine which I was to take back to Seremban and the panniers were packed and treadle engine was also in the corner ready for Graham to return them to 16 Field Ambulance the following morning. The time was around 11am I guess and I thought we had plenty of time before Paul came to collect me at 2pm. Whilst I was pondering, Graham and I were sat in the waiting room having a cigarette when in walked Anna Willing and Judith Kneebone in their civilian clothes bearing coffee and biscuits. It never entered my mind at the time that it was a set up arranged by Graham!

After coffee and some small chat Judith and Graham disappeared into the dental specialist's office which left Anna and myself alone in the waiting room. I was sat on the settee and Anna joined me there. 'Good to see you again' she told me and 'how nice to see you on your own at last'. Everything seemed to come fast and furious from then and one thing soon led to another and it was Anna who introduced me to my first real kiss which she explained was a French kiss. I would not say that that I did not enjoy this French kissing from a woman 6 years older than I was but at the same time I was hoping that it would not lead to anything further.

Her tongue was halfway down my throat and I thought Thank God I was in the RADC and always brushed my teeth three times a day. Stupid thinking at the time!

Whilst Anna's tongue was half way down my throat and the kissing continued my hands were a on her back shoulders. She soon moved my hands onto her brassiere and put them on the back of it and kept her hands over mine. I could not move my hands. I did not know what to do whether she wanted me to undo her brassiere or not. I did not know anything about brassieres of how to undo them. In fact I had only seen brassieres before when my mother hung two them on the clothes line outside and I thought that were some kind of new slingshots or catapults she had got for me to fire my pebbles and ball bearings with, until she explained what they were for. I was not only excited but very worried and embarrassed and thought that I may suffer my first heart attack at the young age of 20. Anna came up for air for a few seconds and immediately started the French kissing again. A moaning and groaning Anna immediately moved my hands down onto her legs.

I looked down and saw that her skirt had ridden up to her waist and that she was wearing stockings and suspenders. She placed my hands on top of her suspenders and placed her hands on the top of mine. Whilst all this was going on I could hear the very loud groans and moans that Graham and Judith were making in the dental specialist's office.

Well I must admit that she was getting me excited somewhat, I still was very worried because I was not experienced in anything like this and thought that if it did go any further then I would prove what a fool I was. I must admit that I knew what suspenders and stockings were but I did not know how these contraptions worked or how you undid them, so if Anna wanted her stockings off then it was she who had to undo her suspenders, or do whatever a woman did. Tights had not been invented in those days and my mother always wore stockings and suspenders to go to work and although I had often seen my mother adjust her stockings and suspenders before leaving the house in order to catch the bus to go to work, I had never seen my mother unhook her stockings from her suspenders. More French kissing with Anna was taking place and Anna seemed to getting a lot more excited than I was. The loud groaning and moaning from the dental surgery next door suddenly stopped and I thought Graham and Judith had finished all their business. In my mind I was perhaps hoping then they would come out into the waiting room and that would stop Anna and me going any further. This was not to be however, for after a few minutes the groaning and moaning started again so obviously Graham and Judith were on round 2!

Anna was getting very, very excited and I must admit that she was getting me excited as well. I thought was this today that I was, at long last going that I was going to lose my virginity to a very experienced teacher. Anna obviously knew that she was getting me pretty excited and she took her hands off of mine and moved my hands up on to her naked inside thigh above her suspenders, keeping her hands firmly over my hands. Again thoughts came into my head and I wondered was this going to be the day this 'Teddy boy had his picnic'. Again I thought, if she showed me all the ropes there was nothing wrong in losing my virginity to a really attractive experienced teacher. Yes I thought let it be today! Let Anna do what she wanted and I would agree and go the whole distance. V Day had arrived I told myself.

Suddenly I heard the door to the dental clinic open with a bang. I saw Paul walking down the corridor, past the reception area and asking in a loud voice if anybody was in. Quick as a flash I took my hands off of Anna's thighs whilst Anna pulled her skirt down and smothered it. We were both sat upright on the settee and apart before Paul came into the waiting area. Judith and Graham soon appeared in the waiting room as well. Paul asked me if everything had been packed and I told him that everything was ready to be loaded into the land rover and that we were ready to go whenever he wanted to. Paul told me in that case, rather than wait for lunch in the Officer's Mess that he preferred to go straight away and have lunch at a Malay restaurant on our way to Seremban. Graham helped me to load the equipment into the land rover which was outside and went off to find the driver. He came back about ten minutes later and Paul thanked Graham for his help regarding the presentation. I thanked Captains Willing and Kneebone for the coffee and then Paul and I got into the land rover and we started our journey back to Seremban.

We stopped at an air Malay restaurant somewhere between Kuala Lumpur and Seremban. Whilst the driver went to park and secure the land rover Paul and I found a table and sat down. The first thing Paul said to me was to remind me how many times he had told me to always make sure the bloody doors were locked at times when I did not want to be disturbed. The door to the dental centre at Seremban was always locked when Paul did some dentistry on the Doc on Sundays he reminded me. I immediately knew then that Paul had suspected what was happening in the dental clinic just one hour before, when he slammed that door open and called out in a loud voice whilst walking slowly down that corridor. Nothing more was said by Paul about the incident, although I was sure that he knew what had happened as sure as eggs were eggs.

Graham telephoned me at the dental centre Seremban from his dental centre in Kuala Lumpur on the Monday morning. Graham knew everything what had happened between Anna and me, and I guess that Anna had told Judith everything and she had passed it all on to Graham. Graham admitted that he had told Judith that I was a very shy virgin and she had told Anna. Graham had arranged the set up encouraged by both Judith and Anna. Graham told me that he was sorry that I had not lost my virginity to an attractive lady like Anna. I was not annoyed at Graham with his set up and I knew, being good friends, that he only had my best interests at heart.

During a couple of weeks later I did receive a scented letter in an envelope addressed to me. All the letter read was 'you never know what you missed'. 'Good Luck in the future'. It was signed A.

For the next few months I often thought how so unlucky I had been not to have lost my virginity to Anna. When I eventually did lose my virginity to the old ugly Winnie the Witch on my 21st birthday on 17 June I thought what an injustice had been done for her to have taken my virginity instead of the lovely, delectable Anna. I soon changed my mind regarding that when Graham telephoned me a week after I had lost my virginity to the witch, with the news that Anna was pregnant and was being kicked out of the QARANC and was being shipped back to Blighty. God, I thought had I have gone the full distance with Anna in the waiting room on that presentation day, I could have well been a daddy by now. I had to wait for another seven years before I had the pleasure of being a father. So losing my virginity to "Winnie the Witch" instead of the lovely Anna may not have been so bad after all.

21

APRIL AND MAY 1958

Compared to previous months April was quite quiet. Captain Churchyard, Cpl Pratt of the Dental Centre and L Cpl Foad of the MRS all returned to Blighty. Capt Wilson RADC, Cpl Harry Woodrow RADC and Cpl Duncan RAMC were their replacements and they all seemed decent guys.

I was still visiting my old haunts at the Mee Lee Bar and the Yam Yam Cabaret with Chicko and Johnny Hart during the week, but I was also with Paul during a few weekends when we were seeing a little more of Diana and the princess.

On the third weekend in April Paul got an invite from the prince to visit his residence for lunch in Seremban. The prince asked Paul to bring Chicko and myself and all the three of us duly arrived at the prince's house on the Saturday for lunch. Over lunch, the prince mentioned that Chicko had told him when he had met him at the Doc's in February, that his job was inspecting the drinking and eating establishments for the Army in Seremban and that he always rode a motor bicycle whilst carrying out his duties. Chicko confirmed that this was true. The prince then told us that although he had several cars and a sports car that he always wanted to learn how to ride a motor bike and he asked Chicko if he would teach him. Chicko told the prince that he would be delighted to teach the prince how to ride a motor bike The prince told Chicko that he would make the necessary arrangements.

A few days later the Doc telephoned Paul and told him that he would like to invite him, Chicko and me down to the estate for a few days and that Chicko should bring his motor bike as the prince would also be coming and that he would like Chicko to give him some lessons. Paul spoke to Chicko and myself and asked us if we could get a few days leave in order to go down to Doc's. Chicko and I both put in for 5 days leave which was duly approved. Paul told us that it was not possible for him to take any leave so it meant that I would be visiting the Doc's without Paul for the first time.

Monday during the first week of May, S/Sgt Meek told Chico that he could take the motor bike up to Doc's and use it up there for a few days. Chicko arrived with his motor bike and we loaded the panniers with our casual clothes and rode off without helmets. Chicko obviously was doing the riding whilst I was riding pillion. The 25 mile journey, especially the last five miles down the sandy track went okay, although I was a little worried as we had no weapons, but we arrived okay at the Doc's in the afternoon and found that he had just one guest, a Welsh guy, named Dai Jones, staying with him for a few days. Over drinks in the evening Dai told Chicko and me that he had served his two years National Service in Singapore a few years before, had met the Doc during his service in the Far East and that he had popped into to see the Doc for a few days whilst on his travels around Asia.

The prince arrived on the Tuesday morning in his land rover with Sgt Ahmed and a Mrs Siti. Sgt Ahmed introduced Mrs Siti to Dai, Chicko and myself telling us that she was a friend of his. On the either side of lunch Chicko gave the prince riding lessons using the five miles of sandy track between the main road and Doc's residence. Whilst the prince and Chicko were out riding I used this time to tour the rubber plantation with my camera, accompanied by Dai, Sgt Ahmed and Mrs Siti. After an early evening meal of an excellent chicken curry, the Doc, the prince, Dai and Chicko disappeared to the bar leaving Sgt Ahmed, Mrs Siti and myself on the veranda. Mrs Siti was a Malay lady and I guess, a woman in her mid fifties and was quite stoutly built. I would not say that she was attractive, but I could not say that she was unattractive either. She wore Western clothes and was quite a talkative person.

It was whilst we were drinking that Sgt Ahmed explained to me in front of Mrs Siti that she was the widow of Police Superintendent Siri who had been murdered by the terrorists a few years before. Sgt Ahmed went on to tell me that Police Superintendent had been the officer in charge of the Police station at Seremban and that he had worked under him until his murder. Since then he had remained friends with Mrs Siti and often helped her when she needed it.

During the next couple of hours the three of us talked about various subjects. Mrs Siti explained that she liked Europeans as she found that most of them had a good sense of humour, whereas the Malays and the Chinese were more reserved.

It was when she asked me what kind of food I liked and I told her that Malayan curries were my favourite, that she told me that curries were also her favourite food and loved cooking curries for her guests. She then asked me if I would like to visit her sometime when she would cook me a special curry. I told her that was very kind of her and that I would love her to cook me a curry. She gave me her telephone number and she asked me to contact her when I was free to come. I promised her that I would.

At around 10pm the prince and Sgt Ahmed returned from the bar and told us that they must be leaving back for Seremban and Malacca. Sgt Ahmed, the prince and Mrs Siti then left. Chicko and Dai were still in the bar, when the Doc came out on to the veranda. He sat down next to me with a drink in his hand and he asked me how I had found Mrs Siti. I told him that I found her to be an exciting lady who was quite knowledgeable, with a good sense of humour. The Doc then asked me if she had invited me out to her house for a curry and I told him she had indeed and that I had accepted and that she had given me her telephone number and that I had promised that I would contact her.

The Doc then told me to think very carefully before contacting her and accepting her invitation. He went on to explain that Mrs Siti was not only very fond of Europeans but that she kept two loaded pistols in her bedroom and lounge. I told the Doc that Sgt Ahmed had explained to me how Mrs Siti's husband had been murdered by the terrorists and that perhaps she kept the loaded pistols in her house in case any terrorists tried to visit her house with a view to murder a police widow. No that is not the reason the Doc told me. The Doc then told me that she kept the loaded pistols in her house in case any robbers broke into her house with the idea of perhaps trying to rape her as well. You mean that she would shoot and kill them in cold blood I asked the Doc. No, No, No the Doc replied very quickly, the bloody loaded pistols are there to encourage the robbers and would be rapists.

Well when the Doc told me that I thought that I certainly would not be taking up Mrs Siti's invitation for a special curry and anything else and I never did contact her!

During the evenings of Tuesday, Wednesday and Thursday after the riding lessons had finished and the prince had returned to Malacca, I spent most of my time at the bar with Chicko and Dai. Dai told his a lot about his experiences in the army whilst serving in Singapore and Malaya a few years before and in turn he asked Chicko and myself a lot about our experiences.

I must admit that Chicko's and my experiences were by far the more interesting. I must say that Dai was a very interesting character whom I took an instant like to. He was also very funny and had a marvellous sense of humour.

Just after breakfast on Friday the prince arrived in his land rover with Sgt Ahmed. Chicko told the prince that he thought the prince had learnt very fast, had been an excellent pupil and that he was more than capable of riding a motor bike on his own now. The prince insisted that he be allowed to ride the motor bike on his own on a test or trail run. Chicko suggested that the prince ride the motor bike down the five mile sandy track to the main road, turn around and come back. This was agreed by the prince. The price mounted the motor bike and took off down the track followed by Sgt Ahmed and Chicko in the land rover. Knowing what the prince was like with his outrageous behaviour, I feared the worse!

About forty minutes later the prince came zipping down the track on the motor bike followed by Chicko and Sgt Ahmed in the land rover. He pulled up by the verandah where I was having coffee with Dai. The prince and Chicko joined Dai and myself on the verandah and Chicko told us that the prince had been excellent and had ridden well and did not need any further lessons. The prince caught me smiling but said nothing. We all had a quick lunch served by one of the maids and during lunch the prince told Chicko that he would like to see me "have a go" on the motor bike before he left for Malacca. No problem I thought, as I had always listened to the instructions that Chicko had given to the prince. Lunch finished and Chicko put me on the back of the motor bike reminding me where everything was on the motor bike. I rode off and I reckon I must have got about 100 yards down the track when I forgot where everything was on the motor bike. The next thing I remember was the motor bike hitting a rubber tree and bouncing off. I do not know what I did wrong all I knew was that both my hands were on the two handlebars and I was turning both in a clockwise direction.

The prince, Chicko and Dai sprinted down the track and picked me up. I was not injured in any way and the bike was not damaged Thank God. The prince, Chicko and Dai were in hysterics of course. I thought afterwards that I was useless at trying to drive a car or ride a motor bike. Possibly the prince, remembering how I smiled when Chicko had told him that he had been excellent on his test ride, thought that "the last one laughing is the best".

The prince thanked the Doc and Chicko and said farewell to us all before leaving back for Malacca in the land rover with Sgt Ahmed. Thanking the Doc for his hospitality, Chicko and I said farewell to the Doc and Dai before riding back to Rasha Camp in the afternoon.

It was Diana's birthday on Saturday 17 May and Paul and I got an invite to the princess's house where the party was being held. Paul and I arrived at around 7pm bearing presents. We were shown into the large garden where everything had been set up for the party. I reckon that there were about 20 guests at the party, all whom I did not know except for the princess, the prince and Diana. I did not see any alcohol being served, so I did not ask for any but stuck with some kind of punch. Later on in the evening the prince managed to get Paul and me on our own. I immediately noticed that the prince's large glass was filled with something which looked like whisky and not punch or any soft drink. Paul mentioned to the prince that it was an excellent birthday party. I told the prince that I had to arrange another birthday party for Chicko, whose birthday it was on Sunday 25 May. The prince immediately told Paul and I that he would like to organise the birthday party for Chicko as he wished to thank him for the riding lessons Chicko had given him. It was at this time that I noticed that Paul was not addressing the prince, as prince, but addressing him as Freddie. Paul told me much later that the prince had insisted that Paul call him Freddie and not prince. Although both the prince and princess addressed me by my Christian name, I always addressed them as prince and princess of course.

Before he left the birthday party, the prince, always a man to make quick decisions and also a very quick thinker told Paul and myself that he would arrange a birthday a party for Chicko at his house in Seremban and that Chicko could bring any of his army friends he wanted. All the prince wanted to know was the number that would be attending by Friday.

I told the good news to Chicko on returning back to my billet. During the week Chicko spent time talking to his friends. By Friday Chicko told me that he would like 11 army guys at his party. The ten soldiers would include himself, S/Sgt Gil Meek his boss and S/Sgt Sexton. The only officer he would like at the party was Paul. I relayed the information to Paul who spoke to the prince. The prince informed Paul that he would expect everybody to arrive for a light lunch by 1pm, then the main party would start in the evening at 7pm.

Sunday 25 May arrived and by 12.45 all of us arrived at the prince's. The light lunch consisted of prawn, beef, and chicken curries with various rice and condiments and with plenty of beer and wine to wash it all down, was served in the large lounge at exactly 1pm. It must have been around 3pm when the prince told us all that he had organised some entertainment for us all. Ever the entertainer and organiser I immediately thought, remembering what the Doc had told me once before.

The prince then went on to tell us all that he had arranged a trishaw race in which we were all to participate in. (For the uneducated, cycle rickshaws are human-powered by pedaling. A person pedals and a passenger sits in the passenger seat).

The prince then told us that he had arranged with the trishaw drivers to lend him 5 trishaws. There were to be 5 teams of 2 men racing against each other over a distance of about 400 yards. The "course" had been marked out and we were to race 200 yards where Paul would be waiting and we were to turn around Paul and race back the remaining 200 yards where the prince would be to greet the winner. The winning team of 2 would receive $100 each from the prince. The prince then told us to pick our teams and that the race would start at about 4pm. The guys started talking and picking their teams. Chicko told me that he would ride and that I would be his passenger. This surprised me as I thought he would have picked one of the lighter guys to be his passenger.

Just before 4pm we went outside and walked about 300 yards to where the five trishaws were laid out, all in a line. The race was to be down the main street in Seremban. Obviously the real trishaw drivers had told some of their mates about the race because quite a few of the public were lined up on the sides of the road. Paul made his way down the road to the 200 yard mark, which was by one of the open air restaurants. The prince told us to go to our "chariots" and get ready. Chicko mounted the bike and I got into the passenger's seat. I looked at the road ahead and when I saw motor vehicles moving in both directions, I was glad that I had a good rider in Chicko. The prince shouted Go and we all went off. After the first 50 yards all the five trishaws were in single file and not in horizontal file. Geordie

Shaw was first at the half way point when he pedaled around Paul and started the race back to the finish. Chicko was a close second and about five yards behind Geordie. The crowd were cheering!

We were about 100 yards from the finish and gaining on Geordie when disaster struck. From the passenger's seat I saw a mad motorist overtaking another car and bearing down on us. Chicko had no option but to swerve and swerve he did, like lightening, right into the 7 foot deep monsoon ditch which was at side of the road. Chicko and I finished up in the monsoon ditch with the trishaw on top of us. It was lucky that there was about two feet of water in the ditch so our landing was not as bad as it could have been. The race carried on whilst three or four spectators pulled the trishaw, Chicko and me out of the ditch. Geordie and his passenger were declared winners of the race. Chicko and I made our way back with the trishaw to the winning line. The owner of the trishaw and the prince agreed that the trishaw had suffered no damage, but that was not the case with Chicko and me. Chicko had was bleeding a bit and had suffered large grazes down his legs and arms. I had blood coming down the side of my face where my face had hit the side of the ditch when we fell. Both our clothes were saturated as there had been two feet of water in the ditch.

The prince immediately suggested that we both go back to camp, get cleaned up, put fresh clothes on and return back to his residence when were fit to do so. The prince sent for his driver and land rover and Chicko and I were taken back to camp where we visited the MRS had a little medical attention, got cleaned up and then went and put some fresh clothes on. We were back at the prince's residence within two hours. During our journey back I kept on thinking not only who would be at the party that night, but what other things the prince had organised! My fears were unfounded as it turned out. On arriving back at the prince's the prince told us that the party was to be stag, with lots of food, alcohol, jokes and laughter and that he had invited nobody else to the party except for Chicko and his guests.

We sat down nearer 8pm than 7pm and the food was superb and the alcohol flowed very freely. At around 10pm one of the maids brought into the lounge a large birthday cake which had a motor bike in icing on top. Chicko was asked by the prince to cut the cake which he did. Chicko then thanked the prince on behalf of us for his marvellous hospitality. The prince replied to Chicko, not once mentioning anything about the motor bike lessons of course. The prince finished his address by giving Chicko his birthday present which was superbly inscribed watch.

From 10pm until just after midnight during which much alcohol was consumed the butt of most of the jokes was about Chicko and me going into that 7 foot monsoon drain. Needless to say the prince thought it was hilarious. Back at Rasha Camp we spoke about the party for weeks on end and most of the guys reckoned that it has been a party of a lifetime!

22

17TH JUNE 1958 - MY 21ST BIRTHDAY

I woke up early on Tuesday 17 June 1958 and was in a very good mood for I had reached the age of 21 and was very much looking forward to my 21st birthday party which Chico and Johnnie Hart had arranged. There was to be about 18 or more of us to celebrate my 21st and Graham Purcell was also coming down that afternoon from Kuala Lumpur to join the party. Doc Holliday, his driver and escort were also due to attend as well and the only officer who been invited was Paul Summers.

During a quiet day at work Johnny told me that S/Sgt Harry Sexton had volunteered along with Cpl Joe Walters to be on duty that night at the MRS, and that Harry had also given his two drivers the evening off and had got a driver from the transport pool to stand in. It therefore appeared everybody from the MRS, Hygiene Unit and Dental Centre would be attending my party, plus the invited guests. Johnny explained the format for the evening and confirmed that he and Chico had booked the Mee Lee Bar from 6.30pm until 9pm for a private party and that a curry buffet would be served. The manager had told Chico that he would open the bar to the public at 9pm that evening. Around 9pm it was planned for our party to leave the Mee Lee and hit the Yam Yam just afterwards. A bit early I thought at the time because we never usually went to the Yam Yam until 10pm or later.

By 6pm I had showered and put on my best blue safari suit. I was looking in great anticipation to celebrating my 21st birthday in style and I appreciated that so many people would be there. Johnny had previously told me that one always remembered their 21st party, where they had it and who attended it. He got that right for sure, but I will always remember it for another very good reason as well. The fleet of taxis arrived outside the MRS just before 6pm and we were on our way!

At the Mee Lee we were greeted like royalty by the manager, who was always wary of Chicko anyway, and who went out of his way to always keep Chicko happy, or else his establishment could be put out of bounds to troops with a result of a severe drop in income. The drinks flowed quite quickly either side of a superb curry buffet Champagne, which I did not like, and still do not like, plus beers and Drambuie chasers. Many of the drinks were on the House and what we had to pay for were paid by Chicko and the lads. I was told that all my drinks were to be free and to keep my hands in my pocket. When drinking my mates always called me "hollow legs" as I had quite an excellent capacity for alcohol, nevertheless by the time we left for the Yam Yam at just after 9pm I was feeling a little tipsy.

On arriving at the Yam Yam we went to out 3 reserved tables. On my table sat Paul Summers, Graham Purcell,

Chico, Johnny Hart, Doc Holliday, Gil Meek and myself. Chicko produced several books of free dance tickets and distributed them amongst all the lads. I was given 4 books containing 20 tickets.

It must have been around 10pm when Paul whispered to me that he had heard the lads had a big surprise for me during the evening. I immediately thought that it was going to be a big birthday cake, because we had not seen any birthday cake at the Mee Lee bar. The surprise as I was to find out about ten minutes later was nothing like a delightful fruit cake. Fruit you might believe but certainly not cake! During the hour from 9pm to 10pm Chicko and Johnny had been dancing with every girl in seats numbered 1 to 10. I did not find out until the following morning that they had told every girl that it was the Virgin boy's 21st birthday.

Paul was standing drinking at the bar with Doc and as all the lads from our table were dancing that left only Gil Meek, my mentor and very good friend at the table. It was then that Gil told me what the surprise was going to be. He explained that all the lads knew that I was still a virgin and that they were all determined that I was going to lose my virginity that evening. I was to be given a choice, either go voluntary with one of the girls of my choosing, in which case they would follow her and me to her residence, wait outside for an hour or so until the dirty deed had been done. The alternative was that they would chose a girl and that I would be frog marched with her to her residence and that they would wait inside until I lost my virginity.

Whilst Gil was telling me all this I looked at the exit and was thinking about a great escape. Unfortunately at the nearest table to the exit sat Geordie Shaw and Andy Andrews, the two MRS drivers who were built like brick shithouses, plus the RAMC Corporals. No chance of any escape I knew!

Gil asked which option I preferred and I told him that if it had to be one then it would be the voluntary one. At the stage I thought that the lads had organised for Gil to be on his own with me as he was detailed to act as matchmaker. Gil asked me which girl I thought I should give the privilege of taking my virginity. I looked at the girls who sat in seats 1 to 10 and whom were dancing at the time. I told Gil that it was a tossup between Randy Rose No1, Tiny Tina No 2, or Sexy Sue No 4. Gil immediately told me No, No, No, you do not choose any girl in seats 1 to 10 as they were very popular with these girls and most likely slept with at least 20 different guys in a month. Gil explained that if I went with one of those popular girls that I could possibly pick up a "dose" or a very serious case of a social disease and who would want a nasty present like that on his 21st birthday.

I asked Gil to give me a suggestion and he suggested No 42 who was named "Winnie the Witch! I looked over at chair No 42, which was the last numbered chair in the cabaret and which was always occupied by the oldest and ugliest girl in the whole dancing hall. "The witch" was sat in her chair and not dancing and even from 50 feet away she looked 50 and she also looked bloody ugly. I told Gil no chance but he then explained that the "witch" seldom danced and that very few guys, if any went with her to bed. No chance of getting any nasty present from her he added. The more I drank and thought about this advice from my good friend Gil the more I thought his advice was perhaps sensible.

The lads came back to our table and Paul called me over to the bar to have a drink. I noticed that the lads had finished their dancing and had come back to our table and were in discussion with Gil. Paul obviously knew what was being planned and he told me that he had seen Gil in deep discussion with me. I told Paul what Gil had told me and what he had suggested and Paul strongly suggested that I should take Gil's advice and go with No 42. Paul added that whilst he could prescribe three "magic bullets" (meaning a penicillin jabs) for me over three days if I caught a minor dose from one of the popular girls but he that could not do anything for me if I contacted a much more serious disease. Doc Holiday, whom I always listened to told me No 42 for you tonight my Boy! So No 42 it was to be.

I was very nervous and frightened and went back to our table with Paul and the Doc to join my mates at our table. It was then Chicko told me that No 42 would be "good" for me, whilst Johnny added that he had slept with every girl who occupied chairs 1 to 10 and that they all performed well. On hearing this I was even more determined than ever that it was to be No 42 for me that night. Although I was quite, quite tipsy at this stage with the champagne, beers, Drambuies and whisky I had drunk I started drinking more beers with whisky chasers. During my drinking I kept on looking over at chair No 42, which was unoccupied most of the time as Winnie now always seemed to be dancing all the time with the lads from our party. Winnie seemed to be doing a lot of laughing and I guess that our lads were making a certain proposition to Winnie. Winnie most likely thought that it was her bloody birthday which had come round so quickly again and not my birthday.

The more I drank and the more I looked over at Winnie dancing, the less ugly she looked and she also looked younger and younger between my drinks as time passed. It was around 11.30pm and the lads told me that everything had been fixed up and that I was to leave the cabaret and meet Winnie who was now outside. I looked over to the exit and noticed that Geordie Shaw and Andy Andrews were missing. I went outside accompanied by Chico, Johnny and Graham. Outside was Winnie with Geordie and Andy and the Doc No last chance of any escape I knew.

Geordie organised an army horizontal "lineup" outside. In the first rank was Andy and Chicko. Immediately behind was Geordie, Winnie and myself, with Winnie in the middle. The last rank immediately behind was formed by the Doc and Graham. I thought at the time that this line up or escort reminded me of a condemned man being led to the gallows! Winnie's shack was only about five minutes from the cabaret and we arrived there at exactly 11.40pm. It is amazing that one can remember the exact time, when he is being led to his execution, despite of how drunk he is.

Winnie, accompanied by Geordie, the Doc took me inside her shack. I was told by Geordie to get undressed which I did by only taking my shoes, socks and safari suit off, and leaving only my vest and underpants on. The Doc and Geordie than left with the Doc informing me that Winnie would take care of everything from then onwards and that he and all the lads would be immediately outside until enemy action had started. I remember Winnie putting me down on my back on the low rattan type bed and taking my vest and underpants off. I fully remembered that the army always told us never to sleep on our back when we had drank a lot as quite a few deaths had resulted in solders being drowned through being sick in their sleep. I was not drunk enough to forget this I told Winnie who assured me that I would not be sleeping or would drown. I lay on the uncomfortable rattan bed and Winnie went to work and jumped on top of me. My weight at the time was around 13stone and as Winnie must have weighed about 15 stone at least I was pinned down and not able to move too much. Whilst Winnie was pumping up and down on me she looked at her watch and shouted it was not yet midnight. A reply came the Doc outside, who asked, in Malay, how everything was going. Winnie replied that everything was okay, that I was being a "good" boy and that she was fully in command. I understood quite a bit of Malay by my time in Malaya so I knew exactly what Winnie and the Doc were talking about.

At around 0.45am with a heavy, breathless, sweating Winnie still pumping up and down on me and me also sweating like a pig, Doc called out again and Winnie replied that all was going well and she was giving me a night to remember. Winnie was certainly right on that score because she did give me night to remember, but not for the right reasons! God I thought to myself how long before this is all over. Winnie had been going like a yoyo up and down for 50 minutes or so, groaning and moaning and I still did not know when she would be finished with me. The Doc called out "Selamat Malam "(Goodnight in Malay) and I presume he left with the lads after that. It must had been well past 01.30am when I experienced a sensational feeling that I had never experienced before and I guessed that at long last I had lost my virginity. I wondered at the time why the sex act took so long to complete with Winnie's and me taking a good 90 minutes. I was later much later in life that the more you drank then the longer it took. Winnie rolled off of me and I immediately turned onto my stomach and went to sleep.

I was shaken awake by Winnie at around 6.30am on the Wednesday morning and told to get up. I was bleary eyed of course and still not a hundred per cent sober, but I sobered up very quickly when I rolled onto my back and saw a grinning Winnie sitting in a chair near the rattan bed. I had never been so shocked in my life for she was as bald as a coot, and her wig was on, what could be described as some kind of coffee table. She looked nearer to the age of 65 than 50 and I thought at the time that my grandmother looked younger. She told me that Johnny had told her to make sure that she got me up at 6.30am so that I would not be late for duty at the Dental Centre at 8.30am. Winnie gleamed at me and said that I was no longer a virgin young boy. She then had the audacity to ask if I wanted a free "quickie" before I left. I quickly changed and went outside and caught a taxi back to the camp.

Back in my billet I had a long shower which took me four times as usual as I washed every part on my body over and over again. I changed into my uniform and went into our dining room for breakfast. Breakfast was something I would never forget either, for most of the lads were there having their breakfast and taking the piss out of me something shocking. I went into the dental centre at just before 8.30am and Johnny told me that after my escort had left Winnie's shack at 12.50am or so that a few of the lads had gone back to the Yam Yam for a hour to finished the night off. He told me that the girls had asked where I was and that they had been told that I had gone with No 42. They could not believe this, as they all knew that it was my 21st birthday and that a few of the girls in chairs numbered 1 to 10 were betting had been betting which one would take my virginity. Johnny told me that he and Chicko had paid the "Witch" $20 (about £2.50) to go with me. I told Johnny that the Winnie the bitch should have paid me $1000 to go with her!

Over the next ten days I inspected my wedding tackle very carefully and was relieved to find that I had not caught no minor disease. Of course the very serious disease did not show until 28 days had passed and I was an extremely happy boy when 28 days had come and gone and to find that I had not caught any unwelcome serious disease. During these 28 days I did not visit the Yam Yam as I knew I would expect much ribbing from the girls in the cabaret. When I finally did put in an appearance, some weeks later it was indeed not a nice experience and all the girls teased me something awful. The most hurtful was when Randy Rose (No 1) my good friend called me a dirty boy and "Calamity" Jane (No 3) called me "grandma's lover".

On my following appearances at the Yam Yam everything seemed was back to normal, and everything seemed to have been forgotten by the girls, who, after all were professionals and although I remained friends with a lot of the girls, had dances with them, and received numerous offers of "sleepovers", I never did bed, or was bedded by any other girl, from the Yam Yam apart from Winnie the Witch.

23

FIRST HALF OF JULY 1958

July 1958 looked like it was going to be a good month with what Paul and I had planned for ourselves but the month was also going to have some very big disappointments.

Paul and I had planned, just after my birthday in June to take a holiday in July touring the East coast of Malaya, which had the best beaches. We had sat down in Diana's house, during the last weekend in June, with Diana and the princess and planned our holiday in detail. By this time I had seen Diana and the princess quite a few times and we were getting friendly, although Paul suggested that it was perhaps getting more than just friendly. We all agreed on a two week touring holiday. It was at this meeting that the princess insisted we drop the 'princess' bit and call her Fatimah, as her real name was Wan Fatimah Binte Wan Ismail. That said and done Fatimah made the rules for the holiday in that Paul would drive her car throughout the tour and that four separate rooms (so there would be no hanky panky) would be booked in every hotel or Government rest house we stayed at. Fatimah being a dedicated muslim also asked Paul and me to refrain from eating any bacon or sausages for breakfast or any pork of any kind during our tour. This we agreed to of course.

Paul and I then had made our plans for our holiday. Paul said that we should put in for different dates for our leave, as if we put in for exact dates, then the CO, who had to approve our leave may suspect that were possibly going on leave together. I suggested that as I had eight weeks leave for the year, which included two weeks accumulated leave from the previous leave year that I put in for three weeks leave whilst Paul put in for two weeks leave. Paul agreed to this and suggested that I put in for leave covering the last three weeks in July, whilst he would ask for the second and third week in July. In fact Paul put his leave dates down as from 12th to 26th whilst I put in for 19 days which covered the period 14th to 31 July, knowing that I could get away on holiday on Saturday 12th as I would make sure that I was not the duty NCO on that day.

When we submitted our leave passes for the CO to sign in June Paul had put on his leave application as touring in Malaya. I had put my leave address on my leave application as Sandes Soldier's Home in Singapore. The CO, as eagled eyed as ever, despite his half-moon glasses asked me what the Sandes Soldier's Home was in Singapore. I told him that it was a convenient, cheap and homely place where soldiers stayed on leave and that the cost was just Singapore $4 (10 shillings) a day which included four meals. The CO complimented me on my research in finding such good accommodation at such a good price and told me to enjoy my leave. The CO duly signed the leave passes for Paul and myself.

During the first weekend in July Paul and I had lunch with the Doc, the prince, Diana and Fatimah in Diana's house. Diana had previously warned us to not mention anything about our intended touring holiday to anybody. It was at this lunch that the Doc told us that he would be going on long leave to the UK for three months the following week. The Doc explained that he got a month's local leave every year and that every three years he was entitled to a three month long leave in the UK and that as this entitlement had arrived to the long UK leave he was now taking it During the lunch I mentioned to the Doc that it seemed being a rubber plantation manager was an extremely good life and with all the pay and the perks and the Doc agreed that it was and that I should seriously think about becoming a rubber estate manager myself and that he would help me in any way he could if I decided I wanted to become a rubber estate manager. He explained that I would start off as an assistant manager, had to speak fluent Malay within three years of being employed and also take three exams over the three years which were easy. I spoke quite a bit of Malay and thought that I would not have any difficulty in being fluent within the three years. The prince, Fatimah and Diana said that they thought the Doc's idea was an excellent one and that I should seriously think about his suggestion. Paul said nothing! The prince also told us over the lunch that he would be also be travelling to the UK and the USA for ten weeks and would be leaving sometime in mid July. Little did I know it at the time that I was never to see the Doc again!

Saturday 12 July arrived and Paul and I took our cases down to Fatimah's in the morning. After a quick lunch Paul and I put all the cases in the boot of Fatimah's large car. Paul got behind the wheel and I sat next to him in the passenger's seat whilst Fatimah and Diana sat in the back and off we went. Our first stop was Kuala Lumpur. We arrived in Kuala Lumpur in the late afternoon.

We found what looked a reasonably decent hotel and Diana booked us all four rooms. After dinner Paul and Diana went into bar and over drinks and started to plan our tour. Paul told me afterwards that Diana had thought the Government Rest Houses were a better bet than the hotels as the Doc had once told her that they were more private than hotels, less rooms than hotels and very few people accommodated in them and that they had a wonderful reputation. There was less chance of all being seen together of course if we used Government Rest Houses rather than hotels.

Meanwhile, whilst Paul and Diana were in the bar planning everything, I was with Fatimah in the lounge. It was then that Fatimah told me that I should seriously think about becoming a rubber estate manager and getting out of the army. She asked if it was easy to leave the army in Malaya and get myself a good expat's job. I told her that the army had a system where a regular soldier could apply to GHQ FARELF in Singapore for a local release. First of all a soldier had to have a written offer of a good job, then he had to have his application approved by his CO. If the CO and GHQ FARELF approved the application, then the soldier would have to pay a certain amount to the army in order to leave and then he could leave within three months, once his replacement had been posted in. So easy I told her. Fatimah asked me if I had sufficient money to do that and I told her that I had. She told me that if I did not have the money then she would pay whatever it cost. It was during this discussion that Fatimah asked me if Paul had ever thought about getting a local release. I told Fatimah that he had never mentioned the subject but that I thought it very unlikely that Paul would ever think about staying in Malaya after he had finished his two years National Service. Fatimah told me that this was very disappointing, as she thought Diana was now in love with Paul! Paul and Diana soon returned to us in the lounge and told us that our first stop would be Kuantan which was about 175 miles from Kuala Lumpur and that the drive would take us four to five hours. Once there it was proposed that we try to book four rooms into the Government Rest House and make that our base for a few days.

After breakfast we set off on Sunday morning for Kuantan arriving there just before 4pm I guess. We eventually found the Government Rest House and Paul and I went in and booked four rooms with the Malay manager for three nights. We were not asked to sign any registrar and we did not pay for the rooms at that stage. He told us that his Chinese cook was an excellent cook and cooked to order and asked us what we would like for dinner. Paul suggested a selection of Malay dishes (curries and noodles etc). We were shown to our rooms and thought that they were just "average" and not too clean. Generally a bit disappointing really after what Diana had told Paul about Government Rest Houses.

After checking into our rooms we went down to the bar and got some coffees and sat on the verandah where we met Robert, an English expat. Robert asked us if staying at the Rest House and we were replied that we had booked in for the evening and that we had originally planned to use the place as a base for a few days. Robert then gave us a bit of a history regarding these Government Rest Houses. He said that these Government Rest Houses were in many places throughout Malaya and that they were all built of wood, had large verandahs and high ceilings with ceiling fans and had usually had between eight and ten rooms. Before Malaya got its independence they were always used by Europeans, rubber planters and tin miners and that they used to be a meeting place for these people he added. Robert continued by telling us that it was always a wonderful treat to stop at a Government Rest House where the food and accommodation was excellent. However, he concluded by stating that this was no longer the case as since Malaya had got its independence these Rest Houses had been taken over by Malays and that they had gone downhill very quickly, with the result that the European ex-pats, rubber planters and tin miners no longer used them. Robert added that he was not staying at the Rest House, but had only popped in for a drink, on his way to Kuantan port, as the bars and restaurants of these Rest Houses were open to the public. Robert suggested that we rethought our plans about staying more than one night and he recommended a good friendly hotel near about three miles away, should we decide not to stay more than one night.

The manager came out to use on the verandah and informed us that our dinner would be ready at 8pm. After a couple of drinks we went into the restaurant around 8pm. The dishes which Paul had previously ordered came along soon afterwards. The food looked okay and tasted just about okay. It must have been around 8.30 midway through our meal when Diana drew our attention to the wooden beams which were situated in the ceiling above us. I could not believe my eyes when I saw a large fat rat, walking across the beam. Suddenly the rat fell downwards right into Fatimah's noodles.

Fatimah moved like lightening, but not nearly as fast as the rat which scuttled off very quickly. Our dinner ended there and then. Needless to say Fatimah was so upset that she was all for booking out the Rest House there and then, but she said she would wait until Paul returned from seeing the manager. Paul soon came back with the manager who apologised. Fatimah told Paul that she wanted to book out immediately and we all agreed that this was the best thing to do. The embarrassed manager informed us that there would be no charge for the rooms or for our unfinished dinner.

We asked the manager for directions to the family hotel which Robert had suggested and the manager gave them to us. We all went off to our rooms to pack. I had only been in my room for a few minutes when Fatimah and Diana came screaming down the corridor telling Paul and me to come quickly. On hearing the screaming Paul and I immediately came out of our rooms which was next to each other and we were both taken by Fatimah and Diana into Fatimah's bathroom. Inside the bathroom were two large ugly frogs jumping around on the floor and croaking away. We left the frogs performing their acts whilst Fatimah packed her case. Once we had got Fatimah out of the room, the rest of us packed and we were on our way to the hotel within minutes. Needless to say the only subjects spoken during our ten minute journey down to the hotel, were dirty Rest Houses, rats and frogs. Not a very good start to our wonderful planned touring holiday I thought!

We found the hotel easily enough and booked into the hotel, for three nights under our correct names, giving our correct addresses in Seremban. Obviously Fatimah booked in under her name of Wan Fatimah Binte Wan Ismail. During our stay we found the rooms, service and food to be excellent. On Monday we spent the day exploring Kuantan. During that evening we met David, another British expat. Over drinks in the bar we told David about our experiences so far. After the laughter had died down David suggested that we avoid Government Rest Houses at all costs, and avoid them like the plague, giving us the same reasons as Robert had. As a much travelled expat who had been in Malaya for over ten years, David recommended that we tour the places and beaches south of Kuantan only for two days maximum and then head off up north on the coast road as far as Kota Bahru which was very near the Thai border, as the beaches north of Kuantan were the best beaches in Malaya, although quite a few of them were isolated.

David recommended only staying one day in Kota Bahru, the capital of Kelantan state for one day maximum, as the place was an extremely religious Muslim place and very little alcohol could be purchased. David ended by stating that we would have to return down the coast road from Kota Bahru to Kuantan after we had finished our touring up there, as the coast road was the only road between Kota Bahru to Kuantan. Paul, whom we had all agreed was the team leader agreed with everything that David had told us and so he suggested that we follow David's suggestions.

We spent Tuesday touring down coast road going south of Kuantan returning to our hotel in the early evening. Paul spoke to the manager of the hotel thanking him for his hospitality and informed him that we would be leaving the following morning on Wednesday 15 July to go touring and that we would like to book a room for one night on the evening of Friday 25 July on the conclusion of our tour. The manager confirmed the booking for Friday 25 July and then we all went off to dinner to be followed by a good night's sle

Before managing to get to sleep I was in deep thought. I thought that this was the first real holiday that I had had in my life. I was really enjoying myself for the very first time in my life being in Malaya, with more money in my pocket than I had ever before; of the tax free LOA that I was getting; of the free cigarettes and the exotic food and so on. Then I started to wonder how it would all end, when Paul got posted back to the UK with me following him after about nine months. Back to the boring, expensive UK I thought, unless I could get a job in Malaya or Singapore and a Local release.

24

SECOND HALF OF JULY 1958

Following breakfast on Wednesday 16 July we went downstairs to reception with our cases and booked out and paid our bill. Before leaving the reception the friendly manager came over to us and took us aside and told us that he had been thinking about our tour and that as he knew the East coast particularly well, he had come up with some suggestions and hotel recommendations in order to make our tour as pleasant as possible and he then produced a typed list of his suggestions. Paul looked at it and suggested that we have a farewell coffee with the manager whilst we went over his suggestions. We all made our way out to the verandah where he arranged for coffee, on the house, to be served.

The manager told us in detail about some of his suggestions and these were, that as petrol stations were far and between on the coast road and that we should always ensure that we stopped, if our petrol gauge was showing half full or under, and fill up whenever we saw a petrol station. He advised us that there so many exciting places to see and many marvellous beaches to visit and he suggested that we go north as far as Kuala Terengganu (KT), the capital of

Terengganu and end our journey there and not to consider going on to Kota Bharu, the capital of Kelantan as the city was extremely religious with very strict customs. On our journey up north on the beach road he suggested that we stop at three places and use these as our bases. We looked at the typed list of his recommendations again and the list read something like.

Travel from Kuantan to Cherating a distance of about 30 miles and stop for two nights on Wednesday 16 and Thursday 17th at the hotel he had recommended. Then travel on from Cherating to Dungun a distance of about 60 miles and stay for two nights on Friday 18th and Saturday 19th.

On Sunday 20th to travel from Dungun to KT, a distance of about 40 miles and spend five nights there at his recommended hotel. On Friday 25th to travel from KT back to his hotel a distance of about 120 to 130 miles.

Looking at the manager's recommendations Paul said that as it looked good that we would initially follow the recommendations and see how it all went. We all agreed. In fact as it turned out we followed the recommendations to the letter and had a marvellous touring holiday. No top travel agent could have given us a better recommendation. Later on Fatimah told us that she was glad that we were not going on as far as Kota

Bharu, as she knew all the royal family there who lived in three or four palaces.

The tour went without hitch apart from one day. We used the hotels as our bases and usually went sightseeing in the morning, stopping for lunch somewhere and then going off to one of the wonderful beaches and spending all afternoon on one of them. We would have dinner somewhere then a few drinks returning back to our base hotel at around 9pm. The hitch came when we left our hotel base at Kuala Terengganu on Tuesday the 22nd, went sightseeing then, had lunch at an open air restaurant and then was told about a lovely beach about ten miles away. We were told that by this beach that there was a small family run hotel which had excellent food and that also there was a beach bar with music, along the beach about a mile from the hotel. We eventually found this beach which was down a mile of rough track. Paul parked the car and we had a superb lunch around 2pm.

We spent about three hours on the beach returning back to the family hotel restaurant for dinner. We had a lovely dinner at around 6pm, had a few drinks and went out to the car at about 7pm for our drive back to our base hotel in Kuala Terangganu. Getting to the car Paul immediately noticed that we had two flat tyres on the driver's side. Obviously we had gone over some glass or other rough stuff when we had come down that rough track.

We had one spare tyre in the boot but not two of course. Paul went to see the manager of the small hotel to find out which was the nearest garage and he told Paul that the nearest garage was about ten miles away but was closed, as most garages would be and would not reopen until 8am the following morning. The manager then suggested to Paul that we all stay the night at the hotel and that he would take Paul in his car with the two punctured tyres to the garage the folowing morning. The Manager told Paul that he had two twin rooms free rooms free so Paul booked one room for Fatimah and Diana and the other room for himself and me.

Paul thanked the manager and then asked the manager about the beach bar along the beach. The manager told Paul that the beach bar which had music and which was popular with the locals and was indeed about a mile away down the beach, but that also we would have to climb over some rocks just before reaching the beach bar. We all agreed that a visit to the beach bar would be a good ending to the day. We went off down the beach at around 7.30pm, walked along the beach and climbed over the rocks and found the beach bar. At the beach bar there were about a dozen locals. We were welcomed by the bar staff with open arms and we all sat at the bar. The locals were very friendly, the atmosphere was great and the music was also great. The guy behind the bar kept the music flowing and he seemed to have all the latest songs. I well remember quite a few of the songs which were; 'All I have to do is dream' sung by the Everley Brothers; 'Who's sorry now' sung by Connie Francis; 'On the streets where you live' sung by Vic Damone and 'Diana' sung by Paul Anka. Needless to say Diana kept on requesting the barman to play 'Diana', but the most requested song by both Fatimah and Diana was 'All I have to do is Dream', which was easily the most played song whilst were at the bar. Both Paul and I bought a couple of rounds each for the locals and needless to say we were both very popular. Whilst Paul and I were on beers, Diana had a couple of gin and tonics and Fatimah tried her first gin and tonic. After a superb night with quite a bit of drinking and singing Diana suggested at just after 11pm that we make our way back to the hotel and we bade everybody farewell.

Leaving the beach bar we crawled back over the rocks in darkness and I slipped on one of the wet slippery rocks and fell into the sea.

I easily managed to get out of the three foot of water, despite the laughter of the others. We made our way back along the beach to the hotel. On getting into my room I put my soaking shorts and T shirt on the balcony rail in order to dry them and then to bed. I woke up in the morning had a shave and shower and then went to the balcony to get my shorts and shirt but there were no shorts or shirt. They had disappeared. Paul said that he could not believe that they were stolen for one minute and he suggested that it was more than likely that the strong wind which we had had during evening had more than likely blown them away.

I stayed in the room whilst Paul accompanied by one of the hotel staff went outside to look for them. They did not find my shorts and shirt. Paul returned back to the hotel room and gave me the bad news. Paul then reminded me that none of us apart from Fatimah had any spare clothes in the car but that Fatimah always had three of four sarongs in the boot of the car as she always liked to change her sarongs during the day wherever she was. Paul then suggested that I borrow one of Fatimah's sarongs, wear it and that we all go down to breakfast and discuss the car situation. Paul went off to see Fatimah and Diana and he soon returned with a beige sarong from the car. I put the sarong on around my waist but could not cover my airy chest. After Paul had stopped laughing we went down to breakfast on the verandah where we joined Fatimah and Diana who burst out laughing. Breakfast consisting of boiled eggs and toast was served by the Malay waitress who did a marvellous job in trying to keep a straight face. After breakfast the manager appeared and told us that he was ready to take Paul to the garage. We got the two tyres off of the car loaded them into the manager's car and the manager with Paul and Diana set off to that nearest garage. Obviously I could not go with them just wearing a sarong so I told Fatimah that I would wait in my room until they came back. Fatimah would not hear of it and she insisted that I sat on the verandah with her until they returned, which I did.

Paul and the others were away for nearly two hours and during this time Fatimah spent most of the time asking me about the future plans of both Paul and myself. It was during this time that I really noticed that Fatimah had really come out of her shell, which I put down to the two gin and tonics she had had the night before at the beach bar and she also kept on holding my hands whenever she could, when she was not drinking her coffee, and telling me how native and good I looked in her sarong. Paul and the others arrived back and Paul said that everything had been fixed and that we were ready to go. I offered to help put the two new tyres on the car but Paul said that it had all been done by himself and the manager and that on returning that he noticed Fatimah and myself laughing and in deep conversation on the verandah and had left us alone. I insisted on paying the manager for the rooms, food and drinks and we all thanked him for his help before departing back to our base hotel at Kuala Terengannu.

The remainder of our touring went as planned and we eventually returned to our hotel in Kuantan on Friday 25th before departing for Kuala Lumpur on the Saturday morning. We stayed one night in Kula Lumpur for the evening before departing for Seremban on Sunday morning the 27th. We dropped the car off in the late afternoon at Fatimah's and had a drink with her and Diana there. We all agreed that we had had a most memorable and superb holiday. Paul and I got our bags and made our way to a restaurant in Seremban where we had a snack and Paul suggested that he leave first for Rasha Camp and that I follow much later. I decided that rather go back to camp the same night as Paul that I would book into a hotel for the night and this is what I did. I spent most of Monday morning bringing my diary up to date. I returned to Rasah on the Monday afternoon.

It must have been around 5pm when I finally arrived back at my billet in Rasah Camp on Monday 28th. Johnny Hart was in the billet and he told me that he had two pieces of bad news. The worst bad news he told me was that Chicko had been sent home on Monday 14th on compassionate leave as his mother had been taken seriously ill and that as he had only two months service left to do in the army he would not be returning to Malaya. His replacement was a Cpl Salmon who had been posted in from Singapore the following day on Tuesday 15th.

Johnny then told me that this Cpl Salmon was a nasty, sneaky bastard who had been upsetting all the staff in the MRS, Hygiene Unit and Dental Centre, since his arrival. The bad news gets worse...... Johnny then went to tell me that Salmon had put the Mee Lee bar and another bar out of bounds to all British troops as he considered the standard of hygiene in those two bars did not meet his standard. Yet more bad news for you he told me. Johnny then told me that Salmon had been in my locker and had taken one of my safari suits out and had worn it over the weekend of the 19th and 20th. Johnny added that he told Salmon that it had no right to go into my locker, (which I never locked) and steal or borrow one of my safari suits. Salmon had then told Johnny that he did not think I would mind, and that as he had a special date with an English schoolteacher who worked in the army school in Seremban that he wanted to look his best. I decided not to do anything that evening even if I saw Salmon when he came into the billet later on. I was still a bit tired from our touring holiday and not only wanted sleep, but I also wanted plenty of time to think and to plan.

Salmon came onto the billet around 10pm just as I was getting ready for bed. His bed was two beds away from mine. He was about the same size as me, but was a lot uglier. He wore thick glasses and his hair was well greased with hair oil. I took an instant dislike to the bastard. He introduced himself to me and then he went off for a shower. I fell into my bed.

I got up on the Tuesday morning at around 10am. I went to for a SSSS before getting dressed and then I went into the dental centre to see if there was any mail for me. The CO and Paul were in the corridor talking when I went into the dental centre and the cagey CO immediately asked if I had enjoyed my holiday in Singapore and asked me the places I had visited. Of course knowing how cagey and devious the CO was I had already read up a lot about Singapore and the places of interest to visit and I rattled quite a few of them off without batting an eyelid. I made a mistake by mentioning that I had visited the Raffles Hotel and had one of their famous curries there along with a couple of pink gins. The CO said he thought that the Raffles Hotel was out of bounds to non-officers and I just replied that I had seen no signs to that effect and that possibly the staff had thought that I was either an officer or an expat.

Later Paul told me that he had his tongue in his cheek when I was rattling off all the places, but had slipped up when I mentioned the Raffles hotel.

I had lunch in our dining room and sat next to Johnny Hart. That slimy sod Salmon was sat opposite me as quiet as a church mouse. On getting up I told Salmon that I would be having a chat with him during sometime in order to clear up some of the bad smells that were around. I think that he knew what I was going to talk to him about and I guess the other lads at the table did as well. I walked over to see Gil Meek in his office. Gil asked me if I had enjoyed my holiday and I told him that I had. Gil asked me if I was up to babysitting for that night and I told him that I was. In that case come early he told me as there are things that I want to discuss with you.

Gil and his wife were going off to the cinema that night at 8pm to see a musical. If I remember right the film was "South Pacific". I arrived at Gil's married quarter nice and early at 6.30pm. Over a beer Gil started to tell me all about Cpl Salmon. He told me that after the sad departure of Chicko that Salmon had been posted in a day later to replace him and that Salmon had volunteered for the posting as he had a girlfriend in Singapore who was an English schoolteacher in one the army schools in Singapore, but that she had been transferred to Seremban and that he wanted to join her. It transpired that the Medical Services Brigadier at GHQ FARELF had been delighted to transfer Salmon from Singapore to Seremban, as nobody in their right mind wanted to be transferred from Singapore to anywhere in Malaya. Gil went on to add that Chicko had been an excellent NCO and was very hard to replace with any normal NCO let alone by a sneaky, miserable, devious bastard like Salmon. Gil added that in the short time that Salmon had been in the Hygiene Unit that he had upset everybody he had come into contact with. Did I know that Salmon had put two bars, including my favourite bar the Mee Lee bar out of bounds to all troops he asked? I replied that I had been already told this. The managers of both bars had been up to see him, Gil told me, asking if they could be put back in bounds as they were both losing a lot of business. Gil had told them that there nothing he could do about the matter.

I then told Gil about Salmon going into my locker and taking my safari suit out and wearing it to see his schoolteacher girlfriend over a weekend. Gil's eyes immediately bloomed and he asked me if I wanted to charge Salmon with stealing, or did I want to report the matter to him officially, so that he could charge him. Could be a Court Martial for the bastard, or a severe reprimand at the least, Gil added quickly. I looked at Gil and asked him if he would do me a favour and do nothing, but to leave the matter in my hands and that I would deal with Salmon. I reckon that Gil must have seen a glint in my devious eye and he agreed to leave the matter with me.

Following lunch on Wednesday I saw Salmon in the billet and I asked him to go outside with me. I grabbed the sweat stained and dirty safari suit out of my locker and joined Salmon outside. Joining him outside and I noticed that he was shaking quite a bit as he obviously knew that I knew he had taken and worn my safari suit and he thought that I was going to hit him. I was not stupid to hit the bastard and leave myself open to a charge and I had other things planned for him. I told him that I knew all about how he went into my locker and stole my safari suit and had worn it over the weekend in order to see his bloody girlfriend and that on returning the safari suit that he had not even bothered to have it washed and pressed before putting it back in my locker. I then told him that stealing was a criminal offence resulting in being charged in front of his CO and getting a severe reprimand or being referred for a Court Martial. I told him if this happened he would either be posted away from Seremban or finish up in the military prison in Changai Singapore or possibly be kicked out of the army on a dishonourable discharge. Of course I reminded Salmon that if this happened he would never see his schoolteacher friend again. Salmon went as white as a ghost.

The colour started to return to the bastard's face when I told him that I did not want anybody on a Court Martial, put in a military prison and dishonourably discharged from the army and that I was not going to do this to him. I then told him what I proposed was, that he would go down to the two bars that afternoon which he had previously put out of bounds and to put them back in bounds immediately.

I would give him the dirty safari suit, that he had put back into my locker, as a gift, as I was going to order three new safari suits, not one suit, but three suits, from the tailor, which he would pay for. On finishing my proposals I asked Salmon what he wanted, a Court Martial or to carry out my suggestions to the letter! As quick as a flash he replied that he would do everything I had proposed and he thanked me for being so considerate. I thrust the dirty safari suit into his hands and I ended our conversation by telling him to stay well away from me in the future and to get on his bike and immediately ride down to those two bars he had put out of bounds and to immediately put them back into bounds to the troops. Of course, I knew that although I had been more than generous with the sneaky Salmon that I was also a marked man by him and that he would try and retaliate in the future at some stage. That is of course if he lasted long enough at Rasha camp!

Gil came over to billet after he finished work at just after 5pm and he asked Johnniy Hart, George Wilkie and myself if we would like to go out for a drink with him later on that evening. We all replied yes of course. Gil then told us that he would meet us in the Mee Lee bar at 8pm that night. Johnny immediately replied that we could not meet there as it was out of bounds to all troops. It is back in bounds I am told by Cpl Salmon, he told us, and the Out of Bounds notice to all troops has been taken down. I kept a straight face and said nothing. We all met in the Mee Lee bar at around 8pm. The manager came over and spoke to Gil telling him that we were the first troops to use the Mee Lee since it had been placed back in bounds. Of course we were served many, many free drinks during the evening. At one stage George Wilkie asked Gil why Salmon had put the bars back into bounds so quickly. Gil was looked and winked at me when he said that he did not have the foggiest, but that Salmon had returned from Seremban that afternoon and had told Gil he had carried out another inspection on the bars and had had a rethink and put them, back into bounds. I said nothing at the time as all I was thinking about visiting the tailor the following day and was wondering what colours I would be choosing for my three new safari suits.

I visited the military tailor the following morning and ordered the three safari suits in beige, light blue and grey colors. Salmon accompanied me a few days later when I went to collect my suits, and Salmon paid for them. Although I had not mentioned, for obvious reasons, to anybody including Johnny Hart about my agreement with Salmon, I suspected that they knew and word had got around the camp, for it seemed over the following few weeks that I was being treated like a hero who had won the Military Medal.

25

FIRST PART OF AUGUST 1958

With the Doc and the prince away there was no more invites to the rubber plantation or to the prince's residences in Seremban and Malacca. When I went out on a couple of the weekday nights it was always with Johnny Hart and we did the usual things like visiting the Mee Lee bar or the Yam Yam Cabaret, our old haunts and the occasional visit to the cinema. Weekends I reserved for going out with Paul when we visited or saw Fatimah and Diana.

It was during the first of week that Fatimah started to telephone me at work in the dental centre, something she had never done before. I usually answered the telephone, being in charge of the office, but sometimes when I was not in the office it was Johnny or George who answered the telephone. Then one Friday evening around 4.30pm, when only Paul and I were in the dental centre, the other lads having left, the duty clerk from the Signal Centre telephoned and told me that there was signal (like a telegram) from GHQ FARELF for us and asked if I would collect it asp. Paul told me that he would stay in the office whilst I collected the signal. I collected the signal and returned to the dental centre about 20 minutes later. Paul was in the laboratory making a pot of tea. I gave Paul the signal and he read it. Paul said that it was just a routine signal regarding the arrangements for the 1st anniversary of Independence Day which was to be held on Sunday 31st August and that no action was necessary. Whilst Paul was reading the signal I finished making the tea and took it into the office. Paul then suggested I lock the dental centre up and that he wanted to speak to me over our tea.

Over tea Paul told me that Fatimah had telephoned me whilst I was away at the Signal Centre. Paul naturally had answered the telephone and was surprised that it was Fatimah telephoning me at the office. He had told Fatimah that I was not in the dental centre and had concluded the telephone conversation with Fatimah after about five minutes. Paul looked at me and smiled and told me 'Now My Boy" some serious talking we must have. Whenever Paul said 'Now My Boy' to me I knew it was going to be something quite serious.

Paul then proceeded to talk to me over the next twenty minutes or so. He did all the talking and I did all the listening and he told me that I should tell Fatimah not to telephone the dental centre as she could never be sure who was going to answer the telephone. He thought Fatimah was becoming too infatuated with me and getting too serious and he suggested that I should back off a bit. He told me that he had noticed she was always wanting to hold my hands during our holiday and he said the next thing she will be doing is asking you to marry her. How very true Paul's words were to become later on!

Paul then told me to forget about becoming a rubber estate manager or any other manager in Malaya and getting a local release from the army. If I did manage to get a job in Malay and get a local release I would more than likely be out on my backside within a couple of years. All these posts held by the Europeans in the government and in the Malaya industries would soon be localised and the jobs given to Malays Paul added. Paul's words were again true as all that was just beginning to happen.

Third point Paul told me. It was okay to go out with local Muslim girls in Malaya but you never let them get too serious with you. You should never marry one and take them back to the UK he added as Muslim girls were not really accepted in the UK and they would be completely out of place regarding their own customs in the UK. Go out with them whilst you are in Malaya, enjoy their company, bed them if you want but always make sure that you take necessary precautions, he added.

Fourth point. You are asking yourself about Diana and me he told me. Paul then said he knew that Diana was also trying to get very serious with him.

He knew that Diana was in love with him, but he also added that these very attractive Eurasian women fell in love with any decent acceptable European, with a view to marriage and a ticket to the UK. This was common knowledge. He said that he enjoyed the company of Diana, who was an extremely intelligent and an attractive young lady, and that he would hope to continue to see her whilst he was in Malaya, but that was no chance that their relationship was going to lead to any altar. If I sleep with her I will always make sure that I take all precautions, as the surest way to that altar is for an Eurasian girl to make sure that she got pregnant and that is certainly not going to happen between Diana and myself, Paul concluded.

Final point Paul told me. Let us both carry on seeing Diana and Fatimah, as we both have enjoyed some wonderful times with them and we both enjoy their company immensely, but let us handle the situation with kid gloves and not to get carried away. Let them know, gently, that we can have a very good friendship relationship only with them and that our relationships are never going to lead to anything beyond that stage. Most important of all was to make sure that we are very discrete and not seen out all together by the wrong people Paul added. Although I obviously did not know it at the time, those last few words of Paul's were going to prove fatal by the end of the next three weeks. Paul concluded by wishing me a good night and told me he would see Fatimah and myself at Diana's the following night at around 8pm.

It was on the 3rd weekend in the month when things started to go wrong. I had spent Sunday 17th at Fatimah's all day and got back to my billet around 10pm. I found a distressed Johnny Hart waiting up for me. I asked him what was wrong and he told me that the CO had caught him that afternoon in the office of the dental centre with 'Juicy Lucy' and 'Dirty Doris' smoking and drinking coffee and had blown his top and told him to get the biddies, who were wearing short skirts, immediately out of his dental centre and that he would see him on Monday morning. Johnny said he feared the worst. Johnny added that it could have been a lot bloody worse if the CO had arrived about an hour earlier when he had the two girls in the CO's surgery and was doing a scale and polish for them.

I suspected that Johnny was doing more than a scale and polish but he was not owning up to more than that. I also feared the worst for Johnny as well as it was known that the CO who was a middle aged 40 year plus bachelor was a woman hater and for him to find local women in his dental centre I could understand how berserk he had gone.

I asked Johnny why he had taken the girls into the dental centre if he was not sure the coast had been clear. Johnny told me that he had heard on the Friday that the CO was going down to Malacca on his boat for the weekend and that he obviously was not aware that the CO had changed his plans. I mentioned to Johnny that the CO always telephoned from the Officer's Mess to the duty NCO in the MRS and asked if the keys to the dental centre were available before he ever came down to the dental centre to do any developing of his films. I asked who the duty NCO was and Johnny told me that it was Cpl Salmon. I immediately got a really bad feeling. I then asked Johnny if anybody had seen him taking the girls into the surgery and he replied that Cpl Salmon had seen him from the MRS. I told Johnny that he was a bloody fool and that when Salmon had seen him that he should have immediately turned around and taken the girls straight out of camp. I reminded Johnny that Salmon was not only a talker and a snitch but was also a devious bastard. Johnny then told me that whenever the CO had telephoned the duty NCO at the MRS previously to ask about the keys, that that duty NCO had always either telephoned the dental centre office or popped over to the dental centre to make sure that nobody was in the dental centre. I agreed that that had always been the case before when all the good guys had been on duty at the MRS but that since Salmon the snitch had arrived a month ago, that was no longer the case. Johnny asked me what I thought would happen to him. At the worst I told him that I thought the CO would charge him, that I would have to type out the charge sheet on Army Form 252, then to march him in front of the CO, read out the charge sheet and then he would have to listen to what punishment the CO was going to award him. Johnny went to bed that night sweating like hell.

Monday morning arrived and the CO came into the dental centre earlier than usual. He did not speak to me but immediately told Johnny to follow him into his office. For the next ten minutes I could hear the CO loudly ranting and raving at Johnny. Johnny came out of the CO's office and told me that he was being posted the following morning, but he did not know where to. He told me the CO did not want to see him again in the dental centre and had told him to clear up all his affairs and settle his accounts in the camp and then pack ready for departure the following day. In the afternoon the CO called me into the office informed me that he was posting Cpl Hart to the Dental Department at BMH Kamunting in Taiping the following morning and that a Cpl Tyson from BMH Kamunting would be posted in to replace him on the Thursday morning. The CO asked me to do the necessary movement orders, issue a train travel warrant to Cpl Hart and to do the necessary Part 2 Orders on Wednesday.

Going back to my billet at just after 5pm I noticed that Johnny was waiting for me and I told him the bad news. I asked him what he had told the CO when he had asked him why he had the girls in the dental centre. Johnny told me that he had told him what I had suggested to him the night before, in that he had met the two girls who had been visiting one of their working relatives in the camp had seen that one of the girls was quite upset and looking quite ill and invited them back to the dental centre for a coffee and a rest. He told the CO that he was only being a good Samaritan. A decent story but whether the CO believed him or not was also a different story. I told Johnny that he had got off light and that if the CO had caught him doing any scaling and polish, or anything worse with the girls, then it would have been a Court Martial for sure. Johnny agreed that he had got off light, but told me that his biggest regret was that although we were the best of mates it was going to be a great pity that we were now being separated.

Johnny and I went down for dinner around 6pm. The dining room was full except for the notable absence of Cpl Salmon. All the lads knew by this time what had happened and that Johnny was being posted. All I could think about at this time was about Cpl Salmon and what kind of nasty things I could plan for the bastard. I was also thinking about my two best mates, Chicko and Johnny, whom I would not be seeing again.

26

FIRST ANNIVERSARY OF MERDEKA

I took Johnny down the railway station on Tuesday 19th for his rail journey up to Taiping and bade a sad farewell to him. I suspected that I would never see him again and as it happened I never did see him again, although I did speak to him a few times on the telephone. On Thursday I went down to the railway station again in order to collect Cpl Bob Tyson, Johnny's replacement who had been posted into us from Taiping and brought him back to our billet. Cpl Tyson was introduced to all the various staff in the Dental Centre, MRS and Hygiene Unit. I spent quite a bit of the rest of the day showing him around the camp, where things were, and introducing him to the personnel he would likely to come into to contact or who he would want to know later on. On Friday evening George Wilkie, the professor and I took Bob on a evening guided tour of the bars in Seremban ending up at the Yam Yam Cabaret. During the evening Bob was told everything about snitch Salmon and advised about his antics.

The weekend of the 23rd and 24th was a quiet weekend and Paul and I spent most of the time at Diana's and

Fatimah's. All over that weekend I kept on thinking about that serious chat that Paul had had with me about Asian women and marriage! Fatimah was still holding my hands whenever she could!

On Monday 25th we received a signal from the Garrison Adjutant which stated that there was to be a parade on Sunday 31st August to celebrate the 1st anniversary of Independence Day. The signal went on to state that every unit in Rasah Camp would be represented and that the dress for personnel taking part in the parade would best Olive Green (OG) shirt and shorts, stockings and puttees. The parade would be in a format of a March Past on the square in front of various VIPs including civilian Malayan VIPs from Seremban. The letter concluded that the MRS, Hygiene Unit and Dental Centre were to supply six personnel, which were to include one senior NCO and names were to be given to GSM Andrews by the end of that day.

The MRS and Hygiene Unit received the same signal. Sgt Gil Meek came into the dental centre later on that morning and spoke to the CO. The CO asked me to organise with Gil Meek. Gil told me that he and Cpl Salmon and himself, would be representing the Hygiene Department and that corporals Walters and Duncan would be representing the MRS and he asked me which two would be representing the Dental Centre. I asked around and both George Wilkie and Cpl Woodrow said that they would like to be on the parade, which suited me fine. Gil told our two lads that rehearsals for the parade had been scheduled for 8am on Thursday and Friday morning and that they had to report to the GSM there just before 8am and that the rehearsals would last for approximately one hour. Gil told us all that there would be quite a number of VIPs at the March Past on the Sunday.

I lay on my bed in the billet on that Monday evening thinking how glad I was that I was not going to be on the parade. For one thing I did not want to be marching up and down and sweating in the heat with Fatimah and Diana watching the parade. Another thing I knew was that the RA Garrison GSM was a bastard, whom I had heard was not only a stickler for boots being bulled to the point where you could see your face in them but that OG's had to be pressed immaculately with the lines in the right place.

The swine also hated the personnel from the MRS, Hygiene Unit and Dental Centre. The more I thought about the parade with that horrible, keen GSM taking the parade, some devious thoughts started coming into my head.

By Wednesday morning I had formed a plan, in my mind, which I thought was good plan, and of course the leading actor in the drama which I envisaged taking place was going to be Salmon the Sneak! The professor was a man whom I could trust and we had done each other quite a few favours since the incidents with the snake and the oxygen. Indeed not only had the professor been out with us to the rubber plantation, but we had gone out drinking together on many occasions and it was me who had convinced him to become a regular soldier. Most important though was the fact he hated Cpl Salmon as Salmon was always picking on him, the professor being only a L/Cpl and the only soldier in our three units under the rank of full corporal. That evening I took the professor out for a drink down in Seremban and told him of my plans and what I wanted him to do. When I concluded telling him about my plans the professor was in hysterics and at one stage I thought he might suffer a heart attack. The professor told me not to worry as he would go and see Vincent Wong, the Chinese guy whom he sold all his snakes to. Vincent had a large shop which sold a very large range of Chinese medicines, and herbs amongst other things and if he did not have the stuff we wanted, then he would certainly know where to get it the professor assured me.

In the camp were several dhobies (laundries). The dhobi which did all the laundry for the MRS, Hygiene Unit, Dental Centre and a couple of other small units and was run a guy named Ali. Ali was the chief dhobi wallah and in charge of the dhobi. Ali and I were firm friends as I always made sure that I gave him a constant supply of those tins containing 50 English cigarettes which he loved and I also supplied him with the odd bottle of Scotch whiskey which he also loved. It was therefore no surprise that I was Ali's favourite and that my OGs and safari suits were always pressed immaculately with just the right amount of starch used. Ali would have done anything for me and I knew it! The system for getting your laundry done was that all army kit was laundered free whilst you had to pay for any non army stuff you put in the laundry.

All dirty laundry was bundled up and collected from the top of our beds where we left it in our billets on Mondays, Wednesdays and Fridays and the clean laundry delivered back onto our beds in our billets two days later. That is except for my laundry as Ali always put my clean laundry, either on hangers in my lockers or on the shelves in my locker. That is always why I left my locker open and only used to lock the one drawer inside my locker which contained my valuables, (camera, money etc).

After breakfast the lads went off to the parade rehearsal on the Thursday morning at around 7.40am leaving the professor and myself alone in the billet the professor told me that he had got the two items I wanted from

Vincent Wong and he gave them to me. The first item he gave me was a bottle containing a colourless liquid which he told me was completely odourless. He told me that Vincent Wong had told him that this liquid was an extremely strong laxative which was capable of clearing a badly constipated elephant and to use the liquid sparingly and that two teaspoons in a cup was more than enough to clear anybody out. The professor then handed me a small package which contained some very finely ground power of some sort. The professor explained that this was an itching power which would suit my needs. I put the two items into my drawer in my locker and locked the drawer. The lads returned from the rehearsals and told us that the GSM had told them to get haircuts before the parade on Sunday and also that their boots were not up to standard.

During the lunch hour I got the packet of itching power out of my locker and I went down to see Ali at the dhobi, taking a couple of tins of fags and a bottle of whiskey with me. I knew that all the laundry which Ali's man had collected from our billet on the Wednesday would be washed and ironed and put back on out beds on Friday at the same time that Ali's man collected the next lot dirty which was to be laundered. I spoke to Ali and told him what I wanted him to do and I asked him what laundry Salmon had in the laundry. After checking Ali told me that Salmon's laundry included two OG shirts and two OG shorts, all which had been washed and were waiting for ironing and pressing. I then explained in full detail to Ali what I wanted him to do, which was to put the powder I was giving him inside the shirts and shorts before pressing and to over-starch all four items. Ali, who hated Salmon immensely as Salmon was always rollicking him and complaining about his laundry told me he would only be too delighted to do all this which I asked him to do and to leave everything to him. I left the laundry a very happy man.

Friday arrived and I was told that the parade rehearsals had gone off okay. After finishing work on Friday evening I went to my billet and noticed that all the dirty laundry bundles from the top of all the beds in the billet had been taken away and the new bundles of clean laundry put on the beds. I noticed a new bundle of laundry on the top of Salmon's bed and I hoped that Ali had done his job. Soon Salmon came into the billet, saw his laundry and put it into his locker before going off for dinner. After dinner Salmon came back and after showering, put on his civilian clothes and disappeared down to Seremban.

After lunch on Saturday the lads who were due to take part on the parade spent a bit of time bulling their boots and checking their kit for the following day's parade. Salmon who hated bulling boots asked the lads in the billet if anyone volunteer to bull his boots for $10. The professor told him that he would do them for $20 and this was agreed. Fatal I thought at the time! Salmon mentioned to the professor that he had no time to bull the boots as he had a date with his school teacher girlfriend and would not be back at the billet until late that evening.

During the evening, when all the other lads had gone down town there was only the professor and myself left in the billet. I had decided to give Fatimah a miss that evening as I had more important things to do. I knew that Salmon was a man of meticulous habits and I was hoping that he was going to stick to one of those that evening. He had previous let us all know that he went for a crap at exactly 8am every morning before shaving and showering. He told us that his system had got used to this and that he always had a regular crap daily at 8am. His second regular habit was always to have a drink of Ovaltine or Bournvita, made with hot milk, before getting into bed at night, no matter what time he went to bed as he said this always ensured that he had a good night's sleep. I was banking on him not to deviate from this practice tonight. At around 9pm I got the bottle containing the laxative liquid out of my locker.

I went to the small fridge in the corner of the billet to find the milk. I knew that Kristian our cook always made sure that we had a supply of milk, sugar, coffee and tea in our billet. In the fridge I found one full pint bottle of milk. I grabbed the bottle, went outside and tipped half of the milk away before returning to the billet. I knew that none of the other lads who returned to the billet from town would ever use any of that milk because none of them ever drank the stuff, or had a coffee or tea at night. I put two teaspoons of the laxative liquid, as directed by the professor into the bottle containing just half a pint of milk and then added another three teaspoons, telling the professor that they were for "the pot". The professor told me that five teaspoons was too much and that Salmon would be crapping through an eye of a needle the following morning. I shook the bottle and put it back into the fridge.

Salmon arrived back at the billet at around 11pm. He noticed that his boots had not been bulled by the professor and the professor handed him his $20 back informing that he had been taken quite ill that evening with diarrhea and that a bug or something similar must be going around. Salmon was not a happy bunny and said that he would spend time on the boots the following morning. I was still lying on bed my pretending to read when I noticed Salmon unlock his locker and take his cup, a tin of ovaltine and his element heating rod heater out of his locker. He went to the fridge, got the milk and filled his cup with the milk and ovaltine. He then plugged the electric element heating rod into the electric point and put it into the glass of milk. Once the cup of ovaltine had heated up he drank it. I went to bed thinking about the shit that was going to hit the fan, or the pan next morning!

Sunday 31st August 1958 and the first anniversary of Merdeka (Independence) had arrived .At 8am as regular as clockwork, on that morning Salmon, made his way to the toilet. Meanwhile, all the lads in the billet were having their SSSS's, and were changing before going down to breakfast. Salmon appeared at breakfast at just after 9am, which was quite late for him and he told us all that he had had a bout of very bad diarrhea and that he must have caught the bug which the professor had mentioned the evening before. Back in the billet all the lads were getting ready for the big parade.

We all put on our best OGs' as we had been ordered to, as best dress was the order of the day whether or not we were taking part on the parade, or attending as spectators. Salmon was trying to bull his boots up quickly but was not having much success. Just after 11.15am the lads who were due on the parade had started to file out of the billet to make their way to the parade square where assembly was due at 11.30am. The Garrison Brigadier with the GSM would then inspect the parade and afterwards at around noon the parade would do a March Past in front of the military and civilian VIPs who would be lined up on the podium and the spectators who would be seated or stood around the square at various points. The Garrison Commander would then take the salute.

At just before 11.15am whilst the lads were making their way to the parade ground, Salmon had another very bad touch of the "abdabs" (diarrhea) and had to rush off to the toilet again. At 11.30 am prompt I was seated next to the professor in the spectator's area watching the GSM bring the parade to attention. The GSM went forward, saluted and informed the Brigadier that the parade was ready for his inspection. I noticed that Salmon was not on parade! A few minutes later Salmon rushed onto the parade square and joined the medical services ranks who were at the back of the parade. I watched Salmon scratching away a lot at his body, whilst the Brigadier was inspecting the middle ranks. At least the itching power was working I told the professor. The Brigadier carried on walking around the ranks and stopping at certain times to speak to some of the soldiers. He eventually arrived at the last rank and I noticed that the GSM spent a minute or two speaking to Salmon. The March Past eventually took place and everything was finished by 12.10pm. The parade was handed back over to the GSM and immediately before he dismissed the parade and I noticed Salmon making a very quick dash off to the guardroom where I presumed the nearest toilet was situated. The rest of the parade and spectators all dispersed for lunch.

At lunch a very sheepish Salmon told us that the GSM had told him that he had been late on parade by 7 minutes, that his boots were in a disgusting state, that he had left the parade before being dismissed and that he was being charged and that he had to report to the GSM's office at 9am on Monday morning. I looked over at the professor who just winked at me.

That evening I went out with Paul and we celebrated the first anniversary of Merdeka at Fatimah's where she was hosting a small dinner party for a few friends. I told Fatimah that it had been a wonderful, wonderful day and she agreed. Of course she thought that I meant it had been wonderful to have celebrated the first anniversary of the Malayans obtaining their independence from the British. Nothing could have been further from the truth! I could not help thinking what nasty things the GSM had planned for Salmon the following morning.

27

SEPTEMBER 1958

On Monday morning on the 1st of September at around 9.15am I was looking out of the window in the office when I saw the GSM marching Cpl Salmon into Gil Meek's office. I wondered what Salmon was going to say when the GSM read the charges out and what punishment he was likely to get. I kept on gazing out of the window and it was about ten minutes later that I Salmon come out of Gil's office and disappear off into the distance. I kept on watching through the window and it was around 10.30am that the GSM came out of the office and make his way back to his own office.

I could not wait to hear the "good" news of what had happened to Salmon so I made my way over to Gil's office, had a cup of tea with Gil and then listened to what Gil told me. Gil told me that the GSM had taken Salmon into the office and told Gil that he was charging Salmon with several offences. Indeed the GSM had the Army Forms (AF 252's) in his hands and gave them to Gil. The charges included being late on parade, leaving the parade before being dismissed, dirty boots and continually fidgeting (scratching) on parade and not standing still. Salmon had been a disgrace the GSM told him. Gil then explained to the GSM that as the Commanding Officer (a Lieutenant Colonel) of the

Hygiene Unit was based in Kluang, and that he was responsible for all discipline in respect of all Hygiene Unit that Salmon would have to appear in front of his CO at Kluang. Gil went to tell the GSM that, possibly the CO at Kluang may want to GSM to appear as a witness as well as being the person who had charged Salmon.

Gil told me at this stage that the GSM and he got on very well together as he was the goalkeeper, in the camp hockey team, which the GSM captained. After more talking between them Gil suggested that he should telephone his CO in Kluang and find out if the CO would require the GSM to accompany Salmon down to Kluang for the charges to be dealt with. Gil explained to the GSM that his CO in Kluang was known as a very fair man, but was not known to be strict disciplinarian.

Gil then telephoned his CO and spoke at length before ending the telephone conversation. Gil then told the GSM that his CO had been sorry that Salmon had embarrassed the GSM and others on such an important parade and that Salmon had let his Corps down. However the CO had told Gil that the GSM's presence would indeed be required down at Kluang, but, the CO informed Gil, that there was an alternative solution that could be agreed if the GSM agreed.

Gil than explained to the GSM that the alternative solution suggested by the CO was that all charges be dropped and in return the CO would post Salmon out of Rasah Camp within the week. Gil then told me that he had more discussion with the GSM and had told him that Salmon had been a pain in the backside and upset so many people ever since he had been posted into his unit. Gil suggested that this was the ideal opportunity of getting rid of Salmon once and for all. The GSM having been given the choice of facing a long day's trip down to Kluang, with the prospect of Salmon only getting a minor reprimand from the lenient CO, or getting rid of Salmon out his camp permanently, agreed to drop all charges providing Salmon was posted. Gil then telephoned his CO again and informed him of the GMS's decision. Later on during the day Gil informed a smiling Salmon that having spoken to the GSM that the GSM had agreed that all charges against were being dropped. Salmon's face changed to one of dismay when Gil then informed him that he was being posted out of Rasah Camp within the week.

Gil informed Salmon the following day that he was to be posted to 16 Field Ambulance RAMC, at Wardieburn Camp, just outside Kuala Lumpur, the following Monday. Word about all this soon got amongst the rejoicing lads and we all agreed that Wardieburn Camp was one of the most primitive camps in Malaya and was not a camp where any of us would want to be posted. On hearing the news I do not know if the professor or I were the most pleased!

I did not play football on the Wednesday afternoon as there was no match that day so I went off on my own to Seremban and spent the day with Fatimah at her residence. It was during that afternoon that Fatimah first started telling how nice it would be to be married and what a super life married people enjoyed. The writing was on the wall I guess, but I did not think more of it at the time.

On Saturday 6th September Paul and I met up with Diana and Fatimah at Diana's place in the morning and spent the day with them. Fatimah suggested that we take a drive down to Malacca the following morning and Paul, knowing that our CO had left the dental centre at lunch on Friday in order to spend the weekend with a friend in Singapore agreed with the idea. We all got in Fatima's car on Sunday morning with Paul at the wheel and took off. Going through Seremban Paul had to stop at the red lights at some road works which were being done, which were opposite an open air restaurant. We were stuck at the red lights for a good two minutes when I looked over towards the restaurant and noticed that Ramasammy the snitch from the dental centre was sat at one of the tables and was waving to us. Obviously we had been seen, at long last. The lights changed to green and Paul drove off and I immediately told him that we had all been seen by Ramasammy the snitch. All Paul said was "Shit!" I then explained to both Fatimah and Diana who Ramasammy was and what he was.

Having spent a couple of hours on the beach with me mainly thinking about Ramasammy we made our way to one of the restaurants on the edge of the town which had been suggested by Diana who told us that the restaurant had a super reputation. We were just about finishing a superb lunch when into the restaurant walked our Padre, the Garrison Adjutant, and another couple of gentlemen. All four of the men acknowledged Paul. Paul explained that the two other men were army schoolteachers who lived in the Officer's Mess with him at Rasha Camp. I knew that all army school teachers had been given officers status and that the married ones lived in army officers quarters, whilst the single ones lived in the Officers Mess. We finished our meal, paid the bill and left the restaurant. Paul and I said nothing to each other at this stage. We spent the rest of the afternoon sightseeing and had dinner at another restaurant before returning to Seremban in the early evening. Paul and I dropped Diana and Fatimah off and Paul mentioned that we were both going to have an early night as we were both tired. Paul and I made our way to one of the quiet bars in the town where we settled down and had a couple of beers.

Paul the reminded me that we had been enjoying each other's company for well over a year and that we had both enjoyed the company of Diana and Fatimah for the past nine months, and had some wonderful times together and that we had never been seen once by anybody from the camp, until today and that we had been very lucky until today when we were seen by at least five people from the camp.

"We are for the high jump" Paul informed me that as sure as eggs were eggs, as one of them would be bound to say something and start spreading rumours. I asked Paul if that happened what could we do and he informed that there was nothing we could do but just to accept the consequences and there will be consequences he assured me. We finished our beers and it was two very worried men who made their way back to the camp.

I arrived at the dental centre on Monday the 8th, obviously a very worried man. Monday passed without incident. I arrived at the dental centre on Tuesday 9th still a worried man. The day passed without anything being said by the CO. Wednesday 10th arrived too quickly and I went to work at the dental centre. Nothing was mentioned by the CO until he called Paul into his office just before lunch. Paul came out of the office and told me that the CO wanted to see me in his office and I immediately suspected the worst. I stood to attention in front of the CO's desk and I listened to what he had to say. The CO told me that he had suspected that Paul and I had been socialising together for quite some time but that he had not had the necessary proof until recently. He reminded me that officers did not socialise with soldiers as familiarity only bred contempt and that under no circumstances did he expect to see either his officers or soldiers in the company of local floosies. I was given a right rollicking by the CO and at the end of it he told me that dental officers were easy to post, whilst chief clerks (being me) were much harder to post. This being the case the CO added, was that Captain Summers and I were not going to be allowed to serve together any longer and that he would be posted whilst I would remain under his command in Seremban. The CO concluded that I was to stop seeing the local floosies immediately and that if I did not then more serious action would be taken against me.

The CO and the dental officers went off to lunch at the Officer's Mess. I had a quick light lunch and got ready for the football match which was to be played on our ground in the camp. Just around 4.30pm at the end of the football match I saw Paul stood on the touch line at the far end of the pitch and I went over to see him. Paul asked me what the CO had said to me and I told him. Paul told me that the CO had basically said the same to him, given him a rollicking and had told him that he was being posted to the dental department at BMH Kluang on Monday 16th Sept.

Paul then told me that he had spoken to Diana that afternoon by telephone and that we were both expected at Diana's house that evening and that we should make our separate ways there. I apologised to Paul for the trouble that I had caused him, and that he was being posted as a result of me. Paul told me not to worry, as that he had enjoyed our company immensely and that we had had some most memorable times together that he would never forget. Paul concluded that it was perhaps a good thing that he was being posted because he thought it was the right time to break away from Diana, whom he knew was getting far too attached to him and far too possessive. Do not ever tell that to Diana though, he added.

We made our separate ways to Diana's house that evening,. Paul was already in the house with Diana and Fatimah by the time I had arrived. Paul had obviously told both the girls what had happened. The two girls were obviously both very upset. Paul asked me if the CO had asked me who the two "floosies" were and I told him that he had not. Paul replied that if the CO had known who the two girls really were and had still called them floosies that he himself would also have been in deep trouble. During the evening Paul carried on talking to Diana and was telling her in as gentle manner as he could that he thought that they would be seeing each other very little during his remaining time in Malaya. Meanwhile Fatimah was asking me what was going to happen between her and myself. I tried to assure that I would continue to see her often as we could but that we obviously had to be extremely careful. Paul was listening to all this when I told Fatimah and he kept very quiet.

It was my sad task on the morning of Friday 12th to prepare the movement order and rail travel warrant for Paul for the CO's signature. Both were handed to Paul. Paul had already told me that he would see me at Fatimah's house on the Saturday evening at around 8pm. A few farewell drinks with the two ladies Paul added. I arrived at Fatimah's around 8.15pm to find Paul in deep conversation with Diana and Fatimah. I noticed that Fatimah was drinking a gin and tonic which was the first time I had seen her drink since our touring holiday the month before.

Shortly afterwards Fatimah took me into the garden where we continued our conversation, leaving Paul with Diana in the lounge. Fatimah asked me for an assurance that although Paul would not obviously be around any longer and seeing Diana, that I would continue to carry on seeing her.

I told Fatimah that I always would want to see her, saying that we could work things out, but that under no circumstances was she ever to telephone me at the dental centre. Fatimah assured me that she would never telephone again and that in any emergency that she would give Sgt Ahmed a message to give to me. Much later in the evening Diana mentioned that she would like to go to the rail station the following day in order to see Paul off. Paul told her that that was completely out of the question and that I would be taking him down to the station by land rover. Fatimah agreed with me. Paul kissed a very tearful Diana a few minutes later and left the house. I left the house some 30 minutes later leaving two very tearful ladies in my wake.

I picked up Paul from the Officer's Mess the following day on 14th September, in the land rover and the driver took us down to the railway station. Whilst waiting for the train Paul told me that whilst had enjoyed his time in Seremban that he had no regrets about leaving Seremban and was looking forward to serving his last few remaining weeks at Kluang in Malaya before his service in the army finished and he went back to the UK. Paul then advised me to have a good hard think about my relationship with Fatimah, whom he said was getting too attached to me, and whom he thought had plans to plan marry me at some stage. Finishing in the army, trying to get a job in Malaya and marrying Fatimah, was bound to end in an unhappy ending or tragedy he concluded. The train arrived and Paul said goodbye to me with tears in his eyes. The trained moved off. I was never to see Paul again. I never ever found out which one of the five people who had seen Paul and I together with the two girls had snitched on us to the CO.

During the following week being quite depressed I did not have much to do with the lads and in turn they left me alone. I suspected that they all knew what had happened. I took the opportunity of visiting Fatimah on Tuesday, Wednesday, Friday and Saturday evenings ad spent the time with her in her house and not moving out of the house. I only saw Diana on the Saturday evening when she came around to Fatimah's. Diana asked me if I had been in contact with Paul since he had left and I replied in the negative.

During that week it was a quiet me who went to work. The CO did not mention the subject again and I carried on with my work as normal.

On Friday morning, 19th the CO called me into his office and told me that we had a slight emergency on our hands. He went on to tell me that Cpl Hart who was supposed go on temporary duty from the dental centre at BMH Kamunting, Taiping to the 3 RAR dental unit at Kuala Kangsar as a leave relief for a week on the 22nd had been hospitalised with a tropical fever and therefore he would be unable to go and that somebody else would have to be detailed to go. Cpl Hart had been detailed for this duty as Taiping was only about 15 miles from Kuala Kangsar. I told the CO that I would be willing to go and that I knew the 3 RAR as I had worked with them before on the dental presentation given by Captain Summers in June and that I had got on extremely well with them all. In fact I really wanted to get away from Seremban for a few days. The CO agreed and I could go and he instructed me to travel up to Kuala Kangsar on Sunday morning 21st. I made the long 200 mile long rail journey up to Kuala Kangsar and I was picked up and taken to the camp I reported for duty on the morning of Monday 22nd and was very pleased to meet Captain Jeffs, who was the Australian dentist that I had met on the dental presentation which Paul had given at BMH Kinrara in March. I enjoyed my week with 3 RAR and the things I remembered the most was that the Australian officers were more friendly than their British counterparts and that they treated you like humans, and indeed called you by your Christian name all the time, and not by just by your rank or surname which the British officers did. In addition the food served up by the Australians was far superior to that which the British army gave you, and that we also had Heinz tomato ketchup and Daddies brown sauce on the table.

Friday 26th came along and I was thinking how good it would be if I could stay with the 3 RAR for a few more weeks instead of going back to Seremban on Sunday, when I received a telephone call from my CO in Seremban informing me that my temporary duty was to be extended by a week. Goodie, Goodie I immediately thought, but I was soon to be very disappointed when the CO told me that the extension of my temporary duty was not to be at Kuala Kangsar, but with the Mobile Dental Team in Wardieburn Camp, Kuala Lumpur. The CO then informed me that one of the dental corporals had had an accident on his motor bicycle resulting in some injury and that he had been given seven days sick leave by the doctors. The CO continued by telling me that he had chosen me as I was already "on the road" and he instructed me to travel down on the train on Sunday 28th as originally planned but to get off at Kuala Lumpur where he had arranged for me to be met and taken to Wardieburn Camp.

I asked Captain Jeffs if I could use the telephone for a private call and he agreed. I then telephoned Fatimah and gave her the bad news telling her all being well that I should be back in Seremban sometime around the first week in October. I eventually arrived at Kuala Lumpur rail station and was picked up by Cpl Eric Martin RADC, a dental technician and taken to Wardieburn Camp and was ready to start another period of temporary duty the following morning.

28

WARDIEBURN CAMP, KUALA LUMPUR

Wardieburn Camp was based just about 20 miles outside Kuala Lumpur and I had heard that it was a very primitive camp, but I was shocked to find out how primitive it was until Eric Martin showed me around. I was billeted with Cpl Martin and after waking up around 7.30am on the morning of Monday 29 September, we put a towels round our waists and made our way to where the toilets and showers were. To describe the toilets as toilets was an insult. The so called toilets were in fact latrines and consisted of 12 thunder boxes situated on an incline in 12 cubicles, which had half stable doors of some type. The wash basins, showers and all the surrounds in the washroom were made of tin and not a single piece of porcelain was to be seen anywhere. The washroom roof was covered by corrugated iron. Eric then explained to me that there was no flushing toilets in the camp, only thunder boxes and that I would soon get used to them.

Eric then told me that the thunder box lids had to be closed at all times when not in use in order to stop the flies, mosquitoes and rats getting into them. Next to No

1 cubicle there was a tank situated in the floor which contained a pump and a fireman's hose. At 5am every morning the hose was put through a hole into thunder box cubicle 1 and water was jetted through the tiled or concrete floor of all the thunder boxes and came out of a hole into a cesspit which was situated just after cubicle 12. Immediately after the hose had flushed out the floor of the thunder boxes a bowser came along at 5.30am and disinfectants and other chemicals were sprayed along the floor of the thunder boxes. Having finished that the bowser collected all the nasty waste from the cesspit situated by cubicle No 12 and the whole process was finished by 6am each morning.

Better to come early every morning and bring your own newspaper, as often there was a shortage of flimsy so called toilet tissue he advised me. My mind immediately went back to the last time I had had to use a thunder box at my mother's house and I did not fancy using them again. I gave them a miss that morning and was dreading the time when I knew I would have to use them.

Eric took me back to the primitive washrooms, which were situated about 20 feet from the latrines, where I had my shave and shower, all in tepid water. Having finished our ablutions we went back to the billet, got changed at went down for breakfast at around 8.30am in the dining room of 16 Field Ambulance. After breakfast he gave me a tour of the rest of the camp and told me that there were various units in the camp and that we were accommodated and fed by 16 Field Ambulance. Another unit based inside the camp was a squadron of 22 SAS who had their own facilities like other units had. After the tour had finished Eric took me to the Mobile Dental Unit where I met L/Cpl Rex James, a dental clerk and Captain Stevens the dental officer in charge.

After dinner that evening Eric and Rex took me to the Corporal's Mess and it was whilst we were sitting in a corner that Cpl Salmon walked in, saw me and nodded at me before going off to the bar. I had completely forgotten that the bastard had been posted to 16 Field Ambulance. Obviously by the look on my face, Eric knew that I had recognised sneaky Salmon and he asked me if I knew him. I told him and Rex that I did indeed know the bastard and I gave them a potted history of the creep. Eric told me that Salmon was part of the Hygiene team that was part of 16 Field Ambulance and that he was a very unpopular man having upset many of the soldiers in the camp, including one SAS trooper whom he had tried to charge for some offence or other. Salmon hated the RADC personnel and was always running down our Corps Eric added. Rex said that I was bound to come in to contact with Salmon quite a bit during my short stay, as not only was he billeted next to the billet I was in, but that he also used the same dining room, latrines, wash room and Corporal's Mess that the RADC used.

Tuesday 30 September came and I made my way down to those awful latrines with a decent supply of newspaper.

Having finished my painful business I had my shave and shower, went back to the billet, got changed, had breakfast and started work at the Dental Mobile Unit. I got on very well with Captain Stevens and the other lads and I enjoyed working with them for the rest of my temporary duty there. Tuesday and Wednesday evening I spent with Eric and Rex at the Corporal's Mess, ignoring a sly grinning Salmon who always seemed to be sat just a couple of tables away. On the Wednesday evening Salmon could not resist the temptation to try and wind me up. I had gone to the bar to order some beers for Eric and Rex and Salmon followed me to the bar and asked me, with a smirk on his face how my girlfriend was doing in Seremban. I asked the bastard which girlfriend, as I had so many. I asked Salmon how he was getting on with his school teacher girlfriend in Seremban, but I got no answer from him. I got the beers and went back to the table and started to think what nasty present I could leave Salmon before I left for

Seremban on Sunday 5th October. On Thursday morning I had to go to the pay office with the other lads to collect my weekly pay and on getting back to the Mobile Dental Unit, Eric and Rex told me that as we had plenty of dosh in our pockets that they were taking me to the Galloway Services Club in Kuala Lumpur that evening.

On arriving at the Galloway Club that evening at around 7.30pm we found that it was quite packed which obviously was due to the fact that it was pay day. We had only just sat down at a table near the door and were on our first beers when lo and behold that bastard Salmon walked in with a Chinese girl on his arm. I immediately thought that either his school teacher friend had ditched him or he was being unfaithful! It must have been around 9pm when four very long haired guys walked into the club, past our table into the Club. Eric whispered to me that they were SAS guys. Rex told that these SAS guys were a law unto themselves and that they did what they wanted around Kuala Lumpur, especially when they had just come out of the Ulu (jungle) from three months operations. Even the Army Military Police (MPs), or RAF MPs were frightened to touch them he added.

Around 10pm one of these long haired SAS guys came over to our table and asked me if I came from Seremban and I told him that I did. He asked me if I recognised him and I told him that I did not.

He then told me that he was the guy who had brought the body of his SAS trooper into the MRS a year before and had handed the body over to me and that I had looked after it and had been responsible for taking the body up to BMH Kinrara. I admitted that indeed I was that guy. The SAS lad, who then introduced himself as Spike to all of us asked me to join him and his mates at their table. I left Eric and Rex at the table and told them that I would rejoin them later.

Spike took me over to his table where he introduced me to his three fearsome looking mates who were called, Dex, Ace and Hawk which obviously were all nicknames. I thought that Hawk had been aptly named as he was a beady eyed man. Spike told them that I was the guy who had taken care of their dead buddy a year before in Seremban and accompanied the body up to BMH Kinrara. From that moment on I was treated like a VIP. They asked what I was doing up in KL and I told them that I was working at the Mobile Dental Unit in Wardieburn camp with the two RADC lads Spike had just met at our table and that I was due back in Seremban by Monday 6 October. On hearing this Spike went over to Eric and Rex and asked them to join him and his SAS buddies at their table. For the next hour we all exchanged stories. Amongst the stories I mentioned was a bit about my time at Seremban and some of the incidents I had been involved in, mentioning my run ins with Salmon. On hearing this Rex immediately pointed out to the SAS lads, the table where Salmon was sitting with the Chinese girl, declaring that is the bastard over there and he was also the swine who tried to get one of your guys charged as well, he added. There was deathly hush! We all finished drinking until around 11pm before that SAS lads told us that they were going on to various bars. Spike told me that he would come and see me the following morning at the Mobile Dental Unit. Eric, Rex and I made our way back to Wardieburn Camp.

On Friday 3rd after breakfast I went to the Mobile Dental Unit and carried out my duties. Just noon Spike came to the unit and asked if Eric, Rex and I could skip lunch and come with him where he had laid some grub on for us and have a chat. We locked the unit up and followed Spike down into the SAS lines where he showed us into a room. I noticed that Dex, Hawk and Ace were seated at a large table where sandwiches and curry puffs had been laid out. We all sat down and food was handed around along with cups of coffee. Spike told us that after they had left us the previous evening and went round the bars that they had discussed various plans to teach slippery Salmon a lesson and that they had come up with four different plans which Hawk would describe in detail.

Hawk then described the four proposed plans. On Hawk's conclusion of the plans I remembered from Seremban that Salmon was always a man of meticulous habits and I asked Eric what time did Salmon go to the toilet. 8am on the dot, every single day and he always used thunder box No 12 Eric told me. I then suggested to the party that it should be plan No 4. Everybody agreed after I had explained why.

Hawk then described in detail what plan No 4 was and what we were all to do. At 7.30am all of us were to be outside the latrines. Four gallons of petrol would be poured down thunder box No 1. A three foot burning wick, soaked in petrol would be put into the hole going into the side thunder box 1 which was used for the water that was jetted through on the daily basis. Spike's men would ensure that all the thunder boxes of the latrine were closed and would that nobody would be using them from 7.50 onwards. When Salmon arrived he would give him a couple of minutes to open the thunder box lid and sit on thunder box 12 and then he would nod to me and I was immediately to light the wick and wait for the fun. Spike would be organising procedures on the morning and that we would all do as directed by him. Saturday would be the day, but if Salmon did not show for any reason, then we always had Sunday to carry out the plan, Hawk concluded. On finishing his plan Hawk asked if there were any questions. A nervous Rex asked Hawk if the plan would really work and Hawk said that they had done this plan before and that he had gone off with a bang. Hawk reminded Rex that the SAS were the best planners in the army and that their plans seldom went wrong. I asked Hawk if we could use eight gallons of petrol instead of just four gallons and he replied that this was no problem and he would make sure that 2 jerry cans each containing four gallons of petrol each would be on site. The meeting finished and we thanked SAS lads before going back to our work. Hawk's parting words to us was that he would see us at 7.30am on the dot, to make sure that we towels wrapped around our waists and that we were carrying soap, shaving soap and razors as normal.

Eric, Rex and I had a quiet evening in the Corporal's Mess that evening awaiting the following morning with great anticipation.

The following morning Eric, Rex and myself all made our way to the latrine and washrooms complex and arrived there dead on 7.30pm.

On arriving I noticed that there were half a dozen guys wearing army shorts all milling around the latrine area. Obviously these were Spike's men. By the water tank at the side of thunder box No1 a canvas screen had been placed around the tank and that a couple of guys were pretending to be working. Nearby was a land rover. Spike seemed to organising things and he came over to us and told us that everything was going to plan. At 7.45am I saw Hawk come out cubical 1 carrying two empty jerry cans which he put into the land rover. At approximately 7.50am one of the RAMC soldiers tried to use the latrines but was met by one of the guys who told him to come back later as the latrines were being repaired, or something along those lines. Spike told Eric to tell him when Salmon had appeared near the latrines and then to disappear quickly into the wash rooms with Rex, and to put some shaving soap of their faces and only come running out of the wash rooms when they heard a bang. He told me to wait behind the land rover until he called for me. Just a couple of minutes before 8am, Eric told Spike that he could see Salmon about 50 yards away coming towards the latrine. Spike told Eric and Eric to disappear to the washrooms.

At this time there were still around half a dozen of Spike's men milling around the place. Suddenly the canvas screen around the water tank was taken up and put into the land rover. I noticed the top of the wick which had been shoved into through the hole at the side of thunder box 1. Spike gave me a box of matches and told me to light the wick on Hawk's signal, to make sure that the wick was burning brightly, before moving off. He told me that I had plenty of time as the wick was three feet long. I was then to get into the wash rooms quickly dab some shaving soapy on my face or start having a shower and to wait for the bang until running out. I obviously could see Hawk from where I was standing. All the other guys in Spike's team seemed to be disappearing into thin air, except for Hawk and Ace. I saw Salmon enter cubicle 12, as I had been told he would. I waited anxiously for the signal from Hawk. A few minutes later he nodded to me. I stepped forward and lit the wick. It started burning. I made my way over towards the wash rooms and entered them. Not more than a couple of minutes later, even before I managed to get much shaving soap of my face, I heard a very large bang. Eric, Rex, myself, with shaving soap on our faces and carrying our razors, and a couple of other lads immediately ran out to the latrines where lots of smoke was rising.

The sight that greeted us is a sight I would never forget in my life. Most of latrine seats had been blown out of the cubicles and were lying on the floor. Smoke was rising from the latrines.

Salmon was hopping around like a Jack in the Box, outside the latrines holding his blackened, red raw and blistered backside. From a distance his backside looked a lot worse than I thought it would be.. The SAS lads were nowhere to be seen. The land rover had disappeared everybody started asking what had happened. Nobody knew, or if they did they were not letting on. Salmon was rushed to the medical centre. Eric, Rex and I made our way back to the wash rooms, had our shaves and showers and returned to the billet.

We all got changed and went for breakfast. One of the medics who came in for breakfast told us that Salmon had been bathed in a gallon of calamine lotion and that he would have an extremely sore backside for a week at least. The lads at breakfast started to discuss what had happened and the best idea that was put forward was that the coolies from the disinfectant bowser had put a new strong chemical down the latrines, and a guy sitting on the latrines had been smoking when he was using the latrines and then dropped the lighted cigarette end down the thunder box, which had caused the explosion or bang.

After breakfast Eric, Rex and I went to work at the Dental Mobile Unit. We all finished work at noon and Captain Stevens thanked me for doing the temporary duty with him. We locked up the unit and were making our way to the dining room when Spike appeared. He asked us all if we had been pleased with the morning's arrangements and we told him that we certainly had. Spike shook hands with us all and told us that if anybody like Salmon caused trouble with the SAS that they would always suffer the consequences. He then told us that the RADC guys were good guys and that were known to always look after the SAS lads and he then told Eric and Rex that if they ever wanted any help of any kind that they knew where to find him.

That evening we all went to the Galloway Services club in Kuala Lumpur and celebrated. Rex mentioned that there was bound to be some sort of inquiry about the morning's incident. I told them both that if we kept our mouths shut that we were all in the clear as we had been in the washrooms when the incident took place and we had sufficient witnesses who could confirm this.

In fact Eric did telephone me in Seremban the following Wednesday and told me that indeed an investigation had been undertaken by the RAMC RSM on the Monday morning and that he had concluded that somebody had dropped a cigarette down one of the thunder boxes onto the strong chemicals which had been swilling around in the channel beneath the thunder boxes.

I went down to breakfast on Sunday morning with the lads and when I noticed Salmon, unable to sit down, was standing up and trying to eat his breakfast, I could not help in giving him a 14 toothy smile! After breakfast I packed my things and said cheerio to Eric and Rex who told me that my short visit to Wardieburn Camp had been such an interesting one. I made my way back to Seremban.

I had no regrets what I had organised for Cpl Salmon. He was a born troublemaker and nasty bastard who delighted getting people into trouble. He had no friends. In fact with the number of friends he had he could easily have held a party in a public telephone box and there would still have been stacks of room for the band.

29

FUTURE PLANNING - OCTOBER 1958

Having finished my temporary duty with 3 RAR at Kuala Kansar and with the Mobile Dental Unit at Wardieburn camp in Kuala Lumpur I reported back for duty at the dental centre in Seremban on Monday 6 Oct, feeling nice and fresh and raring to go. The CO saw me during the morning and asked how my temporary duty had gone and I told him that it had gone very well and also had been quite exciting. He told me that Captain Jeffs of 3 RAR had telephoned him from Kuala Kangsar and thanked him for sending me up on temporary duty, and that he had been exceptionally pleased with my performance up there. George Wilkie, who had taken over my duties as chief clerk whilst I had been away, told me that there had been no problems during my two weeks absence.

I spent the evenings of Monday, Tues and Wednesday during that week visiting Fatimah at her house. We did not want to be seen in Seremban so we stayed in the house like caged mice. We both agreed that this could not continue. Diana popped in occasionally. On the Wednesday evening Fatimah mentioned the subject of marriage again and whether the CO would sign my application to get married. I assured her that the old shithouse of a CO would neither sign any marriage application or any local release application for me, even if I was offered a good job in Malaya and in any event he thought that all the local ladies were floosies and called them as such. Fatimah then went on to ask me if we did manage somehow to get married would we be entitled to some kind of married accommodation. I told her that army married quarters accommodation was excellent and that these quarters contained everything that a married couple needed and that indeed we would certainly be entitled to a married quarter if we got married.

On Thursday morning I got hold of George Wilkie and suggested that we went out for a drink to the Mee Lee bar that night as there was something important that I wanted to discuss with him. Over drinks I asked George if he would like to take over as chief clerk from me. Of course George asked how that was possible and I told him that if managed to get myself posted then he would have to take over as chief clerk because he, apart from me was the only regular RADC NCO in Malaya, Graham Purcell having left Malaya and returned to the UK in July. George told me that he would be delighted to be the chief clerk, but was not sure that he was capable of doing all the duties of a chief clerk. I told George that being the chief clerk of the dental service in Malaya was the same as being a chief clerk of a major unit and that he had already performed some on the minor duties of chief clerk during my two week absence when I was touring Malaya and also during my two week absence on temporary duty.

I went on to tell George that the main duties of the chief clerk were; publishing all Part 2 orders when required; maintaining all personal documents for the officers and soldiers and keeping them up to date; drafting all letters of a non-dental nature for the CO to sign; keeping all secret and confidential documents and maintaining their registers; A good knowledge of the contents of 20 or so manuals we had to keep, especially Queens Regulations, the manuals of Military Law parts 1 and 2, and Pay and Allowances and ensuring that all these manuals were always amended fully up to date; issuing travel warrants and movement orders; doing the travel claims (Army Form) 1771's for the CO and the officers; plus other clerical duties as required. George thought he could possibly become a chief clerk if he had some good tuition. I promised George that he would receive the best tuition possible, from me, of course. I did not tell George what my future plans were at this stage of course.

On Friday morning I typed an official letter to the CO ending with the usual 'shite' that I remained his obedient servant etc and put the letter on the CO's desk by 9am. I had deliberately chosen a Friday morning as I knew the CO was usually in his best mood on Fridays as he usually finished work at noon and then spent the weekend down on his boat sailing or fishing with the padre. It was at 11am when the CO was taking his usual coffee break when he called me into his office, pointed to my letter and asked me why I was requesting a posting. I had practiced my reply the evening before and was ready for this.

I told the CO that not only had I done two years as his chief clerk and that I would like to see a different part of Malaya during my final year and to meet different Malays and learn their culture. I also added that the two biddies or floosies he had warned me to stay away from me, or face severe consequences had not only tried to telephone me at the dental centre, but that I had been told, that during my two week temporary, that they had been visiting the camp trying to find me. I did not want to cause any trouble with the CO or at the dental centre as a result of the actions of these two women, I concluded. The CO reminded me that I was the chief clerk. I replied that Cpl Wilkie had performed the duties of chief clerk exceptionally well during my month's absence from the unit and the CO agreed that he had.

The CO spent a few minutes pondering. No doubt thinking that this would be the ideal opportunity to post me and thus save himself of any problems in the future of having to deal with me or my floosies and the fact was that it was me who was asking for a posting and not him forcing a posting for me. The CO asked me where I would like to be posted to if he agreed to my request. I reminded the CO that Cpl Rogers the dental clerk at the dental centre at Johre Bahru was due to finish his National Service in the very near future and was due to be posted back to the UK on 6 November and that his replacement was due in on 3 November.

This being the case, I suggested was that I be posted to Johore Bahru, in early November and that the replacement for Cpl Rogers be posted into us at Seremban. Cpl Wilkie would then take over from me as chief clerk once I had been posted. The CO told me that he would think the matter over and let me know at some stage.

At 12.30pm after the CO had just finished seeing his patient he called me into his office and asked me to have a seat. He told me he had thought the matter over and that he was going to grant me my request and that he was posting me to Johore Bahru with effect from Monday 3 November and that Cpl Wilkie would take over as the chief clerk. The replacement for Cpl Rogers would be posted to Seremban and he asked me to make all the necessary arrangements and do all the necessary paper work etc. He carried on by telling that I had been a good chief clerk and deserved a nice change of scenery and that I would enjoy Johore Bharu as it was just across the causeway from Singapore and that I would be able to enjoy many off duty days in Singapore.

The CO concluded by telling me to ensure that Cpl Wilkie was fully aware of what all the duties of a chief clerk entailed before I departed for Johore Bahru. I promised the CO that in addition to showing everything to Cpl Wilkie during the day that I would also give him a good two hours tuition every week day evening until I left for Johore Bahru. Good Man the CO told me before dismissing me. I wondered afterwards if the CO on reading my application for a posting had telephoned his good friend the padre and told him about my request for a posting and asked for his opinion before making his decision. If so I thought that there is possibly a God after all!

Once the CO had left I told George Wilkie the good news. George thought I was joking but when I told him it was all true he told me that I was not only a devious sod, but that I must have a very strong ulterior motive and had some future plans for doing it. George was right on both counts of course but I was not going to tell anybody at this stage what they were! We went to lunch and soon everybody knew that I was to be posted. Gil Meek was a little bit disappointed, but Gil said that he was also due to leave Seremban for the UK in December anyway. Gil added that all good things come to an end sometime and that we had both had a marvelous time together in Seremban.

That afternoon back in the dental centre I explained to George that over the next month that he was to watch exactly what I did. That he would read all the manuals, especially the four main ones and that that he would do all the many amendments to the manuals which were always coming in. Look and learn quickly I told him. From Monday to Friday during the evenings that I would be giving him two hours tuition every night from 6pm until 8pm without fail. I impressed on George that all this would be most beneficial to him as when he finally took his corporals course for substantive promotion to corporal that he had examinations on Military Law, Drill, and Pay and Allowances amongst other things. George told me that we were good friends and that he would not let me down. I told George that I knew he would not let me down and that I had every faith in him. Of course I was going to make damn sure that he learned very quickly, otherwise my posting could be cancelled and my future plans would be in tatters. I told George that the evening tuition would start on Monday 13 Oct.

That Friday evening I left George in the billet reading Queens Regulations and I made my way down to Fatimah's. Diana was in the house when I arrived and I told them the news that I was to be posted to Johore Bahru on 3 November. Both girls were shocked at the news of course, Fatimah more so than Diana. I winked at a very upset Fatimah, trying to let he know that there was nothing to worry about. Diana did not seem to be as upset as Fatimah, as this was possibly due to the fact that she had not seen Paul during the past month since he had left for Kluang. Possibly Diana knew that it was all over between her and Paul and that it looked likely that it was going to be all over between Fatimah and myself with the result that she would be able to spend more time with Fatimah again. If that was the case then I thought it was wishful thinking on Diana's part.

Diana soon left the house which left Fatima and myself together. Over the next 30 minutes or so I told a very patient listener what I had done, why I had done it and what I proposed doing. I reminded Fatimah that it was her who had reminded me that we could never go out of the house when we were meeting and that we were like caged mice. It was you I told her that was always mentioning how nice it would be to live together. It was you I reminded her that was always mentioning army married quarters and marriage. I reminded her how attached we had become and that up to now that we never got past the stage of kissing. Fatimah asked me what I proposed to do about it all. I told her that all being well and if George did what I told him and he became the chief clerk then I would be posted to Johore Bahru which was a very cushy posting. The officer in charge of the dental centre at Johore Bahru was Major Black, the officer whom I worked with on R & R leave in the Cameron Highlands and who was not only a top guy, but who was an officer I really liked and who I got on really well with. Once in Johore Bahru not only would be miles away from the CO and his watchful watch dogs, but that we would also be able to rent a house and live together. With Singapore just across from the causeway we could have a really good time I ended by telling her.

Fatimah told me that it all sounded very good and that she would have no problem about renting a house, but that an army married quarter would be a much better proposition! God I thought, Fatimah was determined to get me married to her, before allowing me anywhere near her bed. In any event there was no big decision to went at this stage yet I thought.

30

FAREWELL SEREMBAN

I went into the dental centre on the morning of 13th October to find that a bit of personal mail had come from UK over the weekend for me. There were two postcards from the Doc and the prince and two letters from the Doc and Dai Jones the Welsh guy that I had met at Doc's some months before. I knew that one of the letters was from Dai even before I opened it, as all the letters that I had received from him before I noticed that he always added an 'e' in my surname when writing on the envelope. As usual Dai's letters always asked me what I had been up to and what were the latest incidents that I had been in, or caused. He seldom wrote about what he himself had been doing. On reading the Doc's letter I was quite disappointed to read that he would not be returning to Malaya after he finished his three months long leave. The Doc had written, that during his leave that his father had died following a serious illness and that he was staying in the UK to carry on with his father's business. His letter went on to say that he had contacted his company in London of the circumstances and that they had agreed to release him from contract without any penalty and that Lou would be taking over as the rubber estate manager and that a local Malayan guy would be replacing Lou as the assistant manager. I immediately thought that this was a blow to some of my future plans, as the Doc had promised me that he would help me if I wanted to be a manager of a rubber estate, but there again having read that a local Malayan guy was taking over as the assistant manager I thought that perhaps Paul had been more than right when he had warned me some weeks before that it was only a matter of time before all the Europeans in the top jobs, were replaced by locals.

That evening I started giving George his two hourly tuition on every week day and it would continue until I left for Johore Bahru. By the end of the month George had done exceptionally well and leant much. He had been an excellent pupil, or perhaps I had been an excellent teacher. Either way he had learned a lot and I was to tell the CO as much before I departed for Johore Bahru. Meanwhile, during the following three weeks, after finishing the tuition with George I spent as much time with Fatimah at her house, as I could, plotting and planning. Every Thursday night on pay day, though, after 8pm I took George down to the Mee Lee bar for some well earned drinks. I had not visited the Yam Yam cabaret for some time, for obvious reasons, but I thought that one last visit before I departed for Johore Bahru would not go amiss.

Friday 31st October was a special day. In the morning I watched George make out my railway warrant and my movement order before he went to the CO to get them signed. In the evening Gil Meek had arranged a farewell party for me at his married quarter. I arrived at Gil's place at 7pm, as I had been requested to do so and I found that most of the army guys and were there from the MRS, Hygiene Unit and Dental Centre plus a few of the civilians workers from those units, http://www.bbc.co.uk/sport/cricket/41959648 plus my good friend Ali the dhobi wallah. Ramasammy was an absentee of course. Gil had laid on a food feast with plenty of alcohol of all kinds. As there were a good number of people at the party, quite a few of them overflowed into his large garden area. It was a party, with lots of singing and joking and good fun that I was to remember for the rest of my life. Just before 11pm Gil stopped called for silence at the party as he wanted to make a presentation.

Gil then made a speech telling how it had been a pleasure to have known me, and then said far too many good things about me (which often were far from the truth). He then presented me with a lovely wrist watch which he told me that all the lads had contributed to. How they had kept that secret I never knew. In reply I thanked Gil and his wife for putting on such a wonderful party from an undeserving me and concluded by saying the usual good things. Immediately after my reply Gil announced that the night had not ended as he had organised a surprise for me and that the surprise was a farewell trip for me to the Yam Yam cabaret and that there were two mini buses outside the house waiting to take us there.

Before going out to mini buses I bade a sad farewell to Mrs Meek and thanked her again before giving her a wet sloppy kiss.

We arrived at the Yam Yam just before 11.30pm. I immediately noticed that there were four reserved tables for our party. The manager came over and welcomed us and told me that I was expected to have a dance with all those girls that I knew really well and that I would not need to ask them to dance, but that they would come to my table and ask me to dance. All dances would be free for me, he added. I was sat next to the professor and he told me that Gil, George and he had come down to the Yam Yam a week before and told the manger that I would leaving Seremban for good and that they had asked him if he could arrange something suitable. The manager had informed them that not only would he do this, but that his girls would be informed that it was to be my last visit to the Yam Yam.

I must have danced with at least 20 different girls during the evening. All the very popular girls who sat in seats 1 to 10 asked me to dance and they also asked me if any scale and polishes were likely to be available to them in the future and I told all of them that George was the man to see. Winnie the Witch came over and asked me for a dance and dance we did. Just before finishing our dance she told me that I would never forget her and of course she was right on that bloody score! I was exhausted by the time I returned to the camp at gone past 2am.

On Saturday morning 1st November I had lunch with Gil and George both who told me that they would take me to the rail station the following day. During that afternoon I spent the time packing all my kit and personal possessions. I told George that if ever he wanted to any help, then all he had to do was just pick up the telephone and give me a ring at Johore Bahru.

I had a good chat with George that afternoon and I told him about some of the good times that I had had at Seremban.

I put him in the picture about the girls from the Yam Yam wanting to continue with their scaling and polishing and George told me not to worry on that score. I also gave George a list of very useful contacts. I mentioned to George that over the past few months that I had lost all my best friends, like, Chicko, Johnny Hart, and the Doc and that also Paul was due to leave Kluang for the

UK in early Nov, on the completion of his National Service, and that it had been the time for me to move on and leave Seremban.

What I did not tell George or mention to anybody was that it was as early as August that I had started planning my move to Johore Bahru. In August two significant things happened. The first one was that we received a posting notice from our Records Office at Winchester informing us that Cpl Rogers was to be posted to the UK in November on the completion of his service in Malaya and that a Cpl Evans was being posted in to replace him. The second thing is that I had typed a letter for the CO to Colonel Green the DDDS at FARELF Singapore in which the CO had requested leave from 15 December 1958 to 18 January 1959, stating that he wished to visit his brother in Australia. The CO's application for leave had come back approved. I knew that the CO, who was due to finish his thee year tour in Malaya in June 1959, had wanted to visit his brother in Australia before he finished his tour in Malaya, because he had mentioned the matter to me on a couple of occasions and indeed had asked me if the period over Christmas and the New Year was likely to be a quiet period. I had assured the CO that it was not.

When the CO had approved my posting to Johore Bahru just three weeks before, possibly he had forgotten that during his absence, was that Major Black at Johore Bahru would become acting CO of the Dental Services in Malaya. Major Black who was a regular officer was the only RADC major serving in Malaya. The remainder of the dental officers were only captains, and the majority of them were National Service guys anyway. Perhaps the CO had also forgotten that I had knew Major Black from the time I had spent my so called R & R working with him in the Cameron Highlands. A lot of things could happen when Major Black was the acting CO I thought.

31

MAJIDEE BARRACKS, JOHORE BAHRU

In the early evening of Saturday 1 November I visited Fatimah at her residence. She had cooked me my usual favourite prawn curry and after the meal was over we spoke at great length. I told her that Gil had organised a farewell party for me and that all my friends had been there. I omitted to tell her of course that we had finished off at the Yam Yam cabaret though. I outlined to her about what I intended doing when I had got established in Johore Bahru, mainly looking for a decent house that we could rent. She told me that an army married quarter would be a far better solution. That confirmed my fears that she had more intentions than just settling for anything less than an army married quarter. I asked her where Diana was and she told me that Diana had gone to Singapore for the weekend to see her mother and father who lived there.

Fatimah asked me if it was true that my religion was listed as a Muslim on my personal army records. I told her it was and that both Paul and I had told her that before, but I added that I was not a Muslim and had only had Muslim listed on my documents in order to avoid all church parades in Northern Ireland. Did I have a Muslim name she enquired and I told her that I did not, but had been called Mohammad by the RSM in Northern Ireland, when he used to take the mickey out of me. She continued her interrogation asking if I was in any way religious and I told her that I was agnostic and did not believe in any religion. Was I circumcised she asked. Yes I was I told her.

The interrogation ended and she then told me that she was going to give me a proper Muslim name. She then told me that the Muslim name she was giving me was Wan Nordin Bin Abdullah. She explained that all men were known as Bin and that all women were known as Binte. I knew this of course. I told her that I did not like the name Abdulla and she told me that all "non-believers" who changed their religions to become Muslims had to be called Abdulla.

I quickly told her that I did not want to be a Muslim and that I certainly had no intentions of becoming a Muslim of any kind! She told me that from that day onwards her pet name for me would be "Nordin". I should have realised from that moment by the interrogation that Fatimah was far smarter than I was, and that she was also a better bloody planner than I was! I left Fatimah's at just before midnight telling her she was not to come to the railway station the following day under any circumstances, and that I would be in constant touch with her from Johore Bahru.

Gil, George and the professor took me to the railway station on Sunday 2 November and saw me off. Arriving in Johore Bahru I was met by Cpl Kevin Rogers who took me to Majidee Barracks and got me accommodated in his billet. He introduced me to Cpl Dave Roberts RADC who was the dental technician and who was billeted in the same billet.

The following morning after I had finished my SSSS, had put on my best OG's and finished breakfast Kevin took me along to the dental centre which was situated on the second and top floor of the MRS. I was introduced to Juliana the civilian dental surgery assistant and then to Major Black when he arrived at just before 9am. Major Black took me into his office and told me that he had been looking forward to my being posted into his dental centre and he reminded me of the time we had spent together in the Cameron Highlands. If you ever want anything do not be afraid to ask me he added. Obviously he had never forgotten the episode when I got him those 6 bullets and saved him from serious trouble. I was to ask him for a couple of important things later on and he did not let me down.

The rest of the morning Kevin showed me all around Majidee Barracks and introduced me to the Gurkha RSM and the British Warrant Officer 2 (WO2) in the pay office. Kevin went on to explain that there were over 1000 Gurkha officers and soldiers in the barracks and that there were under 50 British officers and soldiers in the barracks. The British officers and soldiers were treated like kings by all the Gurkhas Kevin told me. Kevin then took me back to the MRS and introduced me to S/Sgt Shillinglaw who was the NCO in charge of the MRS and a few of his staff. Back at the dental centre Kevin went into detail about the MRS set up and S/Sgt Shillinglaw. The MRS had two British RAMC captain doctors, two RAMC corporals, plus eight female and male local civilian nurses, which included three female Gurkha nurses. The MRS was a completely independent unit inside the barracks, with its own Officer in Charge and that the unit did not come under the Gurkha Brigade in the barracks

As you know the dental centre also has its own Officer in Charge which is Major Black, of course and it also has its own CO in Seremban and that we were also a completely independent unit within Majidee Barracks, Kevin added. This I knew of course. The problem is though, Kevin went on to tell me, was that S/Sgt Shillinglaw liked to visit the dental centre office every day, demanding tea or coffee and thinking that he ran both the MRS and dental centre. He is not only an interfering bastard but a pain in the arse, Kevin concluded. I immediately thought how many days it would take me to put a stop to Shillinglaw's antics! After lunch Kevin did a quick handover to me. He also confirmed that Major Black was the best officer that he had ever worked with and that he always took Dave Roberts and himself out for dinner and for drinks down in Johore Bahru at least once a month. After dinner Kevin, Dave and I went onto the Corporal's Mess for drinks. Over drinks for the next few hours both Kevin and Dave told me many things about the barracks and some of the personnel in it, and what to do and what not to do. Dave told me that he played football on

Wednesday afternoons for the Gurkha team, which was quite good team and that if I was decent footballer then he would try and get me a game. That was a bonus I thought, as I was more than a decent footballer. I asked Kevin to tell me more about Shillinglaw and Kevin told me that he was a married man who lived with his wife and two kids in a married quarter just outside the barracks and that he was known to a bit of a ladies' man and that he also quite frequently visited the MRS during the evenings in order to see how his night duty staff, mainly his female nurses, were getting on. Kevin also explained that Major Black was a single officer that he lived in the Officers Mess where he was treated like God himself. I also knew that Major Black had dual qualifications, that of a dentist and also that of a solicitor, but I did mention this to Kevin or Dave.

Tuesday I had taken over the office as Kevin had done his handover to me and he had told me that he would be away all the day doing his farewells and settling all his bills etc. Just before lunch I got a telephone call from Paul at Kluang. Paul told me that he was due to depart from Malaya and would be flying to the UK from Singapore on Wednesday 5th Nov and that he had tried to contact me several times during the past few weeks.

I told Paul that I had been on temporary duty for a month and had been running around all over the place when I had returned to Seremban. Paul asked me if I had seen Fatimah much and I told him that I had, but I left out quite a bit of what we had been talking about. Paul told me he had spent the weekend with Diana in Singapore in order to say a last farewell and that Diana had told him that Fatimah had told her she had planned to marry me. News to me I thought and so much for Fatimah telling me that Diana was going to Singapore in order to see her mother and father! Paul was on the telephone to me for a good hour and I thought that it was just as well that I was not telephoning him when I would have to justify the bill when the Signals office asked for a justification of such a long call. Paul mentioned at wonderful times that we had had together and that he would never forget them.

Paul told me that if I was thinking of doing anything serious with Fatimah to seriously think about it before I leapt, because he thought that Fatimah would never leave Malaya in any event. He wished me the best of luck with Fatimah, whatever I chose to do. I told Paul that I would go down to Changai on Wednesday in order to see him off. Paul said this was not a good idea, as he hated sad farewells, and that the one he had just had with Diana was more than enough. We had said our farewells at the rail station in Seremban when Paul had left for Kluang, so I agreed with him. I was never to see Paul or to speak to him again.

32

FIRST FEW WEEKS IN MAJIDEE BARRACKS

On my first day at the dental centre on Tuesday 4 November I was alone in the office when S/Sgt Shillinglaw came marching into the office. As Kevin had warned me previously, just as soon as Shillinglaw had entered the office he ordered me to get the tea on. I complied. Over tea he told me that he expected me as a junior NCO to stand up when he, being a senior NCO entered my office. I informed the swine that I did not come under him for any discipline of any kind. We had words and he told me not to be insubordinate. I did not want to go to Major Black in order to sort the problem out, though I could easily have done so. I knew that I was more than capable of sorting Shillinglaw out on my own but I wondered how long it would take me.

That evening Major Black took Kevin, Dave and myself to Amy's bar in Johore Bahru for drinks, mainly to say thank you and goodbye of Kevin who was leaving for the UK the following morning.

Wednesday, Thursday and Friday passed very quickly and without any incidents. My clerical duties were so easy and like a piece of cake, especially after my chief clerk duties at Seremban. Shillinglaw visited the dental centre on all three days at roughly the same time 11am.

In addition to his demand for tea, he always went over to the large army metal radio set, which was on top of the metal filing cabinet, and switched stations. I liked certain music and Shillinglaw liked other programmes.

Over the weekend I started to do some serious planning. I got hold of Dave our dental technician and asked him what he knew about electricity. Quite a lot he told me. I then asked him if would fix the army radio up so that Shillinglaw got some kind of shock if he ever touched it again.

Dave started to explain about bare wires of something along those lines, which all went over my head as I knew nothing about electricity. Dave told me to leave everything to him.

Monday morning of my second week came and Dave played around with the radio. He went behind the metal filing cabinet grabbed some wires and played around for some minutes. He switched the radio on at the mains but told me not to touch it. Around 11am Shillinglaw toddled into my office as usual. He was always sneaking or toddling around and I had never ever seen him move faster than a two legged dog since I had met the bastard and I thought to myself that he was going to move a lot faster if he touched that radio. Shillinglaw immediately demanded tea as usual. He then went over to the radio and tried to switch channels. I waited patiently to see if Dave had done his job. Shillinghlaw then put his hand on the switch which changed the channels and the result was electrifying as he came hurtling backwards at around 60 miles a hour missing me by inches. I do not know who had the biggest shock, whether it was Shillinglaw or me. He hit the floor very hard. He eventually picked himself up and was swearing like a trooper. He screamed to me to get that bloody radio earthed properly and he left my office faster than he had come in. I went over to the radio and switched it off at the mains. I knew that Dave would fix everything back to normal by lunch time.

On Tuesday morning the swine came into the centre again at around 11am and demanded tea. I noticed that he did not go anywhere near the radio which was playing. I thought he had learned his lesson not to touch the radio, but he was still visiting the dental centre. More drastic planning was needed I thought. I went back to my billet that night and remembered that I still had more than half a bottle of that colourless, odourless, tasteless very strong laxative which the professor had given me in Seremban. I had never thrown it away, but kept it knowing that at sometime in the future that I may want to use it again.

I woke up on the Wednesday morning full of the joys of spring. Firstly it was our normal recreational afternoon when the dental centre was closed in the afternoon and we played our various sports or had the afternoon off. Secondly I was due to play football for the Gurkhas who represented the barracks for the first time, Dave having got me a trial with them as they were playing a team from Singapore in a friendly match. Thirdly, but most important was that I had planned to put another one of my plans into action. As usual Shillinglaw came into the office at around demanding his tea. He did not go anywhere near the radio set but just down in a chair near my desk whilst I went into the dental laboratory to make his cup of char.

Shillinglaw was very fussy about his tea in that it always had to be served to him in his large China mug and that he liked four spoons of sugar in the cup. I went into the dental laboratory, and waited for the kettle to boil. I put the boiling water into the tea pot with the tea and waited for it to brew. I poured myself a cup of tea. I then got the bottle of the laxative out of my pocket. I remembered that the professor had told me that two teaspoons of the stuff was more sufficient to clear a constipated elephant. I reckoned that the bottle must have contained about eight or nine teaspoons. I put the lot into the tea pot and swilled it around. In for a penny in for a pound I thought. I poured the tea into Shillinglaw's large mug and took it to him. Over the five minutes or so I listened to Shillinglaw telling me all about his army service in WW2, and all the usual bullshit. Did I ever tell you about when I was in Korea and the gooks surrounded our Field Dressing Station he asked me. In order to keep him in the centre so that I could give him some more tea, I said, No please tell me more. Is there any more tea left in the pot he asked me. I assured there was another refill left in the pot and I got his cup and virtually ran back to the dental laboratory to get it. I brought the refilled cup back to him and listened to more bullshit about his army career.

The football match went better than I could have dreamed of. The team consisted of 9 Gurkhas and only Dave and myself being British in the team. We won the match 7-0and I managed to score six of the goals. After a game like that Dave told me that in addition to be a regular in the team that I could expect quite a few invites from the Gurkhas to visit their dining room in order to taste their very famous Gurkha curries.

I went to work on the Thursday morning wondering if the laxative I had given Shillinglaw had worked. Shillinglaw did not appear at 11am for his tea. The morning went well. I went down for lunch in the MRS dining room at 12.30 with Dave. During our lunch Dave and I were asked by one of the RAMC MRS Corporals had we heard the news about S/Sgt Shillinglaw. We told him that we had heard nothing. The RAMC corporal then told us that Shillinglaw had been taken ill with very severe runs of the trots (diaherra) and it was so bad that he had hospitalized and was on a drip in the MRS. The doctor expected him be bedded down for about three days the RAMC corporal added. I consoled myself in thinking that Shillinglaw would not mind a few days being bedded down in his MRS whilst those female nurses he was always chasing were looking after him. Nobody knew that I had been responsible for Shillinglaw's hospitalization as I had not said anything to Dave or anybody else.

I often thought afterwards that I should have found out what that really strong laxative was, as when I returned to the UK I could have marketed it and made myself a fortune, as it certainly was ten times stronger and better than Exlax.

Over the weekend of 15th and 16 November Fatimah had come with Diana to Singapore and were staying at Diana's father's house. Naturally I saw them both in Singapore on the two days, after booking myself into a small hotel in Singapore on the Saturday evening. Fatimah reminded me that we had not seen each for two whole weeks. Diana spent a bit of time joking with me and asking me when Fatimah and I were going to get married. Obviously Diana must had a good time with Paul in Singapore a couple of weeks ago and also, perhaps, thought that if should get me hitched, then perhaps, just perhaps, Paul in the UK, could be persuaded to change his mind and send for Diana and eventually marry her.

I skipped into the dental centre a happy man on Monday 17th. This happy man became dismayed when a much slimmer Shillinglaw came into the office at 11am demanding his tea. God, I thought the swine has never suspected anything or learnt his lesson. I was at a quandary what to do next to stop his troubling visits to the dental centre.
The remaining week passed without any further excitement apart from Shillinglaw making his daily visits

to the dental centre for his tea. On the Saturday evening Major Black took Dave and myself down to Johore Bahru and dinner and a visit to Amy's bar. Sunday was a quiet day. Monday and Tuesday were quiet apart having to put up with Shillinglaw's visits to the dental centre.

I went to work on Wednesday 26 Nov in a good mood as I was looking forward to playing my second game of football for the Gurkhas that afternoon. The morning was quite unusual in that we had no patients on the sick parade that morning so it was nice and quiet and it also meant that Major Black had nothing to do until he saw his first patient at 9.30am. I asked Major Black if I could have a private word with him and he invited me into his office and asked me to be seated.

I asked him if I could have the Saturday off and if he granted me my request that Dave would look after the office and the sick parade on Saturday. I told Major Black the reason that I wanted the Saturday off was because I wanted to go up to Seremban to see Fatimah. I explained that Fatimah was a princess whom I had become seriously involved with. I went to great lengths to tell him about the CO who had called her a floosie and had threatened me with serious consequences if I saw her again and that he had made things very difficult between Fatimah and myself. I was very open in my discussion with Major Black. Major Black authorised me to take the Saturday off and he also reminded me that he had told me that if I wanted any help, or indeed any advice that I was only to ask him.

I played football in the afternoon against a very strong team. We drew 2-2 with me netting both our goals. After dinner that evening I went back to the dental centre in order to type some letters to my mother, the Doc and Dai Jones. It must have been around 9.30pm when I had finished typing all my letters. I switched the office lights out and went out onto the balcony and sat in one of the chairs for a quiet cigarette in the dark. I always did my best thinking in the dark when nobody was around. I was in deep thought about what I really was going to do about Fatima. Was I going to get married if I did would I be able to get a local release in Malaya and get a good job. If not, would she accompany me to the UK after my tour had finished in Malaya, I asked myself.

Suddenly I heard voices below the balcony and I peeped over the balcony and I saw Shillinglaw and a Gurkha female nurse who was in her uniform in deep conversation. I carried on watching them and saw them make their way to one of ambulances which was parked nearby. I immediately edged back towards the back of the balcony, but where I could still watch them. I watched Shillinglaw look around before opening the ambulance doors before pushing the nurse into the ambulance and following her inside the ambulance. He closed the doors. I closed the balcony doors and locked the dental centre up and went downstairs. I thought that I would give Shillinglaw a good five minutes before I made my next move.

I went over to the ambulance and opened the doors to find Shillinglaw naked, except for his shirt and socks, on top of the nurse who was underneath him, laying on a stretcher. The nurse's dress was up above head and Shillinglaw and the nurse were going at it like the clappers.

Immediately on my opening the ambulance doors Shillinglaw had turned his head around and asked who was there. I replied that it was me and that as I had heard noises in the ambulance when passing, that I had opened the doors as I suspected somebody was in the ambulance who could have been stealing something. I then closed the doors as fast as I could and made my way back to my billet. I did not hang around to see if Shillinglaw stayed in the ambulance finishing his business or not. I went to bed that evening a very happy man.

The following morning I made my way to the dental centre 30 minutes earlier than I usually did opening up the place at around 7.45am. I suspected that it would not be long before Shillinglaw appeared, and he did a few minutes later. He did not demand tea this time but sat down and said that he wanted a chat. I got up and locked the dental centre door so that we could talk in private. I am all ears I told the sod. Shillinglaw then went on to tell me what he had done the evening before was a one off and that all men did that kind of thing sometime in their lives. He rambled on about how men were men and that as he and I were in small units inside a large camp containing so many Gurkhas that we should all get on well together and enjoy life, and all that bullshit. In fact I believe that the time has now come when you should address me as Vince and not Staff he told me.

I had anticipated that Shillinglaw would talk along these lines to me, and I had my reply ready for him. I told Shillinglaw, in no uncertain terms that what he had done was disgusting and that those kind of things were not done by all men, especially married men. I reminded Shillinglaw that he was a married man with two kids. I then went into great details about how every Gurkha carried a Kukri, which was a very sharp curved knife which was a combination of an axe and a machete which was excellent for both chopping wood and hacking through dense jungles. I had heard that a Gurkha had no hesitation in chopping a man's wedding tackle off, and rendering him an eunuch , if ever he caught a guy with their Gurkha ladies. What if your wife found out what you had been up? to, I asked Shillinglaw. I took the golden opportunity of giving him a real dressing down and perhaps it was one of the few instances in the British army when a mere corporal did give a staff sergeant a real rollicking. I put the fear of God up Shillinglaw. At the end of my talk and lecture to Shillinglaw, he asked me if I intended to report the matter.
Remembering how the times that Paul and others could have reported Johnny Hart and myself in Seremban, I told a deathly white Shillinglaw that I intended to do

nothing at all and that I would could keep my mouth shut. Shillinglaw could not believe his good luck. I went on to tell Shillinglaw, how he had mentioned that we should all be friends in our small units, look after each other and be on a Christian name basis and I added that that would start immediately. I also advised him that his daily visits to the dental centre and his demand for tea was to cease immediately. Shillinglaw, of course agreed to all my demands.

On the conclusion of our talk I asked Vince if he would like a cup of tea and he replied that he would. I went off into the dental laboratory and made my new found friend Vince a good cup of laxative free tea. Over tea I explained to Vince that I hated all snitches, and that I was guy who wanted only to have a good time in Johore Bahru and to be happy at both work and pleasure. I reminded Vince that what he did was not my business, but that he should be more careful in future. We finished out tea and I reopened the dental centre and Vince left before any of the other staff arrived.

During the rest of my stay in Johore Bahru Vince never once came into the dental centre demanding tea. I did sometimes invite him to have tea with me when I saw him near the dental centre and he always accepted my invitation. Vince and I were always on a Christian basis after the ambulance incident and he left me alone and I left him alone. A kind of truce I guess! As Vince was the NCO in charge of the MRS and in charge of patient's comforts, he frequently did bring me a good supply of tins of cigarettes, telling me that his stock was far too high and that he had to get rid of some of the stock. Those tins of cigarettes were gratefully received and I either smoked the cigarettes or gave many away.

33

MARRIAGE ON THE HORIZON

I went back up to Seremban over the weekend of 29/30th November. I had planned on staying in a hotel on the Saturday evening, but Fatimah insisted that I stayed well away from Seremban itself and that I would sleep in the third bedroom in her house. She hastily added that Diana would also be staying the night (although she only lived in the same street), and would be sleeping in the second bedroom. No hanky panky then I thought, until she got me married.

Fatimah and Diana, the matchmaker, spent the whole night talking to me about marriage. Diana told me that Fatimah and I could marry in a civil ceremony in Singapore providing that either Fatimah or I resided there for at least 15 days before the date of the marriage. Diana added that it was quite permissible for a non-Muslim to marry a Muslim in Singapore, whereas it was not possible to do so in Malaya. Diana said that the residency issue would be no problem as Fatimah could stay with her mother and father in Singapore. Fatimah said that she was not too keen on getting married in Singapore. Fatimah then told me that she preferred for us to betold me because we were both Muslims and that the ceremony would be allowed to take place in her house. I immediately pointed out that I was not a Muslim, but Fatimah quickly replied that according to my army personal records that I was a Muslim and that she had named me Wan Nordin Bin Abdulla. I told her that the army would not accept any marriage certificate which had the name of Wan Nordin Bin Abdulla on it, instead of my proper name. Fatimah told me that she had already spoken to an Imam who was a good friend of hers and he had stated that my real name would be on the marriage certificate, with Wan Nordin Bin Abdulla in brackets. It appeared though that Diana and Fatmimah had been doing a lot of talking and planning themselves during the week, and that Fatimah had also been talking quite a bit to her friend the Imam.

A breakfast of rice and garupa fish the following morning and I thought this was something that I would have to get used to if I did marry Fatimah. Shortly after breakfast Fatimah's friend the Imam arrived at the house. Over Chinese tea the Imam told me that he would be very pleased to marry us at Fatimah's house if I met all the necessary conditions. He asked me various questions like, was I a Muslim, if so what was my name, did I eat pork, was I circumcised. I did not have the chance to reply to any of his questions as Fatimah was like a parrot and answered all the questions. How Fatimah knew I had been circumcised I do not know because she had never seen it. Fatimah told the Imam she would like us to get married in full Malaya dress. I immediately replied that I would not wear any Malay dress and if I was to be married then I would wear a safari suit. The Imam told us that this would be acceptable. The Imam then went on to explain that if the marriage was to take place, that during the ceremony he would quote some verses from the Quron about my duties and that I would reply.

All the time the Imam was talking I kept on thinking about shotgun weddings. Perhaps I did want to marry Fatimah but although we had both mentioned marriage, she more than me, I had never really said that I wanted to get married. I knew that the wedding had been planned when the Imam finally left telling me that he was looking forward to seeing Fatimah and me again in the very near future. Why not I ended up thinking, as Fatimah was a really attractive lady!

The Imam left the house and Fatimah asked me if we were going to get married or not. It looked like I was facing a firing squad with my back against the wall. Finally I told her okay, if that is what she wanted. Good she told me then proceeded to give me a typed piece of paper showing me the words that the Imam would speak at the ceremony with my replies in capital letters. We spent the next couple of hours reading and reading the piece of paper with me having to speak Malay when I had to reply. When Fatimah was satisfied that I had got all the pronunciation right she called a halt. She handed me the piece of paper and told me to read it regularly and to learn it all by heart.

Fatimah told me to give her a date that we were to be married and added that it should be on a Friday. I told Fatimah that before we could get married that I had to get my CO's approval and she informed me that this should not be a problem for me when Major Black was the acting CO. I left the house shortly after lunch to make my way back to Johore Bahru.

On my journey back to Johore Bahru I did a lot of thinking about Paul had warned me about and how deep I had dug myself into a hole. On the other hand I thought how nice it would be to be a happily married man to a lovely girl and living in a nice army married quarter away from the barracks. One thing for sure was that Fatimah and Diana were better planners than I was, and I thought I was good!

The first days of December passed without any incidents. It was a quiet period at work and there was very little to do, quite boring in fact after Seremban. George Wilkie telephoned me regularly from Seremban giving me all the latest news and told me that he was getting on okay. He also mentioned that the CO had told him that he would be going on long leave to Australia on 15 December and that Major Black would be the acting CO during his absence. Of course I knew all this when I had started my planning a good couple of months before. I saw very little of Vince Shillinglaw. The CO telephoned Major Black in the afternoon of 12 December to remind him that he would be going on long leave for a month and that he would be the acting CO and would have to deal with any emergencies. The CO also informed Major Black that Captain Wilson the dental officer in Seremban would deal with all routine matters.

On that second Friday of the month Major Black took Dave and myself out for dinner down to Johore Bahru and we finished off at Amy's bar for drinks. It was over drinks that I mentioned how serious my relationship with Fatimah had become and that perhaps it could end in marriage if I got the necessary approval. I had no qualms about mentioning anything about this in front of Dave, as I knew that if I did eventually marry Fatimah, that he would be the first to know as I would have moved out of the billet into army married quarters. Major Black asked me why I had to get necessary approval before I could get married and I told him that a CO's approval was required in accordance with FARELF Standing Orders. Of course, I took this opportunity to point out that I was unlikely to get the necessary approval from my current CO, who was a woman hater and a confirmed bachelor, and left it at that. It was towards the end of the evening that I mentioned Fatimah and Diana would be coming down to Singapore for the weekend and that I was due to see the both of them. Major Black then told me that he would be in Singapore on the Sunday and that he would like to meet Diana and especially Fatimah for lunch if possible.
Major Black said that he would be lunching in the Raffles Hotel at approximately 1pm with a lady friend and he

suggested that Diana, Fatimah and I join them there if possible. Of course, I told him and a firm date was set.

On the Saturday afternoon I travelled down to Singapore and saw Diana and Fatimah and told them that Major Black had invited us all to join him and his female companion for lunch the following day. They both agreed that it was an excellent idea and that they were looking forward to seeing the major. I returned to my barracks in Johore Bahru that evening thinking of the excellent opportunity that had just come my way. On the Sunday morning I travelled down to Singapore in a safari suit and met Fatimah and Diana just after 11am at a nice cafe. Both girls were dolled up to the hilt and looked stunning. Over a few coffees I told the girls that we were expected to meet Major Black and his companion in the Long Bar at Raffles prior to the lunch at 1pm. I had mentioned to both Fatimah and Diana on a few occasions that Major Black was an excellent officer, was friendly and indeed was the officer whom I had worked with before in the Cameron Highlands before being posted to Johore Bahru. When I mentioned that Major Black was also going to be the acting CO for over a month, I noticed a gleam in the eyes of both Fatimah and Diana. . It was obvious to them as to what I was hinting. At just after noon we made our way to the Raffles hotel, and I was hoping that I would not be refused entry as the hotel was out of bounds to all non-officers in the Forces. The more I thought about this the more I was less concerned I was as I knew that Diana had dined at the hotel many times with her mother and father and that also Fatimah had dined there with Diana has well. Also with the standing and position which Fatimah had, I could never imagine any hotel being so foolish as to refuse entry to her companion.

Fatimah, Diana and I were in the Long Bar of the Raffles hotel well before 1pm when into the bar walked Major Black with a beautiful European girl on his arm. Major Black introduced his partner as Anna, an English doctor working in the hospital in Singapore. It is a small world as they say, and as it turned out Anna worked at the same hospital as Diana's father did and indeed Diana had met Anna on one previous social occasion. Following a couple of drinks in the Long Bar, we had all enjoyed a superb curry buffet. The lunch seemed to go on and on and we adjourned back to the Long Bar for a few more drinks and over these drinks some very long chats.

It was during one of these long chats that Diana, and not Fatimah, brought up the subject of my wanting to marry Fatimah. Of course, on reflection I believe that this had been planned between Fatimah and Diana. It was Anna who asked that if I wanted to marry Fatimah why I had not done so.

Obviously, I was waiting for this opening and I explained to Anna of the problems that I had encountered with the CO and that I had to obtain his permission before I could get married and that he would never give it. Quick as a flash Anna replied that as Major Black was the acting CO then no problem existed. I looked over at the Major, who just smiled at me.

More discussion took place and it was the major who asked Fatimah if she really wanted to get married to me. She replied in the affirmative. The major then asked me if I wanted to marry Fatimah and I told him that I did and as soon as possible. Then it is all settled the major declared and he told me that he expected to see a written application from me to get married on his desk the following Monday morning and that any leave I wanted would be no problem. I thanked the major and did point out that there were likely to be repercussions. Major Black told me to let him worry about any repercussions. The drinks and the chat continued for some time afterwards and by the time we left the Raffles Hotel at way past 9pm, I did not know who were the happiest, the three girls, who seemed to get on a like a house on fire, or myself.

Just prior to us all leaving the Raffles Hotel that evening, I was with Major Black at the bar trying to pay some part of the bill only to be told by him that he was insisting of paying all the bill on such a happy occasion, when I noticed the three girls at the table giggling and laughing their heads off and hugging each other. On leaving the hotel Anna gave me a lovely kiss and wished me much happiness in the future, before departing with the major.

In the taxi back from the hotel Fatimah told me that all being well she would be arranging for us to get married five days later on the Friday. She told me that she would confirm this the following day or on Tuesday at the latest

34

MARRIAGE

On Monday 15 December I went into the dental centre nice and early and typed out two copies of my application to get married and put them on Major Black's desk for his approval and signature. The reason I did two copies is that in addition to the copy for official records I also wanted a copy for my own personal records. The major arrived at just after 8.30am and on entering the general office asked me if I had made out my application to get married. I replied that I had and that my application was on his desk. He asked me into his office and asked me to sit down. He signed both copies and then asked me when I intended to get married. I told the major that providing he agreed that I would like to get married on Friday 19 December in Fatimah's house in Seremban.

The major told me that Anna and he had both been very impressed with Fatimah and that he was glad that we had planned the marriage quickly and that as it was a very quiet period that he was giving me local leave from the 18th until Monday 29th, which would give me sufficient time to get married, apply for a married quarter and to sort everything out. I told the major that I planned on applying for a married quarter on Monday

22 December when I returned to Johore Bahru from Seremban as a married man. Major Black immediately told me that I did not have to wait until the 22nd to apply for a married quarter as he had already spoken to the Gurkha Quartermaster (QM) major in the Officer's Mess the previous evening and told him about my forthcoming marriage and that the Gurkha major had informed him that he had surplus of married quarters and that I could apply for one before I actually got married. Major Black then suggested that I apply for a married quarter by completing the necessary Army Form A10 (Application for a Married Quarter) and to give it to him for his signature and he would then pass them on to the Gurkha QM at lunch time when he went for lunch in the Officers Mess.

I thanked Major Black for being so kind regarding all the help that he was giving me, but advised him that there was certain to be repercussions. Major Black then reminded me of all the help that I had given him in the Cameron Highlands, and also regarding his lost bullets. As regard to any repercussions, the major told me that he was more than capable of handling these if there were any. I left the major's office and went to our stationery cupboard and got Army Form A10, which was an application for married quarters. I completed the form and put it on the major's desk for his signature. Major Black countersigned the form and took it with him when he went to the Officer's Mess at lunch time. The major returned just before 2pm and informed me that he had given my application for a married quarter to the

Gurkha QM and that the QM had informed him that he was allocating me a married quarter which he had arranged for me to take over on Wednesday 17 Dec at 2pm. Although I was officially only entitled to an A or B type quarter, which was either a one or two bedroom quarter, the QM had allocated me a C type quarter, which was a three bedroom quarter. Once again I thanked Major Black for all the help he was giving me.

On Monday evening Fatimah telephoned me and told me that she had spoken to her friendly Imam who had confirmed that he would marry us in her house on Friday 19 December at 11am. I told Fatimah about all the help that Major Black had given us and that he had arranged for me to take over a three bedroom married quarter on the Wednesday afternoon and I explained that we were exceptionally lucky as normally one did not get a married quarter until they were actually married.

On Wednesday Major Black took me down to the married quarter which I had been allocated which was just about 500 yards from the barracks. I was very surprised to find that the quarter was bungalow with a nice verandah and a lovely garden. We met the Barracks Inventory Accountant (BIA) who was due to hand the quarter over to me. The BIA took me into the bungalow and proceeded to check the inventory of the contents of the bungalow with me. All the contents were in very good order and the bungalow was very clean. I then signed the inventory and the BIA wished me luck. Once again I thanked Major Black for all his help.

I telephoned Fatimah on the Wednesday evening and told her the good news about the bungalow.

I had to explain to her that an army married quarter contained not only furniture but everything else one need to live in it, like all cutlery, all crockery, all linen and electric things like a kettle, vacuum cleaner, fridge and so on.

I added that we only had to add our personal things and knickknacks to turn it into a really nice place to live. Fatimah was delighted and over the moon with this news. I ended our telephone conversation by informing her that I would be travelling up to Seremban the following morning

I arrived in Seremban on Thursday afternoon. Fatimah went over the simple wedding ceremony with me. I read from the words I had on my piece of paper and she said that I was word perfect. She told me that her friend the friendly Imam would be coming with his helper and that the ceremony would only last for less than 15 minutes. All I was required to do was to answer, from the replies I had on my piece of paper, when he nodded at me. A piece of cake she told me! At the ceremony would also be three of Fatmiah's guests, Diana, Ahmed and Nor her maid. Fatimah told me that she would be wearing a golden songket, which was a hand-woven fabric

Malayan dress, embodied with golden and silver thread. I would be wearing a light beige safari suit. After the ceremony had finished small snacks with non-alcoholic drinks would be served Fatimah told me.

D Day or rather M Day (Marriage Day) duly arrived on the Friday morning. After a late breakfast Diana arrived wearing a lovely silver silk western dress. I must say that she did look very stunning. A thought did cross my mind that perhaps I was marrying the wrong person. For one thing I knew that Diana always wanted to go to England, whereas Fatimah always changed the subject when I mentioned what it would be like for her to live in the UK. Too late to change my mind I quickly thought. Fatimah went off with Diana to get changed and returned about 30 minutes later and I must admit that she also looked very beautiful and stunning in her Golden songket. The Imam and his Kadi (helper) arrived at around 10.30am and asked Fatimah if everything was in order for the ceremony. Fatimah told him it was.

At 11am sharp The Imam asked me to stand in front of him. He started talking in Malay and then nodded to me. I relied to him from what I had learnt from memory and this continued until the ceremony was finished. All this time Fatimah was stood at the side and nowhere near me.

Just before 11.15am the Imam told me that the ceremony had finished and he congratulated me on being a married man. There were no kisses for the bride or anything like that. Immediately after the ceremony we all went out onto the veranda for snacks and drinks. The Imam's helper soon appeared with the marriage certificate and handed it to me.

I read it and noticed that my proper name was on the certificate with Wan Nordin Bin Wan Abdulla in brackets. Before he left shortly at about 1pm the Imam gave me a copy of the Koran. I thought afterwards that the wedding ceremony was a very short one, and perhaps this is why many Muslims were allowed four wives. I mentioned this to Fatimah and she told me to forget about 4 wives. Fatimah's guests stayed until around 9pm that evening then they left and left Fatimah and myself to ourselves.

Before he left Ahmed had taken me for a quiet drink outside on to the verandah and told me to always be faithful to Fatimah. I looked at him in amazement and wondered whether that was a warning or not. He obviously saw that I was quite shocked and he quickly added that it was just some good advice that he was offering me and hoped that I would not be offended. Ahmed went to tell me that before Diana came onto the scene that Fatimah had another very good friend named Aisah. Aisah was a Malayan girl who married a Malayan man. After a couple of years of marriage Aisah's husband was drinking far too much which she had to accept, but when she found that he had become very unfaithful and had two mistresses she refused to accept that and planned serious action against him. Ahmed went on to tell me that Aisah and her husband lived in a two storey house in Seremban. It is common knowledge in Asia that some Asian wives who find out that their husbands had been unfaithful take very drastic action and that they castrate their husbands using a knife. Aisah decided that enough was enough and she also decided to take drastic action against her husband. I looked at Ahmed waiting for him to tell me what Aisah did. Aisah did not like knives or the sight of blood, so she planned an alternate method, Ahmed added.

Aisah made preparations. She waited for a night when her husband was completely drunk and in a different world. He was in his bed snoring his head off. She then got out the roll of chicken wire and tied one end very tightly to part of his wedding tackle. The other end she tied to a large house brick. She then threw the house brick out of the bedroom window.

Aisah's husband woke up in hell of a shock with part of his wedding tackle missing and which was attached to the chicken wire dangling loosely on the floor. There was blood everywhere. The husband was taken to the hospital by neighbours. It was I who investigated the case actually, Ahmed went to tell me. No action was taken against Aisha and she was never charged with any crime, as her husband was so embarrassed and did not want his friends or women to ever know what had happened.

Aisah told me that she would do the same again if she ever got married again and her husband was unfaithful. Fatimah thought it was marvellous thing that Aisah had done and told her that she would do something similar if ever she got married and her husband was unfaithful man. I could never sleep with an unfaithful husband and I would also castrate him Fatimah told me, added Ahmed. I thanked Ahmed for his advice.

Diana appeared the following morning just after breakfast and whist Fatimah was getting showered and changed she explained to me that I that I would have to forget about eating sausages, bacon, ham and any kind of pork, but that Fatimah would allow my guests and myself to drink alcohol in our house. I cringed at the thought of having to give up those succulent, sizzling sausages for breakfast and ham sandwiches, but thought that Fatimah was well worth giving them up. Fatimah soon appeared and she told me that we should plan to travel down to Johore Bahru the following morning on the Sunday and that Ahmed would drive both of us down in her car whilst Ahmed's police friend would follow us in a police land rover with her personal possessions and her maid.

Early on Sunday we drove down to our married quarter in Johore Bahru, arriving in the early afternoon. Both cars were unloaded and Fatimah's personal possessions and clothes put into the bungalow. We all went out to one of the restaurants in Johore Bahru for dinner. Ahmed and his friend stayed the night and slept in bedroom 2, which had twin beds, with the maid sleeping in bedroom 3. On Monday morning Ahmed's driver took Fatimah, Ahmed and the maid into Johore Bahru shopping for various provisions, vegetables and meats, whilst I went into the Barracks.

On arriving at the dental centre on that Monday morning I saw Major Black and Dave Roberts and confirmed to them that Fatimah and I had got married on the Friday and both congratulated me on becoming a married man.

I showed the major the marriage certificate and he was happy enough with it. I explained to the major, that although he had given me local leave until the 29th, that I had come into the dental centre in order to do the necessary Part 2 order for him to sign and for me to send it off to the various units. I went into the office and typed on a stencil the Part 2 order giving all the necessary details, such as the full name of the woman whom I had married; the date of the marriage, the place where the marriage took place and that the marriage certificate had been seen and verified.

Another entry on the Part 2 Order gave details of my Next of Kin (NOK) which was Fatimah of course and her address of our married quarter. I took the typed stencil to Major Black who duly signed it. I then ran off several copies of the stencil on the duplicator and got them ready for dispatch.

Copies of the Part 2 Order were then dispatched to our records office in the UK, the Regimental Pay Office in the UK, the Regimental paymaster in GHQ FARELF Singapore, DDDS at GHQ FARELF Singapore, the Paymaster in Majidee barracks and the last copy to my CO in Seremban. Before dispatching the Part 2 Order to my (absent) CO in Seremban I telephoned George Wilkie in Seremban and informed that I had got married and he would receive a Part 2 Order giving all the details, the following day. I asked George to make sure that he filed the Part 2 Order away and that he did not put into the CO's In Tray. George told me that that would be no problem because the CO had told him prior to his going on leave that all urgent matters should be dealt with by Major Black the acting CO and that all routine matters by Captain Wilson, and that upon his return he did not expect to find anything in his In Tray. Great I thought! I put all the copies of the Part 2 Orders in envelopes, bade farewell to Major Black and Dave, and then went down to the Army Post Office and posted the envelopes to the various addresses. I then returned to my married quarter.

Fatimah, Nor, Ahmed and his friend returned from shopping with a load of provisions and groceries late in the afternoon I spent the rest of the afternoon chatting with Fatimah, and her two friends whilst Nor prepared what turned out to be a most wonderful Malayan dinner. Over dinner Fatimah told me that Ahmed and his friend would be leaving the following morning and returning to Seremban. Ahmed told me that he and his friend would take the land rover back to Seremban and leave Fatimah's car at the married quarter so that Fatimah could use it locally to do her shopping.

Fatimah could drive and she had a driving license and she said that whilst she did not mind driving her car around the Johore Bahru area, that she had no intention of driving any further. This seemed to be reasonable for the only time I had been in Fatimah's car was when she drove me to the Lake gardens once in Seremban, I was as nervous as a baby kitten and thought afterwards that if ever she drove me again, that I would need to wear at least 5 pairs of underpants. She was certainly not a confident or good driver.

Tuesday morning soon came around and after breakfast Ahmed and his friend took the land rover and departed for Seremban. Fatimah and Nor spent the rest of the day sorting out the bungalow. She told me that I could celebrate Christmas Eve and Christmas Day as I normally would as in Malaya, unlike the Arabic countries all religious holidays were celebrated in Malaya. Fatimah told me that she would like Major Black and Dave as her first guests and she asked me to invite them down to the bungalow at sometime over Christmas. I went into camp on the morning of 24th December and had a couple of drinks in the dental centre with Major Black and Dave and I told them of Fatimah's offer. Both told me that they had already made plans over Christmas but that they would be delighted to be Fatimah's first guests on Saturday 27th December. Major Black told me that he would like to invite Anna if that was possible. I told him that would be an excellent idea.

I returned to the bungalow in the early afternoon and told Fatimah that the major and Dave were delighted with her invitation and that they would be coming for dinner on Saturday 27th December and that the major would be bringing Anna. Fatimah was very excited and over the moon with this news. I celebrated Christmas Eve and Christmas Day with my new wife and we both drank alcohol with Fatimah having a couple of gin and tonics. The food that Nor served during these two days were Malayan dishes but excellent.

Saturday 27th December soon came and Fatimah and Nor spent quite some time in the kitchen preparing some Malayan dishes. At around 7pm that evening, Major Black, Anna and Dave arrived.

Anna looked superb in a lovely dress and so did Fatimah in one of her few western dresses. Nor served the major, Dave and myself beers whilst Fatimah and Anna had gin and tonics.

Dinner was served at 8pm by Nor in the dining room and we all sat down to a most wonderful meal of five Malayan dishes which included a Malayan King Prawn curry, (which I found out afterwards Anna had told Fatimah, when they had met at the Raffles Hotel), was the major's and her favourite dish. It also happened to be both Dave's and my favourite dish as well. One thing

about Nor, is that she may have been quite an ugly bugger, but she was a superb cook and an excellent maid.
After dinner Fatimah and Anna sat and chatted in the lounge whilst the major, Dave and myself went and sat on the verandah.

We could hear much laughter coming from the lounge and it was obvious that Fatimah and Anna were enjoying themselves. Over beers on the verandah Major Black told me that I was a very lucky man to have married such a wonderful lady like Fatimah. I told the major that it was only him who had made all that possible. It was then that the major told me that it was more than likely that he would eventually marry Anna all things being well. It was well after midnight before the major, Anna and Dave bad us farewell and thanked Fatimah for a superb night. A night I will remember for the rest of my life, the major told Fatimah.

Fatimah and I celebrated New Year's Eve over a few drinks and more superb Malayan food. Married life was certainly looking good despite no lovely sausages for breakfast. In fact Nor introduced me to several breakfast dishes like chicken liver cooked in some kind of orange sauce and other exotic Malayan breakfast dishes, in addition to the usual boiled, poached, scrambled, fried eggs.

During the first five months of 1959 married life was excellent and I thought it was never going to end. Of course I kept on thinking what was going to happen when finished my three year army tour in Malaya. Would Fatimah come with me to the UK, or should I be able to get good job in Malaya, get a local release and settle in Malaya. I thought that I would deal with this problem nearer the time. Meanwhile I was enjoying what little work I had to do. I was enjoying playing football. Fatimah was enjoying being a good housewife.

We had many guests during those six months, with Major Black, Anna, Dave and a few other friends visiting us and coming for dinner. Diana and Ahmed from Seremban paid us a few visits as well and stayed for a few days.

Fatimah true to her word only used to drive her car around Johore Bahru with her maid as passenger and never asked me to accompany her. Fatimah loved Singapore a lot and we both used to make the visit over the causeway to Singapore on many occasions. Often we drank and dined at the Raffles Hotel which was Fatimah's favourite place in Singapore. It was during one of our visits to the Raffles hotel that I met Captain Ron Moore, a captain in the RAVC (Royal Army Veterinary Corps). Ron was a guy from Matlock in Derbyshire, whom I had drank with on quite a few occasions in Matlock. Ron introduced me to his best friend in Singapore, a chap called Pete Morris who was a captain in the RMP (Royal Military Police). I was to see them a few times in the Raffles Hotel and we always joined up for a few drinks and had many laughs together. I did point out to Ron that although the Raffles Hotel was strictly out of bounds to soldiers and was only in bounds to officers that I had always been told that Fatimah and I were welcome at the Raffles Hotel at anytime. Forget about all that shit about the hotel being out of bounds Ron told me, in fact I always hear the staff addressing you as captain and Fatimah as Madam. Anyway you look more like a captain than most captains I know, and the staff treat you like royalty, so enjoy yourself, Pete Morris the RMP captain added.

Come the end of May 1959 and Fatimah was starting to ask me what I would like to do on my 22nd birthday on 17th June. I immediately thought of the last birthday, my 21st, I had spent with Winnie the Witch, but put that thought right out of my head. Perhaps a few days in Bangkok to celebrate your birthday would be nice Fatimah suggested.

35

THE REPERCUSSIONS

After a most wonderful five months of happy married life with Fatimah and me living like a Lord, the shit hit the fan (as I knew it eventually would) on Wednesday 3 June 1959. George Wilkie, in a state of panic, telephoned me from Seremban in the early afternoon, as I was just due to lock the dental centre up and go home. He told me that at just after noon a car had been driven up to the dental centre and a very well dressed lady and a Malayan man had got out of the car and come into the dental centre. They came into the office and the man introduced himself to George, telling him that he was the Aide to the Sultana (Sultan's wife) who was accompanying him, and had told him that they wished to see the Officer in Charge. George added that he explained to the Aide that Lt Col Hull was not available and would not be in until the following morning.

George then told me that he had asked what the problem was and that the Aide had told him that the sultana was very worried about her daughter princess Fatimah who had disappeared from Seremban. They had come down to Seremban that morning only to find Fatimah's house locked up and nobody there. On talking to Fatimah's neighbours, they had been told that Fatimah had moved away some months before. On further questioning one of the neighbours stated that it appeared that Fatimah had a boyfriend who was a dental corporal in the army who worked in Rasah Camp, and that possibly she had gone away with him somewhere, because she had seen this corporal loading up two vehicles with a lot of Fatimah's possessions some months before and that neither Fatimah or the corporal had not been seen since. George then told me that he told the Aide that he knew nothing about any dental corporal from Rasha Camp disappearing with Fatimah. George concluded his telephone conversation by informing me that the Aide had insisted on his making an appointment for him to see the CO and that he had booked an appointment for the Aide to see the following morning at 11am, when he found out that the CO had a cancelled dental appointment at that time. I thanked George for all the information and George told me that he would try and keep me up to date with the matter, whenever he found anything out.

I put the telephone down and immediately telephoned Diana. Luckily she was in and I told her what George had told me. Diana was quite upset and told me that she knew nothing about the matter as she had only just returned to Seremban from Kuala Lumpur a couple of hours before. Diana warned me to be on my guard as she knew the sultana, Fatimah's mother was not only a very strong and powerful woman but also a very strict Muslim. Diana promised me that she would try discreetly to find out what had happened and would keep me informed. Meanwhile she would telephone

Fatimah at our bungalow straight away she added. I thought Thank God that our residence had one of the few telephones on the married quarter patch.

On putting the telephone down I locked the dental centre up ad made my way home. One reaching home I found Fatimah on the telephone and immediately realised that she was talking Diana. I let them finish their telephone conversation and when Fatimah finally put the telephone down I could see that she was very upset. I then told Fatimah that George had telephoned me and had told me about the visit of her mother and her Aide to the dental centre and that they were both due to see the CO the following morning. When Fatimah said "Shit" that was the first time that I had ever heard her swear.

Fatimah had previously told me a little about her family, but then she explained about her family in more detail. Her mother was the sultan's third wife. Her father was not strict at all, and although he had bought the house for Fatimah in Seremban, he had had little contact with her over the past couple of years and he had left her to get on with her own life. Her mother, the sultana was a different kettle of fish however, and was quite strict. Fatimah went on to tell me that her mother had four daughters and that she was the eldest and this being the case Fatimah had more freedom and lived in the house purchased by her father, whereas her other three sisters lived with her mother in one of the sultan's palaces. I asked Fatimah when she had seen her mother last and she told me about two years ago when she had visited her in Seremban. I then asked Fatimah when she had spoken to her mother last and Fatimah told me that she always telephoned her mother at least a month and had continued to do so when she had come to Johore Bahru.

Did you ever tell your mother that you had got married and moved to Johore Bahru? I asked Fatimah. Fatimah said that she had not and I asked her why not. If I had told her that I had married a British soldier my mother would have crucified me Fatimah said. Only Christians get crucified not bloody Muslims I could not help telling Fatimah. I asked Fatimah why she thought her mother had tried to visit her in Seremban again and she replied that her mother may have just been in the area. I asked Fatimah why she had not told me all these things before and Fatimah told me that I had never asked much about her family and that as she wanted to marry me she had obviously told her mother nothing, as had she had done so, she would never have been allowed to marry me. I had never had any argument with Fatimah and I knew that I could not start now, as I also wanted to marry Fatimah, and I always knew in my mind that there were going to be repercussions at some time in the future. I then suggested to Fatimah that I tell Major Black everything before the CO spoke to him and let us see how things panned out. Fatimah agreed that this was the best thing to do. In my mind I knew that in the end it was not going to be a happy ending!

On the Thursday morning I asked Major Black if I could speak to him about a serious and important matter before he saw any dental patients. He invited me into his office and I told him of the telephone call that I had from Cpl Wilkie and that the sultana and her Aide would be seeing the CO at 11am that morning and that the CO was bound to telephone him in the afternoon. I jokingly reminded the major that I had warned him that there would most likely be repercussions. I ended my conversation with the major by telling him that I had told him everything, the whole truth and nothing but the truth, of what the CO had done, and also everything that Fatimah and I had done. Major Black then told me not to worry about anything as he would try and sort everything out when the CO telephoned. The major then told me that what he was going to tell me next was unethical and never to be repeated to anyone. I want to know if the CO is going to tell me the truth when he telephones me and when you put his call through to my extension I want you to stay on the line, keep very quiet, and listen and tell me afterwards if he spoke the truth.

The CO did not telephone Major Black on that Thursday afternoon, but George Wilkie did telephone me at my married quarter that evening. George told me that as scheduled the sultana and her Aide had met the CO at 11am that morning. The sultana and the Aide had spent a good 30 minutes with the CO and then left. The CO had come out of his office swearing and foaming at the mouth like a rabid dog.

George then told me that the CO had called him into his office and told him roughly what the sultana and the Aide had said. The CO was at a loss who the RADC corporal the Aide was talking about and that he had never heard of any woman called Fatimah who was supposed to be a princess George added. Had any of our three corporals in Seremban recently got married without my permission the CO asked George. Certainly not George told the CO. Are all the RADC corporals living in barracks the CO asked George and George replied in the affirmative. George then concluded by telling me that the CO had told him that it was a most serious matter and that the sultana and the Aide wanted answers within the next few days and this being the case he intended to make further urgent inquiries. The CO reminded George that the matter had to be sorted out very quickly as he was due to be posted back to the UK on the 12th June having finished his three year tour in Malaya and that the Lt Col Duncan, the new CO was due to be posted in on 8th June.

I warned George that the CO would eventually find out that it was me who was married to Fatimah and that a Part 2 Order had been sent to Seremban. I told George to cover his back and mention this to the CO the following morning. I suggested to George that he tell the CO that he had just "remembered" that a Part 2 Order had come in some months ago mentioning that I had got married and he thought that I had married a woman called Fatimah, and that he had filed the Part 2 Order as the CO had previously told him that he wanted an empty In Tray when he returned from his Australian leave. A weak excuse but better than none I told George. Get that Part 2 Order out ready to show it to him and tell the CO you want to talk to him urgently when he comes in the following morning and who knows he may even thank you for helping to solve his serious problem quickly I told George. George asked me if that is what I really wanted I told him that I did not want him to get into any trouble on my behalf.

On Friday morning the 5th June my telephone rang at about 11am and it was George on the line. The CO wants to speak to Major Black urgently he told me. I knew then of course that George had told the CO what I had suggested. I went into the major's office to find the major having his coffee break and I told him that the CO wanted to speak to him urgently.

Put him through and remember to stay on the line and be nice and quiet the major told me. I went back to my office and put the CO's call through to Major Black's extension.

Good morning major I heard the CO say. We have a serious problem major and then I heard the CO tell Major Black about the visit of the sultana and her Aide. I have now learnt that your bloody corporal is the perpetrator in this matter. Not only has he married a bloody princess but he has got married without my authority, the CO screamed down the phone. That is not 100% true Major Black quickly added. For starters my corporal wrote a written application to me to get married and which, as acting CO I approved, having met his charming wife to be before I gave my approval, and yes he is married to Princess Fatimah. I cannot believe what I am hearing I heard the CO choked. You have been conned by a bigger con man than Houdini and a perpetrator who knows more bloody tricks than Houdini ever did, the CO screamed. Do I have to remind you major that it is the sultans who run Malaya now and not the British government and have since they got their independence and that by allowing all this to happen you have caused an international problem the CO added. How can a bloody British Christian solider marry a Muslim anyway major the CO shouted. The corporal you mention is actually a Muslim and has been for a number of years the major quickly informed the CO. That is certainly is not true major and I think you are clutching at straws the CO belted out. Why do you not check with records office in the UK and his documents colonel, I heard the major reply. Is Houdini living in Barracks or living elsewhere with this female the CO asked. Major Black told the CO that I was living in a nice three bedroom bungalow, which was an army married quarter, just 500 yards from the barracks and had been living there for the past six months. There was a deathly silence on the phone for a few seconds.

So what you are telling me major is that this Houdini is not only married but that he is also living in an army married quarter I heard the CO say. That is correct colonel and I would add that he is not only happily married to a charming lady, but I found, on my visits to his quarter that his wife keeps an immaculate and very clean house, I heard the major reply. In fact I would add colonel that Mr and Mrs Houdini as you call them are possibly the most respected and popular couple on the married quarter patch and they also one of the few who have a telephone and a car.

There was another deathly silence for quite a few seconds before the CO told the major, this marriage is illegal and I am going to get it annulled because a non-Muslim cannot marry a Muslim in Malaya I have been told. I heard the major then tell the CO, I must warn you, as a solicitor, colonel that you cannot get the marriage annulled because both the parties are Muslims and if you try to do so more problems will arise for you and not for the corporal and his wife. This Houdini fellow is not any Muslim and is just a trickster with a sack full of tricks and that you have been completely conned by him major, the CO said. I will make further inquiries and speak to you tomorrow again major the CO concluded. The phone was then slammed down.

Major Black called me into his office and asked me if I had heard everything and I told him that I had. I then told the major that everything that I had told him was true and that I was a Muslim and that our Records office would confirm this when the CO checked, as I knew he would. I also confirmed to the major that the wedding ceremony was genuine and this could easily be proved. The major told me that he believed every word that I had told him and he thought the CO was over acting and trying to cover his back before he was due to leave Malaya in a few days. I am afraid that unfortunately we have not heard the last of the matter and I am a bit worried for you and Fatimah, the major warned me. The major knew that George Wilkie was giving me updates and he asked me to keep him informed of any late developments before the CO telephoned again. I assured Major Black that I would do so.

After finishing work on Saturday Major Black told me that he would be going down to Changi in Singapore that afternoon to meet Lt Col Duncan our new CO and that he would be looking after him on the Saturday night before he travelled up to Seremban on the Sunday. The major then added that he and Lt Col Duncan not only knew each other very well, but that they also had gone to the same university and dental school, but did not think that our present CO knew that.

On Saturday afternoon of the 6th June George telephoned me at our bungalow. I did not tell George that I had listened to the telephone call between the CO and Major Black of course.

George then proceeded to tell me that he had done what I had suggested and told the CO about the Part 2 Order and shown him the order. George had expected a rollicking but was surprised when the CO had thanked him for remembering and told him that he had saved him doing a lot of telephoning around and investigating.

George then told me after the CO had finished speaking on the telephone to Major Black that he had called George into his office and gave him a draft list of all the signals he wished to send, all of which were marked urgent. The first signal was addressed to our Records Office in the UK asking if my religion was listed as a Muslim and if so when did I become a Muslim and also if I was listed as being a married man, and if so to whom etc.

As the CO wanted a reply back that day, and bearing the difference in hours between the UK and Malaya, the CO told George to type up the signal right away for his signature and to take it down to the Signal Centre straight away. George then told me that they had received a signal reply back from records in the UK late that afternoon confirming that I was indeed listed as a Muslim on all my documents and had been a Muslim since April 1956 and that I was also married and that my wife was named as Wan Fatimah Binte Wan Ismail and that our marriage certificate had been seen and verified and that she was also listed as my NOK. On giving the CO the signal, George said the CO went white or grey, was stamping around the office shouting that bloody Houdini was a Muslim all the bloody time he worked for me and I never knew it. Other signals had been prepared and sent off to GHQ FARELF and the Regimental Paymasters in Singapore and the UK and all replies came back confirming that I was married and also in receipt of marriage allowance, George said. There were more signals flying around than confetti at a wedding George added and every one o these signals confirmed what I had told the major. "What are we going to do? the CO asked George. George said he gave the CO a blank look and said nothing. George concluded by telling me that the CO had already sold his boat prior to his leaving shortly for the UK and that the CO had told him that he possibly would be in the Officer's Mess all over the weekend should anybody want him. I told Fatimah, who had been listening to my telephone conversation everything what George had told me.

Fatimah told me that Diana had come down to Singapore in order to see her mother and father over the weekend and that she had arranged for us to meet her in the Long Bar at the Raffles hotel on the Sunday afternoon at noon for lunch.

When Fatimah and I arrived at Raffles Hotel we were surprised to see that Diana had her mother and father with her. Over lunch and drinks I brought Diana's father, the doctor, up to date with the current state of affairs. He was very annoyed to learn that the CO had called Diana and Fatimah floosies and that the CO thought all local women were either floosies, biddies or local prostitutes. Of course I laid it on quite thick.

Monday 8th soon came and when Major Black arrived I told him that George Wilkie had telephoned me at the bungalow on the Saturday afternoon and I told him everything that George had told me. "Good!" The major told me, now let us see what the CO has to say now when he telephones again.

The major told me that he had picked up Lt Col Duncan the new CO up from Changi on the Saturday night and had seen him accommodated in the Officer's Mess in the barracks overnight. He added that he had mentioned to the new CO about the problems that Fatimah and I were presently suffering and that the new CO had promised him that he would try and help if in any way he could, but that he would possibly have to keep himself out of the matter and not interfere if the current CO insisted on dealing with the matter.

George Wilkie telephoned me at the bungalow during the evening to let me know that the new CO had arrived and that the current CO had spent the whole morning showing the new CO around the camp and introducing him to various officers in the camp. During the afternoon both the CO and the new CO had spent the whole afternoon, behind a locked door, presumably going over all the plans for the handover of the unit, George added.

Good old George telephoned me on the evening of Tuesday the 9th December to tell me that he had put two interesting telephones calls through to Lt Col Hull that afternoon. The first telephone call was from the sultana's Aide and the second telephone call was from a doctor in Singapore. George did not know what the calls were about and all he knew was that a very bad tempered and red faced Lt Col had left the dental centre that evening in a big huff. I thanked George for the info.

When Major Black came into the dental centre on the Wednesday morning I told him that Lt Col Hull had received two telephone calls the previous day and that he could expect a telephone call from Lt Col later on.

The major told me that he had wondered why the current CO had not telephoned him so far this week, especially as he had received confirmation from Records about my being a Muslim and being officially married. Perhaps he is thinking of his next move, or perhaps he is busy with his handover to the new CO, or perhaps he has even forgot about Fatimah and me I suggested to the major. Major Black then told me the CO certainly was not going to forget about Fatimah or me, as there was too much pressure he believed coming from the Aide. The major then warned me that perhaps the CO was getting other more senior officers involved in trying to sort out the problem. If this was the case I should fear the worse, he added.

36

WEDNESDAY 10TH 195

Shortly after I had spoken to Major Black on that Wednesday morning of 10 June the telephone rang and I answered, to find George on the other end of the line. George asked me to pass on an urgent message from the CO on to Major Black, requesting the major that he telephone the CO when he was free and to expect a long conversation on several matters. I told George I would pass the message on straight away to Major Black. I informed the major of the message. As it was a quiet Wednesday the major had only a few patients he told me that he would be available to telephone the CO at 11am. I immediately telephoned George in Seremban to let him know that Major Black would be telephoning the CO at 11am.

At exactly 11am Major Black asked me to contact the CO for him, but for me to stay on the line as usual. I telephoned Seremban and the phone was answered by George. I told George that Major Black was telephoning the CO has he had requested. The CO is in his office waiting for the call and I am putting the call through now to him George told me. George put the call through. Major Black had heard all this of course.

Good Morning colonel, I heard Major Black say. What is bloody good about it major? I heard an enraged CO reply. Early this morning I got a phone call from Colonel Green our DDDS in Singapore informing me that the matter regarding your corporal has to be sorted out before I can enplane for the UK the CO shouted. In other words I will not be leaving here on Friday the 12th, the CO added. I do not see any problem colonel, as the corporal you refer to is a happily married man who got married legally and who has done nothing wrong the major replied.

From what you told me before there is no international incident and it is only the mother of the corporal's wife who is complaining and how many times we have seen mother-in-laws complaining about their daughter's husbands, Major Black added.

The sultana's Aide telephoned me yesterday and he told me that the sultana wants her daughter back in Seremban as soon as possible and the bloody husband posted as far away as possible from Malaya, I heard the CO scream. Malayan civilians do not run the British army or arrange postings, Major Black, quickly replied. But I can, the CO shouted and when I have contacted Records office in the UK I am going to request that he be posted as far away as possible, Siberia would be ideal but unfortunately there are no postings there so I am going to request that he be posted back to the UK immediately the CO added. Think carefully before you do anything colonel, because if my corporal is posted back to the UK then he is entitled to take his wife with him and he would apply for an accompanied flight for her, which of course would not be refused, the major said. You are trying to create as many problems for me as that bloody corporal of yours has done the CO quickly replied. No, No colonel I am just giving you the facts, the major said. Just imagine what would happen if you get my corporal posted back to the UK and then you try and stop his wife from accompanying him to UK. For one thing Joint Service Movement Centre (JSMC) would never allow it, plus there would also be an outcry when the News of the World got hold of the story, the major said. There was silence before the CO replied that he would think over the matter again regarding any posting.

Another matter major, the CO said. I had a long telephone call from a very irate English doctor in Singapore yesterday. He told me that he was the father of a woman called Diana who it appeared was the best friend of your corporal's wife. He reprimanded me severely as he had heard that I had been known to refer to these two women as floosies or something worse than that. I told the doctor that I had never met any of the two women he was referring to. The doctor went to tell me that he had met this princess Fatimah or what she is called, and you and your corporal on several occasions in the Raffles Hotel and that he had been impressed by all three of you.

In fact the doctor said that your bloody corporal was welcomed into the Raffles hotel like he was royalty and that he was always addressed by the staff as Captain. What have you to say about that, a breathless CO said.

Before the major could reply, the CO quickly said, I presume you know that the Raffles hotel is out of bounds to all troops who are not officers and this being the case, you as an officer should have notified the Royal Military Police (RMP) and got him barred from using the hotel. Two things stopped me doing anything colonel, the major quickly replied. Number one was that corporal was told by the management that he and his wife could use the hotel at any time they wished and indeed his wife was always addressed as Madam. Secondly one of the corporal's regular drinking partners was an RMP captain, Major Black added.

God, this gets worse and worse the CO screamed. Do I have to remind you major what happened to two other little bloody corporals who thought that they were more important than royalty or officers? Their names were Napoleon Bonaparte and Adolf Hitler and both of those bloody corporals came to a sticky end, the CO added.

There was more silence, then Major Black said, colonel did you manage to confirm that the corporal is indeed a Muslim and is recorded as such on his documents and therefore was entitled to get married?. Yes, Yes I contacted Records Office in the UK and they confirmed that he is a Muslim and has been since April 1956 and that he is listed on all his documents as a married man. This bloody Houdini Muslim fellow was walking around my dental centre for two bloody years and I never suspected a thing. Had I have known I would have posted him sooner. The CO added. Muslim or not a Muslim colonel, I know that he did an excellent job at Seremban before you posted him into me here, Major Black said. How do know that the CO asked. The corporal in question showed me copies of the last two annual confidential reports that you had written on him. In your reports you mentioned that he was excellent at his job, very smart in appearance, excellent at solving problems, and virtually excellent at everything else. You even recommended him for promotion to Sgt although he was only an acting corporal.

The marks you gave him were the highest I have ever seen on any soldier's confidential report. In fact had a layman been reading the reports he would have thought you were writing about the Son of Jesus Christ, Major Black said.

He should not have made copies of any Confidential Report the CO quickly said. He is allowed to take notes only and not make any copies and that just proves to me what a devious man this Houdini is. With regard to his excellent ability of solving problems, you have to remember that he initiated most of those bloody problems himself, I am now led to believe, the CO added. I thought that it was the corporal who requested a posting and it was not you who wanted to post him, Major Black said. Regarding the posting of him to you at Johore Bahru major, it was the corporal who completely conned me when he asked for a posting telling me that he wanted to learn more about the culture of the Malays and to see more parts of Malaya the CO added. Well he certainly did learn more about the culture of the Malays and he has certainly has seen more parts of Malaya and Singapore, Major Black quickly replied.

Major it is no good us arguing over what is now spilt milk and indeed we need to find an amicable solution to the matter of your corporal and his wife quickly, as until we do I am stuck here in Malaya which is completely unacceptable. I have to give this matter some more urgent serious thought and to take further advice before making any further decisions. I will get back to you soon major. Thank you and good afternoon, the CO concluded. The telephone conversation ended. Major

Black called me into the office and asked me if I had heard everything and I told that I had and thanked him for his support. You realise that the CO is not going to get away from Malaya until the matter is solved and possibly you should expect the worse, although I cannot think for one moment what that is going to be, the major told me. I agreed with the major.

Being a Wednesday recreational afternoon and no football I went home to the bungalow in the afternoon and brought Fatimah up to date. Obviously she was quite worried and asked me if they could post me without her. I told her that they could always post me anywhere, but in this case if they did post me back to the UK, then she would be allowed to accompany me.

The telephone rang in the bungalow at shortly after 6pm and it was George on the line again. I told George straight away that whilst I very much appreciated his phone calls to the bungalow that he would have to be careful as when the list of long distant telephone calls came in each month from the Signal Centre that the bungalow's number would be listed and that George would have to answer some nasty questions as to why he was ringing a private number from an army phone. George told me not worry as he was not stupid enough to do that and he always used private phones when telephoning me at the bungalow. George said that tonight he was phoning from a friend's house, who had told him that he could always use his phone when he wanted to call me privately. Also George added Diana had telephoned him a couple of times and not only asked him how things were going, but that he could also use her phone to speak to Fatimah or me, at any time. That was news to me as George had never told me that he knew Diana. Perhaps he was actually seeing her I thought, but I let that pass.

Bad news George told me. George then went on to tell me that after the CO had finished speaking to Major Black that morning that he had drafted out a signal to Records in the UK requesting that I be posted back to the UK immediately. George had typed the signal, the CO had signed it and George had taken it down to the Signal Centre. This signal had been sent off to records in the afternoon with a copy to the DDDS in Singapore. The CO expected a reply by the following morning. I thought that that bastard of a CO had not thought more about the problem, or sought further advice before making any further decisions, although I could not tell that to George of course. It was obvious that the bastard of a CO wanted me posted quickly so that he could leave Malaya himself. George ended the telephone conversation by informing me that the CO was now continually referring to me as either Bonaparte or

Houdini and that he would telephone me the following day at some time to let me know what is happening.

37

MORE SIGNALS AND TELEPHONE CALLS

I went to work nice and early on the Thursday morning of 11th June and as promised George telephoned me just after 8.30am. He told me that they had received a signal back from Records in the UK which basically stated that the CO was reminded that the only person who could request a posting of a RADC solider in or out of the FARELF theatre was the DDDS at GHQ in Singapore, and although they noted that the CO's signal had been copied to the DDDS, had the DDDS approved such a request. The signal had also been copied to the DDDS. George told me that to his knowledge the DDDS had not approved of any such request. George told me that he would telephone me again later on if there was any more news and I told him that I would be staying in the dental centre over the lunch time break.

It was around 1pm when I got another telephone call from George in Seremban George told me that the shit had hit the fan. All exciting stuff George added but it is a pity that it is all about you he told me. Another signal had arrived later that morning from the DDDS in Singapore which had sent the CO into overdrive and into a tantrum George added. George read the signal out to me, which was addressed to the Records Office in the UK with a copy to the CO. Basically the signal informed the UK Records Office that the CO had no authority whatsoever to request any posting for me and he, the DDDS had no knowledge of the matter apart from reading, that morning, the copied signal which the CO had sent off. The DDDS's signal ended by stating that the request by the CO for any posting for me was to be ignored completely and that he, the DDDS would be in communication with UK Records in the near future. I thanked George for the info.

Great news I thought. I knew from my time at Seremban that the CO and Colonel Green the DDDS were quite friendly, but as the DDDS had sent a signal to the CO instead of speaking to him personally on the telephone, I knew that this was a reprimand to the CO.

During the afternoon I told Major Black about the latest signals that were flying around. Major Black could not believe what I had told him and he told me that I had heard the CO promise him that he would give the matter more thought and seek further advice before making any further decision, yet the CO had immediately sent off a signal to UK records requesting I be posted, immediately he had ended the telephone conversation with the CO. The major thanked me for keeping me up to date and smiled when he said Thank God it is the corporals and sergeants who run the British army and not the officers. The rest of the afternoon passed without incident and I went home after work to Fatimah and brought her up to date.

That evening I dug out some 10in x 8in photographs of Fatimah and myself which had been taken at the Raffles hotel. I had developed the negatives myself and printed the photographs in our darkroom at the dental centre. There were quite a few photographs and I chose a lovely photograph which showed, Fatimah, Diana, Anna and her mother and father, and myself celebrating in the long bar at the Raffles hotel. The photo had been taken by Major Black with my Canon camera.

I then asked Fatimah to dig out my Malay dress which I had never worn and a pill box hat. My traditional Malay dress was called a Baju Melayu and consisted of a loose tunic which was worn over light trousers, accompanied with a sampin (saraong) which is wrapped around the waist. The colour was a colourful dark brown with some trimmings. I also asked Fatimah to dig out the beautiful golden songket which she had worn at our wedding. She looked at me in amazement and said, much to her disappointment I had never worn my Malay dress. She asked me what all this was about and when I told her she shrieked with laughter and told me that it was a brilliant idea.

On the Friday morning after a very early breakfast at around 6.30am I dressed into my Malay dress and put a Malay pillbox hat on my head.

Fatimah dressed into her golden songket. I got my Canon camera out and gave it to Nor and we all went on the verandah. The sun was hot and it was a lovely day. Fatimah then told Nor to take her time taking a lot of photos of Fatimah and myself standing up and holding hands, sitting down and laughing etc. After the photo session I got dressed into my OGs and went to work very early arriving there at just after 7.30am. I went into the darkroom, unloaded the camera, and started developing the negatives. The negatives looked good and when I eventually started doing the actual photos I was more than pleased with the end product. Nor was not only a good maid and cook but it appeared that she was a good photographer as well. I left the photos to dry and went back to my office.

Major Black came in shortly before 9am and he asked me if there was any more news. I replied in the negative. There will be soon he assured me. I did not disbelieve him.

At lunch I went back into the darkroom and looked at the dozen photos that I had hung up to dry. I chose two, one of which was of Fatimah and myself stood up holding hands, whilst the other was of the both of us sat down at a table on the verandah, laughing. All the photos were 10in x 8ins.

At just after 2pm the telephone rang and I answered it and was surprised to find that it was Colonel Green, the DDDS on the other end. Colonel Green was very polite and he asked me how I was getting along and so on. I did not mention anything about any problems of course and our telephone conversation lasted for about a minute before he asked me if I could put him through to Major Black. I went and got the major from his surgery and told him that Colonel Green wished to speak to him. The major immediately told the patient that he had an urgent telephone call to take and excused himself. Once the major was in his office I put the call through and then put down my telephone. The major was only on the telephone for a couple of minutes before he put his telephone down and returned to the surgery.

After he had finished with his 2pm patient Major Black came into the office and asked me what patients he was due to see on the Saturday morning. I told him that he did not any, only the sick parade, if any, to see at 9am.

Good the major told me, because Colonel Green the DDDS is coming up to see the both of us at 11am and wants to speak to the both of us. I hasten to add, that the DDDS has assured me that it will be a most friendly meeting, the major added. I look forward to the meeting I told the major.

The rest of the afternoon passed without any incidents. During the afternoon I got the two photos of Fatimah and myself on the verandah, plus the photo of all of us in the Long Bar at the Raffles hotel and put all three photos into a large envelope with a stiffener and went down to the BPFO (British Forces Post Office) in the barracks and posted the envelopes off. The envelopes were addressed to Cpl George Wilkie, Dental Centre, Seremban, BFPO.

After posting the envelopes off I went home with the rest of the photographs that I done in the darkroom and Fatimah was very pleased with them, especially when she saw that we had both looked so well in our Malay outfits. I told Fatimah that I had sent off three photos to George at Seremban and that I would tell him what to do with them the following morning. We both had a superb meal, a couple of Singapore gin slings which Fatimah liked and chatted until the late hours of the evening.

Saturday the 13th arrived and after breakfast and a SSSS I got changed into my very best OG ad headed off to work. Arriving at the dental centre at around 8.30am I immediately telephoned George. I was not worried about making too many telephone calls to Seremban, as it could have been for anything, like a request for stores or for any other matter. George answered the phone and he immediately told me that there had been no further developments since yesterday, but that the CO who was originally supposed to have left for the UK the day before, was still in most foul mood and had been since receiving that reprimand and signal from the DDDS. George said he had heard the CO tell the new CO that not only had his posting and leave been delayed, but that all his immediate plans had been disrupted and that he was now stranded in Malaya without any boat or car all because of that mobster in Johore Bahru.

I brought George up to date with everything and told him that Colonel Green was coming up at 11am that morning to Johore Bahru to speak to both Major Black and myself, but asked George to keep that information to himself. I then told George that an envelope containing three photos would be arriving at the centre for him during the morning, or on Monday morning at the latest and I told George what the photos were. I then told George what I wanted him to do with the photos. I asked George to leave the photos on his desk where everybody could see the three photos. I knew from past experience that the CO was always snooping around the office and was always looking what was on my desk when I was at Seremban. George said that this was still the case as the CO was always picking things up from his desk. God, George declared when he picks up those photos and looks at them he is liable to have a heart attack. George did advise me though that neither the old CO nor the new CO would be coming into the dental centre until Monday. George promised to do what I asked. I was thinking about asking him if he had any further contact with Diana or if he was seeing her, but decided if he was that it was certainly no business of mine. I bade goodbye to George and rang off.

I received a couple of letters from Doc and Dai Jones and I answered them the following morning and told them what had happened to me over the past few weeks. I noticed that Dai continued to spell my surname wrong on the envelope which contained the letter he had sent me!

38

VISIT OF THE DDDS

It was around 10.45 am when Colonel Green the DDDS arrived in his staff car with his driver, from just over the Causeway in Singapore. I was in the general office with Major Black when the colonel entered the dental centre and he greeted us both warmly. The colonel told me that he wished to speak to the major first before he spoke to me and he therefore asked me to stay in the general office until I was called, before he disappeared with the major into the major's office. Juliana the dental surgery assistant served coffee to the colonel and Major Black in the major's office.

Major Black came out of his office into my office at around 11.30am, winked at me and told me that Colonel Green was ready to see me in his office. I accompanied the major into his office and was told to sit down by the DDDS. The DDDS sat behind the major's desk and the major was sat next to me.

First of all the DDDS informed me that the meeting was going to be a friendly one and that he was not there to reprimand anybody, but was only there to offer advice and help. I breathed a sigh of relief. The DDDS went on to tell me that during the past days that certain accusations had been made against me which were untrue and that this was unfortunate and that he was sorry. A complaint had also been made by my wife's mother to Lt Colonel Hull about me in which she alleged that possibly I had married her daughter under false pretences, that I was not a Muslim and that I was not entitled to have married her, all of which were again are untrue the DDDS added. Furthermore, the DDDS added she was insisting of my being posted away from Malaya and her daughter returned to Seremban. The DDDS quickly added that it was not mother-in-laws who posted soldiers in the army and that she should have been told this.

You have to remember what mother-in laws can be like, that DDDS reminded me, they are the butt of all the jokes by comedians in their shows, and indeed I also had a troublesome mother-in-law when I married my wife when I was a young captain, the DDDS concluded.

You may not know that following a visit by the sultana your wife's mother and her Aide to Lt Col Hull in Seremban a week or so ago that many signals have been sent out to various units in an effort to try and solve and problem that may have occurred following your marriage to your wife. Perhaps these signals were sent out too hastily the DDDS told me. I knew all this of course and I also knew that the DDDS was letting me know in a very gentle manner that my CO had been wrong, but of course a senior officer would never criticise another senior officer in front of me. Following some of the signals which were copied to me I found that it was necessary in fairness to all parties concerned for me to get involved and I therefore spoke to the Records Office in the UK, the DDDS told me.

Before I go on further about the Records Office in the UK I would like to add that I have spoken to Major Black about yourself and he has assured me that you have always been an excellent NCO and indeed have always done your job extremely well as your Confidential reports reflect. Major Black has also told me that he has met your wife on numerous occasions and has always not only found her to be a most charming young lady but also a much respected lady by everyone who has met her. This being the case the army has no intentions of trying to separate you and your wife, the DDDS told me.

Back to my contacts with UK Records the DDDS quickly added. Following certain signals that were sent to UK records that were copied to me I found it essential that I contact them. I sent off a signal to them and informed them that I wished to speak on the telephone to the Officer in Charge (OIC) personally and last night I spoke to the OIC. The OIC informed me that he had received a request that you should be posted as soon as possible, but that no reasons had been given for such a request, although he suspected that you had been in some kind of trouble. The OIC then told me that he had ignored the request for any posting and had informed the person requesting the posting accordingly, the DDDS told me.

Of course the DDDS did not mention that it was that shithouse of a CO who had made such a request.

I spoke at length to the OIC the DDDS added and I informed him that you had certainly not caused any trouble, but that there was a situation, which had to be resolved in some way or other, hastening to add that it would be to be unacceptable for you to be given any unaccompanied posting. The OIC took the opportunity of reminding me that you were due to be posted from Malaya in late September 1959, in any event following the completion of your three year tour in Malaya, the DDDS said.

The DDDS then told me that the OIC had advised him that perhaps there was a solution. The OIC had said that I had been penciled in or a posting to the RADC Depot (Stalag 15) in early October following my disembarkation leave, but that should I choose to accept an earlier posting that he could offer me a posting to the dental centre at Chester as they urgently required a

DCA corporal to replace the DCA current DCA who was due to leave the service shortly. The dental centre was in Saighton Camp was the base of the Army Medical Rehabilitation Unit (AMRU).

The DDDS then asked me what I thought, telling me that he had been assured by the OIC Records that there was an adequate supply of married quarters in Saighton Camp and that Chester was not only a good posting but also that Chester was a lovely city. Should I decide to choose Chester then I would be given two week's notice to leave Malaya and would report to Chester immediately following my week's disembarkation leave.

The DDDS then advised me that the ball was in my court, that I could accept the Chester posting and that he would guarantee that my wife was on the same airplane back to the UK that I was on. The alternate was to decline the posting to Chester and accept the posting to Stalag 15 in October with no guarantee of married quarters. The DDDS suggested that I speak to my wife over the weekend and to inform Major Black the following Monday morning of my decision who in turn would notify him.

The meeting ended with the DDDS shaking my hand and wishing me every success in the future. I was then dismissed. The DDDS remained in the major's office for about a further ten minutes before leaving in his staff car back to Singapore.

Major Black came back into the general office and suggested that we go for a drink down to Amy's bar in Johore Bahru before I went home to talk the matter over with Fatimah. We went off to the bar. Over drinks the major told me most of the conversation of what had taken place between himself and the DDDS. Whatever you choose to do I think that you are in a catch 22 situation he told me. The important thing is would Fatimah go with you to the UK if I chose any of the two postings, the major asked me. From what he had gathered when he had spoken of previous occasions to Fatimah, Diana and Anna, was that Fatimah had never stated that she would accompany me back to the UK when the time came, but had only told them that she would make her mind up when the actual time came. Remember, the major reminded me of what Diana had often mentioned - that whilst she would go to the UK at a minute's notice, that Fatimah, being a devote Malay, had always stated that she was worried about being accepted in the UK as a strict Muslim girl. Unfortunately, this being the case I fear, possibly that Fatimah will not want to go to the UK with you. It is a hard decision that you have to make, and it is decision that I am grateful that I do not have to make, as I am not sure that you have been told the truth and the whole truth, the major added.

I mentioned to Major Black that not once had the DDDS referred to Fatimah as a princess when he had spoken to me. The major quickly told me that when the DDDS had spoken to him that he had done so on a few occasions and that he believed he had referred to Fatimah as my wife when he had spoken to me in order to confirm that she was indeed my wife and that our marriage was all above board. He knew that you obviously knew she was a princess of course and did not feel the necessity to mention it. I asked the major if the DDDS had mentioned that perhaps Fatimah may not want to go to the UK and the major told me that he had not mentioned any such thing, but may have suspected it. I also asked if anything about my using the Raffles hotel had been discussed and the major assured me that no such subject had been mentioned.

The DDDS told you that the ball was in your court, but of course the ball is also in Fatimah's court the major added. The major asked me which posting I thought I would choose. Without any hesitation I told him Chester. I then added that I hated Aldershot, hated Stalag 15, that the married quarters around Aldershot were bloody awful and more important was that if Fatimah did accompany me back to the UK that she would also really hate Aldershot and would most likely try to commit suicide. The major told me to talk to Fatimah before making any final decision and reminded me that I had to let him know of my choice the first thing of Monday morning so that he could inform the DDDS accordingly. The major assured me that he was always on my side and would back me up to the hilt whatever my decision was. We had a few more drinks, and I suspected that as major knew that the end was near, he spoke of some of the good times we had had together, before departing from Amy's bar

39

POSTED

I went home that Saturday evening and was quiet when I got in to the bungalow. Fatimah knew that something was wrong and she asked me why I was so quiet. I told her that we would speak after dinner and over a couple of drinks. Dinner came and went and I poured Fatimah a large gin and tonic and a treble whiskey for myself. I explained everything that the DDDS had told me and also what choices the DDDS had given me.

After explaining everything to Fatimah she said that Aldershot was out of the question. That left Chester of course, which pleased me. Fatimah then asked me if I could still get an expat job quickly and then a local release. I told her that this was out of the question for three reasons. The first being that top companies were starting to employ local civilians instead of expats. Secondly there was now insufficient time to get any kind of job and to get any local release. Thirdly even if I was lucky enough to get a job very quickly, there was no chance whatsoever that my CO would approve my application for a local release, but by some miracle if he did, that Headquarters FARELF would certainly not approve it, due to their not wanting any arguments with Malaya royalty.

Fatimah went at great length to tell me that she was afraid that she would not be accepted in the UK. She mentioned that she was a Muslim and was happy wearing Malayan dress, but not Western clothes. Were there mosques in Chester she asked me and I assured her that there were, although I did not know, I presumed there were. After a good three hour chat Fatimah told me she was still undecided whether she would accompany me to the UK, but to ask Major Black to put her on my flight to be on the safe side. I suspected then, that Fatimah, having made so many excuses to me over the past three hours, would not be on that flight.

On Monday the 15th June I got to the dental centre early and waited for Major Black to come in.

As soon as he entered the dental centre the major called me into his office. I told him about the three hours conversation that Fatimah and I had had the evening before and I confirmed that I wished to be posted to Chester. The major informed me that he would inform the DDDS of my decision later on. I will ensure that Fatimah is on the same flight as you are on, when the date is known, but I suspect from what you have told me that Fatimah will pull out at the last minute, choosing to remain in Malaya, the major added. Just before 10am Major Black asked me to telephone the DDDS's office inform and the NCO that he wished to speak with the DDDS. I put the call through to the major in his office and the major told the DDDS of my decision. The remainder of Monday passed without further incident.

On Tuesday 16 June George telephone from Seremban late in the afternoon. He told me that he had received the three photos on the Monday morning, which I had sent him on the Monday morning and as I had requested he had left them on his desk all morning. George went to tell me that later that morning when he was a few yards away from his desk dealing with a dental patient when Lt Col Hull and Lt Col Duncan the new CO had come into the office. Immediately Lt Col Hull had seen the three large 10in x 8in photographs on his desk and had picked two of them up, looked at them and handed them to Lt Col Duncan. I told you that bloody Houdini had gone all native and here he is in full Malay dress, George heard Lt Col Hull rant to Lt Col Duncan. George then told me that Lt Col Hull had picked up the third photograph from the desk telling the new CO, here the little corporal again, acting the Napoleon Bonaparte bit, entertaining his friends in the Raffles hotel. A bloody corporal acting as though he is higher and more important than a senior officer, George heard Lt Col Hull fume. George added that the new CO said nothing but that Lt Col Hull was so red in the face and was spluttering and ranting and raving and it looked like he was doing a war dance before he threw the photographs back onto his desk before storming into his own office.

Wednesday the 17th was not only my birthday, but also a day that I would never forget. As soon as I arrived at the dental centre that morning I got a telephone call from the Signal centre asking me to pick up a signal.

On opening the signal I found out that it had been sent to the DDDS, with copies to my CO in Seremban and to the dental centre in Johore Bahru. The signal basically stated that I was to be posted to the dental centre at Chester and was to report there on Monday 20th July 1959, following disembarkation leave and that actual posting order would follow. George telephoned me later in the day, not only to wish me a happy birthday, but to inform me about the signal. I told George that I had received a copy of the signal. When Major Black came into the dental centre and showed him the signal. At least they are giving you more than two weeks notice the major told me.

I got home that evening and told Fatimah all the news. She did not seem to want to talk about it too much, telling me that I should enjoy the birthday dinner, which she had arranged for me, which Major Black and Dave

Roberts would be coming to. So much for a visit to Bangkok on my birthday which Fatimah had talked about organising, but I thought that this had been impossible due to all the uncertainty which had taken place over the past week or so. The dinner was superb, as always it was when cooked by Nor and no mention of my posting to Chester or whether Fatimah would accompany me was ever mentioned. We did have a quite a few laughs and talked over the times that we had enjoyed, but I must admit that I was quite subdued through the whole evening. Much different from my last birthday with Winnie the Witch I thought!

Over the next week I tried to do a bit of planning and it was on Wednesday 24th, when we had received my actual posting order that Major Black asked me when I intended to book a flight for Fatimah and myself. I was unsure whether if I was required to take one or two week's embarkation leave so I advised the major that I would like to book the flights for Monday 6th July, which would give me sufficient time to arrange all my affairs and also arrange for a couple of MFO (Military Forwarding Organisation) boxes so that I could pack my personal possessions which would be sent to me in the UK by sea.

I booked the flights that morning with the Joint Services Movement Centre (JSMC) for Fatimah and myself. The following morning JSMC confirmed that we would be both on the same flight, flying out of Singapore on Monday 6th July. So Colonel Green the DDDS had kept his word I thought.

I telephoned George later that day to bring him up to date and George told me that Lt Col Hull had already departed for the UK as soon as he had been notified by the DDDS immediately after the signal had come in about my posting. I was a bit disappointed that my old CO did not telephone before he went, but there again I was not surprised!

The next two days were quiet and it was not until the weekend of the 26th/27th June that Fatimah sat me down and did a lot of serious talking. We spent several hours talking about the pros and cons of her coming to the UK and settling down, but on the Sunday evening she told me that after great thought she had decided that she did not want to come to the UK with me at that time, but that she should seriously think about joining me in the UK later on. No amount of persuasion on my part could change her mind, and I knew that finally that I had lost the battle and that I would be returning to the UK on my own. I spoke to Major Black on the Monday and told him of Fatimah's decision and the major told me that although he was very disappointed with Fatimah's decision, that he was not surprised. I then had to telephone JSMC and inform them that Fatimah would not be accompanying me to the UK.

The next few days I spent settling my affairs and packing my MFO boxes. I had arranged the handover over of my married quarters for 2pm on Monday 6th July. On Wednesday Major Black took Dave Roberts and myself out to Amy's bar in Johore Bahru. On Thursday evening Fatimah confirmed that Ahmed and another of his police mates would be coming down with Diana in a land rover on Saturday the 6th and staying the weekend and that over the weekend that they would pack the land rover with Fatimah's stuff whilst he would pack Fatimah's car with the remainder of her items. Once I had left Singapore Ahmed and his police friend would drive the two vehicles back to Seremban with Fatimah, Diana and Nor.

This is what I had suggested to Fatimah a few days before and she was only confirming that all the arrangements had been made.

On Saturday after Ahmed arrived with his driver and Diana. The two guys packed the two vehicles during the weekend. At nights we dined and drank.

There was laughter and plenty of talking about the good old times, but often tinged with sadness. Monday morning arrived and I handed over my married quarter to the BIA (Barrack Inventory Accountant) and got an excellent march out report. Nor and Fatimah had done an excellent job in preparing a very clean quarter over for the handover. The BIA had kindly allowed us all to sit of the verandah until Major Black picked us all up at 5pm in a mini bus which he had arranged. Major Black arrived dead on time with the driver and Dave Roberts and we made our way to Changai airport.

Arriving at the airport I was surprised to see Anna and Diana's father and mother waiting for me. I booked into JSMC and was told of the flight arrangements before I was allowed to go off and join my farewell party. My farewell party and myself had coffee and talked a lot. I counted the people in my sending off party to find that there ten people in the group. Not many soldiers had ten people to see them off I thought. Over the tannoy we got a ten minute warning regarding booking in for the flight and it was then that all my friends moved away and left Fatimah on her own with me. Needless to say she was very upset and crying and was clinging to me like super glue. Over the tannoy came the orders for us to report to the flight desk. I shook hands with all the men and kissed all the girls. The major and Diana had to pull Fatimah off of me. I kissed her and said goodbye and made my way to the check in desk. I never looked back! I knew then that I would never see Fatimah again.

40

BACK HOME AND ON TO CHESTER

After two days on the airplane with four stops I finally arrived back in the UK and took the train up to Matlock and then onto to my mother's house where I would be staying until I reported for duty at Chester on 20 July 1959. Obviously all my family were pleased to see me but I am not sure that the neighbours, like Fred Bond and company, were. It was nearly three years since they had last seen me and now I was a lot bigger, stronger and wiser. One thing was for certain and that was that I was not going to get any more beatings from these neighbours. Some of the neighbours tried to be friendly but I have a long memory, as some of those guys in Malaya had found out, so I kept myself to myself. Fred Bond went out of his way to be over friendly and it was one day whilst I was in the local pub that he stupidly picked an argument with me teasing me that I had left my wife behind in Malaya. I offered him outside and he was foolish enough to take up the offer, but it was he who came out of the argument, wounded, battered and wiser and he skulked off home, much the worse for wear.

I had left all my UK army kit with my mother when I was posted to Malaya as obviously I did not need it out there. When I tried it all on I found that it was all loose fitting and too big for me. I reckon that I had lost over a good stone in weight whilst I had been in the heat and humidity of Malaya. This was soon to be no problem, for when I was not sitting writing daily letters to Fatimah I was in the pub on pints of bitter beer most of the time. My mother helped me to put the weight back on with those sizzling succulent sausages, bacon, ham sandwiches, pork pies and roast pork. By the time I reported for duty I had put a good stone on and my UK uniforms fitted perfectly. The time I spent on disembarkation leave soon passed quickly and it was time, once again to say goodbye to my mother, brother and sisters.

I arrived at the Dental Centre Chester on 20 July 1959 and reported in to Captain Smith who was the OIC of the centre. I was introduced to L/Cpl John Harrison and Cpl Ted Bailey and it was John Harrison who gave me a guided tour of the dental centre and also of Saighton camp. The dental centre was a very nice building with a very impressive set up which contained two dental surgeries (but only was being used), OIC's office, general office, x-ray room, darkroom, plaster room and storerooms. There was no dental laboratory John told me as all plaster models for denture work which we made were sent to the dental laboratory in Aldershot where the dentures, crowns and inlays were made. I was even more impressed when John took me into the attached building which contained three bedrooms, a lounge, and a bathroom. These are our sleeping quarters John told me. The only thing we use in Saighton camp is the cookhouse John added. I had never heard of, or been told that any dental centre had its own sleeping quarters for the soldiers who worked in the centre and I immediately thought how good and private that was. I dumped all my kit in the third bedroom and was again surprised how big the room was. John explained about the set up in Saighton camp. The Army Medical Rehabilitation Unit (AMRU) was the biggest unit in the camp and this was the only AMRU in the UK. In addition to many RAMC personal, there were a good number of Army Physical Training Corps (APTC) in the unit, in addition to some PTIs in Women's Royal Army Nursing Corps (WRAC). Other units in the camp included a WRAC Unit, a Signal unit and a few other units. John then took me on a tour of the camp, where I met various personnel. John concluded his tour by informing me that as the dental centre was a completely independent unit that we did not do any regimental duties and came under our own OIC for discipline. Great I thought, just like the dental centre in Seremban.

The following morning WO2 Sid Halls visited me at the dental centre. WO2 Halls explained to me that he was the chief clerk to the ADDS (Assistant Director Dental Services) and that he was based at HQ Western Command, Chester, which was just down the road. Over a very long chat WO2 Halls told me that he was fully aware as to why I had been posted to Chester and told me that if I wanted any help or advice that I was only to ask him. He went on to explain that I would eventually be taking over from Cpl Bailey in ten weeks' time.

He went to tell me that as he knew that I was only a paid acting corporal that he had arranged for me to do my corporal's course and my trade training class one course at the Depot RADC (Stalag 15), starting the following week. During the course I was to retain my paid acting rank and if I was successful on the corporal's course (over ten examinations of various sorts to be passed) and my class one trade training (DCA 1),that I should be promoted to substantive corporal. I thanked WO2 Halls before he departed. With Cpl Bailey still having ten weeks service left, I immediately knew that my posting had not been urgent as Records had told the DDDS and I smelled a rat straight away.

During the next few days I spent replying to the few letters I had received from Fatimah, Diana and Major

Black, and which were addressed to me at Chester. I had written to Fatimah several times a week when I was on disembarkation leave at my mother's house, and of course I intended to write to her about three times a week from now on. On Saturday I wrote Fatimah a very long letter explaining that I would be doing a couple of courses at Stalag 15, but asked her to address her replies to me at Chester, and not Aldershot, so that no letters were lost. I got all my kit ready and made my way down to Stalag 15 on the Sunday morning, ready to start my corporal's course from the Monday.

During the next six weeks at Stalag 15 I studied very hard and did very little drinking. In addition to studying in the evenings I wrote letters most nights to Fatimah and the odd one to Diana. Before I left the depot Major Cox called me into his office and told me that I had passed both my corporal's course and my trade one training courses with flying colours. Before I left his office he told me as he was the OIC of the Medical Services for the UK football team, that he would be coming up to Chester in early October in order to look at some of the RAMC and RADC players and hoped that I was playing football again by the time he visited Chester.

On arriving back at the dental centre in late September WO2 halls telephoned me and congratulated me on passing my two courses. He asked me to publish the Part 2 Orders straight away and send them out to the various units.

Records Office informed me that I had been promoted to substantive corporal a week later. After a month I took over from Ted Bailey and caught up with answering all the letters which had been waiting for me. I asked John Harrison if the camp had a football team and John told me that AMRU had a very strong team and that it consisted of eight APTC lads, one RAMC lad, one ACC (Army Catering Corps) lad and himself. Very hard to get into the team John assured me. John added that a WO2 Badge Bottle of the APTC ran the team so I went off to see him. I met Badge and introduced myself to him and he asked what position I played and I told him. It will be very hard to get into the team he told me but that he would give me a trial the following week as the RAMC Corporal who played up front was unavailable due to injury. To cut a long story short I played the following week and we won 4-0, with me scoring two of the goals and making the other two. Badge told me afterwards that I would be a regular in his team from then on. You and I are not going to be too popular at AMRU, John told me as AMRU is a medical unit and there will not be one RAMC lad in the side.

It was a pleasure to work at the dental centre Chester and I got on extremely well with Captain Smith and John Harrison. The work was a piece of cake. Most of the evening I spent listening to records, reading or writing many letters in my lovely bedroom, with an occasional visit to the pubs in Chester with John. I avoided the NAAFI and the Corporal's mess on the camp, where most of the WRACs (Willing, Ready, Available, Consenting, or Willing, Ready, Available, Come-on, was my abbreviation for WRAC) seemed to hang out. It was bad enough listening to these girls watching the football games from the touchlines screaming obscene remarks when I was running down the wing in my tight shorts. Of course I could not avoid them when I went to the cookhouse for my meals and although I had offers of dates I always said no. Although I still was frightened of women I prided myself on being a faithful married man. John had warned me that the WRAC girls knew that we had private bedrooms in the dental centre and that he and I were prime targets for some of these girls.

In Fatimah's letters to me she constantly wrote that she was still trying very hard to get me an expat job so that I could join her in Malaya. I replied that if she did manage to get me a job that I would be unable to take it as there was no such thing as a Local Release in the army in the UK and that I did not complete my regular service until late 1962. Diana wrote and told me how unhappy

Fatimah was and she also asked about Paul. I replied to Diana informing her that Fatimah could have come to the UK and could still come under private arrangements. Regarding Paul I wrote that I had not heard from him and that I did not know where he was, except that I knew he had completed his National Service and presumably would be working as a civilian dentist somewhere.

WO2 Halls made regular visits to see me at the dental centre and once he found out that I liked a game of snooker he arranged for me to play with him at his club on a regular basis. I liked the evenings I spent playing snooker with him and he told me to call him Sid and not Sir. Although Sid had a bit of a bad right eye, he was a bloody good snooker player and beat me as many times as I beat him and I considered myself a good player. Those visits to Sid's club also made a nice change to the lonely nights I spent in my bedroom listening to records or writing letters. Over beers after our snooker matches I told Sid a lot about Malaya, my marriage and Fatimah. Following these visits to Sid's snooker club, Sid became my mentor and I thought how unique it was that I always seem to find a senior mentor, like Gil and Paul in Seremban and Major Black in Johore Bahru.

It was in October that I received a telephone call from Major Cox informing me that he would be coming up to Chester the following week to look at a couple of players and asked would I be playing in any match during that week. I told him that AMRU were due to have a match against the Cheshire Regiment on the following Wednesday and that I should be playing. I gave Major Cox the time of the match and told him that we would be playing at home. He told me that he would be at the match.

Major Cox had previously told me that he would be looking at players for his Medical Services team and that he was coming to see the AMRU game so I knew that he was coming to see what John Harrison and I were like. It was a pity that we were playing the Cheshire Regiment I thought, as they had about the strongest team in the whole of Western Command which was not surprising considering that they had nearly 1000 soldiers to choose from. There again I thought our side at AMRU were also a good side and we were unbeaten in the season so far.

Wednesday arrived I missed lunch as I always did when I played football and went and got changed into my football kit and went down to the ground. Before we starting shooting in I saw Major Cox and Sid Halls on the touchline and went over to speak to them. By the time the match had started they was quite a decent crowd, including the usual screaming WRACs. The match was hard and we won 3-2 against a very good side. The bonus was that I scored all the three goals for our side. The match ended and I saw Major Cox chatting away to Badge Bottle our coach. I made my way to the dental centre to have a bath and to get changed. The following morning Major Cox visited me at the dental centre and after chatting told me that he would like me to play for the Medical Services team and I told him that I would be delighted to do so. The major informed me that he anticipated that would be about five or six matches during the coming season. Little did I know it at the time, was that Major Cox was going to be very, very helpful to me in the future in many ways and that he was also going to be another of my senior mentors.

The remainder of the year passed quickly. I did my job. I spent a lot of time writing letters and answering the replies. I did very little drinking. I played football. Before I went home to my mother's for Christmas I attended the camp Christmas party on the camp on Saturday 19th December. There were many WRAC girls at that party in addition to many civilian girls. I reckon that the girls at that party outnumbered the guys by about 4 to 1. The table I sat at had been organised by WO2 Dicky Bird, of the RAPC (Royal Army Pay Corps).

Dicky was a great football supporter and seldom missed a match when I was playing. I had become quite a good friend of Dicky and indeed had spent a few days with him on holiday on the South coast. The remainder of our table consisted of six women. There were no other males on our table apart from Dicky and myself. Dicky insisted of having some photos taken by the official photographer who was present, in addition to taking many photos himself. Dicky gave me several of these photos after I had returned from my mother's after Christmas. The photos were excellent. I should never have accepted those photos as they were to cost me very, very dear within the next couple of months.

Talking about photos, when I was Christmas shopping for Christmas cards in early December with Dicky Bird in Chester we went into a large shop which was selling Christmas cards and postcards. Lo and behold there on a stand were lots of postcards with soldiers and officers in uniform. I was delighted to see there was a postcard of Napoleon Bonaparte in full military dress. I had no hesitation buying two of those cards. I knew that Lt Col Hull had been posted as the Officer in Charge of the Dental Centre at Catterick on his return from Malaya, as I had made it my job to find out where he had been posted. That evening back at the dental centre I looked up the address of the dental centre Catterick. On the first postcard I wrote 'Hope you have a good Christian

Christmas' and on the second card I wrote 'Bonaparte the little Corporal' I then addressed the postcards and gave them to John Harrison the following morning and asked him to post them from Brighton where he was due to visit on Christmas leave a few days later. Of course I did was not stupid enough to sign the postcards or even think about posting them from Chester.

41

TROUBLE ON THE HORIZON

I finished my Christmas and New Year's leave with my mother and the family and I returned to Chester on Monday 4 January 1960 and reported back for work. I must say that the holiday period had been quite quiet and a bit lonely and a lot of the time I spent remembering the previous Christmas that I had spent with Fatimah.

The following day a great stack of personal mail, which included letters and Christmas cards arrived for me. There were over twenty of them and most had airmail stamps on them and were from Malaya. I thought that a lot of these letters must had been held up in the post due to the Christmas rush. If things continued like this I thought I would need a secretary to answer all my mail. I could recognise from the hand writing on the envelopes which were letters from Fatimah, so I decided to open them last. The first envelope I opened was a Christmas card from Major Black which had a letter inside. His letter informed me that he and Anna had planned to get married in the following spring. That piece of news pleased me immensely and I was very happy for the both of them. They were a great couple and I knew that they would enjoy their married life. I replied to the major's letter congratulating them and wishing them every success.

After opening other letters and Christmas cards I opened the two letters from Diana. There was no good news in either of her letters. In her first letter Diana had written that she visited Fatimah every day and that she found her to be often crying and was very depressed. She was not the happy chirpy woman that she used to know Diana wrote.

Diana had written in her second letter that Fatimah's mother had visited Fatimah and stayed with Fatimah for a week during early December.

Since I had left Malaya and Fatimah had returned to her old house in Seremban, Fatimah's mother had telephoned Fatimah at least twice a month and had become very worried about her depression when speaking to her on the telephone. That is why the mother visited Fatimah, Diana wrote.

During Fatimah's mother's stay she had still visited Fatimah every day and she was often party to the conversation which went on between Fatimah and her mother. There was no sympathy on the mother's part and her mother told Fatimah that she could only blame herself for her depression and sadness for getting married to a syaitan putih (white devil in Malay) in the first place. The mother went on to tell Fatimah that no orang putih (white man) was good enough to marry her daughter, even if he was an officer, let alone a stupid soldier. The mother warned Fatimah to stay away from any more soldiers in Rasha camp, otherwise she and her sultan husband would ensure that severe consequences followed. The mother went on to tell Fatimah that she had been speaking to the sultan and had told him to use all his influence to get her sham marriage to me annulled. Diana wrote. All bad reading I thought, but I was not really surprised as I knew what an interfering old bitch Fatimah's mother was. I eventually replied to Diana's letters and told her what I thought of Fatimah's mother.

The nine letters from Fatimah I read last and all were painful reading. She wrote about how lonely and depressed she was and what her mother was continually reprimanding her and blaming her for marrying me. In every letter Fatimah asked me to finish in the army and to join her in Malaya. In my letters to Fatimah I kept on emphasising that I could not finish in the army and that the only solution was for Fatimah to join me in the UK where we would be given an army married quarter and settle down to a happy married life.

Reading these type of letters that I was receiving from Fatimah and Diana did not affect my work, or my football, but it did make me quite depressed when I was alone at night back in my bedroom. If Fatimah refused to come to the UK then there was no solution I knew and I started wondering how it was all going to end.

The letters from Fatimah continued to come at the rate of two or three a week and all her letters were in the same vein.

Letters from Diana ranged from two or three a month. In the middle of January Diana had written to me telling me that Fatimah had remarked to her that I had sent very few photographs to her and what photographs I had sent were mainly of me in my football kit. This being the case Diana asked, could I send her a few photos of myself to her as soon as possible and she would pass them on to Fatimah, at the right time in order to try and cheer her up a bit.

The only photographs I had of myself were those which were taken at the Camp Christmas party by Dicky Bird and the official photographer. Dicky had given me a dozen photographs when I had returned my mother's after New Year and six large photographs which I had ordered from the official photographer. I therefore only had these 18 photographs to choose from. Hardly anybody took photographs those days except at weddings, birthdays and special occasions, so I had very little to choose from. I looked at the 18 photographs and was very pleased with them, they showed me at the table at the Christmas party smiling and laughing and enjoying myself. I chose nine of the photographs, including four large 10in x 8in photographs taken by the official photographer and posted them off, the following morning in a A4 envelope, with a covering letter to Diana.

That evening I sat in my bedroom and looked at the rest of the photographs that I had not sent to Diana. I must admit that I did look bloody good in the photographs. I looked very smart in my uniform and I was laughing a lot, and enjoying myself, but the more I looked at those photographs the more alarmed I became. Every photograph not only showed me laughing but the six girls on the table laughing as well. I counted the number of empty beer bottles on the table and there were over 18 half pint bottles. God what I have done I thought. I should not have rushed to send Diana any photographs, but should have waited and had some proper photographs taken of me, by either a professional photographer, or a mate.

I lay awake for most of that evening hoping that when Diana received the photographs that she would not give them to Fatimah. Diana knew how jealous Fatimah could be and I thought if Diana did give her the photographs which showed me enjoying myself drinking and laughing with those six girls on the table that the shit would really hit the fan. What a fatal mistake I had made I told myself and I reprimanded myself time and time again for not thinking clearly and for being so bloody stupid. Very unlike me not to think things through clearly before I did anything.

42

AVOIDABLE AND ANNULMENT

The letters from Fatimah and Diana kept coming during the remainder of January, but from very early February the letters from Fatimah stopped coming. I suspected then that Diana had passed those photographs of to Fatimah for I was never to receive a letter from Fatimah ever again.

In mid February I received a very long letter from Diana. She had written that upon receiving my photographs that she had kept two for herself and passed the remaining seven photographs onto Fatimah. On looking at the photographs Fatimah had gone into a very jealous rage and had become very distressed. Nothing Diana tried to say to Fatimah could pacify her. In the end Diana had left the house and left Fatimah with Nor, the maid.

The following morning Nor had come to her house and asked her to accompany her to Fatimah's house, as she said that Fatimah was only refusing to eat and drink, but that she was in a suicidal state. She had immediately gone to Fatimah's house with Nor. Nothing she said to Fatimah could calm her down and therefore in the end she had telephoned Fatimah's mother and informed her of the situation. Fatimah's mother, with her Aide, had arrived at Fatimah's house that evening. Diana had written.

Ten days later I received another long letter from Diana. In her letter Diana informed me that the sultana, Fatimah's mother and her Aide had stayed at Fatimah's house for eight days and during those eight days that she had visited Fatimah daily and had witnessed some very unfortunate things. The worst news Diana had written was that I was no longer married to Fatimah. The sultana and her Aide had visited the friendly Imam who had married us and she informed him that she wanted the marriage between her daughter and I cancelled.

The reasons she had given to the Imam, were that I was not a proper Muslim and therefore not allowed to marry a Muslim girl; that the princess did not obtain the permission of her father, the sultan, to marry me, which was required under the state law; that the sultan had not given his permission for the marriage to take place in the Fatimah's house, a residence which he owned.

The Imam had then informed the sultana that has had been not given all the true facts at the time of the marriage, and due to valid three reasons given to him by the sultana, as why I could not marry her daughter, the Imam had then declared the marriage between Fatimah and myself as Null and Void and, on the sultana's request had issued two official certificates to that effect. It was obvious that the Imam was quite afraid of the powerful sultana and had rapidly agreed to her request. On returning to the house the sultana had explained everything to Diana and had given one of the copies of the certificate to her asking her to send it to me with a warning that I was never to contact her daughter again. In her letter Diana had also written that the sultana had told her, that she had already arranged with her husband the sultan that I was to be banned from ever entering Malaya again and that if I did manage somehow manage to avoid the immigration authorities and come to Malaya and try and see her daughter, that I would be shot on sight. Just like the old Wild West with a bounty on my head, I thought!

Diana went to write that she had told the sultana that it was I who had requested that the army to post me in order to solve the problem with Fatimah and that I was only trying to be helpful. That was not true the sultana had told Diana and she had produced two letters from the handbag. The first letter on headed notepaper was from the Malayan authorities to the sultan in answer to his letter, informing the sultan that in view of the problem he had outlined in his letter that they were contacting military authorities and demanding that I be deported as soon as possible and that I should be notified that I was no longer welcome in Malaya in the future.

In the second letter which the sultana had produced, Diana wrote, was written by military Headquarters, although she did not say which one. In their letter addressed to the Malayan authorities they acknowledged that they were aware of the problem and that steps were being taken to post me immediately and that they guaranteed that I would leave Malaya within the month and also that I would be notified that I would not be allowed back into Malaya under any circumstances, Diana concluded. So much for the choice of postings I had been given by Records Office. The offer of the Chester posting had just been a carrot dangled in front of my donkey face. The army was banking on my choosing Chester, and I had not done so I would have been posted somewhere else in the same time frame. They were also banking on Fatimah not wanting to accompany me either. Someone had done a lot of research and decisions had been made way up the food chain, as I did not think that the DDDS had lied to me.

I knew that a sultan had absolute authority over the state and I also knew that after Malaya had got independence from the British in 1957, that the British had no say whatsoever in the affairs of Malaya, so if what the sultana had told Diana was true, and the letter letters were genuine, then it was certainly grave news. I then thought that I could never get the Null and Void divorce cancelled, or indeed, do anything to rectify the whole problem.

A couple of days after I received that letter from Diana, I received a letter from my good friend Sgt Ahmad, who basically told me the same that Diana had told me, but adding that he was sorry about the ending of my marriage to Fatimah and also that Fatimah's mother was arranging for Fatimah's house to be sold and that Fatimah would be leaving Seremban for good and accompanying her mother back to her palace where she would live with the sultana. The news gets worse and worse every day I thought. I was powerless to write to Fatimah, as I did not know the address of the sultana's palace and also even if I did, the sultana would intercept my letters and they would never reach Fatimah. As Sid Halls would have told me at one of our snooker matches, I was truly snookered!

If I thought that things could not get worse then I was about to completely disillusioned, when two letters arrived a couple of weeks later.

The first letter arrived was from the secretary of the sultan, Fatimah's father, on official headed paper. In the letter I was informed that the sultan had annulled the marriage between Fatimah and myself and a certificate to that effect was enclosed. Furthermore the secretary wrote was that the princess Fatimah was now a single lady once again and was now free to marry any man of her choice. The secretary ended his letter by also informing that I had been banned from ever entering Malaya again. He concluded his letter by 'wishing me well in the future'.

I knew then that it my marriage to Fatimah had really ended as I was fully aware that sultans were the ultimate authority of Islamic Law in their states and nothing or anybody could ever change that. I now had one Voidable and one Annulled certificate and I thought that they were certainly making sure that Fatimah was free of me for good.

I opened the second letter, which was from Diana. In her letter she had written that Fatimah's house had been sold and that Fatimah had moved away from Seremban with her mother. She apologised for having given Fatimah the photographs but had only done so because I asked her to do so. She had no idea that Fatimah would become so jealous and distressed. She told me that I should have married her and not Fatimah, and that she would certainly have accompanied me back to the UK and that I would now be living a happy married life with her. She had heard that the sultan had annulled the marriage between Fatimah and myself and that I was now free to get married again. If I wanted any help I only had to ask, and if I wanted anything else that she was prepared to fly to the UK. I only had to ask, she concluded in her letter.

After reading the last couple of paragraphs of Diana's letter I started wondering whether it had been Fatimah or Diana who had been the jealous one. Had Diana been a real friend or a false one I thought. Diana had written that I was now free man and could married again if I wanted, but unfortunately she had been wrong on that score, as I was soon to find out. I went to bed that evening wondering just what other things Diana had told Fatimah.

43

DIVORCE

I was at a loss what to do next until Sid Halls popped into the dental centre to see me in early March. I showed the letters and the two certificates to Sid and he told me that he try and help me and also get me some advice from the right channels. Sid telephoned me a few days later to inform me that he had arranged a meeting for me with an Army Legal Services solicitor at HQ Western Command.

I went down to HQ Western Command to see the legal services officer a couple of days later and I showed him the letters and the two certificates. After reading the letters and looking at the certificates he then informed me that he could do nothing to help me as the Army Legal services were only in a position to advise and help on divorces cases when a soldier was based overseas and not the UK. What a waste of time coming to see this solicitor I thought, but then the solicitor went on to tell me, off the record, that the Voidable and Annulment certificates would not be accepted by the army and therefore I was still a married man. In that case, if I am still a married man and registered as a

Muslim and entitled to have four wives I am still free to marry another three women. Perhaps I could find another three Muslim women or get three English women to convert to Muslims, marry them and then apply for a army married quarter, I told the solicitor. That is not a good idea, neither I'm sure would the army allow you to have three wives in a married quarter, the solicitor told me. He concluded the interview by informing me that if I tried to do all that that I would be once again be creating more history in the British Army. The interview finished and I left no wiser.

A few days later Sid Halls came into the dental centre and I told him what the solicitor from Army Legal Services had told me. No good news then, Sid told me.

Sid then asked me how my football was coming along and I told him that I was due to report to the RADC depot on Tuesday the following week as I had been selected to play for the Medical Services on the Wednesday afternoon. Sid then told me that he had planned on going down to the depot, on RADC business the following week and he suggested that we that we could go down on Monday afternoon in his car and that he could spend the Tuesday doing his business, then he would be free to watch me play football on the Wednesday afternoon and we could return to Chester on the Thursday morning. I thought it was a great idea and immediately agreed.

Sid and I arrived at the RADC Depot on the Monday evening. On Tuesday I met the other lads who were due to play football and we did some training under the eye of Major Cox. On the Wednesday after a very boring match which we lost 0-1, I noticed Major Cox and Sid on the touchline in conversation. After the match Sid took me for a drink in a pub in North Camp and over a few beers he told me that he had spoken to Major Cox about my marital status and he informed me that the major wanted to see me in his office at 9am the following day. The following morning I visited Major Cox in his office and over coffee and biscuits he asked me about my marital problem and I told him the whole story. Before leaving his office Major Cox told me that he would try and help me.

It was two weeks later on a Tuesday when Major Cox telephoned me at Chester and asked me to come down and see him on the Thursday afternoon at 3pm. He advised me that he wished to see me regarding my marital problem and that he had found a solution, but did not go into details. He told me it that was most important that I brought the Voidable and Annulment certificates and any other relevant document or letters with me regarding the marriage and added that I would be accommodated at the RADC depot on the Thursday and Friday evenings.

Immediately after I had put the telephone down that Sid Halls telephoned me. Sid told me that he knew Major Cox was going to telephone me and that he told me that he would be accompanying me to Aldershot and that he would pick me up from the dental centre in his car at 8am on Thursday morning. It was obvious that Major Cox had telephoned Sid before telephoning me.

Sid picked me up at 8am on the Thursday morning and before setting off in car asked me if I had got all the necessary documents which Major Cox has requested. I confirmed that I had. We arrived in Aldershot in good time and Sid and I were called into Major Cox's office at 3pm and told to be seated. Major Cox then informed me that he had been to see the senior Imam at an important mosque in Woking and had spoken to him regarding my marital affairs and had asked him how I could obtain a divorce that would be recognised in the UK. On learning that I was still a Muslim (according to my army personal documents) the Imam had told him that it was no problem and that he could arrange for me to be divorced from Fatimah. Major Cox then told me that the Imam had informed him that an appointment should be arranged for me to attend the mosque with two witnesses and that he had arranged this for 10am the following morning. Major Cox then added that he had also spoken to the Records Office and informed them of everything the Imam had told him and asked whether the divorce certificate would be accepted by them and had been told it would be. Major Cox concluded the interview by informing me that he and Sid Halls would be accompanying me the following morning and would act as the two witnesses.

The following morning Major Cox, Sid and I arrived at a very impressive mosque in Woking and were shown into the office of the senior Imam. I gave all the documents to the Imam and after he had looked at them told me that no marriage certificate was necessary in respect of my Muslim wedding to Fatimah. I informed the Imam that the army had insisted that I obtain a marriage certificate when I married Fatimah.

The Imam then explained to me that he was also some sort of senior elder in the Islamic Council and that it was he would later divorce me from Fatimah in front of two witnesses, which would be Major Cox and Sid. The Imam went on to inform me of various matters connected with various Muslim matters and the procedure for the divorce and what he required me to do. Suddenly he picked up the telephone and spoke to somebody on the intercom. Within a minute two more Imans arrived.

I was asked to stand whilst the senior Imam read from a book (the Koran I believe) and on his signal I said 'I divorce, I divorce, I divorce you Fatimah'. The Imam carried on reading for a few more seconds before declaring that I had been divorced. Two pieces of paper, or some kind of certificates were then produced by one of the Imams, which I was asked to sign and then the senior Imam asked Major Cox and Sid to sign the papers as witnesses. I was then handed the two certificates. The whole divorce procedure had lasted under five minutes. The three Imams then shook hands with Sid and myself and told that we could leave. We went out to Major Cox's car whilst the major stayed in the Imam's office with the Imam. Major Cox joined us about five minutes later, but did not mention why he had been asked to stay or what he and the Imam had spoken about.

I took Major Cox and Sid out for lunch somewhere in Woking and it was over lunch that Major Cox told me that I owed him ten shillings (50p) for the divorce, which he had paid the Iman with a ten shillings note. Cheap at that price I thought and I could not pay him fast enough! If I thought getting a divorce was cheap I was to find out much later on in my life that this was certainly not the case, as divorces from my next three wives cost me in the region of £400,000.

The major then went on to tell me that I should publish the Part 2 order regarding my divorce as soon as I got back to Chester on the Monday, not forgetting to enclose the divorce certificate. Major Cox assured me that the Records office would accept the divorce certificate, but that if there any problems that I was to contact him. I thanked both Major Cox and Sid for their valuable help and support.

Major Cox then suggested that the next thing on my agenda was for me to think about changing my religion again, and do not think about becoming a Buddhist, as you would be required to walk around the camp in yellow robes, he joked. The following morning Sid drove us back to Chester and I could not help wondering if Major Cox had arranged my divorce so easily, why could that army Legal expert not have not suggested something similar. In any event it had been a quite a peculiar past twelve months being both married and divorced in just over a year!

On the following Monday morning the first thing I did when I got into the dental centre was to type out the Part 2 Order and got it signed by Captain Smith and posted it off to Records Office, together with the divorce certificate. I then amended my personal documents accordingly. Records Office never observed on the Part 2 Order and I knew then that I was actually a free, but divorced man. I took the opportunity of writing to Diana to tell her of the latest news but only received a short letter from her a few weeks later, congratulating me on my divorce and asking what I was going to do now, as the ball was in my court. I did not reply to her letter. Meanwhile now that I knew my divorce had been accepted by Records Office and by any court in England, I started to think about what religion I should change to. Perhaps I should think of becoming a Wesley Methodist, as I had been told that they had short church services on Sundays! Unfortunately I did not change my religion quick enough with the result that my next posting would be to Libya.

During the next few weeks a relieved me did my job properly and played football during the day and at nights I read books or listened to my music and kept away from all those WRACs in the camp and women who visited the camp. That was until a WRAC who very young , very attractive and petite gymnast was posted into AMRU on the fitness team. Her name was Donna Reed. Donna and I were soon to get very acquainted within days of her arriving in Saighton Camp...... but that is another story!

APPENDIX

Below is the question asked by a prominent MP in the House of Commons.

TROOPSHIP "EMPIRE FOWEY" (CONDITIONS)

I am very glad to have an opportunity to raise a matter which is of great importance to us all because it concerns the welfare and well-being of a great many young Englishmen who are serving their Queen and country in defence of the free world. My intention is to draw the attention of the House to complaints which have been made to me about conditions in H.M. Troopship "Empire Fowey" during her voyage from the Far East which ended at Southampton in August.

About the middle of July I received a letter from a constituent of mine, Mr. Peter Wright, then a corporal in the Royal Air Force. The letter was written on board "Empire Fowey" at sea and posted on to me by air mail. I propose to give the House an impression of conditions in the ship as they were conveyed to me by my constituent.

I should first like to draw the attention of the House to the question of the ventilation in the "Empire Fowey." My constituent was sleeping in H.2.B deck, which is at waterline level, and all the scuttles were, therefore, permanently closed, and men were sleeping in cots side by side in tiers of three in blocks of 18. Most men preferred to sleep on deck. My constituent says of the morning after: Entering troop decks after a night in the open has to be experienced to be believed. He goes on to describe the filthy smell of sweltering humanity which was quite overpowering even with the majority of the men sleeping on deck. And he invites us to: Imagine this situation ... with the majority sleeping below owing to bad weather conditions in the Indian Ocean. I want next to draw the attention of the House to the question of the recreation space in the ship as it appeared to my constituent. He says: There is one recreation room for all troops below the rank of corporal. Well over 1,000 personnel, I believe. At a rough estimate, I should think the recreation room could cope with 150–200 actually seated. The remainder sit on the floor. If the weather is fine the deck can be used.

Cattle would be better catered for. The final subject on which I wish to quote from my constituent is the most important one raised. I should like to give my constituent's impression before I comment. He says: And now for the final ghastly subject of food. Never in my whole life have I encountered such 'swill'. The menus indicate a fair choice; but the quantity and quality— there words fail him.

He then sets out a time-table of meals in the ship and gives representative menus. The first point to which I want to draw attention is one which I consider to be most serious. The last meal of the day in the "Empire

Fowey" was at 18.00, which is 6 o'clock in the evening, and breakfast was between 7.30 and 8.15 a.m., which left a gap of 14 hours during which the men were without food.

My constituent gives two typical menus for breakfast, lunch and tea. He says, most fairly, that they were quite acceptable and that the quality was either satisfactory or fair. But then for supper the menu was curry and rice, two slices of bread and a cup of tea with the alternative dish, a slice of ham. He comments: You will agree ... that curry and rice is not an accepted dish to the majority of people. In fact, I would go so far as to say that only 50 per cent. of the troops ate this meal. Now for the alternative dish. One piece of ham was offered to me. In actual size 2 in. x 1½ in., a mere fragment; not forgetting two slices of bread and a cup of tea. This is supposed to last a man "14 hours." It couldn't happen in prison. I do not know how he knew that, but that was his view.

He went on to give another representative menu which, again, he said was quite satisfactory for two of the meals, but on the last meal of the day he says this: The vegetable salad consisted of potatoes, carrots, swedes, and peas. —a peculiarly revolting mixture, I always think, which, I am told, is called Russian salad, but people eat it and it is quite a legitimate part of a meal to serve. But my constituent's complaint is this: The whole horrible mess was absolutely rotten, not just a faint smell, but a strong sour, putrid, odour that could be detected three feet away. The Orderly Officer was not available. The Orderly Sergeant stated that nothing could be done. It was pointed out that the men would have nothing to eat except one slice of corned beef, and one slice of spam. This was to last for 14 hours ... Messing representatives have had their say, but alas nothing has happened. All complaints have been formally presented to the proper authorities, all to no avail. He goes on to say: The time now is 10 p.m. and the men are, naturally enough, complaining of hunger. I never thought the British Services would ever reach this sad state of affairs.

I have read out those passages, because I think it is rather difficult to envisage in this atmosphere the state of mind of the men in that ship and I think that we should be ready to recognise just how strongly they did feel.

As a matter of fact, I think that my constituent wrote a very temperate letter, but the House cannot fail to realise the intensity of the feeling aroused. I think that the Minister will agree with me that a letter like that is something that any hon. Member is bound to take very seriously indeed. I immediately arranged to go to Southampton and to board the "Empire Fowey" when she docked. I should like to say how very greatly I appreciate the helpfulness and courtesy extended to me by officers of my right hon. Friend's Department and also by officers of the Royal Air Force and Army who met me.

I was given every possible facility and allowed to see all over the ship and to talk with anybody I wanted. I had a private interview with my constituent immediately and with the Royal Air Force corporal who had been appointed to the committee set up to consider the men's complaints and with responsible officers of the Services and ship's company and the Ministry's own representatives on the troopship. I saw the cafeteria, the recreation rooms and the troop decks and saw the men having their evening meal dished out to them. They had two herrings and mashed "spuds"—which I was told were the best served that trip—tea, bread, jam and butter. I spoke to a number of men, quite at random, and a number of officers and I was eventually most hospitably entertained to dinner, in the officers' dining saloon—and it was one of the best meals I have ever had.

As a result of this letter from my constituent, the visit I made to the "Empire Fowey" and inquiries I have made since, I should like to make certain suggestions to my right hon. Friend. First, on the question of ventilation, it is a very small point, but could my right hon. Friend consider arranging for more frequent changes of mattress covers in these ships to prevent fouling of the air? That would, I believe, be constructive and helpful. Also, I should like to ask him how often the air in a troop deck accommodating 150 men is changed every hour by the forced draught system. Is my right hon. Friend really satisfied that the present system of ventilation in the

Ministry of Transport's troopships is satisfactory? If not, what plans has he for raising the standard?

Secondly, on the question of recreation space, I recognise that the standards have been agreed by all Departments since the war and I know that any change would involve a great deal of expense and difficulty; but I would ask my right hon. Friend whether he is really satisfied that these standards are satisfactory, especially bearing in mind that it is only in these recreation spaces that men are allowed to smoke. I speak with personal feeling and experience on this subject. During the war I served for some time in the lower deck of the cruiser H.M.S. "Achilles", and I served in a flotilla leader in the oldest type of destroyer flotilla for nearly a year, also in the lower deck. So I have had some experience of cramped conditions, though I must say that in my experience we all bore it very cheerfully because we were happy to be in the Service of our choice.

I submit, however, from my own experience and from my observations on board the "Empire Fowey" that the present conditions are intolerable for peace-time trooping. I ask my right hon. Friend really seriously to consider this and to say whether he could not possibly use his influence to have the standards revised.

Thirdly, on the most important question of food, my general impression was that the men were justified. I think that the quality was poor, there was not enough of it, and the men were hungry and angry. I spoke to a young National Service officer whom I happened to see and who spoke most frankly to me. He was not the type of officer one would expect to make any criticism of this kind, but he said, frankly, that he felt that the men had had a thoroughly raw deal and that he had every sympathy with them. I was grateful to him for his frankness, and I think that the House ought to take this unsolicited piece of evidence into consideration.

I ask the Minister not to offer us any prevarications about seasonal fluctuations, potato peelers and points of detail, because I suggest—and I am quite convinced—that the trouble is much more simple and much more radical. I maintain, and I submit to my right hon. Friend, that the present messing rate of 5s. per day for sergeants and other ranks is totally inadequate. The messing rate of 7s. 9d. per day for officers is, I submit, quite adequate, if the excellent hospitality that I was given is any criterion by which to judge; but the men are obviously not now able to be fed as they should be fed as regards either quantity or quality on the present rate.

I believe that this rate was fixed in April, 1952. Since then the price of food has risen by between 10 per cent. and 15 per cent. and it is high time that the rate was revised. I hope that my right hon. Friend will be able to tell us that it is being revised. Any other answer will be mere prevarication, and men in troopships will continue to be both hungry and angry, which is a state of affairs neither of us wants.

The final question I want to ask is one in which I should like to take the matter a little further. I ask the Minister whether, in these days, he really thinks that trooping by ships is satisfactory. I am inclined to suggest that the method is clumsy and wasteful if we want to move troops about the world today. Perhaps the time has come to scrap these ships and to concentrate solely on air trooping which, I think, would be more efficient and more economical.

Those are the four questions which I wish to put to my right hon. Friend. In conclusion—as you said the other day, Mr. Speaker, those are dread words, but I do not think you need dread them just now—I want to make two points. I hope that this debate may result in a satisfactory answer from my right hon. Friend and that it will benefit future passengers in Her Majesty's transports. I hope, also, and this is most important, that the House will, in supporting me, reassure all National Service men that not only are they entitled to make representations to their Members of Parliament when they are in uniform, but that such representations as they may make to their Members of Parliament are seriously and sympathetically considered by responsible Ministers.

POSTSCRIPTS

1960 - In September, after passed my Sergeants course, I was posted to Libya, another Muslim country, in the rank of substantive sergeant. Obviously I had not changed my bloody religion fast enough I thought. The only good thing was that I was the youngest substantive Sgt in the Corps at that time.

1961 - In January I received a letter from John Harrison who had written telling me that a very attractive Eurasian lady named Diana had visited the Dental Centre at Chester and asked to see me but that he had told her that I had been posted overseas a few months before. Diana had told John that she was engaged to me (which was not true) and that she had come to the UK from Singapore on a month's holiday over the Christmas period with her mother and father. John told me that she asked for my overseas address where she could contact me. John knew my address in Libya of course as he was redirecting all my mail to me from Chester, but John was not only a very good friend, but he was smart. John told me that if Diana was really engaged to me then she would know where I was and what my address was and if I had not given her these details, then obviously I did not want any contact with her. In the end John told Diana that I had been posted to the Depot to await an overseas posting and had not heard anything about me since then.

1964 - In February, Major Cox got me a posting to Hong Kong on a thirty month tour. During my service I was to serve a total of four tours of Hong Kong and was due to do a fifth tour when I decided to leave the army. Most soldiers were lucky to get just one tour in Hong Kong and I believe that I was the only soldier in the Army who ever served four tours in Hong Kong. The highlight of my tour was the birth of my beautiful and wonderful daughter – born by my second wife.

1982 - 1997. I left the army and obtained employment as the General Manager of one of the oldest and busiest sports clubs in Asia.

If I was lucky enough to have met, wined and dined with VPs and Royalty during my tour in Malaya, I was certainly very lucky and very honoured in my capacity as GM of this leading sports club to have met, wined, dined and hosted over 200 very famous and international; film stars, tv stars, singers, comedians, footballers, cricketers, rugby players, boxers, jockeys, and other sports personalities and indeed to have become good friends with many of them.

1983 - My Chairman sent me down to Singapore for a week to look at the latest computers. Whilst in Singapore I took the opportunity of going over the causeway by bus to Johore Bahru, expecting to be stopped by the Malaysian Immigration authorities. I was not stopped, but allowed into Malaya.

1989 - I took three weeks leave and arrived in Singapore, accompanied by my third wife and we booked into the Raffles hotel. After a few days in Singapore I hired a car and I drove over the causeway into Johore Bahru. I was not stopped by the Malaysian Immigration authorities. I drove up to Seremban and booked into a hotel for seven days. During the following week I visited all my old haunts in Seremban, Malacca and Port Dickson. Much had changed of course. The houses of the prince, Fatimah and Diana had gone and been replaced by apartment buildings. I made enquiries as to the whereabouts of my former friends only to be told that they had all moved on. Having ended my week's stay in the hotel I went down to the Reception the following morning in order to pay my bill for the week only be told by the manager that my total bill had been settled in full. I informed the manager that there had been some mistake. The manager assured me that there had not been any mistake. He went on to tell me that a well dressed middle aged lady had arrived at Reception in the hotel and asked to speak to him. This lady had told him that she was a good friend of mine and believed that I was staying at the hotel. Once the manager had confirmed that I was indeed staying at the hotel, the lady had insisted on setting my bill in full which he had allowed her to do. On completion of this he had escorted her out of the hotel to her Mercedes car and she had been driven away by her chauffeur.

Driving back to Singapore I could only think that the woman who had paid my hotel bill was Fatimah. I could not guess how she knew that I was in Seremban, or indeed in Malaya. During the following years I visited Malaya on holiday with wife No 4 on one occasion; wife No 5 on another occasion and with my sister and her husband (my old RAF Police colleague from early service days in Malaya) on the third occasion and I never had any problems with the Malaysian Immigration officers.

1992 - I attended a RADC Reunion in Aldershot. During the reunion a recently retired RADC warrant officer told me that when he was in London a few years before manning a RADC Recruitment booth, that an elderly gentleman had approached him and introduced himself as Paul. Paul had asked the warrant officer if he knew me and if so did he know my whereabouts. The warrant officer told Paul that he did not know me, but that he had heard of me, and that he had been told that I had left the army some years before. That elderly gentleman could only have been Paul Summers I thought!

2017 - It is 58 years since I was posted out of Malaya and during those long 58 years I was never again to meet a single person I knew from my army days in Malaya. I did receive letters and postcards from Fatimah, Diana, Major Black, Sgt Ahmed and Dai Jones (who went on to be famous author), but all these stopped after I left Chester.

ABOUT THE AUTHOR

The author served 27 years in the British Army. During his service he was offered a commission to become an officer on three separate occasions, all of which he turned down. During his 27 years service he was never charged with a single offence, either minor or major. He was the first soldier in his Corps ever to receive the Meritorious Service Medal(MSM) and was still the only soldier in his Corps to have received this medal when he finally left the Army. On being presented with the MSM for distinguished service, his citation read " Good, faithful, invaluable and meritorious service, with conduct judged to be irreproachable throughout". On his discharge from the army as a Warrant Officer Class 1 his discharge book stated that his behavior had been "exemplary" and that he had been an excellent soldier with distinguished service and an unblemished record and had been an excellent asset to his Corps and the Army. On leaving the army the author became the General Manager of one of the oldest sports clubs in the world, retiring after 15 years. He presently lives in England with his young and beautiful Asian 5th wife.

Printed in Great Britain
by Amazon